DEAD FOR NOW

By Alex Fiano

GABRIEL'S WORLD ▫ BOOK FOUR

∞

IT'S TIME TO BE PARANOID

Troublemaker Press
Bronx NY

Dead for Now *by Alex Fiano*

Fourth Book in the *Gabriel's World* Series
Copyright 2016, 2019 by Alex Fiano
Published by Troublemaker Press
ISBN: 978-0-9969943-2-3

∞

To the Gabriel's World audience: I thank those readers worldwide who have taken an interest and liking to Gabriel and Joel and the Gabriel's World stories, my friends who have supported *Gabriel's World*, and my unpaid intern FRO. – A.F.

∞

Gabriel's World offers a compelling community of queer and allied characters, in stories that explore the extremes and complexity of good and evil.

Welcome to our World:
Homepage: GabrielsWorld.com
Email the author: gabrielsworld@outlook.com
Twitter: @gabrielsworld
Instagram: gabriels_world_queer_fiction

Gabriel's World: It's Time for New Heroes

Reader Extras: Gabriel's World now has recaps on the *Gabriel's World* website for the s of each book. The recaps offer summaries, commentary, trivia and other insight & info, going into the plot and characters in-depth. Read Recaps of the s on the Gabriel's World website: bit.ly/2wUy6d

Books by Alex Fiano

The Hanged Man

Two-Faced Woman

The Book of Joel

Dead for Now

Hardcore

Previously in the *Gabriel's World* Series:

Book One: *The Hanged Man*
What would you sacrifice to do the right thing?

This is the elemental question Gabriel faces in the first novel. After seeing Gabriel confront a bigot in a controversial viral video, attorney Raymond Booth wants to hire him to probe a disturbing incident at Raymond's charitable foundation. As Gabriel is otherwise publicly scorned and losing clients, he's keen to take on Raymond's case. But then Raymond disappears. Raymond's sister Toni hires Gabriel to find the missing man. Gabriel turns up evidence of abduction–and then Raymond turns up dead.

Gabriel's obsession with the case pulls him into the mystery Raymond wanted him to solve. He begins unraveling a sinister secret connected to the foundation–a cabal tracing back to the origins of Nazism. Gabriel endeavors to uncover the conspiracy of Raymond's murder without losing his license, freedom, or life.

Gabriel also has new developments in his personal life. He meets Alex Shenoy Barclay, a hotshot reporter with the New York *Herald Standard*, who helps him with the investigation and they begin a passionate relationship. But complications arise when Gabriel's former boyfriend Joel returns to help him–and to resurrect the powerful bond between them.

Book Two: *Two-Faced Woman*
Who will catch you when you're falling?

Gabriel is the one falling metaphorically and for real in this second novel with a theme of duality. As he takes on dangerous cases for two extraordinary women, he must find out who he can depend on, how he can save himself, and how he must help others. *Two-Faced Woman* is centered on duality: Gabriel and Joel's new client is Sophie Faulkner, falsely accused of murder; she shares her body with another self, Edward. With Edward's help, Gabriel and Joel begin to unravel what murder victim Leonard Mathers was trying to expose, and who was willing to kill to stop him.

Gabriel is also handling a difficult situation for Joel's friend Geneva Lennon. Geneva is a transgender woman who has discovered that her birth certificate isn't actually hers. Gabriel and Joel must find out who she really is, and in the process uncover the truth of a shocking crime involving Geneva's birth. Meanwhile, Gabriel is suffering from the trauma of the previous summer's events, and is desperate to reconnect with his spirituality. Gabriel is still involved with Alex–and clashing with him over Gabriel's work. Gabriel's reliance on Joel's support is complicated by Joel forcing Gabriel to confront the feelings between them. Gabriel and Joel are targeted by two extremely dangerous men, risking their lives in a face off against a shocking level of brutality.

Book Three: *The Book of Joel*
If the Past Doesn't Kill You, the Present Will

How the past shapes us and confronts us is the theme in this third book in the series. Gabriel is handling some interesting results of the events in *Two-Faced Woman*, and the new nature of his relationship with Joel. For Joel, his burgeoning success as an artist is shadowed by his parents resurfacing in his life.

Gabriel and Joel begin to investigate Joel's father, who appears to be involved in a corruption scheme. A shocking turn of events follows that reverses Gabriel and Joel's roles. They are pitted against a notorious New Jersey killer for hire, and the man who first abused Joel. In this story, Joel's excursion into his past underlies the current investigation. He might be reaching for exorcism of the demons that have haunted him since he was thrown out at 15, or he might be about to fatally collide with evil.

∞

Dedicated to Ioan Culianu and Umberto Eco.

"When decorum is repression, the only dignity free men have is to speak out." -- *Abbie Hoffman*

"We have it in our power to begin the world over again." -- *Thomas Paine*

You are permitted in time of great danger to walk with the devil until you have crossed the bridge. -- *Balkan Proverb*

"Paranoia is having all the facts." -- *William Burroughs*

PART ONE

◆

YOMI

INTRODUCTION: UNKNOWN KNOWNS

From the YouTube Channel "Tom Paine Events," in a video entitled:
Unknown Knowns and Raising the Right Question

Transcript: "In an article, philosopher Slavoj Žižek discussed the concept of 'unknown knowns'--those events which we do not or pretend not to know about, although these events determine action and form policy. Žižek said, "...philosophy as the 'public use of reason' is not to solve problems, but to redefine them; not to answer questions, but to raise the proper question."

"Perhaps the dead are the ultimate 'unknown knowns.' They were present and real at one time, but then faded from consciousness. Yet their death may determine other actions and form policy. Some deaths are ignored. Some are reconstructed to a different truth, although the original truth of the death still exists. In their death, they become a symbol: emotion, love, pride, justice, sorrow, evil. Some deaths are questionable--they are metadiegetic in that their death is a story within a story. Their death does not answer questions, but raises questions about society and what we choose to know.

"In videos to follow on this channel, aside from information and documentation of conspiracies going back over several decades, I will also have a philosophical take on mysterious deaths that have that metadiegetic quality. Are all these deaths conspiracies? Perhaps not. But in a sense the definite misdeeds of government, corporations, and evil interests create a hyperreality in which an actual conspiracy doesn't matter--what matters is raising the questions about an official story. Any official story."

∞

"But it is just the truth that cannot be known of the multitude, for truth is revolutionary." -- *From a 1912 pro-women's suffrage periodical called "The Vote: The Organ of the Women's Freedom League."*

According to Garson O'Toole (QuoteInvestigator.com), this quote is a possible origin of another alleged quote: "In a time of universal deceit, telling the truth is a revolutionary act," which ironically is universally attributed to George Orwell, despite no evidence of his having written or said this.

However, as Ioan Culianu and Umberto Eco have suggested, a misinterpretation can create a reality greater than the truth. Perhaps Orwell would be pleased to own the quote that didn't happen.

∞

From the YouTube Channel "Tom Paine Events," in a video entitled: Unknown Knowns: Alexander Litvinenko ♦ The Spy

Transcript: "Litvinenko was a dissident whistleblower and former Lt. Colonel in the Russian FSB, living in London. In November 2006 he became severely ill and died from poisoning by polonium-210. When he was in the FSB, he had targeted the Russian mafia. As a dissident, Litvinenko had publicly alleged Russian government-sponsored assassinations of journalists and bombings in Chechnya, and he also alleged corruption within the FSB itself.

"Litvinenko had told acquaintances of threats made to his life shortly before he was poisoned. He died horribly of organ failure due to the radioactive compound. Whistleblowers, as we've seen in the US and other countries, have not fared well.

"Speaking out--bringing light to abuse, injustice, and crimes--leads to persecution and death. Those who are guilty are unknown knowns. Litvinenko's death raises the question of how can society better protect and listen to whistleblowers?"

∞

Saturday, August 6, 2011
Warinanco Park, New Jersey, 1:10 pm

A SONG IS PLAYING. Lush, moody, a hit in the Eighties. Joel McFadden sinks in the luxury of the leather seats in his leased Nissan Rogue, although he doesn't turn the music up as he's on his iPhone, using FaceTime.

"You really want this project to happen," Travis Churchill comments on the on the other end of the call.

Joel makes his voice firm. "Yes. It's what I want. I don't care if you pay me for the mural; I want the Milk Center project funded." Churchill chuckles. "Joel, you know you're getting both. My corporate offices here and in New York are going to be even more provocative and energetic with your murals--imagine if...who was it who tried to paint in Lincoln Center? Picasso? If his work hadn't been censored or something."

"Diego Rivera," Joel responds mildly, although he rolls his eyes. "His mural in the Rockefeller Center. *Man at the Crossroads.* Our former governor Nelson Rockefeller ordered it destroyed because it appeared anti-capitalist."

"I know I'm annoying you and I like seeing your face--even annoyed you're beautiful."

Joel glances over at the basketball court to check that Gabriel isn't close enough to hear that. No. He looks back at the screen. Churchill, a nice-looking super-fit white guy in his late forties with wavy brown hair, smiles at him.

"Just so you know, I have it stipulated in the contract your work will not be destroyed--even if it's nothing but dicks. I hope it's more than just dicks, but still. If something happens to me and the board takes over and wants it gone, you can decide what to do with it. *And* I'm making a donation through my foundation to the Milk Center, to enrich your art project with the kids. Soon."

"How soon?" Joel can be blunt with him. He's earned the right.

"Monday. I have to twist the arm of the board, but I'll be picturing you glaring at me impatiently the whole time. They'll do it. I'll call your friend Juanita at the Center to set it up."

"And the donation for basic necessities. Don't forget that."

"Yes, your kids should be able to shower as needed."

"And eat."

"Spartan Foundation is known for its community service, Joel. Look at our rating on Charity Navigator." Spartan Foundation is the philanthropic offshoot of Spartan, the software/app company Churchill designed, founded, and which made him a billionaire. He had just started the company when he first hired Joel as an escort, back in 2001.

Churchill sighs. "Hold on a sec, one of my five other phones is going off."

While on hold, Joel turns up the Breathe song and glances outside at the court again. By extra-sensory perception, Gabriel Ross in turn looks over his shoulder back at Joel. Even at a distance, Gabriel's feelings are clear and Joel smiles faintly. Joel will probably have to fly overseas again soon, and so *Hands to Heaven* fits in with his feelings about leaving Gabriel for a week or so, alone and--

Then Gabriel's close friend Bob Jarvey charges and slams into Gabriel, snatching the basketball out of his hands.

Joel can hear Gabriel's "*What the fuck?*" even in his closed car. Bob is triumphant. "*Too slow, my man. I'm like Wilt in two ways. Only one is on the court.*"

"*Because you cheat, you dick.*" They go back to their strange one-on-one that seems to involve a lot of rough physical contact, like two dogs play-fighting. Both men are white, muscular and of dark Irish descent. Bob is more than ten years older than Gabriel's 37, and at around 6'1, 4 inches taller, but they are evenly matched on the court.

Churchill returns and goes into boring but important details of times, dates, and whatnot.

Gabriel and Bob suddenly bounce into the side of the SUV; the two of them have somehow traveled the ball all the way to the edge of the court and into the parking lot.

Travis looks quizzical. "What's that noise? Are you at some kind of sporting event?"

"I'm at a park in Jersey."

"I bet I know who with. I remember Gabriel at that softball game a few weeks ago. What I like about Gabriel is his confidence. He keeps all eyes on him and he knows it."

And true, a few stragglers have come up to the fence to watch Gabriel and Bob's little show, *Gladiator Basketball.*

For whatever reason, Joel feels a little uncomfortable when Churchill discusses Gabriel. Churchill hasn't tried to come on to Joel sexually since an attack of conscience a couple months ago. But he also seems to have sublimated his desire into sponsoring Joel's art.

"Swing by and pick up the contract," Churchill says. "Or do you need Isabella?"

"No, this is different than my gallery work."

"Good. Come on by."

Churchill could just email it, but Joel knows he wants to see Joel in person and talk. Joel can handle that. Joel wraps up the call, feeling that whatever Churchill's kinks may be, it's worth it for what he can do to help the homeless kids. He opens his window, and skips songs on his sound system, considering what he would play while working on Churchill's murals.

Bob raps on the driver's side window. Joel lowers it.

"Hey Joel," Bob says. "Why you gots to be all business? Give your man a break. He's trying to show off for you. He's *never* this good."

"If I don't react, he tries harder. I like to see how far I can make him go."

"You're mean," Bob responds, laughing. "Are women that mean? I guess so, but I can ignore it for the trim. Gabriel just turns into a helpless fool with the puppy dog eyes."

"Don't hate the player, hate the game." Joel lights one of his clove cigarettes and coolly watches the men go back to the court. True enough, his demeanor makes Gabriel work harder to make an impression on him. Gabriel is fast on his feet and has excellent shooting abilities.

"Now who's too slow, trash-talker," Gabriel says to Bob after making an elegant jump shot.

"I let you do that," Bob retorts. "I didn't want you to look bad in front of your arm candy and not get any tonight."

"You're jealous of my skills." Gabriel looks back at Joel again, and this time, Joel allows a smile that gets all of Gabriel's attention. Impulsively, Joel crooks his finger at Gabriel, who immediately drops the ball and starts towards the car.

"Oh Jesus, this again," Bob complains mockingly. "Time-out for foreplay."

Ignoring him, Gabriel comes up to the window and leans on it. "Hey baby. What's going on?"

Joel meets Gabriel's dark brown eyes with his own blue-gray ones and moves his head closer. "I need to do some things. Can you get back on your own?"

"Too difficult being a sports husband?"

"If you were actually playing something instead of fucking around, I could take an interest. No, I'm kidding you. I really do have to take care of some stuff in order to be free later. You'll reap the rewards."

Gabriel takes Joel's hand and raises it to his mouth, touching the index finger knuckle with his tongue. He bites softly, erotically. Joel pretends this doesn't do anything to him, flicking his cigarette in the ashtray casually.

"I could mug you for that damn thing," Gabriel says, still holding Joel's hand. "The desire for it never ends."

Joel leans forward so he's almost speaking against Gabriel's lips. "Humn. If you behave yourself, I'll let you watch me smoke it later."

Gabriel smiles. "You really want that ass-kicking, don't you? Keep working that smart mouth, see what happens."

"I know exactly what will happen." Joel smiles back. "I can leave you in such a way now that you'll be unable to play any more fake basketball. Unfortunately, you'll only have Bob for company. No relief there unless you turn him out."

Gabriel kisses Joel's hand again. "I can do the same to you...unfortunately, if you're going to see Isabella, she'll notice for sure and offer to take care of it for you. Probably film it too for whatever Jeff Koons-type thing she has in mind..."

Joel never fails to be irritated at any mention of Koons. He says, changing his tone, "I'm going to see Travis."

"Jesus Christ, same situation. I can't win."

"You've already won. Remember whom I'm coming home to."

"Archie. You're coming home to Archie--you're his fun dad. I'm just the sucker dad who buys his food and catnip."

"I can be your fun dad too."

"*Uhhh.*" Gabriel straightens up. "That's it, lost the erection. Don't ever use the word '*dad*' in a sexual way. I need to go to my happy place now."

But he leans back in to kiss Joel on the mouth. Joel smiles and drives away, waving at Bob.

∞

And then the hairs on the back of my neck go up. Various incidents over the past couple years have left me extraordinarily sensitive to things around me being off. Yeah, people are watching Bob and I play the fools. Yeah, a couple look uncomfortable when I kiss Joel. That isn't what I'm feeling.

More like someone's there who shouldn't be. And that I'm under observation. I turn our one on one into boring practice shooting hoops to get the stragglers to lose interest. Then I pace the court with the ball, scanning all directions. An SUV is at the far end of the parking lot; it is dark with tinted windows. Something about it doesn't sit right with me.

When Bob and I are done, we head for his Cherokee in the lot. He's going to drop me at the train station to go back to NYC. I have him stop the Cherokee near the SUV and act like we need to check under the hood.

I pretend to look at the engine. "Can you set your alarm off?"

Bob does, with his remote. I lift my head to watch the SUV. When the alarm screeches, I see a hint of movement inside, and a subtle shift in the frame of the car. More than one person is inside. I nod at Bob and he slams the hood down. As I get in the passenger side of the Cherokee, I notice the SUV has extra antennas. Not obvious--the wires run with the chrome trim of the back window.

Bob asks, "Who do you think your new friends are?"

"Hard to say. As far as I know, neither the feds nor locals have a reason to be on my ass."

Bob laughs. "It has to be *you*, though. I try to stay out of trouble these days. The city of Paterson sure isn't fond of you. I thought those might be agents from the Passaic County Sheriff's office."

"I think they'd be more open about pulling us over and beating the shit of me. Like they did in the jail."

I keep watch as we head to the station, but I don't see anyone following us. I find hard to believe that any official agency would spring for a multiple-car tail. Granted someone could have put a tracer on Bob's car so they could stay out of sight. But why? I'm not important.

My paranoia doesn't get better on the PATH train to downtown New York. I surreptitiously scrutinize the people in my car. Most are summer tourists. But one short-haired man in a suit stands out.

A quote from the Nero Wolfe story *The Doorbell Rang* comes to mind, when Archie Goodwin catches a couple of FBI agents tailing him. "*They were not-looking at me, the way they are trained to not-look in Washington.*"

That describes this guy. He has an iPad held awkwardly in front of him and is studiously not-looking. For fun, I get up and wander over closer to him, as if I want to be near the door. Then I lean over him and rudely look at his iPad. I catch a glimpse of the subway car on the screen--he's using some camera device to help him not-look.

He clutches the iPad to his chest. "Excuse me?" He has a faux-outraged tone.

I look him in the eye. "Technology is wonderful. But has technology helped you find Jesus?"

The two people next to him glance at me warily, in case I'm going to proselytize. But my man drops his eyes to his lap, frowning.

I laugh to myself as I get off the train at the World Trade Center stop. This could all be coincidence. I could be the crazy one. After all, nothing I'm doing is worthy of consideration from intelligence agencies.

∞

In an unknown area of New York, two US intelligence personnel [*REAPER and MORTEM*] send a secure message to their supervisor [*KISMET*].

[SCRAMBLE MESSAGE]
ypW0TgsssP vmtu0mKzOt A7149YE3KB 3SkosB2LTc qSjfFAhwBz

[Unscramble] ENIGMA Project/Eyes Only
From REAPER and MORTEM, to KISMET

This is a follow-up on our collective information regarding subject [*Redacted: Gabriel Ross*] Codename MAGICIAN, DOB 2/15/1974, who is worthy of consideration by our agency lately. Our asset ETERNITY has told us his colleague BEDEVIL is still maintaining surveillance of MAGICIAN. Because of BEDEVIL's interest, we checked on ETERNITY's information regarding MAGICIAN and we are adding to it from our own investigation.

As background, MAGICIAN has few family members. He doesn't appear to be close to his father JEFFREY ROSS, Lt. Col. US ARMY. [See File Appendix] He has a half-sister he does not speak to. His mother KATERINA SHEEHAN ROSS is deceased from cancer, DOD 12/01/2003. MAGICIAN was very close to her and her younger brother DOMINIC SHEEHAN. SHEEHAN lived in the apartment MAGICIAN lives in now on Avenue A in the East Village. SHEEHAN died 09/12/2004. MAGICIAN started his own business with the insurance proceeds from their deaths. SHEEHAN's death was due officially to being caught in a 'freak accident' construction collapse on the CUNY Midtown campus. [SEE File 8745-S/D re: PARADISE]

∞

ONE

From the YouTube Channel "Tom Paine Events," in a video entitled:
Unknown Knowns: Danny Casolaro ♦ The Nexus

Transcript: "Casolaro was a freelance journalist working on a story of how the US government improperly stole a software called PROMIS from its developers. That story developed connections to various other sinister events and conspiracies. As Casolaro spoke to more and more disreputable and dangerous people, the information he discovered and put together became a deep interlocking spiral of government, intelligence, and crimes he called 'The Octopus.'

"Casolaro was in Martinsburg, West Virginia in August of 1991, to speak to a new source. He was found dead in his hotel room. It was declared suicide, but his wrists were slashed to the tendons 10-12 times--too painful for someone to do intentionally. His notes relating to Octopus, which he had brought with him, were missing. Casolaro's death has strong indicia of a fake suicide and is an epitome of an unknown known. A death that has an official cause in spite of the blatant contradictory facts. Casolaro's investigation raises the question of how deeply connected are seemingly random events that formulate government policy?"

∞

Monday, August 8
West 90th Street, 11:27 am

I'M WORKING A CASE with my business partner and best friend, Veronica Gianni. Having decided last year to combine our talents, we named our business Gotham Investigations and just recently rented a new office in the West Village.

Our case started this summer, after I was released from being under house arrest in New Jersey. We're investigating the theft of some antique documents from the New York Archival Institute, a quasi-private foundation that features a vast collection of original documents, plans, maps, and other artifacts pertaining to the New York City area.

We discovered the thief to be Wes Darrell, who is Chief Administrator for the NYC Office of Landmark Designation. Darrell had made numerous deceptive excuses to visit the Institute over the last two years, ostensibly to research various buildings' landmark status. Actually, he was taking advantage of a flaw in the security procedures within the Institute to swipe documents from a poorly-locked storage room and other places. He has been selling the documents through online auction sites.

Darrell had been smuggling the documents out in specially-tailored Brioni jackets with extra-large inside pockets. We found this out by reviewing a few hundred hours of security footage, where we caught Darrell's strange actions on camera messing with his jacket. The video feed is kept on CDs for a five-year period. We later then tracked his actions online in selling the documents.

Before we take the case to the District Attorney, we've been documenting every instance of Darrell signing in to the Institute's attendance book to compare with the video archives. The Institute has an old-school literal book to sign in. This is major part of private investigation work--careful evidence review. We'll likely have to testify about it and take depositions on what we've done, so we're careful.

Veronica and I are in a glassed-in private reading room. I have the book open for June 2010. The book has the name, signature, and the document each visitor officially requests. One of Darrell's requests catches my eye for a different reason. The request is for original plans for the New York Foundation of Art and Culture. I know that place, as my former client Raymond Booth was on the board of the Foundation before he was killed. On a hunch, I flip back pages to earlier in the year, and find that Ethan Nelson, former director of the Foundation, visited the Institute several times. The time frame was just after he was hired. Using my camera phone, I take picture of these particular pages.

Veronica asks, "What's that all about? Oh, Nelson. What do you suppose he was doing here?"

I show her the Darrell entry. "They both were looking at the building plans for the Foundation. You remember Nelson was involved in some fraud involving stolen art, and Darrell is involved in stolen documents. Coincidence? I don't think so."

Ethan Nelson was part of the Tertullian Society, a sinister secret organization that does what everyone thinks the Illuminati does, or maybe the Bilderbergers, or Spectre. I know the Tertullians exist as they killed two of my clients and tried to kill Joel and I last summer. You might say I got too involved in the case, investigating a link between the Foundation, which is a Society cover operation, and a former Nazi.

My friends and I were threatened with horrible things because of this. I had to pretend that I was off the case. But I'm not.

While Veronica continues documenting Darrell's actions, I get up to find the Institute's director, Mischa Frazier. I give her the database number for the foundation plans. "Can we see if these plans are still here?"

Misha leads me to the climate-controlled document room and checks a drawer. "Yes, still here. That's good."

I examine the plans while she has the drawer open. "Do you recall Ethan Nelson looking at these? He was the man who killed Raymond Booth last year."

"Ah, yes. That was your case too, wasn't it? I don't have too detailed a memory, but I recall that he was remarkably arrogant but he thought he was charming. He said he had just begun his job running the Foundation and wanted to know the building top to bottom."

I've had some experience reading building plans. I scan these, looking for anything that would suggest why Nelson would really want to check them out. "Is the building unusual in any way?"

Misha examines the plans. "Well, *this* is unusual. You see here that the basement is built over a previously-existing set of underground passages. It looks like an attempt was made to connect the passages to the basement. The plans say the passages are 'closed.' Probably the passages were walled off."

"That's interesting. Some philosophers have suggested that underground passageways are a Freudian metaphor for the unconscious."

Misha smiles politely at this information. I can't help but wonder what interest Nelson had in the walled-off underground. Misha gives me permission to take a few photos.

Then Veronica calls me. "Darrell is here. He came in and asked what I was doing. I wouldn't tell him, and he left like he was searching for someone."

I leave with Misha following, and go back to where Veronica is in the reading room.

"He hasn't come back," she tells us. "He just kept trying to get me to tell him what's going on here, and then he ran out."

"How did he know we were here?" I look at Misha.

She blushes. "Not through me. Other people here know you're working on this, though."

This is why we tell business clients not to discuss our work, although we can't control them from doing so. Someone can always be an inside man, a snitch. Probably that someone tipped Darrell off.

Suddenly Darrell comes back to the room. He is a medium-sized man in his forties, white, longish graying hair, glasses, sort of dusky skin tone.

"Ms. Frazier, I was--"

He stops and stares at me. Gapes. Like I'm his worst nightmare.

"You," he says, with a tone that matches his expression. "You're here."

His stare unnerves me. "I am. You have some questions or something?"

"I know--I know who you are. Did they send you?"

"Who is 'they'?" I ask in a neutral tone of voice.

He doesn't answer, but looks at the sign-in books on the table.

I don't like the vibe he has, what's crossing his face and his body. I move close to him. "You're going to have to leave."

Before I can get close enough to touch, he turns and shakes his head at me. "You aren't taking me." He digs in his jacket and pulls out a .32 pistol.

I have a sense of danger and because of that, I almost anticipated him having a gun before he reveals it. I grab his wrist and hold it down. "Don't make this worse, man. This isn't something to kill over."

"You don't know," he whispers, with real fear in his voice. He struggles against me. I'm stronger than he is, but his terror makes him a challenge. Behind me, Veronica ushers Misha out the room for protection.

I manage to leverage Darrell onto his knees and even down on the floor on his back, practically laying on top of him. He won't let go of the gun. His body writhes and he grunts from my forcing him to stay prone with one hand, and twisting his wrist with another. I might have to break it.

"Come *on*," I tell him. "Let it go. Let it *go*. This is not worth it. Let me have it. Let me take care of it."

"You..." His eyes are wide and bloodshot. I have to wonder what he sees from how he's looking at me.

Because I have to hold him down, getting him to let go is not easy. Something in him, in his mind, breaks. He closes his eyes. In that instant, I have the gun.

I watch him carefully as I get up, in case he's faking. Veronica has come back in and I had her the gun. I search Darrell quickly for any more weapons. He doesn't resist, keeping his eyes closed.

I move out the room, and shut the door. Misha is waving to a security guard, who is hustling over. "I called the police," she tells us.

I inform the guard, "The room needs to be secure until the cops get here."

"What is he trying to do?" Misha says, shaken.

Veronica and I glance at each other. "He said he didn't want to be taken in," I answer, but it doesn't seem good enough.

"What is he doing now," the security guard asks. "Praying."

Darrell is on his knees, his back to us. He's hunched over. A pill bottle falls from his hand.

I yank open the door and snatch it up. It's empty and it has no label. "What is this?"

He mutters, "You. You aren't taking me." His eyes roll back and he collapses.

I yell over my shoulder, "We need an ambulance..."

"Heart attack?"

"Overdose." I check Darrell's breathing. He gasps, his body heaves. I find he has no heartbeat. I know CPR--chest compression is the main thing to get the blood to the brain. But even so, the chances of survival are iffy. But I do it anyway. When I was certified, the trainer said to compress to the beat of *Stayin' Alive* or *Another One Bites The Dust*, to get to 100-200 beats a minute.

It feels like forever until the EMTs arrive and take over. Darrell is at least still alive.

After this dramatic conclusion we need to go over details of the incident with the police, who arrive with the EMTs. The weirdness of Darrell having a connection to Ethan Nelson, and Darrell's strange fear of me, goes on the back burner for now.

∞

Saturday, August 13
Canal Street, New York City, 3:00 pm

I'm in Joel's apartment in Chinatown with Veronica and our friend Jason Evans, talking music. Jason owns a used bookstore in the West Village and has a bar band on the side, called No Drama. He's recruited me to play more and more. Veronica is big into magic, both stage and hermetic, and sometimes accompanies our gigs doing magic tricks between sets.

Joel is not part of our discussion on what songs to cover, although he wanted us over for company. He is fussing with other things--putting up a collection of original comics under acrylic cover, and a few posters of classic comic covers--mostly Batman.

My personal cell phone buzzes in the middle of our conversation. It's Nic (short of Nicolette) Ronson, who is an editor for an online alternative media, *NYCultcha*. I've been writing articles for them for a few years. I started writing there when they were still struggling to find a presence and a profitable business plan, so I was given free rein to write about civil rights, conspiracies, Buddhism and ethics, and so on. I've managed to keep a following that justifies them keeping me on. The following has now grown in part due to the celebrity I've obtained through my cases over the past year.

Nic says, "You haven't answered my texts, Gabriel. We want you find out who Tom Paine is." Paine is the mysterious YouTube personality who has been uploading videos with scandalous information--facts and documents and connections relating to extremely controversial political stories over a few past decades. The stories, featuring allegations that can and have been substantiated, have gone viral over the last few months.

She continues, "*You* can do that. We'd totally scoop *Gawker*."

I wince inside. "Nic, deconstructing that person's identity is not my area of expertise, really."

"Sure it is," Nic says cheerfully. "You told me you could analyze a great deal by how and what people communicate. Semiotics, you said."

That's what I get for randomly talking about obscure topics. "I suppose I could analyze the videos..."

"I'm surprised you haven't already, since you like this stuff! But do more than that--reach out directly to Paine. I bet he's read about *you*. You're into the same topics. See if he'll talk to you. Even if he just acknowledges your contact, it would be a scoop."

"I don't know..."

"We have tons more traffic on our site now because of you. This is an opportunity to be *the* Tom Paine authority. What if someone else gets contact with him? Or worse, just *says* he or she has contact? No one would know for sure, but there's people out there who say they are sure they know who Paine really is. Some international politicians are saying they want to hunt Paine down for encouraging people to expose more information. Governments are annoyed, major financial institutions are annoyed--why aren't you more excited about this?"

"I am, I just have some other things on my mind. I'll see what I can do."

"ASAP, right? While it's hot. Remember, this is getting the stories out I know are important to you, not just rehashing the latest drug-fueled celebrity outrage. How often does that happen by chance?"

I have to agree with her there. She keeps on hammering her point until she has a definitive promise from me to start working on Tom Paine. I sigh to myself, putting my phone away. *Now what, Gabriel?*

"What was that about," Joel asks, fiddling with one of the covers.

"Uh, Nic wants me to write more stories on Tom Paine. She actually wants me to see if Paine will talk to me, or if I can find out who he is."

Joel glances over his shoulder at me, his expression wary. "That can be trouble."

I agree with him, as we both know I'm actually Tom Paine.

I go back to our discussion of music. Every so often he glances at me. He wants to be with me, involved in my insane life. And for that, I add Icehouse's *Crazy* to the set list. *You gotta be crazy, baby, to want a guy like me.*

Eventually the party breaks up. Since I'm going back to my apartment to feed my cat, I offer to drop off Jason and Veronica. Jason is going back to his bookstore in the West Village, and Veronica to the apartment in Chelsea she shares with our friend Geneva Lennon.

When we get to my black 2009 Camry parked a few blocks away, I unlock it and open the doors...and pause. I pick up a trace of a strange scent.

"Hold on, just a minute," I tell Jason and Veronica.

I look around carefully in the car. The Camry is pretty clean. The few items inside don't look like they did when I parked. An empty coffee cup in the wrong side of the holder. A folder on the back seat, with a few papers poking out. I know I had them tucked in when I left, paranoid about someone looking in and reading them. Even the mats seem a little off--I keep them even and they now look a little crooked.

I state my thoughts aloud: "What the fresh hell is this?"

Jason asks, "Do you think someone's been in the car?"

"Yeah. Things were moved. And something acrid...maybe some kind of chemical was used to test the insider."

I get in and start the car up, because I don't know what else to do, and we have to go on. I tell Veronica and Jason about my experience coming back from Jersey. I keep watching for tails, and I think about sweeping the car for bugs.

I drop off Jason first. At Veronica's building in Chelsea, she doesn't get out but asks, "Why might this be happening?"

The only offbeat thing I can think of is what happened last year. Veronica and I are close friends, and business partners. She's never judged me. But I never told anyone outside of Joel about the Tertullians because I didn't want them in danger. The Tertullians are the reason I do the Tom Paine videos. I had consulted a former journalist in DC, Kent Varney. He entrusted me with a thick stack of notes on conspiracies the Tertullians had been involved in over the past several decades. Then they murdered him too.

"There's something I should tell you about." I pause, wanting a cigarette by reflex. "You may not believe it."

"I will. We all have stories that have something deeper about ourselves--our own Deep Web."

I laugh. "A good metaphor."

"So come in and have coffee. Tell me a story."

∞

[*SCRAMBLE MESSAGE*]
DXCnQMsc2t 5Ct2e2S2ml Ghm69jhbaV 0pRfglaJxp

[Unscramble] ENIGMA Project/Eyes Only
From MORTEM and REAPER, to KISMET

MAGICIAN now publicly acknowledging contact with "TOM PAINE" [presumed pseudonym]. MAGICIAN described this contact in his online articles, and TOM PAINE confirmed it his YouTube channel. Channel being monitored as published. MAGICIAN's personal communications online are PGP, unable for agency to access.

Regarding MAGICIAN's finances, ETERNITY's information confirmed. MAGICIAN has been working class most of his life. He has a GED and Bachelor's degree from CUNY Midtown in Psychology and History. He's been a private investigator for 15 years. This is from the information that's available on his own site, in the news articles about him, and what we have in our databases as well as information ETERNITY collected.

He was solvent for the first five years of his own business, started in 2004, until the economic downturn. Severe struggles from 2009 to late 2010, when good press from the ETHAN NELSON and DONALD MATHERS cases brought him more business.
In last quarter of 2010, MAGICIAN set up partnership with VERONICA GIANNI, a private investigator and friend he has known for 10 years. MAGICIAN and GIANNI have an office on Horatio Street in Manhattan. From documents we've obtained, a private company SMOKING DHARMA invested in their agency GOTHAM INVESTIGATIONS. The company is owned by MAGICIAN's boyfriend JOEL MCFADDEN.

MAGICIAN has had a previous relationship with MCFADDEN from 2006 to 2008, and resumed in 2010. MAGICIAN was, as you're aware, previously involved with ALEX BARCLAY, reporter and editor at the NEW YORK HERALD-STANDARD. That relationship apparently began in summer 2010 during the ETHAN NELSON case, and ended later that year on bad terms.

MAGICIAN has several favorable media contacts: CLARK AHN, crime reporter for the HERALD-STANDARD, CARL MANKIEWITZ, columnist for the NEW YORK SCENE, and WALTER CLEVELAND, celebrity writer. CLEVELAND brought attention to MAGICIAN being wrongfully in jail and abused during the STEPHEN CODY matter. MAGICIAN and CLEVELAND appear to be collaborating on a book about DONALD MATHERS.

∞

"You guys, this is a great story. The *Standard* is starting a video feature for the online version of the stories, and I can probably get something in on this. What do you think?"

Clark Ahn, a 30-year-old reporter at the *Herald-Standard*, is typing up some notes on the Darrell case. Darrell has a court appearance today. He had been in Bellevue under observation, but was making an application to be released on bail. Clark wanted some comments from us, so we dropped by.

"Play it up, Clark. It's all about face time."

Veronica and I are in the media more often, due to some of our cases being newsworthy, as well as my recent situation of being arrested for a murder that I didn't commit. The repercussions of that case--from a former hitman now on the run to a lawsuit against four long-time pedophiles--have the public's interest.

"And so that day, Darrell came over and threatened you?"

We save a few details of our stories for Clark, who is a decent guy and reports positively on us.

"Not quite," Veronica tells him. "It seemed that way, but more that he was suicidal. While we were waiting for the police, Darrell started going into arrest because he had OD'd on some kind of medication. That's why he's in the hospital right now. Gabriel had to give him resuscitation."

"That's so Gabriel," Walter Cleveland comments.

Walter, my would-be biographer and new BFF is a well-known, best-selling true crime writer--the classy kind. For some reason, he's entranced with me and my work. He helped me a good deal when I was in jail, ensuring I had enough publicity to avoid being 'suicided' while in custody, so I have to give him props for that. Walter can be a little pushy, but he genuinely wants to help.

Career-wise, it doesn't hurt. Walter talks to bigtime media, and Veronica and I talk to the local, but my name being connected to his gives us a little of his gravitas on true crime topics. He has written about us in *New York* Magazine and the Huff Post.

Walter is a small man, white-haired and dark-eyed like Derek Jacobi. He follows me around town when possible. He and I are going to discuss our project after talking to Clark. Walter and I are documenting the Don Mathers trial; Mathers is a serial killer I took down last year. Since trials move slowly, our work right now is describing the background of the women Mathers slaughtered. It's one of two books I'm helping with. The other is Bertrand Herrmann's work in hunting escaped Nazi war criminals. Thinking of these books reminds me of the Tom Paine situation.

As if he hears my thoughts, Clark says, "I saw your article online, Gabriel. The *Standard* doesn't think Tom Paine is a good topic to cover. They're afraid to be caught in some kind of hoax. I'm trying to convince them otherwise. Who do you think he is?"

I smile. "Another Deep Throat, I guess." I suggested the same in my article. Joel was furious about that, saying I was tempting fate. When I told Veronica what was going on last week, she disagreed with Joel's evaluation--but that didn't change his mind.

Having inherited Kent's notes after he was killed last year, I wanted to get the information out somehow. I decided on pseudonymous YouTube videos. Joel knows how to cover IP addresses. I know how to use political symbolism. I disguise my voice and provide as many links as possible in order to get others to copy, investigate, and forward.

To say there's a lot of questionable conspiracy-related material on YouTube is to suggest the Pope is connected to the Catholic Church. But my material has support from Kent's notes, my own downlow research, and Herrmann's investigation as well. Herrmann was a former Nazi hunter, who helped me in both the Booth and Mathers cases.

Tom Paine's fame is due to the videos' topics and quality presentations, and the mysteriousness in Paine's refusal to talk to anyone who tries to contact him. The fact the stuff is credible has caused the videos to go viral. The mainstream media is even being forced to acknowledge the videos in some way--though not in a positive one. The media hates anything conspiracy-related, viable or not. Smug journalists and commentators insist everything in the videos is bullshit.

Nic is right about one thing. Even though Paine is not responding to anyone, that won't stop people from assuming his motives and background, and even falsely claiming to be insiders who've contacted Paine. The media is in a state where the public cannot always tell what's true, what's made up, what's plagiarized, and what's deliberately misconstrued. The number of mainstream journalists I trust has dwindled down almost as much as the number of mainstream politicians I believe.

I do not mention the Society by name, but I'm hoping others will make that connection. Clark begins speculating with Walter over whether Paine is in government, and possibly intelligence work. I should, as part of my cover, act like I have more interest in this. If I wasn't Paine I'd be just as freely speculating.

Veronica catches my eye; closer than a sibling to me, she is free to needle me mercilessly.

"There has to be more to the story," she says deadpan.

I try to play off her humor. "If I told you more, I'd have to uh, kill you." My words trip me up. "Well at least I can't say anymore here. Too many ears."

At least *one* too many. Although I thought Alex was off on Saturdays he suddenly appears, as if reading my thoughts. Maybe I better stop thinking so loud.

I hadn't heard anything from Alex Barclay since I chased him from Bob's condo back in June. I broke off my relationship with him in the middle of the Mathers case last year, and got back together with Joel. Alex seemed to interpret that as only a temporary situation, driving me to say terrible things to him to make my feelings clear.

Clark writes crime stories; Alex is editor for political affairs. But Alex is Clark's mentor. I think Clark has figured out the tension between Alex and I. Especially as the last time we were all in the same place I came within seconds of punching Alex in the face. So he's wary as I am when we see Alex walking over.

Alex smiles and sits on Clark's desk. He's wearing a white silk shirt and cashmere sweater vest. Alex is a little older than I, six foot, British and Indian. Longish black wavy hair pulled behind his neck, and a neat beard. He greets everyone with a nod and then focuses on me.

"Gabriel, I'm glad you're here. I have something to talk about with you."

"Looks like I picked the wrong day to stop smoking," I respond, quoting *Airplane.*

My words don't bother him. "And Veronica too, as you're partners. I've been talking with Andy. He wants to have some good press on how he handles the infrastructure of the paper. He wants to hire you and Veronica to review security."

The new owner of the *Standard* is Andy Davidson, a billionaire media man, also British. "You two mates, or something?"

Alex doesn't like me using British slang. He raises an eyebrow, letting me know this, and says, "Yes. He knows my dad from BBC days. I talked you up. He already knows about you, from all the press regarding your do-gooding about town these days...we can borrow some of your integrity, yes? Can I talk to you about it more?"

"He's welcome to call anytime in the near future," I tell Alex, in a tone indicating the conversation is over for me.

It doesn't do any good; he ignores my hint. "Andy is in today. He heard you were in the building. Let me take you both by now. Clark, I'd like you to meet him as well; you haven't had a chance."

Clark is game to have face-time with the celebrated owner. And Veronica and I can't turn down the opportunity regardless of Alex's presence.

Davidson ends up discussing stuff with us for a couple hours; Walter has tagged along, and Davidson is impressed by Walter's fandom of me. Davidson is pretty sharp and asks several pointed questions about investigative work and what we can do for security. He also quizzes me about my past cases. I believe he's already decided he wants to hire us, but is getting a sense of the publicity he can spin.

The meeting wraps up with Davidson saying we'll be sent an offer letter for a broad range of activities and for a fairly lucrative fee. We excuse ourselves afterward, leaving Davidson with Clark and Alex.

Veronica and I are pretty stoked about this, giggling like teenagers in the executive suite hallway. Walter smiles at our antics.

"We can hire Halo as an intern now," Veronica says. This is true. Halo, my other best friend Danny's cousin, is a FTM transgender 17 year-old, attending classes in Boricua College and torn between following Joel in being an artist, or following me in being a private eye. He's begged us to let him work on some cases.

"And maybe Geneva will go to full time." Geneva Lennon is transgender former Army specialist. She now divides efforts between being a part-time op and handling her bookbinding/poster restoration business.

"Davidson really likes pushing the rivalry with the *Times* thing. He's going to change the nature of the paper as a whole, I bet. I hate to say he wants us for the pure celebrity culture factor, but I think so."

Veronica shrugs. "If he does, so what? Yeah, this is no way a typical security job. But the world isn't the same it was ten years ago, five years ago. We're adapting. Take it for the ride and see how we can parlay it. Davidson can afford to have us as window dressing. Are you okay with Alex being involved?"

I roll my eyes. The one drawback to this whole deal is that Davidson insists on his golden boy to be our point of contact for our work. Alex is pleased about this. Me, less than pleased.

"This was too good to turn down, although it will take some diplomacy. But he seemed pretty nonchalant. All that shit between us has to be over, right?" I run my hands through my hair, looking at her for confirmation.

"It should be. I'll handle talking to him as much as possible. It is too good to turn down." Even with favorable publicity a business like our agency, Gotham Investigations, has to hustle for clients in competition with every other PI in the city. The economy remains difficult. The only job creation is for investment banks blackmailing the government for bailouts. I can't put the kibosh on a high-profile deal because of some squeamishness about an ex-boyfriend.

"I'll have to talk to Joel..."

"He'll be all right about it. Just don't tell him if he saw his mom today. You know he Hulks out on those visits."

"Do tell," Walter says. "Gabriel, you have a history with Mr. Barclay?"

"You like gossip too much, Walter. The point is, it's *history*."

"Hmm. I noticed how studiously you weren't looking at him in that meeting. He was watching *you* pretty hard, though."

"I handled Don Mathers and Stephen Cody; I should be able to handle him."

Veronica adds, "Geneva and I will run interference every chance."

We stop talking as Davidson's door opens and Alex walks out with Clark.

Clark says, "Oh, I'm glad you're still here. I had a couple more questions about your case."

Alex casually interjects, "Veronica, love, would you handle it? I wanted to speak with Gabriel a minute."

Out of his line of sight, Veronica makes a face at me. She has little use for Alex and his casually patronizing tone. I nod to her that I'm okay with this.

Once they are out of earshot Alex plays with his ponytail and smiles, slightly awkwardly. "Would you like to see our library?"

I'm a sucker for a library. Always have been. When my mom and I moved to a new town, the first thing we did was join the library. Even before I attended CUNY Midtown, where my uncle Dominic taught, he used to take me to the school's library to hang out.

I like exclusive libraries even more, and I like checking out people's book shelves. Walter got me to visit his home at the Hamptons by mentioning his book collection.

The *Standard* has a reputed extensive private research library. As Alex has a Masters in Library Science he's gotten involved in the maintenance of the collection.

"All right," I say casually.

I see from his expression he knows I'm inwardly craving to go there. Acknowledging this victory, if that's what it is, I walk with him to the elevator bank and down a few floors. We step out into a half-circle reception area. A long, curved Art Deco-style desk stands imposingly in front of couple of frosted glass doors.

A young black man with glasses and braids comes out of the doors. "Hey, Alex."

"Hi, Leo. I'm showing around a colleague of mine."

Leo nods. "Let me know if you need any help."

Alex holds up his ID to a scanner and gains us entrance through the doors. We're now in a carpeted room with a couple of regular desks, computers, shelves with binders, fax and scanner, and some original art on the walls. Three other doors fan out along the back. "It's temperature controlled, of course. Besides copies of every issue of the *Standard,* we have some very rare books. You'd be surprised how many scholars have asked to visit or borrow. It's a careful application process. We won't have what happened at the Archival Institute. And with you here, even less so, right? Now you have the books to protect too."

He glances at me, knowing I take book protection seriously. I nod gravely. "Yeah, of course."

"You'd have regular access, as I imagine you will all over the building. You and Veronica and any associates you vet--Geneva, is it?"

"Yes. We might be taking on Danny's cousin as an intern, but I'll be watching him."

"I trust you. Andy trusts you. He has to, if he's going to let you prowl our halls."

In my mind I'm starting lists of tasks to plan for this giant-ass security job, but I'm interrupted by Alex leading me through the door on the far right.

"Holy shit," I say, unable to help myself.

Alex is pleased at the effect. The room has a soft yellow glow and extends for what seems the length of the building. It's high-ceilinged as well. There's at least a dozen rows of tall glass cases and shelves with antique books. I can almost smell them. The shelves are interspersed with reading tables that remind me of the workstations medieval monks would have to illustrate manuscripts. Prominently displayed is an actual illustrated medieval manuscript. I'm over there to examine it without even thinking.

It's a Bible in Latin, about 15 inches long. The display has it open to the Book of Revelations. The page features an image of a skeleton on a horse.

Alex produces a small key and opens the case. He slips on a glove from a pair inside the case to turn the page. Across the span of the delicate paper is a gloriously evil-looking devil with a dragon's body. I lean over it, staring, afraid to breathe.

"Fantastic, isn't it? Just to feel this history and work off the pages..."

"Yeah, it is." I step back, afraid my presence will cause the book to crumble. Alex locks it up and casually shows me a few more exhibits.

Then we go to the room on the left. This is the news archive. It has copies of every issue since the paper was founded in 1915. The issues are being digitally archived, and a few persons are working on that in the room. The shelves here are gray, but the room has elegant decoration of blown-up front pages over the decades turned into posters. World War II, Kennedy, Nixon, moon landing, 9/11.

The middle room is almost a regular library. Thousands of books--regular books, research volumes, literary works. It's bigger than the others and like the archive, actually two floors. Alex hangs back as I hunt through the stacks, getting a sense of how the works are arranged. There's an intranet catalog but I like finding things on my own.

Eventually I come across an area I could spend a few days in-- books on magic and the occult. At Geneva's urging, I've started formally working on a Masters, and have a thesis underway that involves magic. I pull out a book on magic and the art of memory and become lost in it. Books have a way of drawing you in, keeping you in another realm. Library stacks make me feel like I'm in a world of mystical knowledge.

Since I was inspired to use magic from Veronica's love of it, I'm planning to take her here as soon as we have IDs and to make friends with Leo. My inner thoughts are interrupted by a voice in my ear. "Ah, here you are."

I almost jump. Alex has come up right next to me. He tips my book up to look at the title. "Typical you."

I shut the book and put it back. "I'm studying this stuff."

"Formally?"

"Uh, yeah." I talk too much, out of nervousness. "I've approached CUNY Midtown about collecting my random graduate courses into some kind of master's degree. My courses have been in art history, cinema, religion, philosophy and linguistics. I managed to get an interdisciplinary approval to get a degree in philosophy based upon a Master's thesis and two semesters' work on semiotics and religion in various forms of art."

"Brilliant, Gabriel. I'm glad you're pursuing that."

He sounds sincere. He had pushed me to go back to school, but a more upscale school than CUNY. I had been angry about that. But here I am, doing things my way. And Joel has followed a bit. He wants to take a few college courses, but since he never graduated high school, he has to finish his GED first. He feels a little awkward about it, but lets me help him go over the nuances of standardized tests, as my uncle Dom had helped me and Danny do the same when we dropped out of high school at 16.

Alex continues, "I admire your research, actually. It reminds me of some old tales. You've heard of the Akasha?"

"The ethereal cosmos and essence of the material world in Vedantic Hinduism. That what you wanted to talk to me about?"

Alex smiles. "No, not today. Another time. What I wanted to say is I'm glad you are taking the offer, and that you don't have a problem dealing with me. I'm trying to rectify my own karma with you."

"We're professionals here."

"I know, but I just want you to feel comfortable."

"Well...uh, thank you for the recommendation. That was good of you."

Alex looks as if he wants to say more, and stares into space long enough that I start to feel awkward. Then he looks at the book on magic. "I'll ask Leo to hold that one for you."

He still looks like he's struggling with saying something. The air between us has a sense of expectation for me to step in and ask what's going on. A line from a Fleetwood Mac song comes to mind. *Baby, I don't wanna know.* I don't. Asking is trouble. It's why he wants me to ask. I would hope it's not any suggestion about still having romantic feelings.

I make my voice neutral but not unfriendly. "Thank you. It's a book I haven't seen in other libraries."

He scratches his head. "I'd like to talk about this more. But time to let you get back to your partner and your scribe."

A hint of disappointment. But something else I hear in his voice that stays with me. That he's making his mind up about something.

I decide I'm not going to let that bother me. We leave the library, and he walks me back down to Clark's desk. Veronica and Walter are there, and Veronica comes up to meet me. She looks shocked, and it alarms me. She says, "One of Clark's court sources called. Something bad happened with Darrell."

Clark is on his phone and frantically typing on his desktop; Walter is reading over his shoulder. Veronica and I return to his desk.

Clark ends his call and swivels his chair to face us. "Darrell's attorney left him alone in an interview room for half a minute. Somehow, he got out and slipped past the court officers and made his way to one of the upper floors. He found an open window and jumped."

"*Jesus.*" I wince inside, picturing it. "I guess..."

"Yeah, he's DOA. God, I know this seems really crass, but--"

"No, I know a comment would help. Just give me half a minute..." The half a minute that Darrell took. I shake that off. Clearly, whatever that man was going through was too much for him to handle. Still, I can't help but feel there's is something really, really strange about it.

∞

T w o

From the YouTube Channel "Tom Paine Events," in a video entitled:
Unknown Knowns: Gary Webb ♦ The Journalist

Transcript: "Webb was an intelligent, talented journalist who investigated the CIA-crack cocaine-Contra connection. [Note that in the Eighties, Senator John Kerry had led a subcommittee investigation and found evidence of CIA involvement in cocaine trafficking; this was the time of Iran-Contra] Webb had good sources in the LAPD and intelligence contracting. The details of drugs being used for illicit funding was documented in a series of articles in 1996 for the San Jose Mercury News, and in Webb's book Dark Alliance. However, government refutation of Webb's work (the CIA investigated itself and found no wrongdoing) led to other Big Media disparaging the accuracy of the information and even a something of a retraction of the articles.

"Webb was subjected to a strange and terrible blitz attack by other journalists, who strove to destroy the reputation of a Pulitzer prize-winning reporter, whose stories on the CIA/cocaine/Contra connections were for the most part accurate. Unable to continue his professional journalism career at the same level, Webb committed suicide in 2004. Although some question the circumstances of his death, what stands out is a professional dedicated man was targeted for ruin--by lockstep media and government, to keep unregulated and criminal acts out of the public awareness--unknown knows. Webb's death raises the question of what can you believe is an actually free press?"

∞

Saturday, August 27, Continued
Alphabet City, Avenue A, 8:15 pm

AFTER VERONICA RETURNED to the office, she called Joel and told him about the *Herald-Standard* job and what happened to Darrell, doing me a favor. I had gone to discuss things with Walter for a couple hours, then I went to Bryant Park to be quiet and meditate. I needed to digest what happened, and I suppose Joel needed to digest the news about us working for the *Standard.* Joel hates Alex with a passion. He has good reason to.

Joel was in my place when I arrived home, talking on the phone to his best friend Chris Szala, whom he met while on the streets as a teen. I move furniture while he continues his monosyllabic conversation, watching me arrange the room. Then I turn on my stereo and hold out my hand to him. He ends his call and takes my hand.

Joel keeps his head on my shoulder, but I feel him thinking more than giving in to the music.

"I'm sorry about what happened to that guy."

"So am I. Thank you."

"If you're worried I'm upset about your new job, don't be. It's cool. You're right to take the job. We can cope with it. So you'll be the same with the vice versa and shit, amirite?"

I smile at him, as he tugs at a strand of hair over his ear. He got a new haircut yesterday and is trying to decide if he wants to keep it.

"You know, we're not Hannibal and Clarice. This isn't *quid pro quo.*"

But he shrugs that off. "You think I'm going to be tripping balls on my own jealousy. Just go ahead."

"I do not. I just know it's awkward. And your career isn't causing me any...challenges."

Joel stops to toss his pack on the table and watch my cat Archie jump up to investigate it. "You're okay with Travis's patronage?"

I smile, hopefully deceptively. "I'm an adult, right? We're both adults." Like Walter, Churchill did a favor for me when I was in jail, exerting some influence to get me out on house arrest. Unlike Walter, he wanted in turn for Joel to see him again--professionally. Churchill ultimately didn't go through with that request, but that doesn't inspire me to be his BFF.

But I know Joel is a master at being able to handle himself. I tell him, "Like this opportunity with the *Standard,* what Travis can do for you is a godsend. It's based on your talents, as mine and Veronica's is with this new job."

Now Joel smiles and returns to my arms. If there's anything better than slow dancing with him, I don't know what that could possibly be.

"Hmm," he says against my neck. "So this is what it's like to be adult."

"This is it. James Bond-levels of excitement, huh?"

"In some ways," Joel says, making his voice suggestive and moving against me in a way that makes me nearly shiver in anticipation.

If we can be like this together, it's the perfect antidote to whatever aggravation Alex causes me.

∞

Tuesday, September 23
Horatio Street, 12:20 AM

Gotham Investigation's new business location is on a short block with three other buildings. Our offices are on the third floor of the building on the north end. The structures are old and brick, with 24-pane iron-frame windows.

Veronica is with me tonight--this morning, now. We've been talking shop, and I haven't had a chance to ask her about Mikki. Mikki is my friend and New Jersey lawyer. She and Veronica were dating for a bit, and then suddenly it ended this weekend. I can tell she's all mixed emotions, covering for it with strained chattiness. In her office, I help her put up metal reproductions of 19th Century magicians' posters. The illustrations feature the magis in question bedecked in tuxedos, carrying books of secrets, and surrounded by tiny devils. We take a coffee break, and she consults the extensive book on magic I bought for her last year.

Veronica and I could be twins. Around the same height, same age, coloring. Except her hair is short and brown with burgundy streaks. She dresses masculine, reflecting the masculine part of her Genderqueer identity, but chooses to go by female pronouns. Not because it's easier--we'd respect what she asks, but her using the feminine as a way of defying the traditional default to male. We both had strong mothers who inspired us to defy tradition.

Joel has been in and out of the office. He tends to hang around when he isn't working on his art. Tonight he's going to some party that starts late, because that's what cool people do on a weekday. Joel's gallery agent, Isabella Karimi, a friend of his from way back in his youth, is showing him off to the cool people in NoHo. I'm more or less invited but it's not my thing.

While I'm trying to coax Veronica out of her mood Joel returns to the office, listens to us, and starts badgering her to come with him. She politely turns him down, and he looks hurt.

"Maybe it would do you good?" He tries giving her an expression that often gets him his way, like a cat who knows how to play the guilt.

Veronica places her hand on his face affectionately. "I know you are concerned. I don't really want to party. Go on and go. Give Chris a hug for me."

"I'll tell Iz you said hi."

"Sure," she says flatly. He doesn't notice, kissing me goodbye.

"What's bothering you the most about Mikki," I ask her when he leaves.

"I can't do what she wants me to do. She's getting help from Bob to be evaluated for adoption placement. I'm terrified of having children. What if something goes wrong?"

She sighs deeply, and I take her in my arms. "I understand. I wouldn't be willing to put myself out there for that right now, either. I'm glad it hasn't come up, to be honest."

"I know it hurts her terribly, and even worse, it's a deal breaker for her. That's why we tried to make ending it civil. I want her to be happy, so dragging it on wouldn't help either one of us. I'm going to be alone the rest of my life. That's okay on some level, I guess."

"Not entirely alone. I'll always be here for you." I hold her closer. "No one gets between us. Maybe Joel."

She laughs. "Yeah, that came up in our conversation."

"Mikki cares about Joel. They're always working on his lawsuit."

"Yeah, it's not him, it's me, I think. I've been worried about Joel and what he's gone through with this lawsuit. He has some hurt left in him...of the same kind I've been through. It's real hard to trust again after you've been violated, and when something happens to stir up the memories you have to be really strong not to break down. I guess I mentioned this to her too often for comfort. I had to back off, because I didn't want her mad at him by proxy."

"Huh. I can't see her doing that, but emotions are tricky."

"I always thought she'd say *you* were the one I was too close to. The friend who's the rival with the lover for one's time. You know Mic, though. She's so pragmatic. Not accusatory, just matter of fact."

"We're all screwed up, babe." Indeed, as my best friend and soulmate describes being told by her girlfriend that she is too close to my boyfriend, I feel a pang of jealousy--it *should* be me who's the problem. I realize that's also too fucked-up to even begin unpacking. "Is that why you didn't go with him?"

"No. I don't like those kinds of parties."

"Isabella will watch over him."

"I'm *sure* she will. She rides his jock every chance she gets."

I have to laugh at this.

"Don't tell him. I'm sure she's a wonderful person. I just prefer not to be in the same room with her. She sometimes makes me feel like she believes she and I are rivals for *him,* and starts feeling him up in front of me. He doesn't care, but it annoys me. Is that horrible?"

"No. You can't like everybody, and you two have very different personalities. You don't see me going either, right? Are you going to work anymore?"

"We've done enough. I'm just going to go home; take a pill. Geneva is home taking care of Farrah and Bella. Maybe we'll both zonk out."

Farrah and Bella are their cats. Geneva had been dating Jason, but that had ended amicably. How do people do this amicable thing?

I insist on going outside with her and getting her a taxi, with instructions to call me if she has a bad night.

Afterwards, I stay on the street and consider if I'm going to go back in for more paperwork. Nothing else immediately catches my interest and I don't have anyone to go see. Danny had thought about coming over, but chose to meet the owner of a naked-chest picture he found on Grindr. Bob is looking for adventurous possibilities in some local Ladies' Night festivities in Paterson, NJ. My New York attorney friend Jim is either reaping the benefits of marriage counseling, or suffering the repercussions of same. Times Square no longer has Midnight Movies. I'm alone, unless I go home to Archie.

Since no one is around to rat me out, I cross the street to buy a pack of Camels. Diagonal to our building is a sliver of concrete with a wedge of brick holding a tree and couple of bushes. It divides Horatio from 8th Avenue. And across 8th Avenue is an all-night magazine and smoke shop. The neighborhood is quiet at this time. In the smaller streets nearby--Gansevoort, Jane, and Bank, even more so. It's a different, more intimate world.

I'm not tired, but I'm not going to hang out places alone. I even actually consider calling my father--and manage to shock myself that things have changed enough to where I'd ever have that passing thought. Jeffrey Ross lives in Brooklyn; he's probably still up at this time.

I buy the pack and wander over to the brick wedge with the tree. But before I can light up, I spot something in our building windows across the street. A whitish figure moving around. The building comes with janitorial service, and that tends to be late. No big deal.

Except the person is standing still, and seems to be staring out the window. In my direction. The figure looks like a ghost.

On an impulse, thinking of the SUV in New Jersey and someone having searched my car, I take out my cell and call the office line. The figure turns its head as if hearing the ring. So I'm not hallucinating. Then the figure steps out of sight. I hear the line being picked up, but no voice.

God, that's strange. Being alone on the empty streets adds to the strangeness. "Who are you," I ask.

Silence. Then a slight noise like someone saying *hum* under his or her breath. Then the phone goes dead.

Shaking off the fear, I run across the street and unlock the ground-floor door. Inside is the darkened hallway, which just has an elevator and staircase at one end and a building directory on the wall. I quietly go up to the 3rd floor on the stairs. I don't have my Sig Sauer with me. This wasn't one of those days. Unless every day is one of those days now.

In this building, the stairway and elevator open to a small area in front of our door. I move up to the door and listen.

Whoever's there may have left by now. I crack open the door, which is unlocked. Nothing happens. Some light comes through the windows; it illuminates enough for me to see no one appears to be inside, unless hiding. I go in. The waiting room has a few chairs and a reception style desk that came with the office. Then through another door is an anteroom to Veronica's office facing 8th on the left, then Geneva's work room, the storage room and bathroom to the right, and my office in front facing Horatio.

The bathroom door and two office doors are open. I make a circle of each room, checking silently. No one is in them; nothing appears to be disturbed. The storage rooms are still locked.

I haven't turned on any lights, and the dark seems to reach out to me and crawl on my skin. Then a door creaks ever so slightly in the outside hallway. I go quickly to the waiting room door, and hesitate before looking out. The faint sound of a step near the staircase. I risk looking out. In the dim light, I can see an outline of what seems to be a male head and torso, going down the stairs. He must have left our office and gone up one flight before I came in.

The person holds up a gun, and I duck back. I can still see the person through the crack in the jamb. The person lowers the gun, and seems to stare back at me. Then goes down the stairs. I realize he held up the gun to keep me from following him.

I realize as well my heart is pounding. I go over to a window in my office, open it, and lean out. A second later, the person leaves, now wearing a jacket with turned up collar and a large baseball cap. I can't see the face. The person walks quickly away from me towards 14th Street, well aware I'm watching.

I want to yell at this person, *who the fuck are you?* I want to pick up something and throw it at him--I could probably hit him before he reaches the end of the block. Something keeps me from doing so. An atavistic sense of danger.

My attention goes to checking out the offices to see if anything is out of place. I can't find any indication the computers were turned on, the storage room was breached, anything.

Who was in here? Why? It occurs to me that the person who was here wasn't searching for anything. So not like in the car. Maybe not like being followed from the park. He presented himself obviously--standing in the window where he could watch me and know that I could see him. He did that to get me to come back and see what I'd do.

To see what I'd do. Would I call the police--or try to handle it myself. That thought makes this event all the more disturbing.

∞

[*SCRAMBLE MESSAGE*]
XfVeFHqk0B via9XEvbSc lJ3BtwJ0NA HZmTj5vj7b

[Unscramble] ENIGMA Project/Eyes Only

From REAPER, to MORTEM
--What do you make of them physically, in terms of asset or threat?

From MORTEM, to REAPER
--MAGICIAN is very athletic. He's skilled in boxing and martial arts. I followed him to his gym. He practices for hours. He is also an excellent shot with a handgun and rifle, and has a license for a Glock and a Sig Sauer. He doesn't dress for attention but for comfort. He's very observant of what's around him. He does not appear to have sexual habits that would be a liability, but does have semi-regular marijuana use. He also has some medical issues including insomnia and migraines and possibly PTSD. His criminal record was accessed in New Jersey not long ago, see File addendum. Nothing serious. Of course he was cleared of the murder charge. He is not afraid to get in a fight, and can take the punches as well. He was beaten by three men last summer, had a nasty altercation with DONALD MATHERS which put them both in an ER, and was attacked by corrections officers in the Passaic County jail. That was a civil court matter his attorney MICHAELA CONNOR settled on his behalf successfully.

FROM REAPER, to MORTEM
--I figured as much. He has a temper; I recall from seeing him arguing with some people. That can either make him easy to manipulate, or make him unpredictable. What about his partner?

From MORTEM, to REAPER
--GIANNI has been a private investigator for about the same time. She has family she is no longer in contact with, in Washington State. Her mother died 03/15/1999. Something happened to her in Washington but it's sealed. She has an undergraduate degree in Criminal Justice and a graduate degree in Psychology. She is tough, but not trained in anything other than guns. She's 36, 5'8, good shape, short hair, little make-up, blue eyes. Dresses casual and male, no jewelry other than a pendant/ring. I saw these on her in a coffee shop. Some kind of magic symbol. I believe she's Wiccan or something like that, but no group affiliations. She writes about magic in history. She lives with GENEVA LENNON, the trans woman employee for GOTHAM. Geneva is Army trained [see attached file]. 5'9, dark brown hair and eyes, speaks Arabic fluently, and some Spanish and French. Weapons and overseas operations background. I accessed a court case in Monroe County--a sealed petition to change her birth certificate gender. Source from the court told me her grandfather, a former state senator, arranged for the procedure. The apartment GIANNI and LENNON live in is actually rented to MCFADDEN. GIANNI and LENNON sublet from him. MCFADDEN has his own apartment in Chinatown. He's hard to find any history for--but some of it came out in the CODY case. MCFADDEN is 33, white, 5'8, blond hair, blue eyes. He is known to have been an expensive escort for some time in the Nineties and early Aughts, but not believed to be doing so at present. He has publicity as an artist and an important patron in TRAVIS CHURCHILL of SPARTAN. MCFADDEN associates with known hackers and may be one himself. In the CODY material online, MCFADDEN is from New Jersey, and apparently was sexually abused by the cop whom CODY killed. I think there's a lot more there, but MCFADDEN is very circumspect. He's very difficult to follow.

From REAPER, TO MORTEM

--He's the suspicious type?

From MORTEM, to REAPER
--Very. I tried following him once and he picked up on it and disappeared. Don't underestimate him. He and MAGICIAN and GIANNI met in a coffee shop on Christopher Street near their office. They didn't notice me outright right away, but MCFADDEN detected me again and got them to leave. I pulled a staged drunken harassment street encounter on him and GIANNI a couple weeks ago. He had a switchblade with him and was clearly ready to use it. He is extremely protective of them both and aggressive over what he perceives as any threat. I could even guess he's in love with them both. The man can practically disappear in midair if he wants, but would probably never do so to stay with them.

∞

Sunday, September 25
Westchester County, 10:07 am

My father has invited me to practice with him on a private range that a friend of his owns, north of Yonkers. Since I was a little shaken from the other night, I'm willing to go with him. I consulted both my tarot, which my mom taught me, and I Ching, which my Baguazhang/Tao mentor taught me, and both suggested I learn more about internal and external protection.

Jeffrey Ross is 61 and has shorter, darker hair than me, flecked with gray. We have the same dark eyes, body type, and same alert posture.

"How are things," Jeffrey asks me.

He's taken out a Knight's Armament SR-25 sniper's rifle to show me. I don't like guns the way I do books, but I like knowing about them and how to use them. While I look over the rifle, I answer.

"We signed the contract with the *Standard* and started security evaluation of the building, infrastructure, employees. Davidson even wants an informal input on content, in the context of investigating stories that could affect security or reputation. Of course, once we had our badges, Veronica and I spend a day in the library alone, chatting up the staff librarian, and deciding what stacks we'd tear into first."

"Sometimes I regret not reading more. I did the minimum of school I could to be an officer in the Army, OCS training. They still wanted 90 regular college credits; your mom helped me with those classes. God, what I put her through."

He put her through worse than just tutoring him in English or History, but he knows that and I choose not to push the point for once.

"How is Joel? Be sure to give him my best." Jeffrey asks, opening the back of his SUV.

That in itself is strange to me. I have a childhood full of his snide comments about the various 'fag' activities I liked, and I often overheard him having harsh discussions with my mother about me. Mom was a quiet force who talked him down and stood up for me. But she's gone. I dealt with Jeffrey as little as possible after that...until recently. He's made clear he has changed his feelings about me.

"He's good, thank you. He said to say hello."

At first, when we did this in June, I couldn't be sure I trusted him, but I saw him trying. When I got out of the murder charge, he wanted to see me. We ended up having a couple days of talking. He let me be angry. He let me yell. He apologized. I had to ask myself then if too much had gone by to have a relationship with him. I don't blame anyone for whom too much time has passed, or too much has been said or done. I don't blame anyone who tries to reconnect, either.

"Something strange a couple days ago," I tell him. "A break-in in our offices. But not to steal anything." I describe what happened last Tuesday. After I watched the man leave, I waited in the office for an hour or so to see if anything else happened. Then I finally went home; when Joel texted me later to see if I was up, I told him what happened. He left the party immediately to be with me. I felt guilty for taking him from the party but was glad not to be alone. In the morning, I went over what happened in the office with Veronica and Geneva, and we discussed more security procedures.

Jeffrey lights up a Marlboro and thinks about what I said. "Could this be a rival? Or someone from the media?"

I smile at the idea of a rival PI firm breaking in to steal company secrets. "The media makes more sense. But what could I have that they'd want?"

Jeffrey exhales. "What about someone on a case you're investigating--someone trying to see what you have against them?"

"A good idea. But then, why show himself? That doesn't compute."

"Mm-hm. You're right. Describe what happened for me again."

He takes the SR-25 closer to the range to practice shooting from the ground. As I'm talking, we're both scanning the area by habit, leery of being ambushed.

"He was at the window, he saw you, and just stayed there."

"That's it."

"Then he wanted you to see him, Gabriel. He answered the phone to let you know. This is something else altogether."

"I was afraid of that. I can handle the other prospects. This is different..."

"You can handle that too. You've been doing so. The fact that you can handle all kinds of things is probably why this person was testing you. Maybe he's a stalker. You get any strange mail?"

I burst out laughing. "Every damn day. I barely notice any more. I actually stopped reading comments to news stories I'm in, because I've become inured."

"Maybe you should scan your mail and look for someone who's a little too much of a fan, or too much of a detractor. I still think that religious group you tangled with could be trouble. It's someone who sees you as a target, and thinks you aren't dangerous to him. Provoking you."

That's pretty close to my own conclusions.

Jeffrey asks, "Anything else you might have been into?"

I sigh. We practice for a while on the SR-25, and then switch to handguns.

"I wondered if it was Cody," I tell him. "Really, he should be halfway around the world by now. He got his money out; they said the account was closed. But I don't think he's the type for revenge."

I can still see Stephen Cody in his cabin with his ridiculous knife. He had killed Meese, the man who had abused Joel. But he was going to use the knife on Joel as well. Mr. Zest, a troubleshooter from the Tertullians who was helping me for mysterious reasons of his own worked with me to stop Cody before he could hurt Joel. I came very close to killing Cody. Very close. Joel didn't want me to do it. I let Joel talk me out of it. A part of me feels cheated.

Jeffrey sees the change in my attitude. "What's getting to you?"

I sort the words in my mind, to get them out. "I keep seeing Cody in that cabin. I wanted to kill him. I feel like I should have killed him."

Just saying that makes me feel shaky with a rush of adrenaline.

"Acknowledge what you feel, Gabriel."

I look over at him. "Would Cody still be alive if you had been there?"

"Don't ask me that. I have different experiences. Joel did not want you to kill him, you told me. You listened to him. I didn't have that option in the field. In many ways I still don't, although I have you to think of as my conscience where Kate once was. I doubt this is Cody as well. Hitmen don't work that way. What about that man you asked me to investigate, while you were still with Bob in Paterson? Comstock, or Clement?"

Clement is a man who seems to be connected to MK-ULTRA and the Tertullian Society. Zest warned me against investigating him, and I in turn warned Alex off a story that involved him. Alex didn't get it, which is why I had to tell him off when he came to bother me at Bob's place.

"I ran across him in the course of looking into a matter as a favor to someone. And then I decided to not pursue it."

"A favor to whom?"

"Alex."

"The ex. The one you're working for at the *Herald-Standard*."

"Working *with*. I work for, Veronica and I work for, Davidson and the paper. I mean, they're a client. Alex is a contact. He had a whistleblower to cultivate a story on intelligence abuse, but I thought the whole situation was too dangerous."

"Would that stop him? Why did you think it was dangerous?"

"Let's just say from some previous trouble, I know more about the particular danger more than Alex does. He probably wouldn't stop, but I couldn't babysit him. He seems to be fine; he's still here."

"Granted. But maybe someone hasn't made a move yet. This person being in your office happened just after you were hired--and I saw the article in the *Standard* announcing you and Veronica being hired."

"A threat--to try to scare us off?"

"Scare you, maybe. But just *you*. I'd bet, as a hypothesis, that he waited until Veronica left. Does it make sense?"

"Yeah..." With the Tertullians, anything is possible. Maybe this person is seeing if I'm helping Alex any further. I weigh whether to talk to Alex. No, not for now. I can't trust him. However, I'll tell Veronica.

I wonder where Zest is. After he left Cody's cabin, he stayed out of sight until I was back in my own place and things were settled down. I found him one day in Tompkins Square Park across from my building.

Joel was sure Zest wanted to leave the Tertullians. Zest didn't deny this, but also didn't seem ready to act. "I'm in a holding pattern; I'm not sure what I'm doing," he told me. "But I'm around if you need." He then gave me a number to memorize.

I'm thinking of talking to him about what's going on. "That stuff Clement is supposed to have done, psyops. You have any experience in that?"

"I've seen it in use. I've had it used on me. Torture goes with the territory in my line of work. Giving it, receiving it. I had colleagues who went through it as well. People can do terrible things to one another. Each instance means less and less justification needed for the next time."

"How *do* you get through it?"

He exhales quietly. "When you were a boy and I would take you out to do this, you were good at everything--shooting, reconnaissance, tracking. Just a kid, but you had a natural talent. I never wanted to teach you about the other parts of my work. You have to be strong enough inside to not die. That's most of it. It's not nobility, just endurance.

"Some of these people, they don't just want physical torture, they want your mind. That's the worst. Physical pain is nothing compared to the feeling that you are going crazy. A group of us talked about this. We figured the best bet was to create a separate person. Someone who's in you, but not you. Someone who can take the pain, and give false information."

He hands me another rifle. I look through the site and shoot a few test rounds.

I ask him, "How do you manage false information? Why doesn't the person who's interrogating you know it's not just you lying?"

Jeffrey lights another cigarette, his eyes distant in another time and place. "You have to put yourself away. As far away as you can. Let the other person take over. Hope you're able to come back."

I imagine doing that, and what that means about Clement.

∞

Thursday, September 29
Adams Street, 3:00 pm

In a rural part of Westchester, the man known to Gabriel and Joel as Mr. Zest comes out of the isolated building where he's staying and walks down a dirt road to a small lake.

He wonders how long he has before he must decide the action that determines his fate. He knows the ending is not likely to be good, and very few paths are available. Still, one doesn't hasten an inevitability of this kind.

Perhaps not surprisingly, his solitude does not last long. He keeps various devices around him by which one may communicate; he has them set not to track his location. A mini-tablet inside his jacket beeps to let him know he has a message. When he reads the message, he knows his time has come. Last chance to just leave, or to deal with the Society.

--Maxim;

I have some imminent plans and I need to gather resources for these. I'm hoping that your loyalty remains true to our personal association. I appreciate when you looked into Mesereau further. He seems too interested in my business. I think Jacobs put him on this. However, you might remember I was made aware of a person who could be a good subject for Cognoscenti. You have dealt with him-- Gabriel Ross. What kind of person is he?

–Damon

∞

THREE

From the YouTube Channel "Tom Paine Events," in a video entitled: Unknown Knowns: Dorothy Kilgallen ♦ The Firebrand

Transcript: "Famous writer, TV and radio personality Dorothy Kilgallen had interviewed Lee Harvey Oswald's killer Jack Ruby, and promised shocking revelations in her planned book on the JFK assassination. Kilgallen, an experienced and aggressive reporter, was public and pointed on criticizing the government (especially the FBI) on investigating her as she was investigating the flaws of the Warren Commission.

"She was found dead in strange circumstances, and her manuscript had disappeared. Disappearing manuscripts or notes is par for the course in mysterious deaths. These are unknown knowns, especially regarding stories that haven't been told, like Jack Ruby's. Kilgallen's death raises the question what powers that be might she have been provoking, and what story they didn't want told."

∞

AND STILL ZEST TRIES to stop the force in motion.

--Damon,

I don't think the person you mentioned would be of use to you. I would strongly suggest not approaching him.

It doesn't work, as Zest pretty much knew it would not. Clement is high-strung. He has intense feelings about Zest, thinking of him as a most trusted confidante. However, Clement is also tetchy and impulsive at times. When he has someone in his sights, he's not likely to back off, no matter how much he respects Zest's opinions.

--*Maxim;*

I will always value your suggestions. I have observed Ross. He intrigues me in how he acts. He seems to have certain personality traits that would prove my work to be a success. My protégé Encausse believes the same about Ross.

Yes, this Encausse person. Another unpleasant wrinkle in this Gothic tale. Zest has not yet met Encausse, whom Clement is very fond of but keeps under deep cover. Zest has not cared for years who Clement is or isn't mentoring, but now it has finally become a problem. He sighs. He doesn't like what he needs to say. But what's a lie, at this point?

--*Damon,*

My first priority has always been protecting you. Our relationship demands that. Approaching this individual will be dangerous. More so than you think.

A pause. Then Clement writes back:

--*Maxim;*

Your concern gratifies me, as I'm sure you know what the endgame is. Perhaps you could help us in this task? Not so vulgar as being a bodyguard--but you know this man. You can help us control him.

Zest hasn't used profanity since he was a young man in New Zealand. Since he met Clement, in fact. He allows some now in his mind. Typical of Clement to make the situation worse. More lies are necessary.

--I'm not in the area at the moment. Try to hold off any action until I can scope out the situation.

Clement responds:

--I'll engage in further research.

Zest hopes that this will keep Clement occupied for a while until he can figure out a solution.

∞

Reason to Believe, by Walter Churchill
Excerpted in *New York* magazine Spring 2012

The Tertullian Society, the one that Gabriel Ross clashed with by happenstance in 2010 in the Raymond Booth case, was created at the turn of the 20th Century. It burst into existence like an evil alchemy in the wake of the hermetic revival going on at the time. Around 1900, a frustrated writer and would-be occult adept named Friedrich Schroeder started the Society in Berlin. Schroeder had dabbled in some other sects like the Golden Dawn but ultimately rejected them as they neither appreciated his self-proclaimed superior intellect nor his fascist politics.

Schroeder believed that supernatural powers are available to society's elite, those genetically worthy. He studied the rituals said to be taught in 1st Century Egyptian mystery schools. Those rituals were written down in documents alleged to be authentic knowledge. Purveyors of ancient documents real and fake sought Schroeder out, as he was known to be an easy sell for anything ancient, esoteric, and especially if reflecting his 'masters of the world ' philosophy.

One such document claimed that for those who are elite and pure, the cosmos will open and give them rule upon the world through the old gods...those predating Yahweh, predating the Vedics. Engaging in certain rituals will open time and space to the great beyond. The spirits of the very gods themselves would deign to possess the chosen few and jump-start the world take-over--the inevitable goal of any secret society worth its salt.

Supposedly, this document was discovered by the Church father Tertullian in an underground cavern. Struck by what he read, Tertullian then started the first secret society in Christendom, while covering it up with history's first false flag-- encouraging the great unworthy to cling regular Christianity as a means of mind control, while the smart guys who knew better reaped the rewards.

Schroeder shared his newfound secrets with famed occult master and self-proclaimed "most evil man in the world" Aleister Crowley. Both had strong beliefs that powerful personalities could control others. Both actually proved that right. But two such powerful personalities can't exist together in the same space, sharing leadership. Schroeder eventually fell out with Crowley, declaring him to not be serious enough--too willing to sacrifice principle for fame. And granted, Crowley was nothing if not a fame whore. Schroeder later claimed Crowley stole his ritual, "Babalon Working," from Tertullian rituals. Babalon working was the magic that pre-Scientology L. Ron Hubbard and his buddy rocket scientist Jack Parsons used to attempt to rip open dimensions in our universe. Parsons later accidentally blew himself up in his home lab.

Schroeder met Adolf Hitler when Hitler was a lazeabout youth in Vienna. His influence on Hitler was strong, even stronger than the most commonly-cited influence on Vienna-era Hitler, occult mentor Dietrich Eckart. Schroeder was actually someone Hitler turned to after Eckart died. Not surprisingly, Schroeder was said to have killed Eckart via occult spells. Heinrich Himmler--the real occult adept in the Nazi hierarchy, who perhaps believed Schroeder could kill by spell, encouraged Schroeder to experiment with science and magic. Schroeder began scientific trials on mind control and assassination by spell, sometimes in concentration camps.

∞

Friday, September 30
12th Street, Long Island City, Queens, 7:00 pm

Joel is sitting against a far wall of a ground floor warehouse in Queens. He's surrounded by his phone, his iPad, a small laptop, and a satchel of his art supplies. Chris is next to him, with zis own electronica set up. Chris is a year older than Joel, and over six feet. Ze also is Genderqueer and likes to mix male and female clothing and neutral gender pronouns. Chris is slender and has an unruly mop of curly brown hair and prominent black eyes somewhere between Sophia Loren and Tim Curry. Today ze is wearing cat's eye eyeliner to highlight the Sophia Loren side.

On Joel's other side is Walter Cleveland. Walter's not exactly happy about sitting on the floor, but following Gabriel makes him feel like he's roughing it with the bad boys.

Walter is not sure about the intricacies of gender identities but is talking about the subject with Chris. Chris likes discussing zis experience. "I did some drag when I was young, but I don't feel I'm one gender or the other. They're all the same. I'm like one of those *The New Generation* beings who just transfer from body to body."

Joel said, "The hackers group we were in didn't appreciate that, as I recall." Joel and Chris met in the group back in their teens, where they gave each other code names of Satyricon and Mephisto. Chris also was part of Star Trek TNG and UFO subcultures, but had varying levels of difficulties with some of them due to Chris's nonconformity in gender. Even in groups on the outside of mainstream, convention exists.

"I'm a human avatar," Chris responds. "Those losers couldn't be the wind beneath my wings. But Mephisto got it. I'm the only person he admits is better than he is coding."

They are all at the warehouse to watch Gabriel train with his Baguazhang mentor, Zihou Chiang. Gabriel has brought Veronica along. Gabriel has been teaching Veronica boxing techniques and some of what he knows regarding Baguazhang. Since the completion of the Stephen Cody case Gabriel has been training more intensely. Usually Chiang leads that training in his Chinatown loft, but he's determined they need more space and so they are using the warehouse that Chiang either owns.

"What is this he's doing," Walter asks, his eyes wide in watching the activities in the center of the floor.

Joel stops with his typing and looks up. Gabriel and Veronica are both in t-shirts and athletic pants. Gabriel's hair is slicked against his head in sweat. Chiang is dressed similarly, in all black. He leads the two as if he was handling lions and tigers in a circus arena.

Walter observes how Joel's expression changes watching Gabriel and Veronica, as they focus on Chiang's coaching. He smiles.

Joel glances at Walter smiling at him and blushes. "Uh, according to Gabriel it's an obscure form of Shaolin Kung Fu that involves moves similar to parkour."

"Ah. That's why he's literally bouncing off the walls."

"He wants to be Keanu Reeves in *The Matrix* so bad..."

As the exercises continue, Chiang stops the action and starts it as per his observations, frequently barking instructions at Gabriel, who follows the edicts without comment.

Walter comments, "Mr. Chiang is the only person I've seen Gabriel take orders from. Willingly."

"Tell me about it. I know in part it's because Gabriel doesn't want to mess this up; he wants to be a master of this spiritual discipline. But he isn't even resentful about being told what to do. And believe me..."

On the other side of the room, Gabriel turns, catching Joel's look. He calls out, "You want to get in on this, or something? Come on over."

"Please," Veronica says. "I need someone to make me look better."

Joel responds with a lot of warmth. "No, you two need the practice. I'm busy protecting you in other ways. Plus, I have the pleasure of watching you be bossed around."

Chiang laughs. "I have no doubt about that." Chiang is slightly shorter than Gabriel, with wavy salt and pepper hair, hazel eyes and a trim beard. His accent is a mixture of Hong Kong and the British Isles, with the occasional hint of New York. He is very patient, but he also is very exacting--pushing them to do more with their minds and bodies, and make it a natural flow. "Do it better," he says. "Find the Zen of the action and work with it."

Gabriel and Veronica look at each other a long moment, then begin moving in tandem, working on anticipating the other's moves, the other's thoughts.

"They look great together," Walter says.

"If I believed in reincarnation, I'd think they were twins in another life."

Chris laughs. "Getting all spiritual now. Were *you* there too, Mephisto?"

"Fuck yeah. They fought over me, even." Joel goes back to his computer, smiling. "It probably looked just like this."

"Joel, would you consider doing some kind of martial arts?"

"Not my thing. I fight my own way. Dirty as hell, and with a knife if necessary. I also fight by putting myself in different places, becoming different people."

"Oh, I can imagine. You and he have complementary styles. You're very elegant in life but a street ruffian in action. Gabriel is a ruffian in life but an elegant fighter. But Veronica decided she was interested in the elegant fighting?"

Joel nods, touching his pack of Djarum. "I offered to show her some knife tricks, but she spurned my offer." He tries not to sound annoyed about that.

Veronica is participating in the training because of Gabriel's concern about the Tertullians. Gabriel told Geneva about them as well. He wants everyone to be aware of any danger they face by being close to him. Geneva is Army-trained, but Veronica has very little formal defense training. Gabriel is very protective of Veronica, for both her emotional state after breaking up with Michaela and in her being a target in any way because of the Tertullians. Veronica is protective of Gabriel in turn because of his scare from the break-in and the feeling he has of being stalked.

Joel sat in on a little meeting they had the other day, Gabriel, Veronica and Geneva. Joel was there because he is a silent partner in Gotham Investigations. He has invested a little of the money his friend and former client Jan left him. That investment allowed for the office rental and equipment upgrades.

In the meeting, Veronica and Geneva were both surprised by Gabriel offering to take himself off the partnership and leave the agency to Veronica. He said as a matter of honor he wouldn't cash out but just start again on his own, so she wouldn't be left in a lurch. He feels the danger from the Society is creeping back, and he doesn't want to involve her or Geneva or be responsible for harm coming to them. He said Joel would ensure that the agency is solvent, and said he would figure out how to handle the *Herald-Standard* situation.

Veronica smiled while he described that. "It's very noble. But you aren't leaving." She refused to end the partnership. As his friend, she was staying with him. Gabriel didn't argue but he emphasized bluntly how dangerous it was. Veronica was still absolutely sure she was going to back him up.

Then they both made the same offer to Geneva, to extract herself if she wanted, no hard feelings. Geneva laughed as well. "After what we've been through already? I'm not the type to back down either."

So they're in it together. Gabriel didn't ask Joel about his feelings, as that was not a question. He and Joel have already been through enough to destroy a dozen lesser couples. Fair-weather couples.

And yet right now Gabriel and Veronica are fighting each other. Of course, it's to be able to fight *for* each other. As utterly ridiculous as it seems to him, Joel feels a hint of jealousy at Gabriel and Veronica's closeness; their easy camaraderie. He's close to Veronica but it's more intense. Or something he can't describe.

Joel catches Chris smiling sardonically at him. He makes his face expressionless. But it's too late. Chris whispers to him, "*Yeah*, Mephisto. You want to be their wrestling mat so bad, don't you? Bang-a-gong-get-it-on."

Joel gives him a death glare, but Chris is immune. Having made his point, he turns to Walter to educate him on theories regarding aliens and governmental cover-ups.

∞

[SCRAMBLE MESSAGE]
jFMF1vQhU3 YNXavxrUAl 1Yj0SJEZCE FA5p4ZeB4Y

[Unscramble] ENIGMA Project/Eyes Only

From KISMET, to MORTEM AND REAPER
--Have you heard from ETERNITY of late? I suspect he and BEDEVIL may be going off script.

From REAPER and MORTEM, to KISMET
--Will follow up w/progress report.

--UPDATE: ETERNITY claims to be monitoring BEDEVIL's activities and may have new information on COGNOSCENTI. Will keep apprised.

∞

Monday, October 10
Herald-Standard building, 10:32 am

In reviewing some of the stories from being published in the *Standard* this week one catches my eye, by a reporter named Scott Roman. Something in how Roman writes about a source reminds me of a former *New York Times* reporter who faked a story on African child soldiers. I do some digging and come to the conclusion Roman's story has fake sources, and that this is not the first story the reporter has faked. Veronica begins collecting evidence by contacting the people named in the stories. Once we have enough evidence to prove the allegations, I call Alex about it. He asks me to meet with him in his office, so I go over.

Alex has a stack of files on his desk. He picks up the top one. "Right. This is Scott's employee file. I've been given the protocol of complete candor with you about anyone here. Including myself, of course."

"Really."

"Yes. Whatever you need to know, I can tell you whilst it's related to security."

"So, you can tell me whatever's been entrusted to you--what Clark tells you, for instance. You'll share that with me."

"Outside of trade secrets and confidential business information. You were hired for security. Understand that confidentiality agreement includes any information I give you-- including the fact that I gave it to you."

"Nice."

He raises his eyebrows. "The employees at all levels are aware that no privacy outside that mandated by law or contract is to be expected. Clark is a good man. I know there's nothing to turn up about him. But if he did something..." Alex shrugs. "I couldn't support him. It would be unethical."

"I will let you know should I need more information."

"And I'm in that, too. You can ask what you need to suss out any info." He smiles. "Did you ever run a background check on me?" "Actually, no. And that's funny. A significant part of our business is background checks on people. We make a point of it on the new website. I've done it for Veronica and Bob on personal matters. But not for myself. Outside of reading your stories when we first met."

That gets a bigger smile I ignore, and try to deflect by asking, "Did you check up on me?"

"Yes. I needed to know more about you in order to know if I was on the right track in supporting you with the Booth case. I didn't find much about you online...just the incident in Buckston, and a mention in a couple articles about your uncle's passing."

I hadn't thought about those articles in years. Something in my stomach twists up, by his bringing up Dominic. I also, against my own logic, can't help but wonder what he didn't tell me back in August. He has not attempted to discuss anything but work-related topics. But in every conversation, there's an edge of something not said.

Impulsively I say, "Maybe I'll do one on you now, then. A test case."

"Let me know what you find out." He walks around the desk to hand me the employee file.

I take it and flip through it. "Is Roman here today?"

"Yes. You want to talk to him?"

"Yeah. Is he union?"

"No, so no Weingarten rights." If part of a union, Roman would be allowed to have a union rep with him during any investigation and discipline proceedings. "And we've cleared the issue with HR and Legal."

"Then let's confront him now."

Alex arranges for this and I call Veronica, and have her bring Geneva and Halo to the offices.

Alex brings Roman into the meeting room where I'm set up. Roman is about 35, white, arrogant with an overtone of friendliness. I have a laptop out, with a dual camera system. In another room, Veronica, Geneva, and Halo are watching on a linked laptop. I want Halo to get a sense of how questioning works in this situation.

I start out asking Roman general questions about his employment and past stories. He is reasonably cooperative. I shift my line of questioning and begin to probe in detail.

"This person you quote in the story you just turned in--the one on government contractors. The source says you never spoke to him. Why would he say that?"

Roman opens his eyes wide. "I have a spotless record here. I never got in trouble in school, or any other job. Why are you harassing me? Alex? What's going on?"

Roman is showing two deceptive behaviors. He's trying to make himself look honest with a stiffly executed expression, and deflecting my question by pointing out truths--truths that have nothing to do with the situation at hand. It's always a red flag when the suspect refuses to directly answer the question (as if he couldn't be bothered).

I say in a neutral tone, "My partner and I have reviewed five of your stories. Is there any reason why in all five there are events that have no record of occurring, and sources who don't seem to exist?"

"That isn't...they're true. I just had to protect the sources."

"What about the events?"

"I don't know...I had to protect my sources."

"Why would you say that? How does making up events protect the sources?"

"Hey, you know, I went to the Columbia School of Journalism. Who the hell are you to question me?"

That's another tactic, to try to pull rank by something meaningless. I smile politely. "Tell me this, then. Why might any of your co-workers say that they knew you had fabricated details in your stories?"

"What? Why would I jeopardize my job to do something like that? Make up something?"

He's nervous now. I haven't spoken with his coworkers but his guilty knowledge makes him believe that. And he still doesn't answer my questions directly.

"Is there any reason why we can't find any verifying details to these stories?"

"I don't know. I didn't do anything wrong."

He's about done now, I can sense. My voice remains calm.

"As a sign of good faith, would you go through the stories with me?"

"I'd have to think about it..."

A few more minutes of this and I have him acknowledging what happened. The questioning has to follow a certain structure, I have to listen to his cues to adjust as needed, and keep my tone and face neutral. A confrontational tone would make him close up and being friendly would make him feel like he was in control. Being neutral unnerves him.

I ask him, "I know you didn't do this in all your stories. How many was it? Just let us know."

He admits to several instances of fabricating quotes, sources, and events in the five stories. Alex is extremely angry at Roman, which I can understand. He has a right to be.

While Alex deals with Roman for the time being, I go talk to my associates.

Halo grabs my hand. He's wearing a blazer and slacks today, instead of his leather vest and jeans (copying some guy on *The Walking Dead*). "That was great! Just like on TV."

"It would be less than riveting television, but thank you."

I discuss the situation with them for a while. Then Alex comes by to let me know he's sent Roman sent home for the day, and asks me to come to his office again.

He sits on his desk. I go over to look out the window of his office to the street ten floors below.

"We're going to have an executive meeting in a bit. You were really super."

"Just my job."

"Modest. Because you found this, we can control the fallout. It's not like when someone on the outside finds out first."

"Good. I hope it blows over fast."

"We didn't expect you to find this kind of thing, I admit. But then, I never appreciated you like I should for your skills. You could help people."

I turn around. "I *am* helping people."

"I know. I need your help on something else, Gabriel. My source disappeared. Zach Mesereau."

This has to be what he's been not-telling me. I'm both relieved it's not personal and also feel a sharp vein of fear go through me. Mesereau claimed to have inside information on a MK-ULTRA type operation being illegally run in the US by a rogue element of the CIA. Except that Mesereau was Tertullian-connected. In fact, he was connected somehow to Clement. Alex had wanted me to investigate Clement, who was going under the name Aaron Comstock. Mesereau was afraid of him, Alex said.

"Gabriel, are you okay?" He's leaning forward, frowning.

I try to cover my feelings. "Alex, I'm sorry to hear that. I told you to stay away from his problems. That still holds true."

"I appreciate it. But I'm very concerned. It's been a couple weeks since I heard from him. He recently moved from his apartment to take over his parents' house in Queens. I went by but he didn't answer. He didn't tell me he was planning to leave or anything."

I shrug briefly. "Maybe he had to leave fast."

"Can you help me try to find him?"

"No, I can't."

He shakes his head. "That doesn't seem like you. You've helped me, even if you're mad at me. You look very stressed. Is there something going on with you, someone causing you trouble in your personal life?"

"No. Don't go there, Alex. We're supposed to be beyond that."

"If you say so. But your eyes tell me something bad has happened."

I look away for a moment. "No, not really. No more than usual stressors."

"Well if it's not, hmm, your *personal* life, then what? You started to look into that issue for me with Mesereau, and you got more into it than I asked you too. And then you just stopped. Now you're sitting here looking like the devil grabbed your bollocks. Why did you tell me to drop my story with Mesereau?"

Alex helped me make the original connection to them in Raymond Booth's case. When Zest told me that everyone I cared about would be killed if I continued the investigation, I told Alex that I did stop, for his safety. There was never any reason for him to think otherwise. I never told him about Kent's notes. I never told him what happened in Westchester with Ethan Nelson kidnapping Joel. I never told him about Bertrand Herrmann. I'm not going to.

"I found indications that this was more dangerous. I don't know Mesereau's role, but Comstock is dangerous. Stay away from him, Alex. Please."

Our eyes meet and he half-smiles and gets up. "The fact you're concerned is much appreciated. I'm not worried about me. I need to find Mesereau. At least make sure he's okay." He raises his hands in a what-can-I-do gesture. "I owe him that much."

"Jesus. Did you really get that involved? I guess I'd do the same." I run my hands through my hair. "All right, I still have his file, I think. I'll see what I can find out."

Alex moves closer. "That's good of you. Check out his house. I should have let you check it out before instead of giving you a hard time."

I nod. "Forget it. Just whatever I do or don't find, leave Comstock out of the equation."

Alex takes my hand in a quasi-formal shake. "I wouldn't put myself in any unnecessary danger. Be sure to watch your own back."

∞

When I get home around seven, Archie, my black and white tuxedo-style feline, runs to greet me and determine where I've been, and if I've been messing with any other cats.

Joel comes out of the second bedroom/office, on the phone with someone. He comes up to greet me. I get an open-mouth kiss from him, and hear Isabella's gravelly voice on the phone. He ignores her to attend to our greeting, until she starts yelling: "Are you even listening to me?"

"No," he responds, and goes back into the second bedroom.

I walk into my bedroom, going past a small painting Joel did for me, recreating the FBI "Missing" poster of James Chaney, Michael Schwerner, and Andrew Goodman. The three civil rights workers who were killed in Mississippi in 1963 while investigating voting conditions. It is stunning in its starkness.

Decompression time. Strip off the suit jacket and shoes. I'm thinking I might have a glass of wine to help in the decompression. I head for the kitchen.

He's already opened a bottle and set glasses out. Now that's scary.

Joel hustles out the bedroom again and looks me over. "Where's your jacket and shoes?"

"Hung up, and in the closet shoe rack."

He stops and speaks into his iPhone. "*Siri*, check on any possible saucer landings and alien invasions which may have abducted my boyfriend, and replaced him with a neater duplicate."

I finish pouring. "Nice work with the mind reading on the wine. Can you read my mind right now?"

"Yeah. You're threatening to kick my ass for the 7,119th time, and you'll fail on the follow-through." Joel moves closer. "And even so, you're thinking about what you want to do with me later." His hand goes around mine holding the wineglass.

"That's not mind reading. That's 90% of the time."

He gets right up in front of me, his face close to mine. "What's the other ten percent?"

"Bare necessities. Maslow's hierarchy. Except that things like food, water, shelter, come *after* pleasuring you."

He nods. "Good answer." His arms go around me.

We go to couch. He lies on it, his legs on mine, eyes half-closed and the wine glass dangling from his hand. I sip slowly, watching him.

He watches me watching him. "How'd it go with the reporter?"

"Got him to confess."

"What did you do, give him one of your lectures in obscure Buddhist metaphysics? Yeah, I'd confess too, to get the hell out of there."

He keeps a straight face. I set my glass on the windowsill next to the sofa. "That ass-kicking can be an imminent reality."

"Bring it on, Man of Action."

He called me that when he first got back in NYC last summer, when he was helping me with the Booth case. And reminding me of how important his presence was.

Time feels strange. A year ago, Alex would have been on the sofa, and I would have been feeling awkward about working with Joel.

"Baby, you're tense." He sits up and puts his hand on the back of my neck. "What happened?"

I empty about half the wine glass first, and then take a deep breath and tell him about Alex and Mesereau.

He doesn't change expression, but his eyes get darker. "Am I supposed to be 'adult' about this? Or can I threaten to kick *your* ass for once?"

"You can be what you want. There's always time, up to a point, where I can do something without incurring risk. I know when that point comes up."

Joel shakes his head. "That *point* has left the station, went home, retired and moved to Arizona already. If Harry Potter--yeah, I know you don't like me calling him that--wants to get himself killed, what the fuck do you care?"

"I care because it's who I am."

"You could choose to live a boring life for a while without getting in fires or shot at or jailed. And you have other people to think of. Your partner, your employees, maybe me if that means anything."

"If *you* mean anything? Come on, Joel. Don't be that way. You mean everything to me. What happened to me in the cases was not all my doing."

"But this is different. Gabriel, Alex gets you into the *Standard*, then someone breaks in your office, and now you learn Alex's source disappears--the source who has gotten the Tertullians' attention somehow. Is this all coincidence?"

"Working at the *Standard* is."

"Huh. Maybe someone sees your connection with Alex as deeper than what it is."

I set my empty glass down and look at him. "Do you think that someone is just going to give up? If it's connected to Mesereau, then maybe I need to find out who it is and why he's interested, rather than sitting around hoping it will go away."

"You know who you need to talk to about it. Zest. Dr. Doom."

"Yeah, if he's still around. Let me just look into this some first. Maybe there's a slim chance this has nothing to do with them."

Joel both rolls his eyes and shakes his head. He stares out the window, and mutters something under his breath--*can't get away from that fool.* Meaning Alex, probably.

I feel my face slowly start to burn, and I get up.

He turns back. "Where are you going?"

I look down at him. "It's awkward right now. I know it's my fault. I'm sorry about breaking the mood."

He raises one eyebrow. "Really? I'm not letting him interfere with my night. Sit back down."

I pause for a moment, but he's serious. I sit down again.

He reaches to place his wine glass on the coffee table, then slides off the sofa to get on his knees in front of me. He unbuckles my belt, unzips my trousers, bends over.

I catch my breath, even as the superego part of me has concerns that he's doing this to prove something. The part of my brain connected to my dick has no such concerns.

And still my superego tries. "Would you like to...do you want to..."

I feel the friction of his tongue, and I can't finish my words.

He raises his head briefly. "I'm doing what I want to do." And goes back to it.

Are you gonna argue with him?

Uh, no. No.

∞

Thursday, October 13
CUNY Midtown, 100th Street West Campus, 1:38 am

I start some rudimentary efforts in looking for Mesereau. I ask a NYPD friend of mine to check recent arrests and unidentifiable bodies. I talk to Chris about ways to determine someone's online presence by IP address. I'm putting off doing anything serious until I have to.

Instead today I had a long meeting with my faculty advisor, Anne French, regarding my thesis. She peppered me with questions in preparation for the thesis defense. She knew my uncle Dominic and had worked with him on a philosophy of art course. This is why I asked her to be my advisor. Anne showed me where I could even use some of Dominic's academic articles as sources for my own work. He would have been knocked out about that.

I don't have a copy of Dom's own theses, which were written in the early Eighties. I'm pretty sure that his boyfriend Randall has them. Randall and I did not get along. I would feel a little awkward visiting him--what now--six years after Dominic died, and asking him to give me Dominic's effects. So I've been tracking down some of Dominic's stuff in the college archives.

CUNY Midtown is actually uptown; that's been a running joke for years. The college was originally founded by Caleb Carlson, a 19th Century robber baron. Carlson's other big legacy was Solstice Park in Yonkers, which I know from having a run-with Ethan Nelson there. The college was originally Carlson College. After Carlson's death, and once the college was integrated into the CUNY system, it changed its name due to Carlson's rumored interest in occult magic. It was given the name CUNY Midtown with the intention of moving the university to the East Fifties. But a continuing series of mishaps prevented this. An urban legend has it that Carlson's spirit refused to allow the college to move, angry at the name change. And so it remains "Midtown at Uptown," in its Gothic structure on a sprawling campus north of Central Park, and is rumored to be haunted by Carlson's furious, Satan-loving ghost.

The research library is Carlson Library, and is the largest and most Gothic of the campus buildings. Six stories in height with winding metal staircases dark coves and corners, and rows and rows of dusty books. A newer library, the Anne Hutchinson, is on the Eastern edge of the campus. The two have completely different atmospheres. Only serious scholars go to the Carlson. I've found Dom's work here and spent time copying the papers carefully so I can scan them into my computer at home later.

The library is open all night during semesters but not fully lit in some sections after 9 pm. The stacks of books are tall, the pathways between them dark. The book stacks extend from a back wall to end at a narrow metal grate walkway extending the width of each floor. The accompanying metal circular staircases are at either end of the floors. There are hidden rooms, cubicles, and dumbwaiters on each floor no longer in use. In addition, the floors don't really meet the walls of the building on the south side. There's a gap of about 22 inches, and if you stand in the last aisle, you can look at the drop going down to the ground floor. The floors have barriers of sorts of the edges, about two feet high, with couple of thin metal bars as a brace. Of course, legends have circulated of people falling in the gap, scared by or pushed by Carlson's ghost.

I'm on the fourth floor, and pretty much done for the night. Since it's late, I'm considering a taking a cab home rather than catch the crosstown bus and 6 Train. I pack my stuff into my knapsack and leave the stacks. Stepping on the grate, I glance down and catch a glimpse of someone on the third floor, moving silently.

The figure stops and seems to look up. The grated metal is made up of small diamond shapes, which break up any visual into hallucinatory patterns. Perhaps this is another student working, maybe a little startled that someone else is here at two in the morning.

Maybe.

The figure turns and *backs* into one the stacks aisles. He actually walks backward slowly, still looking up. What the hell?

Maybe you're seeing things. And maybe it's the man who was in our office, trying to see what I'll do when I realize he's following me.

∞

From the YouTube Channel "Tom Paine Events," in a video entitled:
Unknown Knowns: Karen Silkwood ♦ The Whistleblower

Transcript: "Silkwood was a worker in the Oklahoma Kerr-McGee nuclear facility. Having come across evidence that plant safety was being neglected and evidence falsified, Silkwood was planning to meet with a reporter regarding her findings. She perished on the way to that meeting, after drifting off the road in an alleged one-car crash. Her evidence, which she had taken with her, was--guess what--not found.

"Silkwood's death raises the question in how you recognize such unknown knowns. The semiotics of conspiracy--mysterious deaths while alone, a powers-that-be under provocation, documents or evidence that was known to exist suddenly missing. An official story meant to cast doubt upon the bona fides of the deceased, government investigation and dismissal of claims, and something extra--a little strange DNA. In this case, the strange shot of DNA was the subsequent court case brought by attorney Daniel Sheehan of the Christic (now Romero) Institute (who helped expose Iran-Contra) wherein Sheehan alleged FBI investigation of Silkwood, and a judge who supposedly told Sheehan that the information he sought was "sinister" and shouldn't be exposed."

∞

Thursday, October 13, Continued

WHAT I *SHOULD* DO IS LEAVE. Three floors of winding stairs and then through the wide, darkened lobby, and then out the building.

I go down to the third floor and down the aisle next to the one I saw the man back into. No books are kept in the seven-foot high shelves abutting the wall, so that the librarians can store material to be filed away. I can't see anyone through the gap of the shelves. Using the shelves as an impromptu ladder, I climb to the top.

I lean over the top of the shelf. No one is in the aisle. I look back down in mine. He's not here either.

I go back down and head to the grate walkway. It's empty. But *above* me, I now see the figure on the fourth floor. I move to the other end of the walkway. I hear the man walking the same direction.

When I reach the stairs at the south end, I see another person at the bottom--down on the first floor. Standing just in the shadows, waiting.

Footsteps above me. The man coming down from the fourth floor.

I turn left and head down the last aisle. Another step from above. I stop and stand on the top thin brace separating me from the gap. I know from previous misadventures in the library when I was younger that I can just reach the floor above. I hoist myself up enough to reach the bottom brace on the railing. Then I use that to climb up on the fourth floor. I can hear the steps of the person coming down to where I had been.

When I was 19 or so I'd often hide out in the library late at night. Sometimes alone, sometimes with my crush of the moment (all of whom were older and had some risky element to them--all of whom Dom attempted to eradicate from my life). Dom would come looking for me to drag me home. I'd distantly hear the librarian dime me out: "Professor Sheehan, I'm sure I saw Gabriel in the third-floor stacks with a *guest* of some sort..." And then the sound of him jogging up the stairs. I'd already be back at the far wall and doing what I'm doing now--crawling through the spaces at the back of the shelves to get to the middle stack. There's a nearly hidden door set in the wall that doesn't have a handle. It has a lock, but the lock unlatches if you hit the wall next to it just right.

Can I move as fast as I could at 19, complete with knapsack? I'm tempted to confront this person following me, but I go against my instincts. Something about the haunted library discourages risks.

My hand goes down the wall to the spot I know. I hit it with a slight upward motion. A tiny snick sound results. I dig my fingers into a thin crack and pull open the door, slipping inside and closing it behind me.

I'm standing in an areaway, filthy with disuse. Cobwebs and dust hit my face, making me want to panic. Five feet ahead is a narrow wooden stairway that goes down to a back storeroom. That's my destination.

Moving quietly, I make my way down the stairs. Only the fourth floor has the door, God knows why. It was Carlson's design. Danny and I always suspected there was an occult ritual room hidden somewhere in here.

The storeroom is in the far end of the building behind the front desk and admin offices, and mainly holds cleaning items and junk office equipment. That hasn't changed. I push the door open gently and step into the storeroom. So far, so good. I could go out the room and chance pissing off the lone attendant behind the circulation desk. Probably a work-study student handling the graveyard shift. But I continue following my teenage path--going to the lone window in the storeroom, unlocking the ancient clasp, and climbing out.

I'm sticky with dust but no matter. I stay in the shadows next to the building. The 19-year-old me would have been hauling ass for 101st Street and the subway before Dom figured out I wasn't in the building. If lucky, I would get home before him, change and be in bed, and when he returned I'd feign innocence, claiming the librarian was delusional.

The current me wants to see if these mystery people leave. I move around in the darkened grass between the library and the humanities building. A few giant old oak trees offer some cover for me to get to a spot in an alcove that allows me to watch the front of the library.

Twenty minutes later, two men quietly exit the building. They have caps on, pulled low. Both of them look around carefully. Unless they have night vision binoculars or radar, they can't see me.

I realize I'm shivering. The night is cool and damp, but I know it's more from the situation. My phone vibrates against my chest, in the inner pocket of my jacket. Probably Joel.

One of the men holds his hand up to the other and turns slowly, taking in the darkened grounds as if he knows I'm here. He walks on a path that takes him by the humanities building. His walk is very deliberate, pausing at times to stop and scan. The other man follows him at a distance.

I know this has to be the man who was in our office. He is waiting to see what I'll do again. Standing out on a path in shadowed moonlight, remembering that I was reckless enough to go back in the office. Figuring that at the least, I'd be here trying to see him instead of sensibly on my way home.

More phone vibrations. Joel getting mad that I'm not responding.

The man walks closer to where I am. I try to melt into the doorway, become a set of black pixels.

He walks by, twenty feet away. I can only see his eyes, which are highlighted by the moonlight. There's something familiar to him I can't place. It disturbs me, because I know I'm really being stalked.

Then the man speaks. "You are exceptional. I look forward to this."

His words anger and frighten me. I don't respond. This isn't the place. The cold of the stone wall sinks into me, except for where my phone is buzzing hot against my chest. The man stops and waits for his companion to catch up, then nods and looks around a last time. Like he knows I'm nearby, and he's pleased.

I wait five minutes after the two of them have gone out of sight, and then text Joel. He has an account with a car service I rarely use, but this time I want him to send a car for me. I'm afraid to move until then.

∞

Friday, October 14
Wayne, NJ, 6:00 pm

"I'm canceling with Mom," Joel says, exhaling smoke. It's the next evening after the library incident. We're supposed to have dinner with Gloria McFadden in her condo in Joel's hometown of Wayne, NJ.

"No. I'm not going to be trapped in the apartment. I can't do that."

Joel's face gets tense. "Why take the risk?"

"Am I going to give up my job because of this and go all Howard Hughes? Being on the move makes me feel better. I thought about just having you go alone, but no."

"What does this man want with you?"

"Fuck only knows. But he comes around when I'm alone. I just want to be with you and forget for a while."

"And going to see my mother will make this a relaxing, carefree evening?"

"Hell no. But the tension between you two will distract me big-time."

He tries not to smile. These evenings with Gloria are rough. There are things he lets go, and things he can't. I suppose she too has her own issues.

Right now, she's trying to sell her house. Since a murder occurred there, it's not the most marketable property. She doesn't live in the house anymore. She's renting a condo on the outskirts of Wayne. She's talking about buying the condo or another one. She had hinted she wanted to live in New York City near Joel, but he is not going for that at all. He needs some distance. Having to cross a bridge to see her is helpful in maintaining boundaries in a relationship not built on boundaries.

Gloria's condo is set up very nice, and she looks better than a few months ago, when I first met her. New hair, new clothes. The reasons for socializing are like for any family matter. She wants to make us dinner. She wants to feel part of our lives. She wants to continue the drama that she had with Joel for the first 15 years of his life.

I'm not sure what Joel wants. I think he feels that having a mom makes his life more normal. He's ultracompetent in taking care of business, but personal matters are a struggle. He's trying so hard, and sometimes he gives me the impression he's trying to be 'normal' for my sake. I've tried to get across the idea that there is no normal. There may be conventional, but no normal. No amount of multicamera sitcoms with two parents and wacky neighbors can change that.

But here we are. I want to support him, even if I sometimes end up as the buffer between them.

Gloria is a decent cook. She is a little nervous, trying hard to show she wants to be part of 'us.' I help her with the cooking. Joel doesn't help; his version of cooking is maintaining a list of restaurants that deliver in under an hour.

I can keep Gloria going with food talk to ease the strain that is always present between her and Joel. At the same time, I'm checking out the windows to see if anything seems off.

Joel is watching me, knowing what I'm doing. He ends up doing the same. Wandering the apartment, casually checking security without letting her know what he's really doing.

Joel doesn't try small talk with Gloria. His questions are pointed, his answers are perfunctory. Only when he's angry does he speak more than a few words at a time. This comes across as indifference to Gloria, and she tries harder to get him to respond. But Joel gets the effect he wants with carefully-timed silence.

"John says hello," Gloria tells Joel and me, looking at both of us. John Dell is a Wayne police detective whom she's known forever. He worked on the case regarding the murder of Joel's father. Although he turned out to be a good guy and he's a close friend of Gloria's, Joel can't stand him. Maybe because he's a close friend of hers, supplanting Joel when he was thrown out. Luckily Gloria did not try to invite him over tonight.

"Thanks," I say when Joel ignores what she said and looks at his phone. "Give my regards."

"That's kind of you, Gabriel. I'd just like him to meet someone, not bounce around in that house by himself, you know?" She talks while chopping vegetables. "To have what you two have. Joel, maybe you know some nice men..."

Joel gets up and goes over to the back door of the kitchen, which leads to a balcony. "Sure," he says in a fake-pleasant voice. "I know every gay man in the city. In the country, in fact. Through our secret network."

She blushes in embarrassment and turns away to the stove. A moment later she starts talking about something else as if the previous exchange didn't happen. I catch Joel's eye in the reflection of the glass door. I don't like it when he does things like that.

Inside, I feel conflicted. When he looks at her, he sees the mother he wants to have, the mother he wants to love. The mother who was too close to him when he was young, making him her confidante. And also, the mother who told him on the day he was thrown out, "*I can't believe I gave birth to something like you.*" The mother who didn't believed he was sexually assaulted by a family friend. The mother who left him to find for himself on the streets.

Gloria is trying hard to make up for that. The way they both try hard is eerie the way they look alike is eerie. As she continues chatting and moving to the stove, he casually gets up and cleans the counter she just cleaned. He cleans better and quicker than she does, but it's the way he does it. And how he looks at her afterwards.

It's not just him. Larry Meese, the man who abused Joel, also told Gloria about Joel's being an escort. She did not react well, although she has no right to throw stones. She apologized for that later. But as Joel has a streak of stubbornness and anger, she has a streak of martyrdom and passive-aggressiveness. I witnessed a huge blow-up between them not long after the Cody affair was over. They have started therapy together which surprised me. Joel is not fond of therapists. However, this is more evidence of his trying.

Having acted out enough to hurt her feelings, he suddenly feels guilty and dials back to polite. That stays through dinner, a minor miracle. After dinner we go outside on her little balcony.

"Therapy is going well," Gloria tells me.

"That's good--" I start to say.

"Gabriel isn't concerned with our therapy."

"Joel, that's rude. Why do you have to be that way?"

He raises his shoulders. "I'd like you to ask me first before you talk about our personal business."

"We're family, aren't we? Do I have to ask your permission before I say *anything*? Do you think I'd say something to embarrass you? I get it, Joel. I'm just a broken-down alcoholic. Always have been, always will be."

I close my eyes, not wanting to hear any of this.

"I never said that." His voice is calm. "I just don't think you have the discretion to talk about this now."

Her face turns red. "What you *want* me to say is I'm the worst mother ever and totally screwed up my son's life irreparably, even though he's a millionaire now."

Joel takes out his phone and fake-looks at it, then turns to me. "Well, I think I'm good for the evening. What about you?"

He puts down the glass he's carrying and heads for the front door.

"Joel..." He doesn't listen to me. I'm not part of the equation here.

I tell Gloria thanks for the dinner, and she nods, holding back tears. "Gabriel, I'm sorry about this. It's very embarrassing. I thought he was proud of what we've managed to do."

She pauses and holds out her hands. "I wanted to be positive tonight. You see, I had to go to the doctor again about the nerves in my hands. Joel doesn't realize that I can't always do things well because of the conditions in my hands."

She lowers her voice as if she's confiding in me, "The doctor said it wasn't good..."

But her voice isn't low enough to really keep him from hearing, as I suspect she intended. Joel suddenly reappears. "What? What did she say?"

Gloria looks at him reproachfully before answering. "He's pretty sure it's degenerative. Maybe I have to get a home health aide soon. It scares me."

He comes up to her and takes her hands in his own, staring at them. "I'll take care of it. Let me talk to the doctors."

Joel really cares, and he is also terrified that her condition is hereditary. He tries to will her hands to stop trembling by holding them. I've gotten to know Gloria enough to wonder if she's putting on ever so slightly. What she did to Joel will always give him the default upper hand. But his reaction to her illnesses allows her a manipulation that's unhealthy.

Gloria telling him about something else now--she can't find her rings. "In the morning I put them in the dish on the dresser--because my hands felt swollen--and then went to the store. This evening I couldn't find them. Joel, don't give me that look. I wasn't drinking and I'm not hallucinating. I'd swear things have been moved."

That gets my attention. "What things?"

They both look at me. "It can't be that," Joel says. "What would be the point?"

"What? What's going on?"

"Just checking, Gloria. What was moved?"

"Well...the rings. A photo album. Some of my files. One of my wind chimes had fallen in front of the front door, and the back door was unlocked. I know I locked it when I left. Gabriel, what do you think? What should I do?"

I look around down to the grounds below us. The grounds of the condo complex are surrounded by clumps of trees. I go back to the kitchen and turn off the lights. Now the grounds are more visible. Some outside lights illuminate the grass, but the trees are still dark. I climb over the balcony and drop to the ground. Above me, Gloria says something and Joel shushes her.

I just sense someone is around. I hear rustles of the trees and can't tell if it's the cold air or my imagination or disappearing stalkers. I hear cars starting and driving off. Could be people going out, could be disappearing stalkers.

I start patrolling the area in circles, going on and on until I hear Joel's voice when I walk back near the balcony. "Gabriel..."

I look up and see the glow of his cigarette framing his face.

"Just come back up. No one is there." The light disappears as he turns and walks inside.

I go back in the condo's main entrance and head for the stairs. By the time I'm on the second floor, Joel is yanking the front door open, saying over his shoulder, "...and I told you about *five thousand times* stop going through my stuff!"

Gloria answers in a stressed voice, "I was only looking for--" But Joel has slammed the door shut. He meets my eyes briefly and starts down the hall. After a second I go after him.

Gloria opens the door behind us. I tense up, expecting more vitriol. But she skips out and runs to catch up with Joel. She throws her arms around him. "What about next week, honey? You and I can have dinner after therapy."

He nods without looking at her, and lets her kiss his cheek.

"I love you, Joel."

She holds on to him until he gives in and briefly puts his arms around her. "Yeah, okay," he says.

It's enough. She hugs me too, and we leave.

On the way back, he pretends like nothing's wrong, like we weren't even there. But he stays buried in his phone while I drive.

"We should check her locks," I tell him. "Maybe I'll call John and ask him to drive by."

"I checked her locks. I know how to do it. She doesn't need him."

"Don't let your dislike of him get in the way."

"It doesn't. Don't let your gullibility get you so paranoid you can't think straight."

"Excuse me?"

"I'm just sayin' all this happened when you and Anakin Skywalker hooked up."

I consider a few different responses and check them. After working to make my tone not reflect my annoyance I say, "You don't believe me about what's been going on?"

"I'm saying that he's managed to get you in a bad way without even trying hard."

I can't slam my head against the steering wheel the way I want to. And so I have to stay quiet, because one of us has to act sensibly. I let him out when I get to Avenue A. While I head for the parking garage--I've decided to spring for a monthly rental for security--I call John Dell and ask him to check in on Gloria. I tell him I'm afraid of a prowler or peeper in the neighborhood.

Unfortunately, by the time I'm parked and back in the apartment, Joel is waiting on the sofa, legs crossed and smoking, staring at me with a deceptively deadpan expression. A little too deadpan.

"Mom texted me to say Dell called and is coming over. Strange, since I didn't call him to ask him to do so."

"Yeah, really strange. Maybe we should send it to *Fortean Times*."

"Is there a good reason why you did that? To go behind my back?"

"Look up the definition of 'behind your back' and understand what that means. I'm just being careful and you seem to have some difficulty dealing with her tonight."

He looks away, and his voice turns sharper. "Is that right? So I pretend that it's all just wonderful that she's a judgmental nosy bitch."

"Your interpretation of what I say is mistaken. If being around her is too much, then get some distance so you can avoid getting in the kind of dynamic where--"

He swings his head back around to glare at me. "It's not your situation to deal with!"

I feel more than a little stung. Joel never yells or never snaps at me. I struggle to not snarl back at him.

The best I can say is, "That was uncalled for."

"I didn't ask for you to tell me what to do. I didn't ask for you to make security decisions regarding my mother because being an errand boy for your ex-boyfriend has made you a nervous wreck."

I feel blood going to the tips of my ears. "I didn't ask for my current boyfriend to become a sullen brat when he's visiting his mother."

"Then don't go with me. Then you don't have to suffer and watch me do something the wrong way--in other words, not your way."

"Joel, I don't see--"

"You being angry at *your* father is justified. I'm just immature. Jesus, I get it from her, and I get it from you. I do my damndest to take care of people, and in turn I'm told I'm not good enough."

"That is not true, Joel. Don't ever say that." I go over to sit next to him, and he gets up to move away.

"*Not true.* Did you consider that your calling Dell when I said I wouldn't is your saying that my decision wasn't good enough? Just like her asking *you* what to do is telling me I'm not good enough."

"If you feel that way, I'm sorry. I'm being extra-cautious. I don't think Gloria meant it like you're taking it either."

"She likes you. She wishes you were her son. You may be gay, but you're not a whore."

"Joel, don't do this. I know she hurt you, but I think she loves you for who you are, and regrets what she said. Even so, you don't have to accept--"

"I know that. I know how to accept myself. I've been doing it all my life. I have plenty of practice being told I'm not good enough. That nothing I say means anything to anyone."

"That is so not true..."

He sits on the arm of a chair, his back to me, and starts scrolling through his phone. I let it go, give him a chance to calm down. We're both stubborn and opinionated and not willing to give in.

I start taking care of some stuff in the kitchen and Archie comes with me to jump on the counter and play shop steward and supervise. It's only when Archie suddenly raises his head and looks toward the front door that I turn and see Joel getting his jacket.

"Where are you going?"

He's reluctant to answer, and only shrugs.

"Just stay here. Don't do this."

He shakes his head. "I don't want to talk about it anymore."

"We don't have to. It's over."

He glances at me, but says nothing. Still sulking, eyes burning at me, he has the difficulty of negotiating his emotions and the instinct to disappear.

I go over to him. I put my hand on his arm, and he turns away.

"You're going to play this card?"

He won't look at me now. To try to diffuse the tension, I reach inside his jacket and put my fingers where he's ticklish. "You going to keep it up? Humm?"

He twitches under my fingers...almost smiling but holding back. I try it from the other side. I get a yelp out of him. "*Stop...*"

I stop, and turn his face so I can see him. "You need to stop, too."

He looks at me. Without speaking, the '*fuck you*' in his expression is quite clear. I shake my head. "I'm not letting you get away with that."

I hold him closer; he tries to slide away but I'm not allowing it. I speak in his ear. "No, it doesn't have to be this way."

I back him up against the wall, put my head against his, hold him for a minute. "C'mon. You don't need to be alone; I don't want to be alone. We can work through this."

He sighs suddenly and drops his head to my shoulder. I hold him closer. His chest hitches like he's trying not to cry.

"C'mon," I whisper, and stroke his hair, gently kissing the side of his head. I keep murmuring to him, tracing my fingers on his hair. "It's okay, baby. You know I love you. You know I need you. You know you mean everything to me. I'm sorry for anything I said or did that gave you a different idea. No more fighting." I say it over and over, meaning it more each time.

I feel him returning to himself some; he settles against me. When people try to run away, sometimes what they really want is to be held tightly. I have to let him know through my embrace that I love him, crack through the wall he throws up. And as I coax him further into lessening his defensiveness, my touch with him takes on a different tenor. I have my lips on his ear, and let my hand drift down to the small of his back.

Joel is caught between responding to the desire in my touch, or the thoughts shot-putting around in his head. "I don't think I have the mindset for it tonight; there's so much going on."

"It's a good way to forget. Just forget about what's going on."

He lets me put my mouth on his neck, and I slide my hands under his shirt, to continue caressing his back.

He resists, but only nominally. "Uh...I'm sorry about earlier."

"I'm sorry too."

"I'm scared about what's going on..."

"I'm scared too."

"Worried..."

"All of that." I slowly reach down between his legs. "What else are you?"

He doesn't answer in words, but in sighing and pressing against my hand...

Sometime later in bed and exhausted...we're bathed in the residual heat between us...he's tucked in against me, facing me with his head under my chin. I keep my fingers gently entwined in his hair.

He should be asleep, but digs his fingers in my back like a cat. "Is this what it's like to be adult?"

"This is what it's like to be you and me."

∞

[SCRAMBLE MESSAGE]
rBRuc4mQcV DrgQUWoECd Z01ZPoJR8A oIKq8qDQcr

[Unscramble] ENIGMA Project/Eyes Only

MORTEM and REAPER, to KISMET

--Reconnaissance of MCFADDEN residence and secure sweep of area complete. Determined that GLORIA MCFADDEN has no connection to MAGICIAN's work and visit was purely social. Note that BEDEVIL was possibly running concurrent surveillance.

∞

Wednesday, October 26
Forest Hills, Queens, 11:51 am

And for a time, a week and a half, thing calmed down. I did not sense anyone was following us or trespassing in our places. Gotham has an abundance of business that needs attention. We work on our business as Joel works on designing the mural for Churchill and an art program for the Harvey Milk Center for homeless LGBTQ youth.

For a time, life is what we need it to be. But things you don't want to deal with don't go away because you just hope they will. So finally, Alex catches up with me and Veronica in the *Herald-Standard* building while we are supervising installation of security devices and software with the IT department. He drags me aside in an impatient manner. "Gabriel, are you going to check Mesereau's home? See what you can find?"

While I'm a little ticked he so casually suggests I break into someone's house, I have been known to trespass now and then. But I still feel I need to find out what is going on with this whole affair, for my own sake. So while Geneva is interviewing a couple of new clients, Veronica and I depart into the wilderness of Queens to Forest Hills.

Mesereau has a nice corner place, freestanding in a block of duplexes. It's one-story with a basement and a fairly tall black iron and brick fence surrounding the street-facing sides of the property. The back and inside has a thick wooden plank fence.

We're in a rented car, catty corner next to a park. I'm observing the house through a very sensitive high-powered scope no bigger than a child's kaleidoscope. We've taken turns doing this to see what we both see, and what each other might see differently. While I scrutinize the house, Veronica sweeps the neighborhood with cameras temporarily attached to the car, and a monitor on a tablet. Then we switch. We wonder if anyone else has the house watched.

It's that prospect--that someone may be tracking who comes to the house--that dictates utmost caution. Mesereau doesn't answer his cell number nor the landline in the house. We see a mail carrier stuff envelopes in a box on Mesereau's door that is already full. This indicates that Mesereau is not there, or at least not available to answer.

I have been able to determine what kind of security system he uses. He's got the place wired but no advertisements. He has cameras as well.

This kind of set-up can be connected to a smartphone. Someone really worried about break-ins will want to have the ability to see the camera feed on the phone. I have the same set up now for my own apartment, and fixed it up for Joel and Veronica's.

I also know how to disable it. This involves some hacking, which Chris helped me with. I don't like doing this, but it's expedient--better than cutting wires that may trip other alarms. In a few minutes, using a burner laptop. I access Mesereau's desktop remotely, and find the website for the security company. Once in his account, I get the security code, and also check out the house from the camera feeds. We see that no one is in the house. It looks okay, but the kitchen has some mess as though someone left in a hurry.

Time to go in.

Dressed in work-type jackets and caps that could pass for movers, cable installers, contractors or similar persons who would have metal invoice clipboards and kits with tools, we approach the back of the house. The locks also can be remotely disabled, so no need to pick this time.

Inside, the kitchen does look like something happened--bad. Blood smears on the floor and wall. But although a few objects are in disarray, it's not that bad. There wasn't a fight here.

We double-check to ensure that no one's inside, hiding in closets or bathrooms. I've been burned about that before. Then we're back in the kitchen.

∞

In another area of the city, Clement receives a signal that Mesereau's computer has been accessed. He gets in contact with his protégé, Encausse.

"They're at the house," he says. "I can see them."

∞

From the YouTube Channel "Tom Paine Events," in a video entitled:
Unknown Knowns: Gary Underhill ♦ The Informant

Transcript: "Gary Underhill was a military man with intelligence connections. Underhill believed that JFK was murdered by the CIA due to the Bay of Pigs fiasco and JFK's plan to restrain the agency's powers; he also suggested accused assassin Lee Harvey Oswald was a patsy, as Oswald claimed. Underhill told a friend he was in fear for his life due to what he knew.

"In 1964 Underhill was found dead due to a gunshot to the head-- official story, suicide. Witnesses to the scene said the shot was to the left side of the head, though Underhill was right-handed. [Similar to alleged JFK autopsy witness Navy Lt. Commander William Pitzer, who died from a gunshot suicide in 1966 to the right side of his head, although he was left-handed.] If indeed assassinations, Underhill's and Pitzer's deaths raise the question of whether the persons involved are incompetent, or trying to send a message to silence any other witnesses?"

∞

BOTH MEN ARE ABLE to see what goes on in Mesereau's house via the security cameras. Then then the cameras go dark.

"He turned them off," Clement says.

"Hold on. Okay, he's accessed Mesereau's account and changed the password."

"Can you do anything? He must be going inside."

"We have the one extra camera. It's a risk because he might see the light. But we'd be able to track them somewhat."

The camera Encausse operates is in the kitchen, affixed to a doorway leading to the rest of the house. The camera has a wide view of the kitchen and the back door.

A few moments later, the two men can see Gabriel and Veronica enter the house through the back door. Instinctively they are back to back once inside--he scans the room in front of him, and she scans the backyard out the window. Gabriel is chewing gum absently, but his eyes are alert. He looks up but doesn't see the tiny camera. Veronica uses a small handheld device to check the room for something, perhaps recording devices.

The two look around carefully, speak to each other. They see the blood stains. They both leave, presumably to check the rest of the house.

Eventually they return to the kitchen and study blood stains. Clement says, "You think he can find out what happened?"

"Yes. He's that good."

Gabriel and Veronica are only talking right now.

"Too bad we didn't set it up for sound," Clement comments.

"Agreed. But you saw they swept for bugs. He's way too paranoid. Keep that in mind. He won't even talk so you can read his lips."

"Ah, but every trait that seems so aggravating now will be so useful after Cognoscenti."

Gabriel and Veronica are still discussing something.

Clement asks, "Why not search more?"

"They're trying to figure out what happened."

∞

"He was injured somewhere else," Veronica says. "He came back here to get something vitally important, and left."

"I'm with you. The stuff in the fridge is going bad, he didn't take any personal belongings. Just something he knew he'd need, and that he figured was worth the risk."

"Money, passport, account numbers, keys..."

"He might have had a go-bag. But where? No dust is disturbed, no marks to indicate it was anywhere out in view."

Veronica meets my eyes. "This is the only place with the blood. He didn't go anywhere else in the house. It was here."

I get up and start at the first drops by the door. Two trails, one coming in, one leaving. Smears by the alarm, and smears on top of the smears.

Drips near the sink and along one side wall. The wall is half rough-pebbled paint on top, and half intricately patterned tile, each tile eight by five. "This part of the wall--the tile--looks recently installed. It's only on this wall, and doesn't seem to serve the purpose of being a splash guard."

We both get up and look at the smears on the wall. I turn my flashlight on. Veronica traces the pattern of smear up to a point about three feet high. To the left, a microwave cart has a bloody palm print. "He leaned on this. So he crouched here."

Then we see the smear that looks like it was wiped away--but not completely. And it ends abruptly under the tile, as if the tile was laid over it.

We glance at each other. I reach over and press the tile hard. A door, about two feet square, swings open.

I do my best Muldoon from *Jurassic Park* impersonation. "Clever girl."

∞

Clement exhales. "Damn. He *is* good. They both are. We totally missed that."

"He has an instinct. It's too bad we can't see what's in there."

The camera is situated where the two watchers can only see part of the hidden door that swung open. The space, whatever it is, faces the opposite way. Veronica takes a photo of the inside of the space with her phone. She and Gabriel talk for a moment, then he holds up his light to illuminate the space so she can photograph it again.

Then Gabriel takes a pad out of his tool bag. He gets as close as possible to the space. He appears to be drawing something.

∞

The space is empty, and yet it is not. Mesereau once had at least two things in there. A document and a key. He might have had more--the space is about three inches deep. Whatever was in there pressed against the bare wooden wall structure, and humidity and glue in the wood slats caused the document to get tacky and stick against the wall. The key was stuck to the wall too--probably pushed into the tack. The key left a sharp outline. The document was peeled away but a faint image remains. I feel like I know what the document is. Veronica photographs both. I draw the key as a backup. I have training as a locksmith.

"You can duplicate it?"

"Yeah. It's bigger than a typical house key or apartment key. I doubt it's a safety deposit box."

She checks her phone. "That paper--it's a building plan of some kind. Probably where the key unlocks. He wanted a visual reminder."

Veronica stares harder at the outline. She has exceptionally good vision. "And there's names under the paper. Maybe it was folded over."

I've finished the drawing, and put it away. Now I turn the flashlight back on. "Comstock-Clement. Jacobs-Hu...Damn. The real names and the code names. The rest of Jacobs is cut off. Cirlot and Voirol under Jacobs. I can make out a D and a C. D next to Cirlot, G next to Voirol. And under Clement is...*Encaus?*"

"*Encausse,* probably. A question mark. Mesereau knew the code name but didn't know who Encausse really was," Veronica says. "The historical Encausse was a magician in the 19th Century. These names look divided. Sections, maybe. Divisions? Departments?"

∞

"Clearly," Clement says with some excitement, "we need to know what they found."

"Next step. It has to be very careful..." Encausse stops as they notice that Gabriel is staying very still. He's looking over his shoulder. He says something to Veronica.

Now Gabriel opens a small laptop, and waits for it to warm up. While he does, he gets up and searches under the kitchen sink.

"What is he doing now?"

Veronica watches the laptop, facing away from the camera. She tells Gabriel something.

"Shit," Clement says, "They can see our camera."

Gabriel comes back with a bottle of bleach and a bucket. He proceeds to pour the bleach on the inside of the tile space, and then scrubs at it with steel wool. Veronica is packing their stuff.

"Son of a bitch."

For a second before they leave, Gabriel looks up and looks directly in the camera, raising his middle finger. His eyes flash defiance.

In spite of Gabriel having destroyed the evidence in the tile space so they can't come back and find it, Clement is taken by Gabriel's defiance. "Oh, God. He's going to be so good in this experiment."

"Next steps," Encausse says. "Getting what he has may not be so easy."

∞

[*SCRAMBLE MESSAGE*]
kqn754LoI1 nxc4JyQrUa YT9B7JIXkk ifeGNI38tX

[Unscramble] ENIGMA Project/Eyes Only

From KISMET, to MORTEM cc REAPER
Activation of operation is a go.

Thursday, October 20
Battery Park City, 9:00 pm

In a very dark corner of a cocktail lounge called Exposition, a white man around 60 sits in the booth that is furthest away from the front door. Another man, somewhat younger, joins him.

"At last. It's good to see you, Maxim." the older man says, lifting a glass of whiskey.

Zest has a class of expensive white wine. He sits across from the other man. "You too. I'm very interested in latest developments."

The older man, Damon Clement, stirs his drink. "Let me tell you more about Cognoscenti. The technology is electromagnetic-based. I have "profiles" of various brain types and personalities I have collected over the years, and that my mentor had. With these profiles, I can program Cognoscenti to direct electromagnetic impulses via transcranial direct current stimulation or transcrainial magnetic stimulation, depending. The profiles provide stimulations specified to a type. That enables me to coach the subject with a projected 93% percent success. My mentor came so close. Very close. Drugs, hypnotism, yes. But he needed one step more. The CIA wouldn't fund it. But he left me his research to build upon."

Zest is nods. "And you feel it's ready."

"It's time. Maxim, you feel like things are changing?" He leans forward across the table. "Jacobs is plotting something. He'd like to shut us down anyway. I feel certain this Tom Paine is some kind of false flag. You notice that the stories have to do with mostly my work. Not his."

"I can try to find out more."

"Good. I need any and all information. I'm moving on him. And the rest of them. Cirlot and all of them. But I need a good man to be my Jason Bourne, if you will. Ross fits that picture. I think it's fortunate that Ross was mixed up in the business with Ethan Nelson, as Nelson was my original pick."

"He certainly had the psychopathy. But he was unstable."

"Like a Sirhan Sirhan, yes. You remember how you brought him to me to find out the information you needed. He broke rather easily. I need someone who won't break. I can see that in Ross. In fact, I may create a new profile based upon him."

"Ross might be unstable in a different way. He is not suitable ideologically to the philosophy. I know you have people within who'd be willing to help you with your experiments. More than willing. I know how devoted your people are."

"That's the *thing*," Clement says, and his black eyes show animation, hunger. "The fact he isn't willing is what makes him intriguing. He has a way about him...I've seen it. If I could turn it, use it for us...he could be like *you*, Maxim. I don't know if he could ever reach your level of skill, but he can help me with Jacobs."

"Some of your people are very skilled."

"I am protecting my people. We can't sacrifice *good* people when we can have a trained soldier do it for us. And even so, none of my people are quite like Ross."

Zest nods. "You are committed to going through this."

Clement leans back. "I know Jacobs and his ilk don't own you. Yes. It's happening. We will have the old ritual, and put it in motion. I know Cognoscenti can work. You see, happened with my predecessors--Galton, and my mentor Henry Helms--was good. To be able to hypnotize, to be able to induce amnesia, to be able to create a new personality. They came close, but they didn't have *consistent* results. Their methods weren't individualized enough. Cognoscenti creates that consistency. With this, I hope to show my protégé Encausse some great things, as he's been such a great help to me."

"You've never introduced him to me."

"Not because of my intent, but you've been busy for the Production Faction. I recruited this one a long time ago, and stayed in touch. We've been getting together recently to put the plan in action. He's not the only one. I've chosen very carefully who I bring in to us, and I'm not vetting them with Jacobs. They are loyal to me."

"I see. Be careful that doesn't bring attention to you. You wouldn't be able to get all of them at once. Understand I want to keep you out jeopardy."

"Hum. Well, I am very pleased that you are looking out for me. You were always the best. I trained you that way."

Zest doesn't show any reaction, just sips at his wine.

"But here's the great part. All of them, everyone in the Society, has a tell. The last part of the training I give everyone is the tell. While they're under, I give them an imprinted message that if they ever try to leave us, they'll send the tell unconsciously. I put out a message--social media makes that ever so much easier--and that triggers the tell when they see it. I have a record for every person trained and what his or her tell is. They won't be aware they're doing it."

"You mean a post-hypnotic suggestion."

"Exactly. It works very well. Not that they know, and not that many leave. I'll show Ross how to track them down."

"I had no idea about the tell," Zest says flatly.

"Safety precaution. You underwent the whole training too." Clement shrugs. "I'm sorry about that. I should have trusted you more. You're different; you've always been mine."

Not reacting is more difficult this time. "Of course. Where is Encausse right now? What's his day job?"

"I'll let him tell you. Well, you'll know when you meet him, I suspect. He really wants to lay low right now. He's heard of you, and admires you, but he's very cautious. He has to be, as being in our Society without dealing with Jacobs' sector is very dangerous."

"Please tell him I would very much like to meet him. He'll have to know how to contact me in any case. I've been keeping track of Tom Paine, but I don't see it as a false flag. Jacobs would not take the chance to have connections go back to him or the other directors."

A waiter passes by and Clement holds up two fingers to get them refills. "All right. You know him pretty well. Then it has to be Mesereau. He was planning something. Now ostensibly, he was going to expose Production Faction in some ridiculous way--to the media, of all things. He's found out about some of our operations and is focusing on those. I guess that's more interesting than what Production does. But now he's gone and in hiding."

"You can't find him? What about the tell?"

"I'm working on it. He has to get the message first. He may be wise enough to resist going out for now, but he's hurt. Sooner or later he'll be out and he'll have to check on things. Of course, I have back up."

Once the drinks appear, Clement takes out his phone and shows Zest the camera feed from Mesereau's house. Gabriel and Veronica finding the panel, Gabriel glaring at the camera before he leaves. Zest watches impassively.

"He's being cautious too, but I'll catch up with him. Next steps. Damn it, I have to run...the office is calling me about some such nonsense and I have to keep that facade going." Clement finishes his drink quickly, stands and holds his hand out to Zest. "We'll talk, Maxim."

Zest stays in the booth for some time, playing the video in his head of Gabriel in the house. Thinking of his own next steps.

∞

[SCRAMBLE MESSAGE]
soxQSIuKR3 p2zJ5IOZPx tnVsVAxmXX sYvQJZ5FoV

[Unscramble] ENIGMA Project/Eyes Only

From MORTEM and REAPER, to KISMET
--Note that Project Q is active regarding BEDEVIL. MORTEM has
been tapped to proceed with contact and possible integration with
COGNOSCENTI venture. ETERNITY suggests BEDEVIL is
moving on plan with MAGICIAN.

∞

Reason to Believe, by Walter Churchill
Excerpted in *New York* Magazine Spring 2012

William Galton was a physician and a protégé of Schroeder. He
supported the Nazi party, according to various acquaintances. When
Schroeder died mysteriously in WWII, supposedly in an explosion
while conducting one of his experiments, Galton escaped Germany to
Switzerland. He later claimed he was forced to assist Nazis. He even
hinted that he tried to sabotage Schroeder's experiments. Yet he
developed a core group of followers who maintained Schroeder's
rituals principles. Seeing where the opportunities lay in the new Cold
War era, Galton and some of his most dedicated followers moved to
Canada.
While working in a psychiatric center Galton given free rein to test
drugs and hypnosis and electroshock therapy on patients. At the time,
psychiatrists were rarely questioned on methods, and were even
considered humane for their tireless work in subjecting the mentally ill
to radical experiments.

Galton didn't have much real success, but he toyed with an idea for a machine that could control minds. He started a private organization called Synarchest. Synarchest was an exclusive spiritual retreat. It promoted a seemingly harmless spirituality for wealthy persons, a type of positive-thinking/ EST/vague Christianity cover. But it had a second purpose--as an undercover operation for both the Society and certain intelligence organizations. Both were very interested in the possibility of that mind-control device.

Galton had a special mentee of his own, Henry Helms. Helms was trained in psychiatry by Galton in Canada. Helms later relocated to the US. Helms is the person who in turn recruited and trained Damon Clement. They all were part of Synarchest. Like some mystic malevolent family tree, Galton, Helms, and Clement each tried hypnosis, drugs, religious practices and various types of machines to induce mind control. The intelligence agencies were always supportive of each, because the cover of Synarchest centers around the world allowed them access into countries to smuggle goods, money, weapons. But the Society's loyalty was not toward the government. They used government money to conduct dual experimentation.

More unsuspecting persons were needed to experiment on. Programs were set up in colleges and mental health facilities, such as Wildemore in New Jersey (which is now closed and abandoned). The experiments involved psychic torture, drug-induced stupor. Forced waking and electric shocks, forced sleep and induced nightmares...

∞

Friday, October 28
Midtown, Herald-Standard Building, 4:30 pm

I need to work on a section of my thesis, and I'm still wary about going back to CUNY Midtown for now. Having checked that things in *Herald-Standard* security are running smoothly, I've taken a couple hours to borrow some of those magnificent books.

I'm deep into some analysis but also mindful I need to leave soon to play a gig with Jason. It's at an East Side bar that just underwent refurbishing, playing from 8 to midnight. I've insisted that as many of my friends as possible come so I can watch over them.

Yet I'm drawn to read as much as possible, having found a first edition of Ioan Culianu's *Eros and Magic in the Renaissance* in English translation. Culianu is describing the Platonic soul-body distinction and relations, as understood by the ever-empirical Aristotle. The soul and body do not, cannot, communicate with each other without some intervening apparatus. The soul transmits information to the body through an instrument known as the *prōton organon*. It is located in the heart, and is made of the same substance of the stars--*pneuma*, or spirit. Conversely, the body provides messages to the soul through *phantasms*. The apparatuses of phantasms are absolutely necessary for the soul to understand anything corporeal. The phantasms then, as I see it, are the semiotics between body and soul...

A hand comes down on my shoulder suddenly, and it takes everything I have to not scream. Instead I look up like it's nothing.

"I heard you were here," Alex says.

"You have a better security network than I do."

"I doubt it. I was looking for you." He pulls up a chair. "One thing I like about this place is it's both quiet and private. In fact, it's no doubt why you're here. Sorry about that."

I shrug. "It's okay. You got me here."

"Thanks. I wanted to check up on if you've found anything about Zach. I'm still trying to see if he'll respond to an email drop or online message, but nothing."

I lean back, playing with a pen. "He's not anywhere online that I could find. No financial transactions with any of his known accounts. I called his office and they say he took leave. And I did go to his house--yeah, I know you were going to ask that next. Something's happened. There's blood in the house."

Alex's eyes widen and he grabs my arm. "What? You mean, like a crime scene?"

"Not that much, but he's probably seriously injured."

"God, I knew something was wrong. I'm so glad you checked. Was there anything that could be a lead about where he went to?"

I have no idea what Mesereau's story is, but I figure the fewer people who know what Veronica and I discovered, the better. Since Alex did not act that wisely with Mesereau in the first place, I don't think he needs to know for now. Until I actually find Mesereau, if I can. I'm planning to make a key based off the drawing I have and then double-check my suspicions regarding the document.

"Maybe. I'm going to follow up."

Alex inches closer. "What is it?"

I put on my tactful voice. "Let me check it out, and then I'll bring you up to date."

"Gabriel, don't be ridiculous. This is my source. We need to find him. I can get him to some kind of safe house. I'll ask my dad for some contacts."

"You should go ahead and ask. Alex, remember I told you this was a dangerous case. I'm not bullshitting you about this. It is dangerous. There's people connected to it...they might be watching what's going on."

"Who, the Mafia? The CIA?"

"I wouldn't be so afraid of them. This is different. I want to you to restrain your instincts and just let me check it out first."

He looks annoyed. "You don't trust me?"

Now I get annoyed. "Don't go there. I'm thinking of your safety. If you try to find him, you'll attract attention you don't want."

"From whom?" He puts a hand over mine. "At least tell me that. If the danger is that imminent, shouldn't I know?"

He has a point. "The Tertullians."

Now he really frowns. "Them? They're back?"

I slide my hand from under his. "They never went away. You remember what we read about them. They are connected with this. I'll tell you this much. Comstock is. Do not try to contact him, no matter how tempted you are."

"Oh, my God." He breathes heavily. "No wonder you've been distressed. You found that out when I asked you to look into Comstock."

"I came across indications. It's why I wanted you to stop."

"Zach must have discovered how they are participating in these government experiments."

"Or he was colluding in them. Look, you don't know what his story is, really. That's another reason why it's not good for you to go after him. He could be in the Society and have had a falling out with his buddies."

"Why would he try to tell me about what's going on at the agency, then?"

"Because they're a bunch of fucked-up Nazis. You remember you were given a warning about your job for helping me in the Booth case. Someone here could be a listening ear for them. This all started after you took him on as a source." I realize I'm echoing Joel's words. "Clark was working on this story too. I hope he's safe."

"Yes, we haven't done anything on the story lately. Zach approached me because of my past exposés. He felt I was enough of an advocate to trust. I can't believe he was just using me for some operation--what would you call it? False flag?"

"Even if you don't believe it, act as if it could be true. Especially as strange things have been happening. I have to be careful, and you have to as well. Don't talk about this here. Even with us running security, I'm pretty paranoid."

Alex takes a moment to think over what I'm saying. "Are you sure you don't want to share what you found out with me? We can investigate it together. I promise what you say goes. I wouldn't cock it up. I realize you're much more capable to handle this than I am."

I bite my thumbnail. "Not right now. I'm gonna see what I can find out discreetly, and then, well, maybe. Not because I don't trust you, but because I don't want to put you in danger unnecessarily."

"I'm keen to take the risk. Not like last time. Things are different now."

"Okay, well, I'll let you know. How about, in case Mesereau's on the up and up, you see if you can get your father to find those contacts?"

"I was thinking of taking a short leave anyway, to look for Zach. I'll go to London instead and get Dad to set me up. I'll be in touch, then."

I figure he's going to shake my hand or something, but he hugs me instead. At least I have things stable for now until we can find out more about what that key goes to.

∞

Saturday, October 29
East Village, Midnight

The bar is called First Act. Our band has taken its final encore. I'm at a table with Joel and Isabella and Chris. Joel is going to some after-hours party with them and I don't want to stop him; I promised I wouldn't be alone.

Danny is up at the small stage talking to Jason. He's part of the book club we have in Jason's shop once a month, and they're talking books. Danny beckons me to come over. Jason and Danny step outside the back door of the bar and I follow.

Jason produces a joint. "I was thinking we could just relax for a while. You look like you need it."

"Smoke right here in the alley?" I smile and take a hit.

"This is just the beginning. I have some primo shit if you're down for it."

I sigh. "Might as well."

Danny smiles. "My place. I don't want to encourage you to smoke regular cigarettes, but I really need one."

Halo had been staying with Danny until he got a dorm room at Boricua. Halo knows 20,000 other young persons, and most of them were tramping through Danny's apartment in the past few months--holding impromptu discussion groups, wrestling hook-up matches, and drag ball practice. Danny's relieved to have the place back for himself.

We quickly confirm plans then go back inside. I look for Joel. They have clearly been joking around in preparation for whatever they're doing later. Isabella is actually on Joel's back; he's holding her and she has her legs around him. All three were laughing about something before we came in. I almost feel like an intruder.

They look at us. Isabella says brightly, "What are you guys doing now?"

I say, "Uh, not sure. We might just binge-watch something on Netflix."

"Well, if you pillow-fight or play strip poker, would you record--"

"Iz, shut up." Joel sets her down on the floor. "We're gonna go soon," he tells me.

"Us too."

He takes my hand and pulls me aside, then puts his arms around me. "Everything okay, baby?"

"Of course." I kiss him.

"For a second, you looked funny."

I draw his face to me again and whisper, "Just use condoms, that's all I ask."

Joel's expression when I say that makes me laugh.

He says with sharp, subtle sarcasm, "You smell like reefer. What are you and Dan going to do, really? Toke up? Be sure to clean afterwards in case there's a raid."

"Don't you worry, lover."

"Yeah, don't worry, lover." Chris is suddenly behind me and drapes zis arms around my shoulders. "Mephisto, you going to leave Danger Man on his lonesome? If you neglect him, I'll have to steal him away."

I pretend to give zis words some thought. "Hmmm. I'll have to consider that. Chris *would* listen to me more..."

Joel takes Chris's hands off me. "Gabriel seems to have a playdate. He and Dan are no doubt going to reminisce over their youth-gang roots, and get *high*." He says the last word in the same tone of voice one might use saying, "*Mistreating orphans*."

Chris doesn't bite. "Rough trade is sexy, baby."

"Come on." Joel kisses me and whispers in my ear. "I'm still worried. Please for fuck's sake, don't do anything stupid."

"Not a problem."

He doesn't believe me, but I've insisted he go. So he pushes Chris along impatiently to where Isabella is waiting.

Jason has finished loading his SUV, and we get in and drop off the music equipment at the bookstore, then go to Danny's building near Chrystie Street.

Inside, Jason produces a bag of Chronic. I'm good with it. It helps with my pain issues--especially the migraines, which tend to pop up out of tension.

"Joel looked rather disapproving." Jason starts chopping it up with a plastic card.

"He doesn't like drugs of any kind, tries to keep me on a short leash with weed. I pick my battles. Changes in my habits worry him." I get beers out of Danny's fridge and bring them back. "And with what's going on lately I understand that."

Jason lights up the joint and passes to me. I sigh after holding it in. Danny puts *Archer* on Netflix, and after a couple episodes we're nearly breathless from the giggles.

Then there's a soft knock at the door. That sobers me a little. I never like it when people get in a locked lobby door without being buzzed in, although it's not hard to do.

"You order something," Danny asks me jokingly. "Or did the Witnesses follow you here?"

He gets up and goes over to the door. I hear him ask some muted questions. I get up too, feeling adrenaline rush through my chest. Then Danny closes the door, steps back and looks at me.

"This guy says he needs to talk to you right now."

The tension grows in the room as I look through the peephole, and sober up even more.

"Give me a minute," I tell Danny, who frowns at my tone of voice. I open the door and step out.

∞

S I X

From the YouTube Channel "Tom Paine Events," in a video entitled: Unknown Knowns: Michael Hastings ♦ The TruthTeller

Transcript: "Hastings was a principled, contentious reporter who burned to expose truth--such as events in Iraq in the Green Zone, an article about then-General Stanley McChrystal in Rolling Stone that led to McChrystal's resignation, and the 2012 presidential election. Hastings ran full tilt on his crusade to expose hypocrisy and media-access culture, where truth is secondary to obtaining a good interview with a high-powered figure.

"Again, a journalist questioned, scorned, and disparaged by his peers because of his probity. Towards the end of his life Hastings was said to be stressed and reckless but not suicidal. Hastings also alluded to a new important story he was working on. In June of 2013, Hastings' Mercedes appeared to go out of control and crashed into a palm tree in Los Angeles--then exploded. Hastings had serious concerns he was being investigated by the government, which the FBI (unusually) denied publicly. Richard Clarke suggested Hastings' car crash was consistent with a cyber-attack. Rogue journalist or prism of truth? Hastings' death raises the question of why freedom of the press so often means freedom to embed/sell-out to an official position, and freedom to disparage a man doing his job."

∞

I ASK MY VISITOR, "What's going on?"

Zest says, "I wanted to touch base with you. There's trouble."

"I guess it's urgent if you're willing to show yourself to my friends."

"I'm glad you're out of your own place; it's under watch. I was waiting for a chance to catch you out--I can't be seen with you."

I nod. "Did you just come back?"

"I haven't really left the area. You're in danger, Gabriel."

"Damon Clement, I'm guessing."

Zest's expression turns graver. "How do you know?"

"He's been in our offices, and in the CUNY Midtown library, both at times when I'm alone. He is definitely watching me, although he hasn't tried to hurt me, I think. I got the impression he was testing me."

Zest stares at me a long time. His face goes dark, and his eyes get distant. "I've been trying to divert him."

"It's not working. Is that Jacobs' plan?"

"Jacobs has not contacted me. Clement and Jacobs do not take orders from each other. However, having contact with this Tom Paine is risky. Jacobs has no doubt noticed those videos. But that has nothing to do with Clement. He's interested for other reasons."

"You said he and Jacobs aren't good with each other. Who is good with Clement? Someone named Encausse?"

Zest steps back and looks around. But no one is in the hallway. "Yes. How did you hear of him?"

"I was looking into it. Not to piss them off, but to try to help someone."

"Encausse is his protégé. I've never met the person. I need to do something--I don't know what. It will take some time to explain the circumstances. I want to do that because I think you need to know in order to understand this situation."

"You know I don't underestimate them. Nor do I discount anything you tell me. What are you trying to divert Clement from?"

"If you know his name, you know what he does. At least, what the government thinks he does...Gabriel, don't go out unless you need to. I wouldn't even go back to your apartment for now. Let me look into this. Be *very careful* until I get back to you. Take this number. No one else has it. Put it on speed dial."

I take my phone out my pocket and do so.

"Gabriel, if anything--*anything* looks like it's going to happen, call me immediately. Even if you can't say what's happening. Let me have your GPS." He holds out a small thin metal square that looks like a device to boost cell phone reception. "This will track you. Only I'll see it."

I'm leery of this and hesitate to accept it. But he takes the phone out of my hand and puts his device on the phone. It's magnetic.

"Trust me. I'll try to stay around you as much as I can. We need to talk more, but I have to check some things out to be sure we are safe to do so." He meets my eyes. "I'm more or less a dead man right now. You don't have to be."

He abruptly turns and goes down the stairs.

I go back in the apartment and find Danny going back to the sofa, having spied on the conversation through the peephole. He's not embarrassed about being caught. He asks, "Who was that?"

He and Jason only show concern. I never told him about the Tertullian Society. Even Chris and Walter, who saw Zest briefly a few months ago, do not know who he is.

"He's a confidential informant for a few cases. We have to be on the downlow."

I say it casual enough and he accepts that, although I see him glancing at me the rest of the night as if wondering what's going on he doesn't know about. I have to wonder that too.

∞

The New York Scene/Thin Blue Line Column by Carl Mankiewitz
Tom Paine's Revolution

The *Scene's* favorite troublemaking private investigator, Gabriel Ross, continues his correspondence with mysterious YouTube provocateur Tom Paine. Paine has confirmed on his channel (*Tom Paine Events*) that Ross is his go-to spokesperson. Paine has given Ross some specific details on political incidents over the past 50 years. (See below for a summary). Ross has kindly shared these details with me.

Paine has been gathering a strong online audience approaching 200,000, and many of these fans copy and discuss Paine's videos and documented information. Paine encourages sharing and adding to the initial information he has--just stipulating that anyone who adds, documents credible information rather than speculating wildly. And to refrain, like some conspiracy-based talk show hosts and websites, accusing every event on Earth as being a 'false flag' set up to instigate the New World Order. Paine doesn't hold to NWO, false flags, birthers, or presidential 'hit lists.' Ross quotes him as saying, "A false flag operation outside military is extremely difficult. Better to have a real incident, and just use the media tendency to scoff at conspiratorial elements and portray anyone who asks questions as a nut."

Is Paine asking too much? Not to the burgeoning RIP (Revelation Interpretation Provocation) movement, a loosely-connected group who have been following Paine's videos righteously. The group has become a phenomenon like Occupy, with international connections (especially in the countries that the videos concern) and a strong online presence (via forums set up through TOR).

The RIP online has started to hold rallies in London, Stockholm, San Francisco and New York. They have their own eye-catching avatar that's being used in graffiti, websites, and posters. As Anonymous is identified with the Guy Fawkes mask, RIP has a radical version of the Maneki-neko cat. The 'beckoning' cat is usually seen in Asian restaurants as a symbol of luck. But the RIP version has the cat raising its fist defiantly, wearing a slave collar, and holding a protest sign. The message on the sign changes periodically. Yesterday, I saw one that said *Rise Up Against Your Oppressors.* RIP would like Paine to show up at a rally, or Ross to speak at one. Ross says he'd prefer to keep a lower profile but encourages the RIP activists to push forward with their questions as much as possible...

∞

Monday, October 31
Horatio Street, 8:02 pm

Halloween. The idea of people dressing up to pretend to be malevolent monsters is disconcerting. People behind masks. Trick or treat.

Revelry is going on a few blocks east of our building on Broadway. The annual Village parade has started, and a few celebrities are supposed to be in attendance. With the window open we can hear the crowd, but due to the parade being such a people magnet our block is pretty quiet. Once the parade is over people will drift this way but for now, we're on our own. The muted noise from the crowd on Broadway actually makes the quiet here more eerie. Add to that we're the only people in the building right now.

I went to my apartment briefly this morning. I took Archie to Veronica's apartment to stay with her two cats. I grabbed my laptop, my guns, Kent's notes, and my locksmithing equipment. Right now, I'm using my key-making machine to create a version of the key that was in Mesereau's secret space. I have a blow-up of the photo Veronica took and my own sketch, to compare.

We did a minimum of work today while planning where we could go to wait for Zest to talk to us. I instructed Joel to check that Isabella and Chris's places are safe. Joel is coming over here as soon as he can--I wanted him to check on his mother as well.

Jim and Mikki have taken their own precautions. I've given them a vaguer explanation about a threat. Neither are surprised, but they want to help. I have no idea what to tell them. I just hope I'm the only target.

I work on the key while thinking about the days ahead. I'm considering something radical--to talk to Mankiewitz about what is going on. I would have to stay away from those I care for in order to go public. I wouldn't out myself as Paine, but maybe say just enough to make any further stalking cease. Then I would just avoid flying or driving anywhere for a while. I would like to give Clark the story as well, but the *Standard* is reluctant to get its hands dirty with conspiracy theories. I've called Walter and told him I may need to entrust him with certain information if anything happens. I plan to talk to him at the end of the week. And while it scares me, I've called Mankiewitz and told him I want to meet with him on Wednesday.

As I finish the key Veronica goes around the office securing everything. She's installed a program on the computers that will encrypt everything if the computer is turned on without a password, and it will erase everything on the hard drive with one wrong attempt on the password. She's also installed a combination on lock on the storage closet and similar locks on the file cabinets.

I put away the equipment in the storage room and lock the key in the safe that is kept in the storage closet, in a hidden section of one of the file cabinets.

The noise of the parade gets a little louder, making us both nervous. Veronica looks out the windows in my office for a few minutes.

"Gabriel, I don't like this. A van just pulled up."

I'm over there immediately, and grabbing my Sig Sauer off my desk. Veronica is licensed to carry, and I've been training her on my Glock. She picks it up now.

Shots come high through the windows, suppressed.

We drop to the floor. I try to cover Veronica. But the shots are too high to hit us, just meant to rattle us. We move, keeping low, from the office to the common area. Outside our suite door we hear someone rattle the knob.

Then the door bursts open. We both start shooting. It's not a time to consider the righteousness of the action.

An invasion happens so quickly it's hard to keep your mind up with what is happening. People in black; they have some kind of protection from the guns. Our shooting makes them break for the sides of the reception room but they do not stop.

One of them says, "Get him out."

Veronica is up faster than I, and starts blocking them as Chiang has trained us. I follow her. It's happening too fast to say if we can hold them off and make it to lock ourselves in an office, or be able push past them. Or just take them down with us. Fighting in a studio hand to hand is not fighting with people in Kevlar uniforms. But staying in motion keeps them off guard. Baguazhang-style is good for multiple attackers.

To be able to hold them off takes a sense of where their vulnerable areas are outside of the protective gear, and how to move just ahead of where they reach. Fighting fiercely in this confined area, things in the office are getting smashed. But I only hear that noise in the background of my mind, concentrating on grunts of the men as my fist or foot connects with them.

Then one of the men manages to hold a gun against Veronica's head. She tries to twist away, and a shot goes off that grazes her. Another man grabs her arms.

I stop and back up, holding up my hands. "Leave her out of this. Whatever you want, it's with me."

Those two men drag Veronica out the office without comment. She's still struggling to punch and kick her way free. The others--four men--approach me. They have goggles or shields on their faces, gloves, body armor.

I call on everything I have to stop them, in some hope other help will come. I hear Veronica scream somewhere in the building, and my fury at that gets me loose enough from the men to escape to my office. I kick the door shut and lock it. They start slamming themselves against the door.

While I have a chance, I switch my phone on and press the speed dial. I hear a click as Zest answers. He says, "I'm nearby, almost there."

"They're doing something to Veronica--protect her."

The men slam against the door again, cracking it.

"Gabriel--"

"Just protect her, damn it."

The door breaks. I hold up my Sig Sauer and when I see the black clothing, I shoot. They duck back. But even so, they've crashed in and knock me down. I feel something at my feet stinging. Then my entire body convulses and I can't move.

One of the men says. "Take him out."

Then some hideous clamor starts outside in the hallway. Their heads turn. A moment later, as I'm barely able to take a breath, I hear another one yell, "Someone's taken the woman upstairs."

"Forget her," the first man says. "Get him out now."

I feel relief that Zest must be here. Then a hood goes over my head, and three of them pick me up. I try to yell, afraid I'm going to suffocate.

"Be careful with him."

I still can't move, frozen from the Taser effect. But the feeling begins to wear off as I hear the building door open, feel the cold night air, and then hear doors to a van sliding open.

A couple shots go off again in the street. The men holding me loosen their grip; I rip off the hood, break away from them and tear down the street. I head toward 13th Street and any possible traffic. I hear them running behind me, and the van gunning its motor. Two cars coming the other way barely miss me, swerving. The van drives over a sidewalk to pull across the street, blocking it, and men jump from the van.

I grab a lamppost in a desperate measure to hang on, even as I feel something sharp in my back. A needle. With the adrenaline rushing, whatever it is begins working in under a minute. I dig my fingers in, but they get weaker and weaker. The men drag me back, with my nails scraping the metal of the lamppost.

One of the men puts an oxygen mask over my face. Fear makes me breathe deeply. My world turns black.

∞

Horatio Street, 9:30 pm

Joel is very anxious by the time he reaches the office building. He spent the day with Chris and Isabella until he drove to Wayne go over Gloria's condo. She was out but came home to find him putting in stronger locks. She had a ton of questions he ignored, but he called Dell and asked him to come over. Dell then had a ton of questions Joel ignored, and ultimately he abruptly left them both as he was not getting responses from Gabriel or Veronica in the last hour. He finally tried calling Zest, and didn't get an answer from him either.

The lights are off in the hallway and the door is open. Joel hears something from Gabriel's office and steps in. A radio is on and crackling as if it's between stations. Joel snaps on the ceiling light switch next to the door.

The light buzzes, flickers on, then fizzes and pops. *An electrical problem....?*

The light finally gets one bulb working. Enough to see the offices have been thrown into chaos. In the strobe light Joel's not believing what he's seeing.

"What the..."

He steps gingerly into the reception room, with an immediate sense of dread. Chairs are overturned, items knocked off shelves. Posters are ripped from the walls. Plants have been uprooted and apparently tossed across the room.

Joel does a 360, then panics. *"Gabriel!?"*

He starts to search the wreckage and hears a noise behind him.

Zest is standing behind him. "Come with me, Joel."

Joel follows Zest up the stairs to the next floor where Zest has broken into an empty office.

Joel draws his breath in. Veronica is laying on the floor, unconscious.

"Jesus! What happened?" He gets down on his knees beside her. He sees bruises on her face, and blood on her face, head and leg.

"She was shot in the leg, and grazed in her scalp. It's not life-threatening, but I want to treat her."

Joel takes out his phone and Zest stops him. "No ERs. They'll bring in the police."

Joel frowns and then looks around. "What--where's Gabriel?"

"He's gone. With Clement."

"What the fuck do you mean--"

"Clement abducted him. He came here and invaded the offices. Gabriel signaled me to help; he wanted me to protect Ms. Gianni. They had already dragged her out and were going to harm her. I was able to get her away. There are a couple men in the back hallway who are disabled. I've called for help with that. We need to get her to some place where I can treat her."

Joel is speechless. He puts his hand on Veronica's face, and she moans.

Zest says, "Gabriel wanted me to take care of her. We need to do so."

"Yeah, okay...I have my car outside."

"Good. Don't worry about the office. I'll have people taking care of things in here to minimize police involvement." Zest picks up Veronica's prone form, and heads for the elevator.

Joel leads him outside to his SUV. Zest lays Veronica on the back seat. He then stops and looks around the deserted street.

Joel asks. "My place okay?"

"Yes."

Joel drives to Chinatown, and calls Geneva to have her meet them there. He feels himself slipping into panic, and tears coming. Zest stares out the windows.

"I'll find out where Gabriel is. I'll have to get some help."

Joel wipes his eyes. "I'll help. Geneva will help. What's going on?"

"I don't know where Gabriel is, but...I know what's likely happening."

"*What?* What is happening? Why does he want Gabriel?"

"He thinks Gabriel is useful to him. Joel, while I'm looking, tell people whatever story you can to keep it quiet. As I said, I'll have the building cleaned up. With the Parade going on, what happened in the building probably wasn't noticed. It's in Gabriel's best interest that this incident doesn't attract attention of the authorities. Not serious attention."

"They kidnapped him. They don't expect the police?"

"No. Missing is one thing. His being reported missing is not important to them. But if *any* possible connection to the Society is exposed, the Society will kill Clement and Gabriel."

"But the Society--"

"Not them. Him. Clement acted alone, or almost alone. Much like I'm doing."

"You can find him?"

"Yes." Zest doesn't have confidence--he has surety. Joel is somewhat relieved by that surety.

"I have to be careful so Clement doesn't know I am doing this. He believes certain things about me. I have to be careful because if he suspects at all that I've been helping you, he'll kill Gabriel."

"Okay. I get the picture. So you find him. And then we rescue him?"

"Yes. I'll set up an operation. I have people I use outside my regular work."

"And us."

"I'll say yes for now, although you must be discreet. I don't have to explain things to you about that."

"No. I wouldn't endanger him. What is Clement trying to do?"

"I can't say *exactly*. I will tell you when I find out. I'm 95 percent sure that for now, he is not in danger of being killed. You need to know that. Clement wants him, and doesn't want to harm him unless he must. Trust me on it, please."

He doesn't say don't worry, because he knows better.

Joel lets Zest out at the building door with Veronica. He parks the SUV in a garage, and runs back to explain what is going on to Geneva.

But Zest is already in the loft with Geneva, and has given her a short version of the events. Geneva has summed up the situation quickly and brought over a homemade medic kit she and Veronica have for emergencies.

Zest uses the tools in kit to find the slug in Veronica thigh, stitch her wound, and dress her other injuries. Zest has penicillin and morphine with him. Whether he carries that all the time, he doesn't say. Geneva strokes Veronica's head once she's on the bed, still unconscious.

"You did a damn good job," Geneva tells Zest.

"Thank you. You might guess I've had practice."

Joel goes through several cigarettes, watching him. He too goes over to Veronica. "I'm sorry," he tells her sleeping form.

"She'll be all right. None of this is your doing." Zest's voice is quieter than normal.

"I could have been there."

"They wanted Gabriel. If it meant killing her, they would have. Had you been there, that would have applied to you as well. Joel, I'll need you to help when I find Gabriel."

It's not exactly comfort, but the intention is there. Don't go down the mental road of

blame and guilt. It won't help, and will make things worse.

"We'll keep it together," Geneva says. "He needs us to. From what Mr. Zest says, Gabriel would be glad Veronica is safe."

Later, repeating the conversation with Zest in his head keeps Joel from freaking out. *Zest can do this,* Joel tells himself. *He'll find Gabriel.*

∞

PART TWO

DIYU

∞

SEVEN

From the YouTube Channel "Tom Paine Events," in a video entitled: Unknown Knowns: Frank Olson ♦ The Experiment

Transcript: "Olson was a decent man doing his job as a biochemist and director of planning and evaluations in the US Army Chemical Corps Special Operations Division. In 1953, Sid Gottlieb, father of the CIA's MKULTRA program, arranged for some government personnel to be unwittingly drugged with LSD during a social occasion. Olson was one of those drugged without his knowledge, and apparently he suffered severe psychological distress from the experience.

"Coerced into seeking treatment in New York City, he fell to his death from a 10th story hotel window--or was defenestrated. The window was closed and according to Olson's son, who spent decades investigating his father's death, the setup of the room made the official version of Olson's actions in committing suicide impossible. Olson was an unwilling part of an experiment in mind-control, an unknown known and a known unknown. His death raises the question of how can we ensure that the death of a man who was a keystone to understanding the dirty and unethical programs our intelligence agencies (with a black budget not subject to public review or sunshine laws) remains in the forefront of consciousness--as those programs doubtless still continue..."

∞

Somewhere else

DARKNESS. Cold wood floor under me.

I'm breathing loud. I can't see anything, but my head is spinning. I feel pain in my arms...trapped behind me in handcuffs.

I open my eyes as wide as I can... it's still dark. No, something is over my eyes. My semi-consciousness is laced with panic. I reach with my fingers, trying to get a sense of where I am. The handcuffs are linked to a chain. The chain goes to a thin pipe running along just above the floor.

I wait, wondering if someone is watching me. My mind fluctuates between panic and nausea. I know I've been drugged, and it's hard to think. Very hard. I can't remember where I was before, or with whom. I remember having a gun, struggling, running being dragged away...

Time goes by. Then I feel the presence of another person; a light on me. The blindfold is lifted briefly. I jerk away by instinct. Then the blindfold is ripped off. I still can't see anything; the room is dark. Someone's shining a flashlight on me. I can't see the person with the light in my eyes.

"What do you want?" My voice sounds angry and scared.

No answer. The man, I feel it's a man, stands over me. I only can make out an indistinct silhouette. Like the silhouettes I saw in the office and the library. This makes my heart pound. Then he turns and walks away quickly. A door shuts.

Alone again. No sense of how big this room is, if anything is here. A long time goes by as I fight to get my system normal again. Veronica...is she here? No...I'm sure she escaped. I hope she escaped. I try to remember.

I try to get a sense of my surroundings, now that the blindfold is gone. *Push yourself to understand where you are, see what you can do.* That would be my plan. *With every problem, there's a way out.*

But I can't do what I want to do. Whatever I've been drugged with just makes me weak. I end up dozing...and wake suddenly with my heart pounding in terror.

I had hoped it was a nightmare, but I'm still chained on the floor. A man, maybe the same one, is here again. It's still dark in the room. I feel a strange touch on my head. His hand. I inhale sharply, accidentally slamming my head against the wall to get away from him.

A light goes on. It makes me wince. But I can see him.

He's in a black shirt and black pants and a white coat. And a mask. The mask is white, vaguely resembling a drama mask, with thin slits over the eyes.

It's so surreal I have to wonder if I'm hallucinating.

The man with his expressionless mask reaches down and touches where I hit my head. "Don't do that. I'm not going to hurt you. I want you to get on your knees, all right?"

I get up, with difficulty. I realize how weak I feel. All parts of my body feel heavy, like dead weight. The man helps me to my knees. I hear him unlock the chain from the pipe.

"I know you want to hurt *me*. You can't do anything with your hands locked behind you. Just bear with me and you'll be okay. If not, this is going to go worse."

Right now, my body feels so strange that I can't trust my reflexes. "Okay."

"Good." He lifts me to my feet. I try to get my legs to move under me; to find a purchase on the floor. My eyes have adjusted; I can see the room is the size of a large house bedroom. No furniture. The floor is old wood. The windows on one side are blacked out. There are two other doors. The one furthest from me is closed. Some light is coming in from another room connected to this room, through a cracked door. It's a few feet from me.

He asks, "Are you going to give me trouble?"

"No." My voice sounds strange, flat. Stressed.

He unlocks the cuffs from behind me. I bring my hands in front of me and look at them. I hear him rattling things around in his hands.

I turn quick and try to hit him on his neck. At the right angle, it would take him out.

Except I don't turn quick. I can barely move, and then my hand won't lift where I want it.

I can see him better now. Even with the mask, I can tell he's a white man close to 60, maybe. Short gray hair, a little taller than me. He doesn't react to my movement at first. He just stares at me. He seems familiar.

Then he reaches out with both hands and pushes my chest. I fall to the floor. It scares me how weak I am.

The man crouches next to me. "Even if you want to start trouble, you can't." He then recuffs my hands in front, and connects these cuffs to the long chain attached to the pipe.

He opens the door to the nearest room.

"You can go in there."

I see the other room is a bathroom. There's window, but tied to the chain I can't reach it. The chain is just long enough for me to reach the toilet. Next to the toilet are pipes from what used to be a sink. The toilet has no tank lid or seat. Nothing to use as a weapon, just like in jail.

I hear him walking away. Hesitantly, trying to get used to using my hands again, I urinate. I can barely stay upright.

I'm still wearing what I was the last time I can remember. In the office. Jeans and a long sleeve t-shirt.

When I go out again, he's frowning. "I'm sorry I have to do it this way."

"Are you going to tell me why I'm here?"

He walks over and actually strokes my head. I cringe from his touch.

"Not yet. I'm so sorry."

I try to switch tactics. "Can I have some water?" I make my voice uncertain.

He stares at me. "I'm sorry. Not yet. You have not yet learned." He raises a hand and two other men come in with a white opaque box, about the size of a trunk. It has holes on the top. The men haul me up and disconnect the handcuffs from the chain. I realize in horror they are going to put me in that box.

I struggle against them, but I can't do anything effective. They fold me into the box in a fetal position on my right side.

"You don't have to do this," I say in panic. "You're a reasonable man."

"You need to learn, Gabriel. I am *fond* of you, in fact." He looks down at me in the box. My heart is racing and my breathing gets heavier.

"Don't hyperventilate. It will make the situation worse. As I'm fond of you, I let you use the toilet before you went in the box. Consider that."

He gestures to the men, and they put the dark green lid on the box. The holes are big enough to get light and air, but my panic rises.

Calm down Gabriel calm down there are worse things that could happen he's trying to break you.

The lights go off.

I start shaking from the feeling of helplessness and fury. There's a cliché in movies, where the captured person yells helplessly. If you imagine being in this position, you don't think you'll break and do that. But it happens.

"Who are you? What do you want from me?"

No one responds.

I work on calming myself. *You can get through this. He didn't kill you so he wants something. You have to survive. Like Dad said. You have to survive.*

Some of my strength comes back. In the tiny amount of space I have to move, I test the integrity of the box. Something clamps the lid shut, but since it's plastic, it would have to give with enough pressure.

I start kicking. A few minutes go by. I'm making the box rock back and forth. Doing something about my situation calms me down. I think I feel the lid open slightly.

Water hits my face suddenly, making me scream.

His voice above me. "You need to stop. I can keep pouring water in this box. Consider that. Show me you can listen, Gabriel."

∞

Hours and hours later. Despite my best efforts to maintain a calm mind, I've lost a sense of time. I barely have any about space. Logic. Sooner or later something has to happen. *You can't stay here forever. This is absurd.*

But maybe not. It happens. People get kidnapped by maniacs. Usually children or women, but it's not unfeasible that a man could be kidnapped and held for years. Or like in Guantanamo. If you're an enemy combatant or an "enemy combatant" don't expect to see the light of day anytime soon.

What are you thinking??!!??

My mind goes to Joel. I know I'm alive, but he doesn't. All he knows is I'm gone. I don't know what he'll do. We never discussed this. We never discussed--what happens if one of us disappears? *That's not a normal relationship discussion.*

Except in my life, apparently it is. Now.

He will do something. With Zest, most likely. I know Zest got Veronica safe. I have to believe that. Just like me, he won't sit around and wait. If Zest knows where I am, Joel will make him tell me. But Joel will worry. Knowing he'll worry is agony for me. It's worse for me to think of him worrying than being in this box.

"I'll get out," I tell him. And then start crying.

I try to send him mental messages I'm okay. Then just try to send him messages where I am. Maybe my mind can be a GPS.

And then I break down again. *If something happens...he knows I love him, right? He'll always know that, right?*

My mind clears enough to try to think about what they want from me. Clement. Clement is interested in me. Clement, who tested me--tested my reactions. Clement, who worked on experiments for intelligence agencies. Mind control.

Son, you're in trouble. If I wasn't sure about it before...

The lid is abruptly off the box. Some masked person leans over me with a needle.

∞

I wake up and I'm on the floor in the dark. Chained to the pipe, but I'm not in the box. My hands are cuffed in front of me. I try to drag myself up a few times to go in the bathroom and check if I can stretch the chain. A white sheet of plastic covers the window. I can see light through it, but nothing that tells me where I am. And then the light dims. I try to listen but hear little. No city noises, no suburban noises.

Then a bird flies by in shadow, and it startles me. It looks like an owl. Sitting on something outside the window. Although I don't know owls and their habitat, I get the sense that this is a rural area.

I have managed to calm myself. The dullness of nothing happening helps. *You're still alive right now*, I tell myself. *Every day, every minute you are alive, it's a victory. It is an opportunity.* Joel had been telling me more about when he lived on the street. He said that's what got him through, to wake up alive each day.

I work on getting control of my mind. I concentrate on going through a book in my head, one I've read so many times I could practically recite it word for word, the way the poets did with the *Iliad*. I make up reviews for the book. Imagine the movie and who I'd cast in it.

I find myself checking to see the owl, who remains near the window. The owl is not the men in this room. The owl is an innocent being without the evil humanity can demonstrate. I think I hear a rustle of wings. It disappears and I want to cry. *"Don't leave me."* It's my only link to something not horrible.

Then the owl comes back later. And I'm so relieved. I end up falling asleep, and wake up suddenly, feeling nauseated, like I need to vomit. I get on my knees and dry heave. Tell myself to calm down, or I'll choke. No panic. No matter what happens.

∞

The New York Scene/Thin Blue Line Column by Carl Mankiewitz

Investigator Missing: Tom Paine Contact Had Promised More Serious Revelations

Gabriel Ross, the 37-year-old private investigator and Tom Paine confidant, is missing. Ross had specifically promised to meet with me a couple days ago, and I have not heard a word from him. Trust me that he's not like that. Repeated attempts to contact him have only led to voicemail or no response. I contacted his Gotham Investigations partner, Veronica Gianni. She said she was ill, and would not comment on Ross. Ross's significant other, artist Joel McFadden, says Ross is 'unavailable.' Granted, I've only known Ross a year, people, but he does not duck out on contact. He'd say something about what is going on. The fact he's the official mouthpiece for Tom Paine--whose videos are getting more and more provocative, and encouraging demonstrations to demand information--makes me nervous. And I'm not given to speculation...

∞

He's back.

The door to the room is open; the light looks blinding from a hallway. *From the looks of the hallway. This is a house of some kind.*

He's back in his mask, crouched next to me, staring at me. "You should get up, take care of yourself."

I try to and can't stand.

"I'm sorry," he says, and even with the mask it seems like he means it. "It's okay. Go slow, and come back when you're done."

I crawl to the bathroom. I recognize that other than the water poured on me in the box, I've had no food or water. Urinating doesn't come to much. But I have so much difficulty moving, I almost piss on myself.

Eventually I make my way back, breathing hard. He looks almost concerned, but also as if he's noting details. Like a scientist.

Deprivation is torture. Sensory deprivation, water deprivation.

He walks out again. This time he leaves the door open. I try to crawl to the doorway, but I can't reach more than halfway across the room. I don't see anything outside the door other than a blank wall.

Some men in dark olive uniforms--military? They have the same mask on. They push a large rectangular screen against the wall across from me. It's the size of a 60-inch TV. They turn it on and a strange noise comes from it. It reminds me of EVP, ghost voices coming from outer radio frequencies. The noise becomes horribly loud. The screen lights up with a pulsating yellow light. The room is dark other than this horrible yellow light. I have to turn away and cover my ears.

Bombardment is torture.

I already hated torture, but now I begin hating every person who ever tortured another person. Ever. No matter what the purpose. No matter what the excuse. There is no excuse. There is no military reason good enough. There is no god worth that much. The Nazis tortured people, innocent people. Doctors participated. Mengele, Ishii in Japan. The US plea bargained with Ishii so the results of his medical experimentation wouldn't get to Russia. The Allies tortured as well. What does that mean when the different sides use the same method?

Calm down. Clearly, Clement wants you to break. I can feel myself wanting to scream. I'm not entirely sure if I am screaming or not. Feeling weak, alone, being watched by men with no faces. They're wearing headphones so they can't hear this noise which pulsates along with the light. The worst is having to crawl to the bathroom again, without being able to cover my ears. I imagine that the light is radiating me.

The toilet has a little water in it. I may have to drink that. I know it's not the worst thing in the world. It's survival. And somehow that makes me collapse on the floor. "*Stop it stop it stop it.*"

The noise stops and the lights go on. I lift my head. And then two men are picking me up. I fight against them, and it makes me dry heave.

"Hold on," he says. Clement. He waits for me to stop heaving.

"You need to learn. Show me what you can take."

The box is back. That makes me struggle more. But they shove me in, and once the lid is on, ice water is poured in. I choke on it, gasp, start hyperventilating and choke more.

Then something makes me stop. *Get a hold of yourself.* It still takes a couple minutes but I stop gagging and bring my breathing down. *He wants to see what you can take. That means he'll let you out.*

Through the box I hear him say, "Good...good. I'm really sorry about this, Gabriel."

∞

Hours later. I'm out of the box, and I don't remember being drugged. Clement is here again. I sense it, and roll over to look at him in his mask and earplugs.

The screen is back. The lights and sound go on. It makes me cringe inside and want to scream, but I'm reminded: *he wants to see what you can take.*

I don't do anything. I don't look at the screen but I don't move. *Rise above it rise above it...*

Ten minutes. Twenty minutes. Clement leaves. I still don't react. I get up to go to the bathroom, and return to the floor. The noise and light are tearing at my nerves, and I'm nauseated, but I hold it in.

At least an hour. I don't really have a sense of time but it seems like an hour. Clement comes in. He raises his hand and the light and sound go off. My ears still ringing.

"Good," he says. "I knew it." He holds a water bottle in his hand, outstretched to me. I have to take time to lift my hand. I'm afraid he'll leave because I'm taking too long. My hands and arms feel so heavy.

Finally, I have the bottle and almost drop it. Getting the cap off is hard, but a surge of fear that I'll die from dehydration makes me twist it, and almost fall over. I don't ask him anything while I work on drinking. I don't care why I'm here anymore. I need to get out. That's all. From the sound of his voice, I've seemed to accomplished something. I don't know if that's good or bad.

His black eyes gleam at me through the slits of the mask. His tone becomes conspiratorial. "I know you want to escape. You can't. There are cameras everywhere. You've been with us for some time now; you're not in the US anymore."

I don't believe that. He's trying to scare me. He nods at my expression.

"You don't think so, but it's true. Before you get better, we need you to...help us, you might say."

"Help you with *what?*"

His voice gets slow. Too slow to hear. I don't know where I am any more. I hear the pulsating noise but I can't move. There were drugs in the water. Not just sedatives, but something to make me lose a sense of reality. It makes me want to leave my body, get away from this place. *Go. It's okay.*

I imagine that I'm somewhere else. I hear voices. I swear I hear Joel somewhere, and I have to think that he knows something is wrong and is looking for me. He has to be.

Then I hear Clement's voice. I feel hands on me I can't get away from.

I know I'm awake when I feel two men lift me up. The light and noise are turned off. I can't move much...*opiates,* I think fuzzily. He has me drugged to not have any strength, combined with no food for however long.

Aside from the two men holding me, I see Clement. He's frowning at me through his mask. Another man is walking around the room. He's white, maybe late thirties. Big, muscular. He wears a black vest over fatigues, dark sunglasses, brush cut. His mask is different, dark green with a downturned mouth. Like an angry god.

The Muscle Man says, "I want you to know something. You're helpless here. You'll cooperate. If you don't, we'll have 72 hours together, after which you won't be recognizable. I'll cut your balls off. I'll cut your eyes out. You'll wish you were dead if you don't listen to me."

He stands behind me. "I believe in progressive persuasion."

I feel the punch coming before it does, in my lower back. The pain makes me suck in air. I feel it radiate from my body in waves. Then he walks around in front and I know he's going to hit me again. When he hits my face, the other two men let go. I fall to the floor. Then they hold me up again.

The puncher frowns at me. He doesn't know I've been beat up before, and I'm not afraid of pain.

He walks out the room and comes back with a portable charger.

He presses a button and sparks crackle from it. That makes me gasp by reflex. In an almost business-like manner, he touches my chest with one of the clamps. It hurts horribly for a moment, then he steps away. He starts walking around me.

He touches me with the clamps again. I'm breathing hard, but I don't scream. I know what it feels like now. I look over at Clement, who has his fingers on his chin, studying me. *He wants to see what you can take.*

The Muscle Man snaps his fingers, and the men with him throw ropes over a pipe hanging from the ceiling.

"Oh, do we have to do this?" Clement shakes his head.

Muscle Man retorts, "I know what to do."

He pulls my arms behind my back. I feel lengths of rope being wound around them. Then he pulls me to my feet.

"You're a tough one, huh? Not for much longer."

The two men tie the rope over the pipe to the rope behind my back. I try to brace myself.

He comes around again to face me. "You think you can take it? We'll see."

At some signal they haul me up.

The pain is more than anything, ever. I can feel my shoulders separate, my arms starting to come away from the sockets.

I know I'm screaming, but I hear nothing. *It can't last it can't last itcan'tlast can'tlastcanltlast*

Clement snaps, "Take him down!"

I end up on the floor again. The ropes are cut, but I don't feel my arms.

The men leave, except for Clement. He very slowly puts the chains back on. And puts his hand on my head for a second.

"You did well. I'm so sorry," he says.

Sorry.

The door is shut, and room goes black.

As the adrenaline ebbs, I start shaking and have dry heaves again. I feel like I may never stop.

But my mind goes back to what he said. It sounded unrealistic and yet I can believe it. And yet something doesn't ring right. I don't know. I don't know if I'm thinking right anyway. I don't know what to believe. But my mind tries to hold on some kind of control. Some kind.

What might be a few hours goes by. The pain stays in my body after I feel my arms again, but I can handle this. It reminds me I'm still alive.

I start to remember I'm Buddhist. And that what I'm going through is nothing compared to the horrors people have endured in war and genocide. People who were "disappeared" in Argentina, in Cambodia, in Iraq. It doesn't make me feel better, but I try to be more resilient. I'm not a martyr, but I can try to stay alive.

The door opens...the light and sound again. I try to cover my head. They come in and pull my hands away, lock them behind me. I chant to myself the entire time.

The light and sound go off. The green-masked torturer comes back. He has the charger again. And the ropes. I know how it feels and remind myself it will not kill me. They don't want to kill me. They want me to suffer and break. I keep chanting. It makes the green-masked man angry.

I get lightheaded from the pain and fall down. He yells at me. I pass out.

The light and sound go back on.

I crawl without using my hands to the bathroom, just to get my head around the door jamb, and be able to see the window. It's night; I wonder if the owl will come back. The owl seems like the one thing I can count on. A symbol of survival.

I wonder if I can find the strength to beat my head against the old tile wall until I'm unconscious or dead.

Then I'm dragged back in the room. The light is off, so I know what's coming. They pick me up again. The Muscle man is waiting.

When I'm dumped back in my room, I crawl to the bathroom. I hear beating wings and see the owl perched somewhere outside. She turns her head to look at me.

You are doing right, she says. She has Veronica's voice. *Stay strong. He doesn't know.*

Clement is beside me in the bathroom. I've vomited on myself.

"Oh my God, I'm so sorry."

I don't want to ever hear those words again.

He kneels down. "He's so awful, so awful. What he did to you."

He reaches for my head and strokes it. "So awful." Then he moves closer and puts his arm around me. He takes his mask off. I can see his face, his black eyes, clearly.

I'm so angry. I know what he's doing. I want to kill him. I can't stop shaking and he holds me against my will.

The owl says, *Go with it, Gabriel. Play him.*

I slowly let my head go to his shoulder; it takes everything I have mentally to get past the revulsion. He pulls me tighter. "I know, I know. I'm sorry."

We stay like that. My hatred for him grows, and yet some part of me wants to give in for real. His hands on me seem to feel sincere in affection. I'm aware of the loneliness and need to be comforted. I'm repulsed by my own thoughts, and feel the beginnings of losing my mind.

No. Play him.

I allow myself to sound like I want to cry. It's not hard, and I start crying for real.

He says, "If you can help us, then you don't have to see him again."

"What do you want help with?" My voice sounds strange. Trying to sound like I'm giving in, but my anger still underneath.

"We'll go over that. You have to trust me that I'm going to help you."

He has another bottle of water. I know something must be in it, but I'm dying of thirst. I drink it too fast and immediately puke up the water.

He gets up and comes back with a towel and cleans me off. "I just need you to help me."

And he has something else. Orange juice. I recognize it from the color, the label on the small carton. It looks so magical, so foreign. I look at it the way the conquistadors must have looked at the cities of gold in Mexico and Peru.

"Be careful," he says softly, holding the carton for me. "Don't drink fast this time."

At first, it's gloriously sweet, and then I almost throw up again.

"Careful, now. I don't want you to be sick."

It's real juice. I can't tell if they put something in it. But for a minute, I feel human as it goes through my body.

The simple act of drinking juice makes me feel human, too human. But moments later, I pass out. Maybe I'm in some kind of low blood sugar fit. I wake up and see the green-masked torturer standing in front of me, still in his mask. My body tenses, waiting for the shock.

"No need..." I hear Clement's voice. "He'll be okay."

And I almost feel *grateful.* I hate myself for feeling grateful. *That's what he wants you to feel.*

The light starts again. Now, with the tiny amount of energy from that juice, I can take care of this. I won't let him have me. I can choose my fate. I sit up, crawl in the bathroom, take a breath, and slam my head against the wall.

It hurts like hell. I have to do it harder. I slam my head again.

Suddenly Clement is next to me. "*No, no, no*. Don't do that. *Don't do that.*"

I try to lash out at him--my hands, my feet, anything. Take him with me. I start crying again, uncontrollably.

I hear the owl's wings beating, and her voice.

Don't do it. You can survive this. He wants to see what you can take. You can beat him, Gabriel.

"Turn off the light," Clement says.

The evil thing goes dark. I feel like I can still see it. I stop and stay still, concentrating on listening to the owl's beating wings. Clement doesn't appear to hear this.

"Gabriel, I don't want to have to bring the box back..."

A sick fear envelops me to think of the box. "You don't need to. I'll help you."

"All right. You help us, and I don't need to send the other man in here, I don't need to use the light. Consider that."

He looks me in the eyes. "Do not hurt yourself. I will not hurt you."

"Just tell me what you want."

"We'll talk about it."

He suddenly pulls me up, and unlocks the chain from the pipe. I'm too disoriented to try anything. I feel helpless, like an accident victim. Like a mental patient in a ward. I'm one of the characters in *One Flew Over the Cuckoo's Nest.*

Clement puts a hood over my head, and pulls my arm to make me walk with him. "Come on with me."

We go out the room. Under my bare feet, I can feel a wood floor. Then some distance down, what feels like stone or tile.

Clement steers me into a chair. It feels like plastic, metal legs. The hood is taken off, and I catch a glimpse of a white-ish room and machines of undetermined usage.

A couple of other people are here. I guess they are people. They are in white suits with hoods, some kind of cloth/paper thing. Their masks have no human characteristics. Large black circles over eyes, grey face, points where the nose and mouth should be. They look like insects. One straps my arms to the chair, which is uncomfortably like a dentist chair.

The insect people stick things to me I recognize as electrodes. Small and large. Stuck to my chest, legs, and many to my head.

"Remain still, Gabriel. This will take a few minutes. You will be the imprimatur of my creation, Cognoscenti."

"What are you doing to me," I ask helplessly. My voice breaks.

No answer. I can hear one of the machines being turned on. My body tenses. *You're going to be tortured more.*

"We are just going to talk." I see him wheel up a screen about the size of a desktop monitor. I'm scared it will be that light and noise again.

"No, it's okay."

The screen turns yellow. It doesn't pulse, it flows. It looks like silk on the screen. Golden yellow like the sun.

"Watch it, Gabriel. While you watch I want you to tell me some things."

He asks me questions like he's interviewing me. My name, my age, my address. Since he's been stalking me, these aren't secrets.

The questions get stranger. What I like and dislike. What makes me sad or angry. I stop answering, shake my head. He asks about people in my life. I don't answer.

He asks the same questions over and over. I become so tired; I want to fall asleep. I close my eyes, and a minute later feel a needle in my arm.

"What are you doing?"

"I'm going to make this easier. You are almost there, but you need some help to cooperate."

I have to imagine this is sodium pentothal...if it's scopolamine, I'll pass out.

The room begins to waver some. My heartbeat feels loud.

"Watch the monitor again. Don't close your eyes. I want you to tell me about yourself."

∞

Eɪɢʜᴛ

From the Tom Paine Events Channel on YouTube, in a video entitled:

Unknown Knowns: Oscar Romero ♦ The Beatified

Transcript: "Archbishop Romero was assassinated in 1980, while at the pulpit in El Salvador. He had been urging the Salvadoran Army to stop targeting its people. He is thought to have been gunned down by a right-wing death squad, which were pretty common in Central America at that time.

"Romero had asked publicly for international assistance in stopping the genocidal (and this was the United Nation's term) war in the country that was causing thousands of deaths every month. Initially conservative, Romero had turned more sympathetic to liberation theology after being affected by the murder of a local priest; this priest had advocated for assistance to the desperately poor in the country. Romero could not get any international leaders to help. He could only tell the Army from the pulpit that they did not have to follow orders that were contrary to God in killing their fellow citizens. No one specific been determined to be the killer or killers to this day. Romero's death--which he foresaw, raises the question of can a group keep on with embodying the spirit and principles of a movement once a leader has been murdered, and how to remain true to the principles?"

∞

Sodium pentothal is not magic truth serum. For it to work, you have to know what you're looking for when you interrogate someone. I start talking, just making up random shit. Even if I say something truthful, he won't be able to figure it out.

He folds his arms and glares at me. "I want to know what is important to you. Who is important to you?"

I begin telling him the plot to *The Sound of Music,* including the song list.

He walks out and leaves me alone for a long time. I almost fall asleep.

When he comes back, he says, "If you want water, or any kind of food, you're going to talk to me, Gabriel. I *can* get in your mind."

He has a bottle of water, and when he tries to put it to my mouth, I spit it out. I can see he's angry and impatient. He tilts the bottle in my mouth, forcing me to drink. I try to spit out as much as I can, and end up in a choking fit.

Once that's passed, he waits. I feel some hallucinogen coming on. The light comes on as well.

Clement is staring at me. He's sitting in a swivel chair, clasping his hands.

"All right, Gabriel. Let's try again. You have books, right? Many, many books. I've seen them. Tell me the titles of the books, all you can remember."

It seems innocuous. As I start to mention titles of books, the yellow pulsation in the small screen seems to get larger. His questions float up and surround me, almost becoming physical.

Who are you?
What are you?
What do you like?
Who do you love?
What is meaningful to you?

And I finally feel like I'm leaving my body as I wanted to before, lost and floating in these questions.

∞

I'm back in a room. A library. CUNY Midtown? No. The New York Public Library Schwartzman building? No. But it's familiar. So much under glass. I realize I'm in the library in the *Herald-Standard.* Everything must be okay. Nothing can happen bad in a library.

I'm in a t-shirt and pants. I'm a little cold but not too bad. I hear a pleasant hum. Almost like innocuous background music.

I'm in front of a large book in a glass case. It's a medieval illustrated Bible. The illustration on the left page looks like me--me as St. Stephen, with arrows sticking out of my body. On the other page is an illustration of Dominic as John the Baptist, crying in the wilderness.

And then Dominic is in front of me. *He's not dead anymore. Good. I have a lot to talk to him about.*

Dominic says, "Gabriel, you were unfairly persecuted. That isn't going to happen anymore."

Dominic has Archie in his arms. He lets Archie jump down, and Archie proceeds to scratch his claws on a book I'm sure is mad-expensive.

"Arch, don't do that." Archie, as per cat nature, puts his ears back and scratches more furiously.

"It's okay. Let him. They can't tell you what to do here."

Dom's voice sounds strange and flat, although he looks normal. He's dressed in a suit he wore for a staff photo at CUNY Midtown; I have it in my photo album at home. "What do you mean, Dom?"

"You *were* the Annunciator. It has to be different now. Now you are the Avenger. You can do that. I trust you to do that."

The glass case disappears but the book remains on a pedestal. Dom turns pages of the book without touching them. "Here you are as the Annunciator. You tried to tell people what was right." He shows me an image of myself in front of the Virgin Mary, who looks like Veronica. Pages turn. "Now you will be Michael." The vengeful warrior Archangel. Dom points to the black and white illustration in the style of Doré. Myself with a sword, reaching up to Heaven, standing on a jagged mountaintop.

"You can take vengeance for others, Gabriel." His voice is still flat, but mixed with a strange bloodthirstiness Dom never had in life.

"Revenge is not right, Dom. You told me that. We talked about Anne Frank--"

Dom gives me an annoyed, impatient look. Then he's gone--disappears in front of me. I look at Archie. He runs down a corridor. I try to chase after him, and fall down on a carpet black as forever.

I struggle to get up.

"Gabriel, I need your help."

I look up and see Joel standing in front of me. "Oh, my God. Joel, are you okay?"

"Of course. I need your help." He's looking down at me. He's wearing a leather jacket and jeans that I remember from a photo on his website. In that photo he's standing next to a painting of his. He has his hand on the painting now, just like in the picture. "Gabriel, I was going to paint you as the Avenger, the Avenging Archangel, but you don't want that. Why? Tell me why."

I feel scared again, and look around the library. "Joel, be careful. What if they're around? They might find us."

"Who?"

"The Tertullians. I know they were after us. I must have escaped but we're still in danger. Did you find Veronica? Is she all right?"

He looks blankly at me for a long moment before answering. "Yes. She is okay. Do not worry. I want to talk to you about my painting--"

I get up and put my hands on his shoulders. "Later, baby. Let's be sure we're safe first, okay? I'm not going to let anything happen to you."

He stares at me curiously. "Yes, I understand. What are you afraid of?"

"What they can do. What they can take away."

"What would you do to stop them?"

"Joel, I'll protect you with my life. You know that." I grab for his hand.

He stares at my hand holding his, and then smiles. "That's beautiful, Gabriel, really. You aren't an avenger. You are a *protector*."

"Yeah, you know I'll do anything for you. Joel, come with me. We need to..."

"Gabriel, look at the painting."

He's exasperating me. I look at his damn painting while thinking *we need to get out of here--why do you have to be this way?* The painting is of me as a Bodhisattva. The Bodhisattva image is from one of the books in my own collection. *Unlike Joel to be so derivative. He doesn't copy, he has new interpretations, like the "Missing" poster. The Bodhisattva here is like a child's paint-by-numbers. A fake.*

I say to myself, "If the painting is a fake, then maybe--"

"Gabriel," Joel says sharply, "Look closer at the painting."

The painting turns silky yellow, and holds my eyes helplessly as it pulsates.

∞

I wake up and see I'm back in the room. *What happened? He hypnotized you.*

I had no idea was susceptible to that. But I realized it happened. Telling Clement the titles of my books put me under. What did I say? How long did it go on?

I have the unpleasant feeling I was talking about myself. I have a vague dream about people I love, but they were acting wrong. We were at cross-purposes. They were fake. False flags.

He was in my mind. A strange feeling, like having had the police search my place. Everything is poked through. Cabinets and drawers open. Things rifled through. The most intimate objects cursorily examined and tossed aside.

Clement is in the room. Smiling down at me. "Very good, Gabriel. We had a good talk. We'll have a better talk tomorrow."

He leaves a bottle of water beside me, and a couple of apples. The door shut behind him, leaving me in semi-darkness.

In movies, you see people who have been starved attack food like animals, reminding us that we are in fact animals.

I restrain myself from that; I'm trying to think. He's going to hypnotize me again tomorrow. I have to protect myself. He's making me talk about myself. He's making me talk about other people. Protect the people I love.

I hear the owl's wings beating, and see her shadow outside the window. Her name is V. I know it.

Remember what your father told you, she says. What my father told me. *You have to become another person.*

"Who...how?"

Ryan, she says. Ryan. My middle name. As with most middle names it's almost meaningless except when being written on some document. An application, a legal paper. Now it has a purpose.

V tells me, *Ryan is a different person. Ryan can be the person to talk to Clement.*

I try to imagine what Ryan is like, to let him take over...if I can do that.

∞

I'm in the chair. The light goes on and I feel the needle again. This time it makes me warm. At ease. A change.

But I hear my heart beat hard--so hard I imagine it's going to stop. And yet, it doesn't hurt. Things go black.

Suddenly I'm aware I'm reciting a list of something. Streets in Manhattan. From Battery Park to Inwood.

"That's very good. I want you to tell me what you don't like."

"I don't like darkness. I don't like that light you kept on me."

"You want light--like the sun."

"Yeah...I want to go outside."

"We can do that. Just talk to me. Tell me what I need to know."

I'm sure it's Clement talking to me, but the tone of the voice changes. Now I get the impression the voice belongs to a huge faceless being. A circle of beings. A council of beings. Just outside my vision--they are in another dimension and so I can't see them clearly. Of course--no wonder I can't see them. But they want to know about me. If I tell them, perhaps I can move on. That is the purpose of every book of the dead--to give you the correct answers to move on.

The voice speaks and I hear an echo--male/female/old young. The voice asks, *what is most disturbing to you?*

Now I'm in a white mist, like I'm floating.

"Pain...other people's pain."

Then you want to be part of other people avoiding pain, and finding peace. Helping them move on.

"Yes. Whatever I can do to help."

Have you helped people before?

"I tried to. I think I did."

Do you want to be where there is sun?

"Yes, if I could."

Do you want to be alone?

I don't want that man with the charger near me. I don't want the insect people. And yet...the idea of being in a black void where I'm totally alone--for all time--terrifies me.

"Please don't leave me alone."

The white mist I'm in abruptly turns dark.

"What happened? Where are you? Why did you leave?"

Something red appears in front of me. A shape that becomes what I was afraid of as a child. A demon. Rising tall, ten--twenty feet. Dark souls in the background screaming. The demon is standing over a pit. I used to be scared of that pit as a child, the one that Satan rules over.

The screaming gets louder. I try to think of prayers I know, and none come to mind. The dark form of the demon gets closer and his limbs grab my chest. I feel the talons inside. Ripping my insides, tearing them out and eating them while I'm still alive.

Reaching for my eyes. I can't see any more. I start screaming.

Then I'm in the library, with Joel. He looks at me with mild annoyance. "Gabriel?"

I grab him and pull him close, looking around for the demon, to protect Joel from the demon. It's strange because Joel doesn't feel quite right. His face doesn't seem to change from that expression he had in the photo. His voice is flat, just like Dom's. I try to adjust it in my mind to make it like the one I know and love.

"What is happening, Gabriel?"

"I want to protect you from the demon."

"And who else?"

"Why ask questions, baby? We need to go."

"It's important." He pats my shoulder awkwardly. "I need to know who's important to you."

"You already know."

"I need to know again. Who influenced you?"

"My mom..." I stop. Why does Joel need to know this? He already does.

Now he takes out pictures and shows me. "Who do you care about?"

I see my mom, and Dom. Then Joel shows me pictures of my friends. Veronica. I'm scared for a moment seeing the look in Joel's eyes. Something is wrong.

"She'll be able to take care of herself," I say. I don't want to make her more vulnerable.

He nods, like no big deal. He shows me other pictures. Danny, Jim, Mikki. Bob. Geneva. Jason. "Joel, did you take these out of my apartment?"

"I need to know."

"They are all able to take care of themselves. Why do you ask?"

"I just want to understand you." His image fades in front of me and comes back.

"Christ, Joel, what is going on? You're not right."

Joel frowns. He almost disappears in front of me. Like a computer glitch.

"Gabriel, I'm in trouble. I need your help. Your protection."

"What do you want me to do?"

"If I...had someone I needed you to protect, would you do that for me?"

"Who is it?"

"A friend. A dear friend."

That's all I hear. The stress from worrying over what's happening to him gives me the bad headache. My head pounds intolerably.

When the blackness clears, I see my mom. It's strange; although she seems to be real in front of me, she looks like she did in 1980, in photo of her I have in my apartment in the living room.

"Gabriel, we need your help."

"Mom, what happened?"

"Gabriel, we need to know what you found in Zach Mesereau's house."

I frown at her. "How do you know about that, Mom?"

"I do know because I'm your mother."

"I can't tell you. I don't want you hurt."

"I won't be hurt. You'll protect me."

"The less you know, the better."

She looks angry at me. And then I hear V, the owl. *Gabriel, don't listen. It's not your mother.*

I stare at my mother. She never looked so angry. She grabs me and shakes me. "It's very important you tell me what you found in that house. You need to protect us. Listen to me Gabriel!"

I back away. "Something's wrong with you. Just like Joel. You'd never act this way with me."

She suddenly begins crying. "Oh, honey, I was just worried. Gabe, please, help me out. Just tell me what was in the house."

My mother didn't call me Gabe. No one has since I was 5 and insisted that my name was Gabriel, and Gabriel only. She's a fake, too.

"Mom, I want to help you," I say carefully. I try to think of something they will believe. "I saw a picture of Damon Clement."

"Really, was that all? What were you drawing when you were in there?"

The owl cries in my mind. *Don't let them know, Gabriel.* "A map. A map that was once in the space, but it had been taken. I could see the outlines."

"Do you remember the map?"

"No."

"Does Veronica have it?"

I laugh and make my tone superior, to deflect their attention from Veronica. "No. I'm better at doing this than her. I destroyed the map."

"Why would you do that?"

"It was dangerous. Mesereau is dangerous."

"You're right. You need to protect a friend of mine from him. Would you do that?"

I look at her. Her image fades in and out, like Joel's. "You're not my mother. Whoever you are, stay away from my mother. You know nothing about her."

"Is that right?"

And then the demon reappears. He takes my mother and bites into her neck. She screams as blood pours out.

The demon says, "Is this what you want?" He digs his curved teeth into her and bites through her shoulder. I can hear the bones crunch.

I start screaming and run toward the demon. He falls down under my blows. And then a yellow light comes from his eyes and I hear him roar. His talons reach for my eyes, and his tail wraps around my legs to drag me in the pit with him.

I wake up on the floor, gasping. I'm back in the room, chained to the pipe. I feel the floor, then see it. I'm not in the pit. My eyes haven't been ripped out. I breathe against the floor, and feel my breath come back to me. My throat hurts terribly.

Clement appears. "I know you would like some water."

I have a moment of clarity, much like awaking from a night terror. "What did you do to me?"

"You'll be better soon. I promise. I'm sorry about what you have to go through."

He kneels down with a water bottle. I know it has drugs in it, but I have to drink. Or die. And I don't know which is worse.

He reaches for my head and strokes it. "You want to help. I know you do."

"Help *what?!*" I say desperately.

"Trust me. Just do this."

I end up drinking because I don't want to die of thirst. Maybe dying of an overdose would be better.

I dream about myself. Telling myself whatever he's doing, go along with it. V speaks to me as well, behind the bathroom window. *You can survive this; we will find the way...*

∞

The New York Scene/Thin Blue Line Column by Carl Mankiewitz
More Questions Arise in Private Eye's Disappearance

A movement is on the precipice of taking off. A collective that is tired of official stories and being made out to be wingnuts, when real evidence existed to prove a point. Some international groups (overseas, conspiracies are more believable) have made pointed comments asking why Gabriel Ross has dropped out of sight. Is he hiding? Is he dead? Or is the entire Tom Paine thing a hoax?

Although in the Raymond Booth case I had some doubts about Ross when he said he gave up the investigation, I never really believed he did. In Ross's defense, he had the injuries and hospital bills to show for his refusal to back down. He also has a big mouth and is consistently courteous. So his not being here--and not in any area jail or hospital (I checked) is disturbing...Anyone who knows Ross is not giving any satisfactory answers--either *I don't know* or *No Comment* or *I'll get back to you*...If you're reading this, Gabriel, what's going on?

∞

I wake up in the chair with my body on fire. I can't see the fire but I feel it. The fire goes to every nerve ending.

Something pounding in my brain. *Do you want to help?*

No. Never. I'll never help someone who does this.

Then the fire stops and I feel nothing. I'm on the floor of the white room. I can't move.

You can't get up, voices say to me. *Do you like feeling like this?*

I'm paralyzed. I can't even move my fingers. I hear someone screaming in the background.

The voices insist, *Tell me what the worst thing is.*

No.

Tell us about who you love. Tell us about them so we can help you. So they can help you.

No....

Then V's voice breaks through the other voices. *Do not think of anything.*

But I can't help it. I see the demon from childhood. The one I was afraid of when I was a boy, and given to visions of Hell. The Hell my father believed in at the time. The Hell in paintings by medieval artists with infernal wisdom.

The demon returns. Goat feet, red body, black eyes, horns. Taller than I, with a human face under the red. He stands in front of me, in front of my chair. *Hell is the lack of God. There is no 'god' in this place.*

A screeching sound, now in stereo. A pit opens before the demon. The people in the pit reach up. I can see their hands, black and scarred. Faces without eyes, just bloody gaps. They're reaching through a grate over the pit, and find my feet.

The demon watches as I'm dragged to the grate and the pit. The hands pull at me to bring me in the pit. I can't move, I can't stop them. They'll take my feet, my hands, my eyes. They have parts of them that are missing, and the demon has promised me to them to replace those parts.

If you want this to stop, Gabriel, tell us about your friends, your loves...

I find myself screaming.

The demon is real. He wants me to grasp at his goat-legs, to beg him to let me out before the people in the pit devour me.

Suddenly water flows in from somewhere. It fills the pit, then rises around me.

I'm afraid to be in water. I'm afraid of drowning.

The water is over my head. The lid to the pit opens, and bodies float out, bumping into me. I can only see the water rising higher, and me not able to move. My chest is aching. I cough violently, and the water goes in my lungs.

Even as I'm drowning, I see V, perched on a tree in the room. Next to her is a man. He's me, but a black and white version to my color. His hair is shorter, darker. He's wiry and thinner. He's standing next to a set of shelves. Shelves holding books.

V says to me, *it's not real. It's not happening. Let Ryan take over, Gabriel. Let go. They're in here. All your memories, all that you love are in these books. And the books have locks. They can't get to them. That's all you need to know now. Remember you can leave, as your father said.*

I tell V, *They want to know about me. About what I found. About who I love. I can't tell them.*

V cries and spreads her wings. *Ryan will take over for you now. He will handle them. Hide it. Hide it. All they have is the body. Just the body. The body can be used. I will watch out for Ryan. Ryan will pretend he is their protector.*

Take over. Take over *please.* Then I feel the migraine start pounding in my head. The migraine, saving me. Even the demon cannot get through the points of white that fill my head with pain. I tell myself to disappear. I have to protect myself and protect the people I love. I have to go.

Something is prying at my brain, trying to make me talk. The voices are urgent, seductive, powerful. Offering relief, escape, even love. I know I can't resist being taken over. Because I can't resist, I have to hide.

Go. *Hide in the library.* Where-where-where. Not the *Herald-Standard.* The old library in the Bronx where my mom worked. I'm there hiding in the stacks. With the locked books.

And I black out. Into whiteness.

∞

Clement sees that something has changed in Gabriel's face. The tension disappears and he becomes sedate. Clement puts down his microphone.

Gabriel says in a different voice, "What do you want from me?"

Clement responds, "Let us in. Open yourself."

"Go ahead, I can tell you everything."

Clement tilts his head inquisitively. "Who are you?"

"Ryan."

"Where is Gabriel?"

"I don't know. I only know someone here needs my help. My protection."

"And would you help us?"

"Yes."

"Do you have that map?"

"I do. But I have to be careful with it. I need to protect others."

"Will you tell us about who you know, who you love?"

"There's only me. I have no one else. I'm all you need. I'm here for you."

Clement smiles. "Ryan, my name is Damon Clement. Call me Damon. I'm going to tell you about a man I need you to protect me from."

∞

One of Clement's helpers comes up to him. "Encausse is here."

Clement goes downstairs to meet his protégé. He grips the other man's hand. "It's going well."

"May I see him?"

"Certainly." Clement leads the way. They go upstairs and Clement unlocks the door. "We just cut his hair and shaved him. He was looking rather messy."

"He always does," the other man says. "I couldn't get him to change."

Inside, they both scrutinize the man on the mat, leaning against the wall. His hair is cut short enough to show recent scars. He doesn't react to the visitors other than to look at them.

"You're sure he doesn't remember anything?"

"He is no longer himself, no longer Gabriel. He calls himself Ryan. If he did remember, I imagine his reaction to seeing you would be quite different."

Clement's protégé smiles. He walks closer to Ryan, then crouches next to him. He observes the manacles--which have replaced the handcuffs and allow Ryan more movement--the chains from the manacles, Ryan's posture, and his eyes, which show confusion.

"Quite different indeed. But then, he should have listened to my suggestions in the first place."

"Who are you," Ryan asks. The owl, V, had told him to go along with Damon. Be his protector, be his friend. Do not let them know someone is hiding inside. V watches over Ryan. She is outside the windows talking to him, but Damon and his people cannot hear her.

As long as you are not going out this building and hurting anyone outside, you are okay. I will tell you when to stop. For now, go along with Damon.

"Ryan," Clement says, "This is a friend of mine. You will protect him as you protect me."

"Yes."

"Are you sure you understand?"

"Yes, I do. What's his name?"

The protégé holds out his hand and takes Ryan's hand in the cuffs. "Ryan? My name is Alex Barclay. A pleasure to meet you."

∞

NINE

From the Tom Paine Events Channel on YouTube, in a video entitled:

Unknown Knowns: Kenneth Michael Trentadue ♦ The Mistake

Transcript: "Trentadue was arrested and jailed for parole violations. He was interred in FTC Oklahoma in 2005, shortly after the Oklahoma City bombing. Trentadue was found hanged in his cell not long after. His death was ruled a suicide.

"However, Trentadue's family, upon seeing his body, were shocked to see Trentadue was covered in cuts and bruises. Bureau of Prison officials and a Department of Justice inquiry maintained the suicide story. This was in spite of two medical examiners who insisted that Trentadue was murdered.

"But if so, why? One reason speculated was that Trentadue looked too much like Richard Lee Guthrie Jr. The two men had the same distinctive tattoo. Guthrie was a suspected co-conspirator (John Doe #2) in the bombing. Timothy McVeigh apparently said he believed Trentadue was mistaken for Guthrie. Guthrie also died in federal custody, again a suicide by hanging. Another inmate in a cell near Trentadue told Trentadue's brother he heard a violent struggle the night Trentadue died. That died himself in his cell from suicide by hanging. So the story goes. Sometimes people don't die from assassination, they die to cover up an aftermath, or a mistake. Simple life-ruining false accusations isn't enough, as was done to Richard Jewell (Atlanta bombing) and Steven Hatfill (Anthrax attacks of 2001). The question raised by Trentadue's death is, what is so wrongfully hidden that a mistake can't be admitted or rectified?"

∞

ALEX GETS UP and walks across the room with Clement. "It worked, then."

"Indeed it did. All the patterns were sorted by Cognoscenti until finding the right basic match for him. Then it was a matter of making him go over his life until we found the fundamental core of his being. He is a *protector.* He's protecting me. He will be an excellent protégé."

Alex's expression is slightly nonplussed at Clement's pride and affection for Ryan. "Of limited use."

Clement smiles, putting his hand on Alex's shoulder. "He's not the same as you, Encausse. You are special to me. Ryan is a superb vehicle, but he is limited, yes."

"And he won't tell you about the map."

"He's very cautious. Was Ross cautious?"

"Sometimes. Hotheaded, at other times."

"I suspect Ryan has aggravated characteristics of Ross's traits. He's protecting me from dangerous knowledge. An interesting aspect to consider."

"If that's so," Alex says, "Let's test it out."

Clement gets the machine going again. The yellow light has Ryan under within seconds. Alex watches impassively.

Clement crouches down next to Ryan. "Ryan, look at this man. Listen to the *message,* Ryan. I'm adding to the *message.* You love this man, Alex. We also call him Encausse."

Alex, moving next to Clement, raises his eyebrows. Clement says to him, "Just go along with this. He needs to protect you too, right?"

Then he turns back to Ryan. "Look at him, Ryan. You're glad to see him. You love him, remember? He was in danger, but you helped get him out of it."

As Clement had told Alex to go along with it, so too does V tell Ryan to go along with it. So Ryan looks at Alex, allowing his expression to be intense with feeling.

Alex turns to Clement, saying in a low voice, "How does that work, exactly? He believes anything you tell him?"

"He believes I'm his dearest friend, so my words can be trusted. Also, he's using some of Gabriel in some way--emotions, memories, experiences--just reconstructed to the reality of who he is now. His mind is searching for something to make sense. On some deep level he senses you and whatever, uh, you shared. So it's easier to turn it positive...granted he may also project what he feels about that other man he was involved with. That man isn't here but since you are, he thinks you must be the proper recipient for his feelings. It's how his mind copes with what is going on."

Alex nods, although he looks irritated again when Clement mentions Joel. He watches Ryan staring at him, then gets down on the mat with him. He smiles encouragingly. "Ryan? It's so good to see you."

Ryan reaches out one of his manacled hands and Alex embraces him. He holds on to Alex, and Alex strokes his head. He tilts up Ryan's face and kisses him.

"I was afraid something happened to you," Ryan says.

"I know. I'm glad to be back with you." Alex holds Ryan's face close to him. "Ryan, you won't let anything happen to us."

"I'll never do that."

"Someone's trying to kill me. Me and Damon. Can you help us, love?"

"Yes." Ryan's fingers dig into him with the intensity of his feelings. "Alex, I'll protect you with my life. You know that."

"Ryan, I need you to tell me something."

Ryan puts his hand on Alex's shoulder. "Later, baby. Let's be sure we're safe first, okay? I'm not going to let anything happen to you."

Clement is pleased to see that Ryan repeats the same words he used when he thought Joel was with him. However, Alex takes hold of Ryan's jaw tersely. "Listen to me, Ryan. I need you to tell me *now*."

"Yeah, you know I'll do anything for you. Alex, come with me. We need to leave."

"No, we're not leaving. Tell me what the map was."

"The map...?"

"In Mesereau's house. You found a picture of Damon, and a map. What was it?"

Alex digs his fingers in tighter.

"Alex..." Clement's tone is warning.

"It's a test," Alex responds.

Ryan tries to draw away. He's conflicted from knowing he can't hurt Alex--he was told not to, and he knows it's important to do what Damon says. But he can't understand why this man who is supposed to love him is hurting him. *It's okay,* V says. *You can get past it.*

"Alex, please stop."

"I'll stop when you tell me what I need to know. What is your problem, Ryan? You can't love me very much if you're going to fuck around like this."

Ryan works on something to say that will pacify this man. They want to know what was found. That's fuzzy in his mind.

Lie, V says. *We told him about a map. Give him something to believe about the map.* "It was...a map to a building."

Alex shakes him once, sharply. "*What* building?"

"In the city."

"More *specifically?*"

"I don't remember."

Alex, his expression gone cold, slaps Ryan's face hard. Ryan raises his hand in response, but only touches where he was hit. Alex says, "Tell me now, before you cause us to get killed. Is that what you want?"

"I was just trying to protect you."

"To do that, you'll do what we say. Where is the fucking building?"

Clement interrupts. "Stop, now. Don't go too far. You'll interrupt the mind pattern I'm setting for him. Be patient. I will use some pictures to get the info we need."

Alex sighs and sits back. Clement leaves the room. Ryan looks at Alex. In his mind Ryan searches for specific memories and can't find them. Only feelings. What about places? Ryan has flashes of a city, an apartment, a building. Alex talking to him in the building. They're looking at books.

No, V says. *Don't worry over this. Just be cautious.*

Alex ignores Ryan's frowning expression and lights a cigarette. He checks his phone for messages. He says idly, "I asked Joel where you were, of course. Since you haven't been back to the *Standard.* I called him and emailed him. He keeps saying you're out of town. But I can tell he's losing it."

Ryan looks away. "I don't know what you're talking about."

"No matter. I do, that's what's important. I keep asking if something happened he hasn't told anyone about. I say I'm going to the police. He has to respond to me so I don't go to the police. Let him suffer for once."

Ryan looks at him, his eyes burning. "Alex, I just want to protect you. Why are you acting this way?"

"You have yourself to blame, love. Always thinking you were smarter than anyone else."

Ryan starts chanting softly. He doesn't know where the words come from, but they seem to help in calming himself.

Clement returns. "You shouldn't talk to him about anything other than what's prescribed."

"I don't use his name. That part of him is gone, just as you said."

Clement opens a folder and flips through the photos inside. "These are some known Society locations." Then he says to Ryan, "I want you to look at these pictures. Tell me if any of these is the building in the map."

Ryan continues chanting. Alex reaches over and grips the back of Ryan's head. "Shut the fuck up and look at what Damon is showing you."

Ryan becomes briefly enraged from Alex's hurting him, but settles himself. *V said to protect Damon. Damon said to protect him. You love him. You love them both.* Ryan looks at the photos. One stands out to him.

Not that one, V says. *They can't know about that one. Choose another.*

Ryan forcefully touches another photo--a corporate office type building. "This one." He makes his voice sound convincing.

Alex releases him. Ryan rubs his head. He feels the rage again, but forces it down. Damon does not want him to hurt this man, Alex. Just protect him.

"Excellent," Clement says. "Jacob's building. That makes sense." He turns to Alex. "Mesereau must have some knowledge of something there. An entrance, something hidden...maybe he's there now."

Clement smiles at Ryan. "One more thing. What are these, Ryan?" He picks up the stack of notes found in Gabriel's office. Clement had come up and briefly looked around the office as the men were getting Gabriel into the van. The notes had caught his eye as looking out of place in the office, and flipping through quickly he saw that some articles and photos were familiar.

Ryan stares at the notes. "I don't recognize them."

"Answer him, Ryan." Alex's voice is harsh enough that Ryan burns inside.

V says, *it's okay to go along with them. They have answers they want to hear. You are doing right.*

"I found them."

"In Mesereau's house?"

It's important to lie, and make them believe the lie. "Yes."

"Do you know what they are?"

Ryan stares at the sheets Clement is holding up. "I can't understand the writing."

"All right."

He and Alex move away to talk quietly in a corner of the room. Clement takes a deep breath. "This worked perfectly. These notes he found...Mesereau must have had contact with that DC writer."

"Kent Varney. Of course. Varney was going to tell *him--*" Alex indicates Ryan, "--about the Society. But he was killed."

"They found Varney's notes. But he must have had a second set, and given them to Mesereau. He was going back and forth to DC at the time."

"Mesereau was betraying Jacobs."

"Now that is hilarious, in a way. If only I knew to put Zest on him then. Ah well, now we know something even Jacobs doesn't know."

Alex looks over at Ryan. "All that nonsense he was into turned up something useful after all."

Ryan watching them, frowning intensely.

Clement says, "You want to leave him this way? You know, once Jacobs and the others are taken care of, you can do what you want with him."

Alex makes a wry face. "I doubt it's worth the effort. His rentboy would be looking for him."

"You think that matters? By the time we're ready for Jacobs, Ryan will eliminate anyone we tell him to."

Alex casually walks back to Ryan. He gets down again, and smiles at Ryan, who smiles back. Alex takes one of Ryan's hands, and moves in closer to him. *Go along with it Ryan; it's okay. This is survival.*

Ryan accepts his kiss, no anger, no recrimination.

"Ryan, you would do anything for me?"

"Yes. I love you."

"Umn. Yes." Alex moves his hand down Ryan's body. "You want me to fuck you?"

Ryan hesitates. "We're being watched."

"That doesn't matter. I want you to answer me."

"Oh, uh..."

Alex pulls him close again. "Tell me."

"Yes." Ryan feels this is easier to say as Alex sounds much better than before.

"Be careful," Clement says. "You might tell him too much."

"This is for my pleasure; I'm not interfering with the operation."

Clement shakes his head. "Just be careful."

Alex leans over and says things in Ryan's ear. He asks Ryan some intimate questions, making him say the answers. Then he switches tactics and tells Ryan a few terrible things. "Do you understand?"

"Yes," Ryan replies.

"Good. Forget this happened, Ryan. Forget I told you that."

Ryan frowns, and Alex's expression goes cold again. "If I want you to, I'll tell you when to remember. Take it somewhere and put it away."

Ryan finds this strange. Why tell him and then then him to forget?

Send it to the library, V says. Ryan flashes on the library. The library in the building has something to do with Alex. V is right. It's safe to put Alex away there. Where he can get to it if he needs to later.

"Is that all," Clement asks as Alex gets up.

"I don't know that I want to be bothered with him when the plan is complete. But I left it open if I wish." He lights up another cigarette.

Damon half-smiles. "I thought one of the reasons you were going to take him to Europe in the first place was that you wanted him with you."

"I did. He disappointed me deeply. He's a tool at this point. A means to an end, Damon. The project comes first. Knowing I could is worth more than doing it. What will you do next with him?"

"He'll take care of Jacobs for me. I want to know why Mesereau had a map to Jacob's building, and so we'll work on that, but nonetheless the first objective is Jacobs. Then I plan to add to Ryan's adaptation. I have a brain implant here; it's computer-connected to Cognoscenti. Then I don't have to use hypnosis or the drugs. I wasn't sure if I would have to use it or not right now, but he's come along so well I've held off."

"A brain implant? Does that work?"

"Yes, it's a simple operation that can take place in under an hour. It goes through the nose. I'll be able to computer-control him. Jose Delgado's 'stimoceiver' implants in the Fifties could only increase or decrease aggression. I'll be able to design and manipulate Ryan like one would a video game. Some labs are doing this now for military, to use transcranial pulsed ultrasound in helmets to control fatigue, stress, or pain. But they can't redesign the mind like I'm doing. That's the step everyone failed at, but Ryan is my success."

Alex leaves shortly thereafter, and Clement goes back to observing Ryan. He gets down on the mat with him. Ryan is no longer a threat, so it's safe, but just in case--until Ryan has completely adapted his personality--the cuffs are necessary. Ryan doesn't seem to mind.

"He was a little rough with you. I'm sorry," Clement says.

"He said some things I'm not supposed to remember."

"He's still coming along. He's my friend, and yours too. I'll need to talk to him a bit. He doesn't appreciate that you are doing us such a great favor--bringing the true Society back to light. When we have the ritual, it will purify you. You will see a light brighter than a thousand suns, and people who will love you, because you are protecting them. Doesn't that sound wonderful, Ryan?"

It's okay to like him and be happy about it, Ryan. It is survival.

"Yes," Ryan smiles, genuinely. "When, Damon?"

"Soon. I promise. I care for you, and your great mission, Ryan." Clement strokes his head. "You are my friend first, and I know you are loyal to me. I will always appreciate your sacrifice, for making Cognoscenti truly worthwhile."

∞

Damon is back.

Ryan has been practicing what Damon asked him to practice, writing over and over in a journal. The rules about the *message.* When the *message* can be *sent, added, forwarded, canceled, deleted, aborted, and retrieved.* Every time Ryan writes what Damon wants, he feels better.

V comforts him and supports him. Is he deceiving Damon? *No. It is survival.* Is he friends with Damon? *Yes, it's okay to love him and do what he says for now.* Damon has asked him to do terrible things to protect him. *Say what he wants to hear. You will protect him. I will tell you when to stop.*

Damon gets down on the mat with Ryan.

He asks gently, "What is your name, and who am I?"

"My name is Ryan. You're Damon Clement. You are my friend."

Damon watches Ryan for a long time. "That's right. Where do you live?"

"Here."

"That's excellent. What is the *message*, Ryan?"

"I want to *protect* people. I have a mission to protect people."

"What is the *message*, Ryan?"

"There are some demons, disguised as people, who want to hurt you. I need to stop them. I am strong enough to stop them."

"To *send* the message."

"To find and kill the demons."

"To *delete* the message."

"The demons have come in where we are. To kill them all."

"To *add* the message."

"Other persons I need to protect."

"To *forward* the message."

"To protect you, but not kill anyone."

"To *cancel* the message."

"To stop hurting someone if you say so."

"To *abort* the message."

"To sacrifice myself."

"To *retrieve* the message."

"To...uh, forget all of the other instructions."

"Yes, you are so good. I doubt I'll use *retrieve*, or *abort*, but one never knows." He unlocks the chains and takes Ryan to the white room. Under the white hoods, the people seem to be smiling. They greet Ryan by name.

Ryan looks questioningly at Damon, who nods. "It's okay, Ryan. I'm rebuilding your memory for you."

Okay, then. Ryan sits in the white chair. The yellow light goes on in the machine Damon calls Cognoscenti.

"Ryan, remember the *message.* You want to protect people. More than anything, right?"

"Yes. I want to *protect* people. I want to *protect* you."

"I need your help, Ryan. I need your strength. I need your skills. You can do so much. Can you help me?"

What do you want me to do?"

"You've been trained to protect. Your body, your mind. You know how to hurt someone to protect another, don't you?"

Ryan hears urgency in Damon's voice. "Yes. Yes, I can."

"As far as you can go."

"Yes, if it's for...if it's right."

"It's right. It's for who you love. You do love me, don't you? Isn't that in the *message?*"

Ryan has visions then. A sun lit paradise. Ephemeral music playing. Damon holding my hand. A man of wisdom and kindness, he's sure of it. But vulnerable. Others don't understand what good is, and would hurt him.

"I'll *protect* you."

The straps around Ryan disappear. "Him," Damon says, pointing. "He's trying to hurt me. He's been working with the demons."

Ryan looks to where Damon is pointing. A tall man with short hair and a dark green mask. Very muscled.

Go ahead, V says. *In here it's okay.*

The man rushes at Ryan, and hammers at Ryan with his fists. But Ryan knows he's been trained better, somewhere. Not just artfully, but with a mindful purpose. To think while he fights. He can foresee what the green-faced man is going to do before he does, and soon Ryan is beating him, tripping him up. He stops when Damon raises his hand.

The masked man walks away, then turns to say to Ryan, "You aren't that good."

What he says means nothing. Ryan looks at Damon.

The muscled man comes back near Ryan and says, "You can't stop me. You're too weak."

Damon says, "*Forward* the message, Ryan."

Ryan feels a rage coming over him as Damon speaks. He grabs the masked man by the throat and slams him against a wall. The man gasps in surprise and his mask falls off. Ryan's hand squeezes his windpipe.

The other man's eyes roll back, gagging, struggling for breath. His voice breaks. "*Enough. Tell him enough!*"

Damon laughs. "You thought he couldn't do it. You better tell him."

The man looks at Ryan, his eyes bugging out. "I'm not going to hurt him, I promise."

Ryan doesn't know if he should believe him, even with the fear in his eyes. "I can't take the chance."

Damon says, "Tell him the *message*, idiot. Before he kills you by accident."

The man says, "*Cancel* the message. *Cancel* it, Goddamn it."

Ryan lets him go.

Damon says, "Excellent, Ryan. If he keeps up, would you kill him?"

"I would protect you as necessary. If he would kill you, I'd stop him."

The man sweats under me, in pain. He glares at Ryan as he rubs his throat. He seems like he's going to attack again. Ryan changes his stance to be on guard.

Damon gets between us. "No, you are to leave Ryan alone. He's better than you, but you helped him be that way. Accept your part."

The man puts his mask back on and curses while Damon laughs.

∞

Damon is back in Ryan's room. "What is your *purpose*, Ryan?"

"To be with you. To protect you and our friends."

He smiles. "Yes, that's right. That's so beautiful."

He has water and food for Ryan, and strokes his head. "I'm going to take you to be washed. Then we're going to talk about the mission. About the place where you will meet the sun people, and what you're going to afterwards."

∞

The New York Scene/Thin Blue Line Column by Carl Mankiewitz
Gabriel Ross's Disappearance Focal Point of Rallies

Gabriel Ross once told me that even if an event isn't true, if it stands for a greater truth the initial truth doesn't matter. And so whatever reason Ross has disappeared, he has become that greater truth. Because Ross was the primary contact for Tom Paine, and he's fallen off the face of the earth, no news has come out regarding Paine. Even Paine is mostly silent, although he's posted a couple of short comments on his YouTube channel.

The grassroots RIP movement been putting up grainy, stark, black and white "Missing" posters of Ross around the city, and in their rallies, as a symbol of people struggling to reveal the truth who have been repressed, disappeared, or killed. Ross as revealer--as a man who was interested in Gnosticism, he'd appreciate that...

∞

Somewhere Else

Clement is obsessed with making Ryan see the demons, feel the demons. When Ryan is in the chair, Clement creates a dark black-red shape to engulf Ryan's body. *Be what he wants,* V tells Ryan. *Let him believe. It is survival.*
"Do you care if you drown?"
"No."
"Because it's for me."
"Yes. I want to be with you. I want to protect you."
I feel a hand reach in me. "Take out what you want."

"Come with me," Damon says. He leads Ryan to the ledge of a bright white building, looking down into clouds. Ryan feels he isn't really there--that Damon has created this building. Then Damon points behind them. The red, pulsating horned demon is behind them.

"Protect me Ryan," Damon says.

Ryan steps in front of Damon, facing the demon. "Stay away!"

The demon comes closer, his dark mouth opening to show sharp white teeth. "I'll kill him."

Damon says, "Help me...forward the message, Ryan."

You can do it, it's okay, V says.

Ryan runs to grab the demon.

The demon growls, "If you want to protect him, you'll have to sacrifice yourself instead. To abort the message."

You can do this, Ryan. This is not what it appears to be. Go ahead.

Ryan stares in the demon's black/red eyes. "I can do that, but I need to know Damon is safe."

"He is safe."

Damon says, "I'm safe, Ryan. Abort."

Ryan steps off the ledge, and feels like he is floating over the clouds. Behind him, Damon purrs: "Yes. Feel the greatness. See, if you sacrifice yourself, you don't really die. That's the beauty of it."

Ryan throws back his head to look at the sun. The sun throbs with life. A dozen, and hundred voices cry out to encourage Ryan to continue his work.

Damon speaks to him from somewhere beyond the clouds. "Whatever you sacrifice, you are rewarded because you protect others. That's the beauty of it. You will go with these people, the people who love you. The people you are protecting. The people of the sun."

"I will do what I have to, to protect you; to protect them."

"We will soon be with them for good."

At last, Ryan thinks. He won't have to worry any more. Instead of being told who to hurt, he can be with people who love him. He can't wait.

∞

Damon has helped Ryan clean up. Ryan feels stronger than ever, eager to get going to see the sun people.

"Excellent," Damon says. "I'm so sorry about what you've been through up to now. We're leaving soon for the Sun People. But first, I'm going to take you to visit a man. A demon. His name is Jacobs. He is trying to hurt us, and we need you to take care of him. To *delete* the message."

He leaves Ryan in the room. Ryan stares after him, the words echoing in his head.

Man/demon.

Delete the message.

Jacobs. Delete Jacobs

We're going to the Sun People.

But first...delete. A man.

Ryan realizes something is under his foot, annoying pressing into the flesh. A spring. A tiny spring that popped out of a crevice on the floor. Or maybe tracked in by the workers in the white suits. It sticks to his toes.

V has returned. She is in the room, on the inside of the window sill. She flutters her wings. *Keep it,* she says. *The spring. Keep it.*

Ryan wants to laugh about it. Such a tiny thing. "Okay, V," he whispers to her. He picks up the spring and slips it between his fingers.

Damon is lying.

Ryan suddenly has a mental image of someone familiar. A man in a library, surrounded by books. Ryan looks over at V. "Who is this?"

The person you are really trying to protect. Damon is lying. He is not taking you to any Sun people. He wants you to kill a man.

"Kill..."

You do not do that. It is time to leave him, Ryan. The spring is a key. You can pick the lock of those shackles.

"No. V, you don't understand. Damon is coming to take me away to the sun."

No. You don't do that. You know you don't kill people. He wants you to kill this man. You don't do that. Pick the lock, you know what to do.

"I don't..." Ryan's fingers mold the metal to a familiar shape. Now the metal is mostly straight, with a tiny bent portion.

It's a key, V tells him. *You can pick locks with it. You were trained in that.*

Ryan sees the man in the library, sitting among the books. He looks up. *Do it. Get out.*

"Who are you?"

V is beside him now, holding his eyes with her own. *The one inside you. Who you are protecting. He is you, you are him. You are protecting him because he needs to hide. But he would not kill, and you will not kill.*

"Jacobs. He wants me to kill Jacobs. But V, Jacobs is a demon..."

He lies--Jacobs is a man. He is using you. You are protecting the one inside you because this man lies--because he's using you. You've done a good job protecting, but you cannot kill for him. Do not listen to him anymore.

"How do I know you're right?"

You know me. Pick the lock. When it works, you know this is true.

Ryan puts the pick in one of the locks and turns it experimentally. Then he feels as if someone is guiding him to how to move the pick and to cover with his other hand, as cameras are in this room.

Then Damon is back. When Ryan hears his approach, he rubs his hand that holds the pick to further disguise it.

"Yes," Damon says. "It's going to be good."

Ryan feels the lock open on the cuffs and coughs to cover the sound. The sensation of the lock opening is like a revelation to him. *When it works, you know this is true.* "Damon, why am I going to kill Jacobs?"

Damon looks at Ryan, startled. "He is a demon, Ryan."

"How do you know?"

"I know. That's what's important."

Ryan shakes his head. "I just want to be with you. We're going to the place with the Sun now, right? You're my friend, that's all we need to do."

"Ryan, I need you to do this one thing for me first. And then we'll see the people of the Sun. You have to protect me by killing Jacobs."

Just as I told you, V says.

"I can protect you without killing him."

"No, Ryan. You have to do this sacrifice. Or we can't go to the Sun people."

He lied to you. He was supposed to take you to the people of the Sun. And now, he wants you to sacrifice yourself, to do something you cannot, should not do.

"No," Ryan tells Damon. "I'm no killing him." Something in Ryan's voice is different; he hears it, and Damon hears it.

"Ryan...this is important. Jacobs must be killed." He reaches for Ryan's arm.

"No!"

Damon stops and stares at Ryan. After a minute he says, "All right...Ryan, I didn't want to do this, but we're going to have to delay the Sun people. I'm going to need to give you something."

"No more. No more drugs!"

"This is different. I'm going to put a special key in your head. You'll be able to see some beautiful lights, and I can be a voice in your head from now on. You don't have to worry about decisions."

"No."

"It will be okay, Ryan. I have the key with me, and a little operation that will be over in a couple hours."

Ryan sees the man in library in his head. The man jumps to his feet, and the books fall over. Shelves and shelves of books. *NONOnononononononono....*

Ryan becomes angry and alarmed at the same time. He looks at V, who is spreading her wings and crying. *He lied to me,* Ryan says to her silently. *I suffered over and over again. To help him.*

V cries again. *Ryan, he's going to hurt you. You need to leave now.*

Damon says, "So let's get you ready to go in the lab..."

Ryan shakes off the cuff in one swift motion, and punches Damon in the gut. Then he works the other cuff as Damon doubles over.

V is crying. *Get out! Don't let him tell you anything else.*

Damon holds up his hands in real fear. "I swear...I *will* take you, I won't hurt you, Gabriel...uh, Ryan. We will go to the Sun people. Right now. Don't worry."

Gabriel. "Uh..." Ryan grabs his head. Strange images come in of the man in the library holding his head as well. *I'm Ryan. I'm not Ryan. I'm someone else, and Damon wanted me to kill someone. But I don't kill people.*

The thoughts become too much, stabbing inside Ryan. Still holding his head, he starts to scream. He, and V, and the man inside his head all scream.

∞

TEN

From the YouTube Channel "Tom Paine Events," in a video entitled: Unknown Knowns: Fred Alvarez, Patricia Castro, and Ralph Boger ♦ The Resistance

Transcript: "Alvarez, his girlfriend Castro, and Boger were shot to death outside Alvarez's home in 1981. Alvarez was a leader of the tiny Cabazon Indian Reservation in California. An investigation decades later led to an arrest of a prime suspect, but the charges were dropped. From what official and unofficial investigations surmised, the murders were due to conflicts over using the tribal land for weapons deals and/or casino deals, by shady characters (whom Danny Casolaro later investigated) involved with the tribe and also the government. These murders raise the question of how do you prevent outside interests from controlling your destiny?"

∞

Wednesday, November 9
Chinatown, Canal Street, 7:00 pm

JOEL IS IN THE MIDDLE of arguing with his mother on the phone--she's upset that Joel has not visited her and canceled therapy for the foreseeable future--while he's walking out the door of his apartment building.

Danny is waiting right outside.

Oh, shit. This isn't going to go well.

Danny gives him the death stare as Joel begins trying to get Gloria to hang up, making his tone conciliatory. Of course, Gloria is reluctant to end contact without definitive answers about seeing him.

"I don't know. I'll get back to you," he says to Gloria, stopping resignedly in front of Danny.

She's resistant. "Is something wrong? You're really being dismissive with me."

"Everything's fine. I've just got a lot of appointments today. I'll call you later."

"Are you sure? You didn't last time."

Joel closes his eyes, resisting the urge to throw the phone under a passing bus. Danny is still glaring at him, and he defiantly meets Danny's gaze while making his voice harder. "I said I would and I will. I have to go. *Now.*"

"Tell Gabriel--"

"Yeah." Joel ends the call and shoves the phone in his pocket.

Danny doesn't bother with niceties. "Where is he?"

"I can't tell you."

"Fuck that. Don't make me knock you out here on the street."

Joel feels his temper rise. "Don't make me make *you* regret saying that."

The fragile truce between them is frayed. Danny's looking for every reason he's ever had to distrust, dislike, and disbelieve Joel. And yet Joel feels a little bad for him. Joel has knowledge Danny desperately wants, and thinks Joel is being cruel, while at the same time worrying himself sick about where his best friend is.

Danny continues, "What the fuck is going on? I'm not leaving until you tell me. You can call the cops, I don't care. I will not let you pretend you can't tell me where Gabriel is."

Joel turns over some factors in his head for an executive decision. He doesn't care if Danny goes back to hating him. It's whether Danny will make more trouble if he knows or if he doesn't know.

Danny continues his rant. "There's even people online asking where he is, because of that Tom Paine story. I'll get them to go look. I'll call Walter Cleveland and have him publish something."

That's all we need--Walter posting about Gabriel's disappearance in the Huff Post.

He opens the building door. "Come in."

"No thanks. You can talk to me here."

"Goddamn it, Dan. Despite what you think, I'm not playing games. I can't talk about this outside. Just come in the fucking lobby."

Danny follows him in. The tiny lobby is only big enough for a freight elevator and stairway. To the right is a line of mailboxes. A few newspaper deliveries lie on the floor underneath.

Joel drops his messenger bag on the floor and takes a deep breath, running his hands through his hair. "He's in serious trouble."

"I'll check out everything you tell me."

"You can't check this out. It's not that kind of situation."

Danny steps back and takes out his pack of Marlboros. "All right, just before he disappeared, he was playing that gig with Jason at the bar. You went out with your friends for the night. Gabriel and Jason went to my place to smoke. Well, this man comes to the door, an older guy. Almost sounded British. Very formal; he looked like a real *serious* character. I've never seen Gabriel sober up so fast. He said the man was an informant, but this guy was no informant. The next day Gabriel put in a new lock on my apartment, and told me to have Halo stay with me. Is that man threatening Gabriel?"

"No. He's trying to get Gabriel *out* of trouble. He's...as serious as he looks. Another very dangerous man abducted Gabriel. This man, the one you saw, he's going to find Gabriel and get him out."

"*Abducted him.* When?"

"Halloween."

"And you saw no need to tell me?"

"What would you have done?"

"Called the police; the FBI. Like I'm going to do now."

Joel takes hold of his arm. "Dan, no bullshit, you'll get him killed. These aren't people you can call the cops on."

"But this guy you know, *he* can take them on." Dan's sarcasm is 100 proof.

"Yeah, he can. He's part of them; part of the organization."

"And he's helping you? Why?"

"You really want backstory now? I've already told you more than Gabriel would."

"Gabriel doesn't always make the right decision in keeping everything to himself. How do *you* know so much?"

"These same people tried to kill me. When Gabriel was investigating the Booth case last year."

"The case he gave up but didn't really give up. Don't look surprised--I've known him over twenty Goddamn years. I know what he was doing. He crusades his way into trouble."

Joel frowns at Danny's expression. "I didn't get him into this. He didn't get himself into it either. If I had to blame anybody, it was Alex and some fucking story *he* was working on that started this, and Gabriel trying to help *him*. If you know Gabriel so well, then you know this is not a simple situation. And you know I'm not going to let anyone risk his life. I'm telling you all this because I need you to stay quiet."

"I'm not staying quiet. You can't make that decision--"

"You're not listening, Dan. I *have* made that decision." Joel gets closer to the other man. "If you think I'll let you leave here and make this worse...to put him in jeopardy going to the police or stirring shit in the media...that isn't going to happen."

A long minute passes with the two men staring at each other.

Eventually, Danny says, "I'm trying to give you a chance. The only reason I'm not turning you inside out is you know more about what's going on than I do. I'm not going to call the cops, but I'm not just standing by either."

Before Joel can reply, Danny abruptly leaves, letting the front door slam behind him.

∞

Alphabet City, Avenue A, 9 pm

Joel finds himself speechless, seeing Jeffrey Ross at Gabriel's front door. *Not this too...*

Jeffrey has gotten in Gabriel's building without buzzing, but no big deal for him. He and Gabriel share the same skills.

"Where's my son, Joel?"

"Uh..." Outside of Danny, Joel has told everyone else--Jason, Bob, Mikki, Walter...as well as Gabriel's editor and teachers, either that Gabriel-is-sick, or Gabriel-is-out-of-town. Veronica and Geneva back him up on those. Mankiewitz keeps running stories questioning why Gabriel's disappeared, but Joel is taking this one day at a damn time. Sometimes one hour at a time.

"Um, he's out of town, Mr. Ross. A complicated case, he's undercover."

Joel expects Jeffrey to give him a perfunctory "*Tell him I was here*" and then leave. Instead, Jeffrey puts his hand on the doorframe and stares at Joel.

"I tried getting in contact with him, and he's not responding. Danny called me..."

Oh shit--again. Joel is helpless as Jeffrey moves past him into the apartment.

"...and he seems to think that Gabriel is in serious trouble and you know more about it than you're telling, and that I should look into it."

Jeffrey stands in the middle of the living room and looks around. "He's not here, you're lying, and I have reason to be concerned. Now I want answers." Jeffrey turns to meet Joel's eyes. "Not to mention you are scared to death; I *see* that. What's going on, son?"

Joel tries to speak. Jeffrey moves on to check the rest of the apartment, still talking. "Danny didn't give me any details, but I can tell he doesn't believe what you told him. I thought maybe at worst Gabriel is just hiding out from some trouble."

"Uh, it's more than that."

Jeffrey goes back into the living room. "Tell me."

Joel thinks about what to preface his explanation with, then remembers what Gabriel told him. Gabriel had asked his father to look into Clement. "What I told Danny was true. That man--Clement. The one Gabriel asked you about. He kidnapped Gabriel."

"Why?"

"I don't know. But a man I know--I trust--is looking for him. Clement's been here. He's taken things--photographs. I'm not sure what else."

"Is that man you trust in the same work as Clement?"

"I'm not sure what Clement does, but my...friend, his name is Zest, he's not military. He's in something else. Uh, private...civilian. A secret organization Gabriel knows about and is trying to expose."

Although he speaks calmly, Joel has to turn away and put his hands over his eyes.

Jeffrey goes to the kitchen and finds a bottle of water in the refrigerator. "That sounds like my son. How did it happen?"

Joel collapses on a chair. Jeffrey hands him the bottle of water. "Catch your breath, Joel. Come on, drink this, and tell me what happened."

Joel describes what happened Halloween in the office.

"How is Veronica?"

"She had a concussion in addition to the gunshot wounds. She's pretty traumatized. Geneva is helping her keep the office together. She feels guilty about Gabriel, but if what happened was reversed, he would feel the same about her."

"Yes, I know. I understand now. You were afraid to tell me?"

"I was afraid to tell anyone. This organization..."

"Gabriel's conspiracy theories are true. That's why I didn't want him reading that shit when he was a kid. Sometimes you can know too much. Don't worry about me. I'm not the type to make the situation worse. Not with him. When was the last time you heard from Zest?"

"Friday. He's looking for the place where Gabriel is. He has to be careful, so he doesn't...so he doesn't scare Clement into doing something drastic. They know each other, but Clement doesn't know Zest is helping us."

Joel sees something dark go over Jeffrey's eyes. Just like Gabriel when he becomes angry.

Jeffrey says, "I'm not good at comforting people, I'm sorry about that. If Zest is right, Gabriel's alive. And we'll know where he is soon."

"He'll find out if anyone can. This guy, he's like every movie bad-guy fixer you've ever seen, but he's on our side."

"Huh. Well, I'll wait a little longer before I start doing something myself. If Zest calls, tell me first. I'm going with him to get my son."

Joel doesn't argue with him. Jeffrey grabs Joel's shoulder. "You're as strong as Gabriel is. And he knows that. He'll need that."

Then he leaves.

∞

Monday, November 14
Chelsea, 4:00 pm

It's been a strange day, in an already strange situation. It begins with Veronica walking around outside her apartment building, holding Joel's hand. The bullet wound is her leg is healing but she still some residual pain. She's also frustrated from lack of action.

Veronica says, "Those notes that they took--they were important to Gabriel. He said he was decoding them."

"Yeah. Hopefully those assholes don't know Gregg shorthand."

"You should tell Zest to look for them when he finds Gabriel."

"If it's feasible. Well, there's another copy."

"Where? I want to look at them and see if I can continue what he was doing."

Joel frowns. "Why, V? Right now it's not..."

"I need to do what he would do. He wanted to protect me. I want to make sure what he was doing stays relevant. The audience for those videos want more stuff. I've been looking at Tom Paine's channel and seeing how the story is catching on."

"You're talking like Gabriel is gone," Joel says, his voice guttural.

"I have to do something while we're waiting. It will make me feel better to keep on with his stuff. Maybe it will help you too. It's taking action against them."

There's a slash breaking through her short hair, a slice where the other bullet creased her scalp. The angry red mark doesn't seem out of place in her slightly punk look. But Joel is worried that her concussion from the bullet affected her.

"You think I'm brain-damaged." Always intuitive, she scares him now reading his mind.

"Never. I just...want you better. You know along with Gabriel you mean everything to me."

She leans against him. "Then tell me where those notes are, baby."

"Stubborn like him. No wonder you're soulmates. I'm just along for the ride."

"You're scared too. You haven't been able to work. I saw you have Gabriel's Xanax. That's how you're sleeping."

"I'm afraid to sleep--afraid Zest will call. But I have to sometimes."

"He's okay. I know it. I'd feel something otherwise."

"Okay." He smiles. "How is it you would and not me?"

"He and I are highly attuned to each other. We knew each other more than once in other lives. I know you think that's crap and it's your prerogative, but we know it."

He leads her to a coffee shop on 9th Avenue. They get tea and sit by the window.

"I don't--I'm not scornful of what you all believe. I just wonder where I was when this was going on in your former lives. I shouldn't even be saying such horrible things while I'm out of my mind worried about him."

"You're human. Even under stressed and worried, we can't help but think what we think--get angry and even have crazy questions. The mind has to cope. Gabriel said to me once--granted he was drunk when he did--that you are an ethereal being who was sent to save him from something. So, while you're pouting like a baby about not being there with him four or five hundred years ago, apparently *I* can't save him. So there's that."

For a moment, Joel feels a rush of adrenaline from hearing her describe Gabriel's words. He wants to smile. "When did that happen? And did you agree with him?"

"Some night last year when you weren't around and he missed you. Before you got back together. He was struggling with himself--it was right before Thanksgiving and his fight with Danny. And I sort of agreed with him. Except I also find you a pain in the ass that makes me wonder what I did in my previous life to suffer through you trying to avoid answering me right now."

"All right, all right. We have to go to Brooklyn. To the man who he has been working with on a memoir."

"Good. I want to meet him." She checks her phone to see if Geneva has messaged. Joel watches her. He feels strangely conflicted and desperate with not knowing what is happening with Gabriel. And that drives him to ask an utterly irrelevant question.

"Why did you sleep with him?"

Veronica looks up at Joel. She is direct whenever possible. "He told you about that? It was while you were overseas, a year or so after you left. A time when both of us were very lonely and sad. And somewhat inebriated. We got over-affectionate and it seemed like the thing to do. You know it's not unheard of."

"Yeah, it's not that. It's just..."

She raises her eyebrows.

"If anyone, I thought you and I..." His voice trails off, and he feels even more ridiculous bringing the topic up.

"Joel, the reason why it happened with Gabriel is because he and I could walk away from it without bad feelings. That couldn't happen with you and me. We're practically in an emotional affair as it is."

Joel blushes, feeling guilty for having even raised this issue. "Michaela must hate me."

"No. She knows life around me is chaotic. She knows you and I are overly-tight because I let it happen. I can't settle down very well. She wants kids and I can't be a mom. We agreed it was better. Let's go to Brooklyn."

Joel gets his SUV from the garage. About an hour later, Bertrand Herrmann opens his apartment door and looks down at them. He's in his seventies and over six feet. His gray hair is a little long, and his beard is very short. Behind him, his bulldogs whine because they smell Joel and want to play.

"Joel. Something is very wrong." Herrmann smiles at Veronica. "I'm not saying you are wrong, miss. Only that this is unusual."

"She's with me. This is Veronica Gianni. She's Gabriel's partner and she knows about *them* and about Tom Paine. Gabriel is in trouble."

Herrmann looks over their heads, scanning the hallway. He's very sensitive to trouble. "Were you followed?"

"I left my car in Park Slope, took a cab to the library, and then we took a bus here."

"*In ordnung*," Hermann says, opening his door. "Let's hope we are secure."

Herrmann sets up tea for them, as Joel and Veronica greet the bulldogs and the six cats in the apartment. Gabriel's favorite, Jonah, is a young adult now but still playful. He pushes in front of the dogs and demands attention from Veronica, a new conquest.

Joel tells Herrmann what happened to Gabriel. Herrmann seems rather grave. "This reminds me of working in Berlin in the Seventies. No one could be trusted. Sometimes people disappeared. While you think no one cared about Nazis then, in fact there were always networks around. People would say something to the wrong person, and end up knifed in an alley."

"Uh," Joel says, looking stricken.

"*Entschuldigung*, I know you're worried. I fear for what they want with him. This man who is searching for him--can he be trusted? A man from that organization?"

"I have no choice. I can only believe that he tells the truth about wanting out of the Society, and is going to live up to his word."

"Does this man look haunted? From how you describe him he seems haunted."

"Yeah. If he wasn't doing this, I could see him walking off a bridge, know what I mean?"

"Haunted is good for sincerity. The weight of his actions play on him now. But in this organization, there's no point of return once you are in."

"Bertrand, if he's lying--I don't think he is, but still--are there any possible contacts you may have who can find out about Clement? Where he might possibly be holed up?"

"Maybe, if he goes to the same place and his habits are known."

"It's been over two weeks. I'm getting tired of waiting."

Herrmann rubs his face. "*Ach.* I have to do something. Now that I know, I can't *not* do something. Is your number safe, Joel?"

Joel produces a burner phone and gives Herrmann the number from it. "We'd like the notes too. They took his copy."

"I have three copies. One in my safe deposit box. Two in my safe. Is this the right time?"

"I want to stir up some shit on his behalf," Veronica says.

"He would like that. But it might be reckless, young lady. Veronica. He took precautions for you."

She turns her hands up. "That's why I need to do this."

"A matter of honor. I understand that." Herrmann gets up and goes over to his safe.

∞

Not long thereafter, Herrmann calls Joel. "I have found out something. People who know people, six degrees of secrecy. It doesn't matter, you want the bottom line. I don't know where exactly, but apparently Clement is supposed to have gone to Spotsylvania, Virginia. That is about it, but it is a lead."

"Thank you," Joel says. He starts to call Zest, and thinks about it. Then he goes to Veronica's office and talks to her and Geneva. "Do I tell him? Could we do it ourselves?"

"If we could find it. Narrow it down." Geneva frowns. "Let's look at the logic. What are your concerns with Zest?"

"He might be lying. He might want to kill Clement, for instance, and Gabriel too."

"He could have done that a thousand times before."

"Maybe he needed to do it this way. Like with Ethan Nelson. A set-up."

"True," Veronica says. "I've been concerned about the time factor. If Zest knows Clement so well, why has it taken him this long?"

Joel lights up. He's smoking Gabriel's Camels. "He would say...I don't know what he would say. Let's ask him."

Joel calls Zest and says they need to talk. Zest agrees to be over within the hour.

When he arrives, he nods at the group. "I am awaiting word on what I hope is a lead."

"*We* may have a lead. From a source you don't know of."

Zest nods again at Joel's words. "Tell me and I'll check it out."

Veronica says, "What has taken so long up to now?"

"Ms. Gianni, Clement assumes I'm very close to him. He is planning a coup of sorts. The details aren't important at the moment. In order for him to trust me, I can't let him know I'm inquiring about him."

"Sure, I get it. But if you're so close to him, why is calling him and saying, *Hey, what are you up to,* so bad? He must know that you know he has Gabriel."

"He isn't responsive at the moment. Probably only to his protégé."

"Encausse."

"Correct. I don't know who that is, but I'm trying to find out that as well. Damon is very paranoid. He has reason to be. He also in essence lives in his own world. I had asked him not to take Gabriel, but he went ahead anyway because he is insistent on his plan. He may feel I'm angry at him because he went against my advice, so he's going to want to prove his plan works before he answers me. If he asked me for protection, I could be there in a minute. But if I try to without his request, he might think it's Jacobs."

Joel looks annoyed. "It can't be that hard. He has places he uses, right? For whatever he's doing?"

"Many. Some are closed down. Some are hidden. Joel, if that information can help locate Gabriel, you know you need to tell me."

"If you've been honest with us."

Zest contemplates them all. "I have little means of demonstrating sincerity. You know that should Jacobs be aware I'm here, within minutes I'll be shot. They wouldn't bother with pretense, because I'm too dangerous."

"So you say."

"You do remember Nelson agreeing to that."

Joel stubs out his cigarette. "This could all be an elaborate lie."

"It could. I can tell you this. It's all I have to give you. In Switzerland I have a box. I'll give you the account number. You can verify it. The password is my name, my real name. No one uses my name other than Jacobs and Clement; very few people even know it. It's too dangerous. Over the last thirty years I made it that way. Therefore, using it will cause many things to happen. The box has information on Jacobs and the three other directors in the Society. And Clement. You may do with it as you wish."

"No one? What about your family?" Geneva looks doubtful.

"My family is dead, or might as well be. There are no records of me beyond a certain year. No photos. I do not exist, which is why my name is dangerous."

Joel exchanges glances with Veronica and Geneva. "I don't care about exposing them if Gabriel's dead. I want him alive."

"As do I. This is all I can offer. You're going to have to figure out if you can believe that."

"Give me the number."

Zest tells Joel the account number and the institution. Veronica verifies it exists, using one of the burner laptops.

Zest calls the bank on speaker. He says he wants to verify no inquiries have been made on his behalf. The account does not have a person's name, only "Metaword Enterprises."

"That was a game I played when I was young," Zest tells them. "A very early Role-Playing Game that involved some science fiction and war elements. It's where I chose the name you know me by."

The mechanical voice asks for the password. "Maxim Atwood," Zest says.

The other three, regardless of suspicion, feel something like a chill when hearing him say his name. *No going back now...*

No one has made any inquiries about the account, and Zest disconnects the call.

Veronica, Joel and Geneva turn to each other. "What can we live with?" Veronica asks. "I think telling him."

Geneva nods. "I agree. Then tell him."

Joel lights another Camel. "Fuck. Okay. He's in Spotsylvania, Virginia."

Zest's eyes widen and he gets up to stare out a window, almost agitated. For him, that's demonstrated in his slowly running one hand through his hair. "That's where I underwent his treatment a long time ago...well, no matter. I know the place, certainly. Give me twenty-four hours. I will have a team go down to verify, and to breach it. Are you going with me?"

"Yes," they all say.

"Ms. Gianni, you are not able to walk very well. I would suggest you stay. As a matter of security, you can keep my information should you need it."

"I don't want to be here wringing my hands."

"You can do better than that. Clement is monitoring the news. Some rumors abound about Gabriel being too quiet. That's fine, as it was inevitable. Information is useful if it is controlled. Try to get in touch with Tom Paine, as Gabriel was doing. Tell him you have some information regarding...let's see, Mendel-Malthus."

Mendel-Malthus is a notorious US and multinational investment banking firm. Big with obtaining important institutional clients. Big with manipulating the market and misleading investors. Big with financially blackmailing the US Government to bail it out and engender regulations and decisions in its favor--helped by the revolving door of Mendel-Malthus execs who go on to government positions, and then go back to the Cthulhu-like maw of the company.

The three keep straight faces. Zest does not know about Gabriel being Tom Paine. "What kind of information?"

"A connection to Banca Mediterraneo Centrale Internazionale. A former German officer, Hans Dietrich, funneled money from the BMCI to Mendel during the war. Dietrich was a Nazi. If you find a picture of him in the BMCI records, which are available in an archive in Rome, match the picture to a man standing next to Mengele in that Auschwitz scrapbook that was discovered and published. Dietrich is that man. It proves he was a Nazi. In addition, his DNA is likely on the effects of a man who was killed to cover up the connection, Antonin Natale, who supposedly committed suicide in the early Eighties. Dietrich claimed he didn't know Natale. Even better, BMCI has a secret contract with Mendel regarding international securities--the complex orders that led to Mendel's part in the 2008 meltdown. I can get you documents later."

Veronica is writing down the information. "How does this help?"

"It throws Clement off the scent. If Paine publishes, then they know Gabriel isn't Paine. Also, that no one is close to finding out where Gabriel is."

Joel catches her eye and nods. He'll have Chris help her with that.

Zest gets up. "Joel, you and Ms. Lennon. Anyone else?"

"Gabriel's dad. He was or is Army intelligence. He's the type of man that's difficult to stop. Danny, Gabriel's friend, wants to go, but he's a hothead. I can't control either of them."

"I'll speak to them. Meet me at the West Side piers in 24 hours and let them come as well to the meeting area. Do not have any phones on your person that are under your name. Ensure you are not followed."

∞

The New York Scene/Thin Blue Line Column by Carl Mankiewitz
Signs of Life from Tom Paine

Tom Paine is back with more stories. The video conspiracy theorist is reporting on wrongdoings of national and international financial institutions in connection with the economic meltdown of 2008. The great Cthulhu Mendel-Malthus is the major player. See below for those stories. What I was wondering is if Paine heard from the still missing Gabriel Ross. Paine has said that something sinister is up with Ross's disappearance, and until we hear more to not forget him. Not a chance.

∞

Monday, November 14
West Side Piers, Chelsea 4:00 pm

Joel has his SUV in a parking lot. He and Geneva and Veronica are waiting outside the car. Danny is with them. He's stolid and silent. Joel looks exhausted because he is. He hasn't slept much. Keeping things going is wearing him down.

Zest suddenly appears next to the driver's side. Joel lowers the window. Zest says, "I found him. Your information was good."

Joel exhales. He and Veronica and Geneva embrace each other. Danny also looks relieved, but he's still angry.

Zest continues, "He is alive. The safe house is an old stone house in a rural area. One of these places that intelligence agencies like to leave looking abandoned for the benefit of outsiders. It hasn't been used officially for some time. The CIA isn't involved and Clement doesn't want them to know he's doing this. He has a minimum crew, aside from the device he's been using on Gabriel."

Danny says, "I don't like the sound of that device."

Zest lights a cigarette. "It's not the biggest problem; we can deal with at length, after the emergency is over. We must be discreet. Clement's not expecting to be interrupted, though, so we can take him by surprise. I have people surrounding the area. We should go now."

Jeffrey Ross shows up then in the parking lot, walking over to them. He introduces himself to Zest, and the two men step aside and talk for a few minutes. Then they return to Joel's car.

Zest speaks to Danny. "Mr. Martinez, I know your feelings and your desire to go. Too many people shouldn't leave the city, however, in case you are all under observation. It's why I asked you to be discreet in showing up. I asked Ms. Gianni to remain because she is injured. She is also the safeguard in case I'm not trustworthy. She should have support and protection as she takes care of the task to get suspicion away from Gabriel."

Danny nods but says, "I would like to be there with you to get him."

"Getting him out is half the battle. I'm not doing it so much as my team is. Mercenaries outside of the Society who are loyal to me. Afterwards, he's going to need treatment. He'll be safe, and you will be able to see him. Mr. Ross will be going with us." He indicates Gabriel's dad.

"It's okay, Danny," Jeffrey says. "I know how you feel, but he's right. I'm looking out for the situation. Gabriel would want Veronica protected."

Joel takes out one of a bunch of burner phones in a gym bag. "Take this. I'll keep you updated on everything."

Danny takes it. "All bets are off if I hear anything different than he's safe."

"It will be for me as well, Danny," Jeffrey says.

Reassured to a degree, Danny relents, accepting the situation. Joel gives Veronica his car keys, then he and Geneva exit the car to get in Zest's with Jeffrey.

Then they are on the road, in a SUV Zest obtained. Zest explains as he drives, "My team is meeting me in the area. The only thing we don't have is a place to take him afterwards."

Joel says, "You mean a hospital?"

"Not a good idea. Not in public. He is going to have to recover in safety."

Jeffrey speaks up from the back seat, where he is with Geneva. "I have a place in Bethesda. I have to go to DC a lot, so I invested in a townhouse there. It's pretty quiet."

The tension as they drive south is almost unbearable for Joel. He smokes constantly, promising himself it will be the last one. Zest keeps classical music playing softly in the SUV. He switches from major highways to two-lane roads, and keeps watch for any potential tails.

"We're halfway there, about. The house is not too far from a Civil War battlefield," Zest says almost conversationally, after a couple hours. Joel is taken aback, but then realizes Zest is trying to calm him. Jeffrey and Geneva have military experience, and Zest has whatever he has internally--enough to know how to handle nerves in an 'operation.' Joel could reach in, reach back to the Numbness, what used to get him through bad incidents as a youth. But he gave that up to change his life. So now he's wired with nervousness.

Geneva and Jeffrey had briefly discussed some Army places they were both familiar with, as well as experiences they both had. They're assessing each other. Joel notes that Jeffrey also observes Zest carefully.

Jeffrey catches Joel's eye. "You've been in bad situations, Joel..."

Joel turns to look at Jeffrey. "Yes. Things that required clarity, skills, whatever. Life or death. When I was younger, and...more recently. I don't panic."

"This is true. He's quite capable," Zest says.

Jeffrey asks, "You were there?"

"Yes. The only one more capable than Joel is Gabriel himself."

For the first time Joel notes the concern in Jeffrey's face. "Good, good. I never saw Gabriel in action. But as a boy he was very courageous, intelligent and strong. I know he hasn't changed from that--how he took care of things when he was arrested showed his strength. I know he can handle this."

Joel's hands shake. *He's telling himself this to convince himself Gabriel is okay. I have to believe the same thing.*

He says, "There's camera feed of what happened in the office. It took everything they had to capture him. Uh, where is your place, Mr. Ross?"

"It's on the outskirts of the city. It's three bedrooms, end of a cul de sac. Sometimes I let people use it, but it's empty now."

Zest only stops for gas at Fredericksburg, a few miles short of their destination. It's a short break. They'll be in Spotsylvania around 10 pm. But they use the opportunity to walk off the tension as best they can and mentally prepare.

As they get closer to Spotsylvania, Zest says, "This place is supposed to be haunted. That maybe is true. Not just the Civil War, but it's rumored the Lost Colony of Roanoke was taken there--and disappeared a second time."

"That's something Gabriel would find interesting," Joel comments. He tries to smile, but he's having a hard time keeping still.

Zest checks a phone he has. "My team is near. When we get him out..."

Joel turns his head and stares at Zest.

Zest glances at him. "We *will* get him out. Clement and his team inside have no idea about me being here. They do not have heavy security. It's not that kind of operation."

Jeffrey says, "But that man Clement is dangerous."

"Indeed. He is, but not to us. His is a danger to those he targets."

Joel lights up again. "He targeted Gabriel."

"Gabriel is still alive."

"You know?" Joel feels tiny tears come to his eyes. "Do you know for certain?"

"Yes. I needed to know exactly where he is in the house. There's equipment that can do that. Infrared. My team has it. From what they saw, we know six people are currently in the house. Clement is probably one of them. I can't let him see me *as* me, but I'll take care of that. Gabriel is the seventh person."

Joel stares at him. "How do they know it's him?"

Zest takes out his own cigarettes, delaying his answer. "They can tell the person is chained to something."

"Jesus..." Joel feels chilled. Geneva gets up and gets next to his seat.

"It'll be okay. He's alive, Joel."

"I'm scared; I can't help it."

Jeffrey reaches over and takes Joel's shoulder. "I know. I am too. To think of Gabriel in there with this person. He knows, though, that you would be here."

"What did Clement do to him?" Joel asks Zest. "Do you know any of that?"

"Yes. I don't want you to focus on that now--but after, yes, we'll need to deal with it. You should know this much. He's likely been subjected to some physical torture, and a particular type of psychological experimentation. He's remarkably resilient. But torture is trauma. And I also know that kind of torture. It depends upon how his mind acts in defense."

His voice drops, betraying something. Something in his experience shakes his cool exterior.

Then he recovers himself. "Keep in mind when we take him out, most likely he is not going to react like himself. This is why I'm glad Mr. Ross is here."

Joel goes from horror to guilt. "I should have stayed with him."

"Clement wanted to take him, Joel. You did nothing wrong. No way can you prevent something like that." Zest checks his device. "We're turning off now. We'll be in the area in five minutes."

∞

ELEVEN

From the YouTube Channel "Tom Paine Events," in a video entitled:
Unknown Knowns: Ioan Culianu ♦ The Scholar

Transcript: "Ioan Culianu was a professor at the University of Chicago. He was a beloved professor and brilliant writer, mixing politics and mystic religious concepts in fiction mystery stories and exploring concepts of hyperreality and other dimensions--trying to bring together Earth and magic. He was also a Romanian emigre, and at the time of his death in 1991, a strong critic of the political situations in Romania past and present. In 1989, the Ceauşescu regime had fallen and people hoped a democracy would arise. However, the political machinations appeared to be more of a coup, due to apparent connections to the old fascist Iron Guard of Romania. Culianu was cautious and justifiably paranoid of the Iron Guard and the Securitate, the Communist secret police in Romania. Yet he was also outspoken against them in interviews, and in his column for Lumea Liberă, an emigre newspaper. In fact, Culianu's biographer Ted Anton described how in the US some foreign-language periodicals feature investigations into cultural-political issues that have led to threats and possibly murders of journalists.

"Culianu was assassinated by a shot in the head in a University bathroom; the killer is still unknown. Culianu had been threatened prior to his murder, and friends and colleagues were threatened afterwards. Why? Interestingly, Culianu was a protégé of Mircea Eliade, also a Romanian religious scholar--but one who was suspected to have ties to, and was championed by, the fascist Iron Guard. Culianu was executor of Eliade's papers and could not find definitive proof Eliade had ever supported the Iron Guard. Still, the Iron Guard considered Eliade to be one of them, and may have had concerns about Culianu's handling of Eliade's unpublished work.

"Culianu earned the wrath of the right-wing faction--viciously so, from how they degradingly and vilely spoke and wrote about him after the murder. He was also reviled by the remainder of the Securitate, and a strange disinformation campaign against Culianu after his death was said by some to be a Securitate type of operation.

"In an excellent article on Culianu, Anton asked--could a scholar be that dangerous to others? Yes. Scholars believe in investigation, in open minds, and in pursuing principle. One who was raised in a repressive regime would feel the principle of freedom and accountability even stronger. Culianu's death raises the question of if his death a warning to others, a means of silencing his protests, or both--and can one ever be safe from repressive forces?"

∞

Monday, November 14, continued
Spotsylvania, VA, 10:15 pm

THEY WATCH FROM A DISTANCE about a hundred yards from the stone house. Zest had given Geneva and Joel handguns, just in case. Jeffrey has his own sidearm. They can't see Zest's team; the men are shadows in the darkness. The then shadows move *en masse*. The best operations aren't dramatic. They go quick and quiet.

Zest has a miniature radio in his ear. He's all in black, and a hood over his head. He has a device around his neck, to change his voice. A precaution for anyone who may hear him speak, as no one is supposed to be killed here unless it can't be helped.

A small boom from inside.

"Noise grenades," Zest tells them. He listens to the radio in his ear. Then he indicates they should move in. "It's clear."

They all jog towards the house. The front door opens, and a man completely in black like Zest waves them in.

They see a few more men in black, and other persons in fatigues or white medical-style clothes lying unconscious or semi-conscious, with wrists bound in ties.

One of the men says, "We stayed clear of the room where he's in just in case. It's locked and someone's in there with him. But it has a camera set up on that laptop." He leads them up to the second floor and down a hall to a mostly empty room. The room has a folding table with a laptop, microphone, and some related equipment. There's also what looks like a large screen TV monitor, sitting in the middle of the floor and aimed at the other door in the room.

"In there," the man says. "We tried to access the laptop, but they shut it down."

"I'd like to see inside that room," Zest says. "Can we get into it?"

Joel looks over the equipment. "Give me a minute. I'll get it on."

∞

Clement lies dazed on the floor, but is trying to pick himself up. When he tried to grab Ryan to stop him from screaming, Ryan punched him in the face. Ryan did stop screaming and now paces back and forth around him like a panther guarding its kill.

A sudden commotion downstairs. Moments later, an assistant calls Clement. "Someone's trying to breach...are you all right?"

Clement manages to get to his knees. "Yes...go out and stop them."

Clement ends the call and looks up. "Ryan, you misconstrued what I said."

"I'm not listening to you. The demons aren't real. You want to put something in my mind. You want to use me."

"No, no, no, I'm sorry. The demon is here, Ryan. And it is real."

Ryan stops; his attention snaps into focus. "Where? I'll take care of it."

"I know...I know you will. You'll help me, won't you? Ryan-- you'll protect me? We'll leave immediately for the people with the sun. But the demon is trying to kill me."

Ryan meets his eyes. "I won't let that happen."

"Yes, you're strong. You're what I knew you would be." Clement's voice drops to a low seductive sing-song. "You're all I have. I'm sorry I confused you. You're everything to me, Ryan. Please help me, Ryan. Please stay to the *message*."

Ryan turns to the window. V tells him, *you don't have to listen to him anymore.*

The noise in the house gets louder. Whoever the intruders are, they're advancing.

"Ryan..." Clement reaches to his back, and retrieves a gun. He holds it up to Ryan, grip first. "You need to shoot the demons who come in. We have to get away, you and me. To the people. I promise. If you shoot them, they won't die. You won't be killing anyone. We can go away."

Don't listen to him, Ryan.

"It's okay in here," Ryan says. "Remember? We're not outside. I can help in here. I'm not killing anyone."

Ryan...you have to get out.

"I can do this. I can protect everybody" Ryan takes the gun and looks it over--flicking off the safety and cocking it. He steps in front of Clement and aims the gun at the door.

∞

Joel is successful with the camera set-up. "Hang on...here, here! He's in there. Oh..."

They all see a high-angle shot from somewhere left of the door, no sound. A room empty except a thin mat on the floor, another door leading to a bathroom.

Clement sitting on the floor, talking to Gabriel. Gabriel is thinner, wild-eyed, and his hair's been cut very short. He's holding a gun aimed at the door. Joel immediately turns and heads for the door. "Gabriel..."

"No." Zest grabs Joel's shoulder and holds him back.

"But he's gotten..." Joel stares at Zest and then back at the screen. Gabriel's eyes are wide and his posture is a firing stance. But Clement, behind him, doesn't look scared. He appears to be encouraging Gabriel to shoot.

Zest turns to Jeffrey, who is studying the screen of the laptop. Jeffrey looks back at Zest. "He's under something--drugs, hypnosis."

"Assume he does not know who we are and will not recognize us."

Joel's intake sounds sharp in the room. "Would he shoot us?"

"Yes. Clement will tell him we are the enemy. Don't go to the door." Zest scans the equipment and picks up the microphone, turning the switch on.

He turns on his voice filter and speaks into the microphone. "Your people are disabled. Just you left. Come out, you on the floor. Leave the other man."

Clement grabs Gabriel's arm and pulls himself up. Gabriel doesn't react or change his stance. Clement flicks on an intercom.

"This house is wired to explode. Get out, or we'll all go."

Zest turns off the mic. He speaks to his team over his radio, then tells the others. "I believe he's lying. He values himself too much. They're checking the structure for any such signs. But Joel and Ms. Lennon should wait outside."

But both are shaking their heads. "I agree, it's a bluff," Geneva says.

Jeffrey is watching the screen. "He's buying time."

They can hear Clement encouraging Gabriel to shoot anyone who comes in, but he's calling Gabriel "Ryan."

Gabriel is shaking his head and staring at a corner of the room, and talking to something they can't see--something that isn't there. "It's supposed to be okay in here, what do you mean?"

Clement says. "Ryan, you need to listen to me--"

Gabriel turns and yells at him. "Stop talking!"

"What is going on," Joel asks everybody and nobody.

"There's a part of him resisting this," Zest replies, as if he recognizes the process. "But it's not stable."

"He looks like he's trying to listen to someone, but there's no one there," Geneva observes.

"Someone else is there to *him*," Jeffrey says. "That's the thing. He's hallucinating. I wish I knew who it was he sees. That man is calling him Ryan. That's his middle name."

Zest tilts his head, listening to his radio. "Let's get him extracted. My team can't find any evidence of explosives."

He gives instructions to his team, and a minute later. They hear a 'pop' type sound. On the laptop screen a projectile breaks through the windows. It's a stun grenade. The screen goes white at the same time the explosive noise reverberates inside.

When the light flash lessens, they see Clement is on the floor again, covering his head, writhing from the effect of the grenade. Gabriel is still standing though, as if he was unaware of what was thrown in the room.

He looks to the corner again. "All right," he says. "But I'm still protecting..." He approaches the door to the room and opens it.

Joel feels his body shot through with adrenaline as Gabriel steps out. He looks the same and different at the same time.

Clement is trying to crawl behind him. "Ryan, wait for me."

"Ryan," Jeffrey says to himself, watching his son.

Gabriel glances sharply at him, then dispassionately at the others in the anteroom, as if they weren't there, or perhaps were mannequins. The gun remains in his hand, but is not pointed.

Zest says, through his filter. "You will stay there. Both of you."

Gabriel looks at Zest. "Who are you? You're not the demon."

"*He is,*" Clement says behind him. "Shoot him, Ryan."

"Ryan," Jeffery says in an authoritative voice. "Don't listen to him. He's lied to you."

Gabriel tilts his head at Jeffrey, scowling in confusion. "I know you."

"Yes. Ryan, that man is lying to you."

Clement reaches the door. "Ryan, the *message.* You have to *delete the message.*"

Gabriel turns and stares back at him.

"*Delete the message.*"

Jeffrey says, "Don't listen--"

Gabriel lifts the gun with both hands. Everyone backs away. His eyes are wide, he starts breathing heavily.

Gabriel swings the gun around, but doesn't focus.

Jeffrey has his hands up. "Don't do it. Look at me."

Gabriel turns back to his father. "I know you."

"Yes, you know me. No demons are here with me."

Gabriel's hands are shaking. He starts edging toward the door. "I have to *help people.* I have to *protect people.*"

"Let me help you, Ryan."

Clement interjects, "Ryan, *delete the message.*"

"He isn't the demon," Gabriel says to Clement without looking at him. "He's not trying to hurt you. I can't hurt him." But he doesn't put down the gun.

Desperate, as Zest is moving closer to towards him, Clement yells, "Abort the message. Ryan, *Abort.*"

Gabriel shudders, then begins backing out of the room into the hallway, pointing the gun at the group. "Stay away from me."

"Ryan, don't leave," Jeffrey says, as Clement keeps yelling, "*Abort, Abort!*"

Zest is able to get to Clement, and in a swift move with Geneva's help, puts restraints on him and injects him with a sedative. "Don't leave Gabriel alone," he tells the others.

Jeffrey steps in the hallway, following his son. "Ryan. I'm your dad. You remember me, I know. Your name is Gabriel."

Gabriel is shaking wildly. "No, no, no, no." He's moving toward a door at the far end of the hall, creeping backward, keeping the gun at Jeffrey. "I don't want to hurt you."

"You're not going to. I'm going to help you."

"No. I have to abort."

"You do not. The man was lying to you."

"I'm protecting him. I'm protecting everybody. It worked before." Gabriel reaches behind him and opens the door. He slips inside and starts going up a set of stairs.

Zest, in the hallway, speaks on his radio. "Stop him, block him. Don't shoot."

They can hear Gabriel say, "Move! I mean it."

Jeffrey is already up the stairs, which go to the roof. Gabriel is on the flat roof, surrounded by three of Zest's team. "Ryan, what did the man tell you to do?"

"Abort. Abort the message. It's what I have to do to get to the Sun people."

"What is abort, Ryan? What do you have to do?" Jeffrey circles around the other men, who stay several feet away. Gabriel looks over their heads to the edge of the roof.

"I have to sacrifice myself. Damon said if I just jump, it will be okay. I'll go to the Sun people."

"There are no Sun people, Ryan." Zest is now outside with them. He takes off his hood, and his voice is normal again. "Do not abort. *Retrieve* the message."

Gabriel looks over his shoulder. "How do you know?"

"I know. I've been there."

Gabriel frowns at him. "I know you."

"Yes. We've met before."

"How did you get here?"

Zest smiles gently. "We found you."

"I have to abort. It's the only way to protect…"

Jeffrey's voice is low and urgent, "Ryan, you were talking to someone in that room. Who was it?"

"The owl. Her name is V. She's been with me the whole time. She said Damon was lying. But I don't know. I don't know. I was supposed to be his friend. I was supposed to protect the man inside my head. I just want to go away. I don't want to kill anyone."

Zest takes a step closer. "You can't help by aborting. *Retrieve the message.*"

"He said I couldn't *retrieve* anymore."

Zest nods. "That's what he was lying about. You can. You see these people?" He points to Joel and Geneva, who have carefully climbed on the roof.

"I don't know them."

"Ryan sent them here, Gabriel. *They're* the ones you need to protect. *Add* to the message. You can do that."

"If I abort, I can protect everyone."

"That isn't the way. I need you to protect these people. You remember me. You remember your father."

Gabriel drops the gun and puts his hands to his head. He screams from deep in his chest, a howl that reverberates in the dark, cold, Virginia countryside. His wailing scares the hell out of everybody from the vibrating inhuman quality. Except Jeffrey and Zest, who grab Gabriel and pull him back from the edge of the roof.

Gabriel suddenly stops screaming and almost collapses, but the other two men hold him. He looks up at Jeffrey. "Dad? Did I do okay in the woods? When we were practicing what you wanted to teach me. I never knew if you liked me or not." His voice sounds decades younger.

"Of course. I was always proud of you." Jeffrey comes up and puts his arm around Gabriel. "I'm proud of you now. You did just right."

Gabriel now seems to have a problem standing on his right leg. "I got hurt. I don't know how..."

"We're going to go. You're going to help protect these people."

Gabriel glances at Joel and Geneva. "Okay. I will."

Zest says to them, "He has no idea what's going on, and we're going to get him out, but bear with him. He's in shock; he probably still has drugs in his system, he may be having a psychotic break trying to deal with this."

Gabriel tries to say something, then looks away from them. "I'm afraid the demon will come back."

Zest responds, "It will not. We've seen to that."

"There was no sun, was there? Or people who will love me. He was lying about that, too."

"Come with us now. We have people who love you."

Gabriel has some difficulty walking, from his injury. He leans on Jeffrey.

"We're going down the stairs." Jeffrey puts his arm under Gabriel's, taking weight off Gabriel's injured leg. His face is icy with repressed rage, but he keeps his voice calm. "Let me help him. You take point."

Gabriel says nervously, "Are you mad at me?"

"Absolutely not. I want you to lean on me when we go down." He helps Gabriel navigate the stairs. Zest, Geneva and Joel follow. Jeffrey leads Gabriel to the stairs going down to the first floor.

Jeffrey turns for a second to look back at the door to the room where Gabriel was held. "Clement is still in there."

"Yes, unconscious. My team is going to scour the place. I know there's some of Gabriel's belongings here."

Something flickers across Jeffrey's face.

Zest says emphatically, "We need to get Gabriel out."

Jeffrey nods, and begins moving Gabriel down. Zest signals his team over his radio, and they ensure a path is clear for them all to go out the front door and back to the SUV.

∞

Inside the car, Jeffrey is in back with Gabriel and Geneva. Joel has gotten back in the passenger seat. Gabriel stares at everyone without speaking.

Zest gets in the driver's seat. "The team will leave in a few minutes. We're going straight to Bethesda."

"Right on," Geneva says.

"It's going to be okay now," Jeffrey tells Gabriel, who's shaking again.

"Dad?" Gabriel's voice sounds like he's about ten years old.

Then he begins to cry. Jeffrey holds on to him, letting him cry. Then he falls asleep.

"He doesn't know who we are," Joel whispers. He wants to cry himself. *But he's out. He's out. He's safe now. That was the hard part.*

Jeffrey says to Joel, "He'll get better. He's drugged, right?"

Zest answers. "No doubt. One of my team will do a sweep to see what's there before they leave. I believe, since Gabriel's mind is strong and this was not a great length of time, he'll recover. He just needs the opportunity.

Joel takes a moment to call Danny and let him know they have Gabriel. When Danny asks how he is, Joel hands the phone to Jeffrey, since he doubts Danny would believe him.

After talking to Danny, Jeffrey turns to Zest. "Thank you for rescuing my son. You're right. I am aware of some of these tactics myself. It's not easy, but he'll get himself out."

"You're welcome."

Geneva leans forward. "Mr. Zest, were you ever military?"

He glances in the rearview mirror. "Not quite. I've worked with military; the Society is private sector."

"These people you're with..."

"My help is genuine. As I said, if my people knew I was helping Gabriel, I'd be dead."

"You sound interesting. Whatever you were in, you here helping."

"I had to. I'm doing what I can to rectify."

"Your soul is not dead, however. Not when you are going so far to rectify this situation."

Zest smiles. "You assume I have one. Mine was traded in a long time ago. 1978, to be exact."

"The year I was born."

"Perhaps you got the best part of that year." He smiles again.

"You were recruited that year, is that it?" Geneva says.

"Indeed. A man I admired, respected, even loved." For a moment, Zest's voice is flat.

"Clement."

"Yes. I found out when it was too late, about who he really was and what he wanted."

"What are you going to do now?"

"Ensure Gabriel is safe. After that, I'm going to leave and go somewhere."

"Escape?"

Zest sighs. "No, Ms. Lennon. There's no escape."

Joel sits up straight. "You're really committing suicide? That's harsh."

"People have right to choose how they may leave this world."

"Oh my God, don't do that." Geneva reaches over the seat to put her hand on his shoulder. "It doesn't have to be this way, whoever they are."

"Ms. Lennon, I cannot live on the run, looking over my shoulder."

Joel turns to him. "They did this to you. If you don't care, then don't care in a way that stops them."

Zest smiles. "And what would you suggest, Joel? Going to the *New York Times*? Or its rival the *Herald-Standard*? People sympathetic to...my organization are in both places."

"We can think of something."

"Can we? Let's just get Gabriel safe for the present time."

∞

TWELVE

From the YouTube Channel "Tom Paine Events," in a video entitled:
Unknown Knowns: GEC-Marconi ◆ The Scientists

Transcript: "Twenty-five scientists who worked in GEC-Marconi in Britain died mysteriously between 1982 and 1990. These persons worked on the Sting Ray torpedo project and the US's Strategic Defense Initiative-related projects.

"They died under mysterious circumstances--strange suicides or unexplained deaths. Single car crash. Self-inflicted gunshot. Hanging. Falling out a window or off a bridge. Electrocuted. Carbon monoxide. These deaths raise the question--if connected and due to their work, what about this kind of work can lead to so much despair and death?"

∞

Tuesday, November 15
Bethesda, MD, 3:02 am

NEARLY TWO HOURS later they reach the quiet street with the townhouse.

Zest parks the car in the little driveway next to the townhouse. "I recommend he be sedated. He's in for a bad night."

Gabriel has actually fallen asleep on the drive to Maryland. It isn't an easy one. He mutters constantly and suddenly wakes up, startling everybody, and then drops off again.

Zest continues, "I have the information from my team. Clement had him on Rohypnol, DMT, and Oxy derivatives. Probably the entire time. He'll be detoxing."

Jeffrey gently wakes Gabriel. It's already starting. Gabriel opens his eyes and stares at him while shaking. "Uh...Dad...I don't feel well."

"I understand. Just come with me. I know you don't feel well, but you're safe."

Zest studies them over the seat. "I can have a doctor check on him, get you some things. I think it's a good idea if we watch over him for the time being."

"Sure." Jeffrey opens his door. "Come on Gabriel. Hold on to me."

Jeffrey helps Gabriel to the door, and unlocks it. He waves at the others to come inside. Joel follows first. The townhouse is cool and dark. Jeffrey pauses after turning on a hall light and disarming the alarm system.

"I want to check things out first. Haven't been here for a few months. Gabriel, do you have trouble standing? I'll take you to the living room."

"Okay," Gabriel says flatly. He's sweating now, pain creasing his face. "My leg hurts bad. And my arms."

"I'll help you," Joel tells him.

Gabriel looks sidewise at him, as if he's suspicious of Joel's motives.

"Gabriel," Jeffrey says. "Let him help you."

And Gabriel acquiescently turns to Joel. Joel slips his arm under Gabriel's right shoulder.

Gabriel winces and says, "I'm sorry. Oh God, this hurts."

"You don't have to be sorry." Joel isn't sure what else to say. He remembers last summer when Gabriel carried him out of the warehouse in Westchester, back to Gabriel's car. To get him away from the man who was going to kill him. This is no different.

Except it is. The lack of familiarity in Gabriel's eyes, the wariness of a stranger.

Zest had said, while Gabriel was asleep in the car, that they not push him to try to remember anything. "He'll need to be assessed as to what was done to him first."

Now, when Jeffrey returns, Zest says, "Mr. Ross, do you have any colleagues with this experience in handling this sort of experience, so to speak?"

Jeffrey's face turns dark. "I do, but I don't know that I can trust them, since Clement was connected to intelligence. I don't know who to trust."

"We need to find someone, the sooner the better."

"I know who," Joel says.

Jeffrey, Zest, and Geneva all look at him. Only Gabriel has his attention elsewhere, as if he's unaware they are discussing him.

"Chiang, his martial arts mentor. Gabriel said Chiang has a history in this kind of thing. That's why he's in the US, to get away from his past."

Zest gives a short nod. "Call him, discreetly."

Jeffrey then asks, "Can you all stay for a while, to help watch him? Joel, I know you will."

"Sure I can," Geneva says.

Zest and Gabriel are looking at each other. Zest says, "I would like to stay. As I know what he went through, I can help when Gabriel's mentor arrives. You can get him here, Joel?"

"He'll do it for Gabriel."

"Can I sit down," Gabriel asks suddenly. "My arms really hurt like this."

"Yes, of course." Jeffrey leads him to the wide staircase. "What happened to you?"

"Uh...this man in a green mask pulled me up." Then Gabriel rolls his eyes, and seems to have a moment of clarity. "In the Middle Ages, they called it *Strappado.* Savonarola suffered through it." Gabriel laughs suddenly, then gets angry. "Why do I know that, and not who all of you are? You're all *staring at me.*"

"Gabriel," Jeffrey moves close. "You know me."

"Yes...Dad. I know..."

"And you know I'm not going to hurt you. That's over. Trust me. Okay? You're not going to feel well for a while, but I'll take care of you."

Gabriel nods and turns red, as if he's embarrassed. Jeffrey says to Joel, "Please take him upstairs now."

Geneva and Joel help Gabriel move up the stairs. He won't look them in the eyes, and just mumbles thanks when he's on a bed.

Downstairs, Jeffrey lights a cigarette. "I don't have Gabriel's book knowledge. What is Strappado?"

Zest describes the torture.

Jeffrey grimaces. "Oh, yeah. I've seen it. I know it. Not under that name. Is your team still at that house?"

"No."

"I'm going back. Watch him while I'm gone."

Zest reaches out and takes Jeffrey's arm. "When Clement wakes up, they'll bug out. They won't be there when you get there."

"You don't know for sure."

"I do. I know him."

Jeffrey stares at Zest. "Then I want to know where he's going."

"Let me take care of him."

Jeffrey shakes his head. "I get it; but I'm not that kind of person--not like Gabriel. I get the idea you tried to protect Gabriel from something. But I'm past that. You and I have likely done the same things in different contexts. But no one does this to my son and walks away. I'm not being pacifist about this."

"Not now, Mr. Ross. Let's get Gabriel back to us--that's more important. Clement is not going to in any sense *get away* with it. You have my word, and I hope now that Gabriel is here my word means something. But no purpose served to put yourself in harm's way right now."

Jeffrey Ross is used to making executive decisions. He doesn't argue. "All right. I'll trust you on that for now. For now."

They go upstairs. There's three bedrooms. "Joel, can you and Geneva bunk together? Good. Zest, you can have one. I'm staying with Gabriel. I don't want him alone.

Jeffrey goes in Gabriel's room. Gabriel has almost dozed off again, and Jeffrey takes a pill from Zest, who has a supply of meds with him, to give to Gabriel. Gabriel's passivity in accepting what's given him is disconcerting.

"Xanax," Zest says.

"He took a lot of that when he was going through a bad time last year."

Jeffrey looks down at Gabriel and then at Joel. "This gives me an opportunity to take care of him. I didn't do much of that when he was young. You probably know that."

"He found it meaningful to reconnect with you. It was hard, but I saw it in his face. Like I am with my mom."

"Good. It's what I wanted. And I see in your face how worried you are still. I know how much you care about him. It reminds me of Kate...It makes me sorry for some things I said to him a long time ago. Well, what's important is what we do now."

Joel nods, and leaves the room. Geneva is on the bed in the other room. "I imagine you can't sleep well."

"Or at all."

"I'm glad I'm with you. It's hard to be alone."

"Who will stay with Zest?" Joel smiles briefly, but can't hold on to the humor long.

Geneva strips to her t-shirt, and massages his shoulders. He gives in to that, and then bursts into tears. She continues rubbing him as he cries.

"Why are things like this?"

"Sometimes you can't do good in this world without catching hell. I saw that overseas."

"It's not fair."

"To you or him?"

Joel lifts his head. "Him. Maybe me. God, we had what--a few peaceful months since he got out of jail. I thought that was going to be the rest of our lives."

"Are you okay with this?"

He turns to look at her. "I'd never leave him. I don't care what happens. That isn't it. I'm just..."

"Tired. You're tired. Lie down for a while." She continues rubbing his back, and calls Veronica on a safe phone to update her. Joel is comforted listening to their easy rapport. He's glad he brought them together. Geneva puts the phone on speaker so they both can talk to her. She's in Danny's apartment, and he joins the conversation to get more details.

Despite exhaustion settling on him like an avalanche, Joel can't sleep. He periodically gets up and checks in Gabriel's room. Jeffrey is asleep in an easy chair by Gabriel's bed. Gabriel is sedated enough to sleep through the night. Joel finds Zest isn't asleep either. He's downstairs staring out the sliding glass doors leading to the backyard. He goes outside to smoke, and Joel joins him for few minutes. They don't talk, both lost in thought.

Around two am, to do something, Joel calls Chris, who is keeping Joel's phones. He gets Chris to find Chiang's phone number. Then in spite of the hour, Joel calls Chiang and leaves a message.

Ten minutes later Chiang calls him back.

Joel briefly explains the situation.

"The demons have returned for him," Chiang says. "In human form. Where are you?"

"Bethesda."

"I'll come down there, unless you're coming back up."

"He's not going back right away." Joel gives Chiang the address.

The morning makes up for the relative peace of the night. Joel wakes up sharply out of an uneasy doze. He hears something like crying, and immediately goes to Gabriel's bedroom.

He finds that Gabriel is awake and shaking, covered in sweat. Joel walks over to him. "Hey. What's going on?"

"I feel like I'm dying," Gabriel whispers.

"You're not, you're not." Joel takes Gabriel's hand and holds it.

Jeffrey had been out getting water; he comes back now. "Let me see if Zest can get a doctor. He's in withdrawal."

Jeffrey leaves to go talk to Zest. Joel finds a washcloth in the bathroom attached to the room.

"I'm sorry," Gabriel says through clenched teeth as Joel wipes his face. "I'm just in so much pain right now."

"It's not your fault."

Gabriel glances up at him, lost. "I don't understand what's happening..."

"I know. I know it's bad. But it will go away. I promise."

Gabriel tries to say something, maybe "thank you," but can't find the words.

Geneva pops in. She is talking to Veronica again. Joel can hear Veronica's voice faintly.

Gabriel raises his head, forgetting his misery. "That's V, my owl's voice. Is she here?"

Geneva stops talking. "I'm talking to Veronica. She's a friend of yours."

"The owl's name is V. Is that her?" He sounds hopeful.

Joel dabs Gabriel's head with a washcloth. "Put her on speaker."

"Should we do this?"

"For a minute. See if it helps."

Geneva tells Veronica that Gabriel had heard an owl and somehow connects it with Veronica. She is not surprised and more than willing to be the owl. Geneva switches the phone to speaker.

"Gabriel?"

Gabriel stares at the phone. "Where are you? At the house?"

"I left when you did."

"Do you...do you know what happened?"

"Yes. You did what you should have done. And you are safe now."

"I...I was scared of what was happening."

"But you were strong enough to get through it. You will stay strong now."

"I feel sick. I don't understand why I don't know what's going on, who these people are."

"Gabriel, listen to me. They will take care of you. Bit by bit, things will get better. You have to trust me."

He tries to answer, but becomes too sick to talk, but is upset when Geneva turns the speaker off. "I don't want her to go away."

"She'll be around when you need."

Geneva leaves and Gabriel breathes heavy, curled in a fetal position.

"I had a few hangovers like that."

That startles Joel. Jeffrey has returned.

"No matter how bad it was, even when his mom was super-pissed at me, she took care of me. I'm glad he has you, Joel. I miss Kate so much...anyway, Zest's doctor will be here shortly."

"Should we get him in a shower?"

"Let's try."

Gabriel's still shaking and incoherent, but he hears his father and manages to sit up. They maneuver him to the bathroom.

Not surprisingly, he immediately vomits uncontrollably.

When he's curled on the floor after, Jeffrey strips the stained t-shirt off him. "Any chance you brought him clothes?"

"Yeah, I was afraid to and afraid *not* to."

"Be prepared, Joel. It's going to get worse while he's detoxing. Why don't you go find those clothes, and let me take care of him?"

"I've been through him being sick before."

"Not like this, son. You ever see someone detox from opiates and lose complete control of himself? Forgive me, Joel, but he wouldn't want you to see him like this."

Joel backs away, giving in. Something like an hour later, Joel is waiting in his room with Geneva. Trying to tell himself the worst is over.

A little later they hear Gabriel's voice getting loud. They both rush over and find Jeffrey helping Gabriel to the bed. Gabriel's managed to make it through a shower and is in a clean t-shirt and shorts. He's still shaking and is still in so much pain he can't do anything but curl upon his side.

They think he's going back to sleep. But then he surprises them all by sitting up and looking angry. He climbs out of bed, and starts pounding the walls.

"I know you have something! Why won't you make this stop?!"

Jeffrey gets an arm around him, and wrestles him back to the bed. Gabriel struggles with him, yelling. Joel can only watch Jeffrey remain calm and repeat that Gabriel has to get back in bed.

Zest comes in with a doctor. She's dressed down, to not stand out in the neighborhood. She proceeds to do a fairly thorough examination, ignoring and talking gently over Gabriel's curses and insistent pleas for a painkiller.

She then speaks with them away from Gabriel's hearing, although they can hear his angry voice from the bedroom, doing a good imitation of the demon in *The Exorcist*.

The doctor smiles ruefully. "As you can see, he's going right into the thick of it."

Jeffrey says, "What's the best option to get him clean fast?"

"We can do URD. It means putting him under for some hours."

"What is that," Joel asks.

"URD is ultra-rapid detox. A method of breaking an addict from opiates by flushing the system with a chemical, Naltrexone. It requires general anesthesia."

"He's not an addict."

"Okay, but he *is* addicted at the moment. I have to warn you of risks. Sometimes the patient dies. Maybe from the reaction to the anesthesia. It's rare, but it could happen. We wait for him overnight, for him to fast and to be in full withdrawal, and start it tomorrow morning. Then put him on buprenorphine. We could just do buprenorphine, but it would be over a period of time."

"Excuse us," Jeffrey says. The doctor nods and steps away.

Jeffrey sighs. "If it wasn't for the amnesia, I'd say go with the safer option."

"He needs to be safe. I'm his health care proxy."
"None of this is on the record, Joel. But I'm not fighting you. I'm worried about his safety too--but not just from the drugs. I want to try to get him working on his memory."

Zest says, "Yes. He's not in immediate danger, but the risk that remains from Clement needs to be contained, so we need him back to himself. He's going to suffer, no matter what."

The other two look at him as it sounds as if he's speaking from experience, but he doesn't elaborate. "Has Gabriel been under general before?"

"Yes," Jeffrey nods. "No problems."

Joel bites his thumbnail, thinking. "This is...I don't know. I don't know how to make these decisions."

Jeffrey puts his hand on Joel. "I know. Gabriel and I and Dominic had to discuss Kate, when she was close to the end. But this is not that situation. Whatever we do, we have to think of his best interests."

"I know what he would do," Joel says. "He'd want his mind back and take the risk. Although he wouldn't risk anyone else that way. I guess I have to respect that."

The doctor is told to set up the URD. She goes to make arrangements, and says she'll be back in the early morning.

A couple minutes after the doctor leaves, Gabriel starts pounding on the walls again, and kicking something. Joel goes back in the room and takes hold of Gabriel's hands gently. "Don't do that."

Gabriel's face is red, and he's sweating again. "Do you have something? Anything? Just make it go away. I don't know why you're making me go through this."

"We're not--I swear it will get better."

Gabriel locks eyes with him, and Joel has the strangeness of looking at someone he knows so well, so intimately, and who sees him as a total stranger. Gabriel yanks his hands away from Joel. "Who the fuck are you? If you don't have any painkillers, then get the fuck away from me."

Instead, Joel gets closer to him, and puts his arms around Gabriel. He feels the strain, the anger, rolling off in waves. Joel holds him tight, bringing Gabriel's head down to his shoulder. "It's okay."

"It's not..." Gabriel mutters. "Please *help* me."

*Don't cry don't cry don't cry...*even as Gabriel cries, suddenly, explosively, not caring.

"I can be strong for you," Joel says softly. "I'm not going anywhere."

Jeffrey is in the doorway, watching. "You want to go out for a few minutes? The rest of the day, and the night, is going to be rough."

"I can take it," Joel says. "I'm good."

∞

Friday, November 18, 2011
Bethesda, MD, 7:17 am

I wake up and stare at the walls of the bedroom. It's blue. I like blue. It's soothing. I can feel cold air coming through a crack in the window. Winter coming on; lying in bed and reading. I want to read. I'm just not sure what. I tried reading some of the books my father has, and they seem familiar but I can't remember what happens in them.

My door is open, and I'm startled to see someone in the doorway. It's the younger man. He's staring at me intensely. About my height, and body frame, blond, longish hair, dressed nice. Blueish eyes and a faint growth of beard.

I say, "Uh, hello."

He closes his eyes briefly. "How do you feel, Gabriel?"

"I feel like I'm sick, I guess. What was your name?"

He walks in. He's staring at me still. It makes me a little uncomfortable. I have the sense he wants something, but I don't know what.

"Joel," he says.

I shrug. "I'm sorry. I just don't get what's going on. What day is it?"

"Friday. You're a lot better from just like two days ago. A lot."

"If you say so. I feel pretty fucking rotten, so I guess I must have been really fucked up then...was I screaming?"

"Yes." I get the sense he's trying not to smile. "But we put up with it."

I guess he thinks that's funny. I can't find anything funny right now. I just want to go back to sleep.

I don't even know what I would find funny.

Try. Think of something. You can't stay like this.

But he throws me off being here. "You're staring at me."

"Sorry." He sits next to me on the bed, and puts his hand on my head. I have to admit it's soothing. Somebody cares. And I'm helpless. I don't know what's going on, I don't know who I am, so I have to trust these people.

But I know my father, that's something. I guess if he says Joel is okay, then I have to believe that.

I get a sense from him I can't describe. He wants to say more. I want him to say more, since I'm frustrated over knowing nothing. A giant gaping hole between remembering being in the woods with my dad twenty-odd years ago, and now. I look at my body and wonder what it's capable of, where the scars came from on my arms and chest and neck. Why I chose the tattoos I have. Who I've been with.

I know I'm not right. I'm too thin, and I look different, even though I'm not sure what I look like normally. My head feels strange-- my hair so short I feel naked.

"It's okay for you to have coffee today."

"Oh my God, yes."

I look up at him. I want coffee like it's the sweetest drug in the world.

"I'll get it; just be careful. You're having trouble keeping things down."

The prospect of coffee is enough for me to sit up. Since Joel is out of the room, I can find some clothes to get dressed in. I can go to the bathroom by myself, have some privacy for a few minutes.

But by the time I'm back, I'm shaking. *I'm sick and dying and they're not telling me why.*

Zest stops by the door to the room and says Good Morning. Why do I have a vague idea who Zest is, but nothing about the man who comes in with the coffee? In the transfer of the cup, our fingers touch, and he watches it.

"Who are you," I ask.

"We know each other. You'll remember."

I work on keeping the cup steady in my hands.

Suddenly my father appears, and behind him is a Chinese man in his fifties, dressed in a jersey and jeans, with longish graying hair and a light trimmed beard. While there is a faint familiarity, I don't really recognize him either.

Yet he seems to know me. "Gabriel." He has a subtle accent. "Of all your training, I didn't think this would be called upon."

He holds out his hand and I shake it. "I'm sorry, I don't know who you are, although I feel I should."

"Zihou Chiang. I've been teaching you Daoism and martial arts for some time. You don't recall any of this."

"No."

"I might try some acupuncture with you. Some other remedies. But I'd like you to get up and follow me."

"I'm sick. I can't go anywhere."

Chiang abruptly takes the coffee out of my hand. "*Xuéshēng,* Get up, *now.*"

For some reason something in his voice makes me get up. And then I'm mad at myself. "Are you kidding--?"

He interrupts me. "*Now.* Let's go."

It's imperative. I follow him, seeing that both my father and Joel are surprised at this.

Downstairs is a sparsely furnished living room. Chiang hands me back the coffee as he walks around me, looking me over.

Jeffrey says, "I think that Gabriel used something I told him about. Some tactics to work against psyops. To put away memories, people, somewhere safe in your mind. To become another person and forget who you are. It's happened to other people I worked with."

"I've seen it as well. But at the same time, I get the idea that this person who had him wanted him to be someone else as well."

"Right. It's kind of messed up. Clement was trying to turn Gabriel into a soldier to kill on command. Gabriel turned himself into another person, Ryan. Ryan both protected him so Gabriel could disappear in his mind, and Ryan also absorbed Clement's hypnotic control. Poor Gabriel doesn't know whether he's coming or going. He got jolted out a little when we rescued him but something is still keeping Gabriel from getting his full memory back."

I'm frowning at them. I don't like to be talked about, and I have no idea what this stuff is about being another person.

Chiang takes the coffee and sets it on a small table. "Face me."

I get in front of him. I feel sick as a Goddamn dog, like collapsing, but I can do it.

Chiang shifts his posture slightly, and something in me follows his stance, almost automatically.

Chiang glances at Jeffrey, Joel and Zest. "Without trying to sound too much like the mysterious Asian stereotype, the body does have a memory different from the mind. One might think of it as a separate functioning DNA."

He bows to me, and I bow as well. Somehow, I can feel what he's talking about. Because he's my teacher, I bow lower.

Chiang picks up a pad of paper and a pen, and draws a symbol on it. "You remember this?"

I glance down at it, and an images creep into my head. Drawing the same symbols in sand. "You said, "Do it again. *Better.*""

Chiang laughs. "You *would* remember that. You don't like being criticized. What were you supposed to do better?"

I take the pad from him, and copy what he drew. And then other symbols that come to me.

"Not bad," Chiang says. He turns to the others. "He hasn't lost his memory. It's locked away, as you guessed. What I'm going to do is another form of hypnosis to counteract what they did."

Chiang takes an ottoman across from me, and gestures for me to sit in a chair. I take the coffee with me. My father and Joel sit on the sofa on the other side of the room. Zest is in the background, with Geneva, the woman who seems to be a friend of mine as well.

Chiang takes out various things from a satchel. "I want to test you on light, sound and motion. Do any of those bother you?"

"I don't know."

He turns on a flash, and I see a room, all in white. People reaching for me. Demons reaching for me. I'm drowning as dead people grab for me. I fall out of the chair, and the coffee goes everywhere.

I try to run out the room. My father is already up and putting his arms around me. "Okay, Gabriel. It's okay."

I'm shaking uncontrollably. I want to help clean up, but I can't move.

Chiang says, "That was probably like what they used. What about this?" He holds up a small metronome.

I glance at it cautiously. "That's okay."

"Good."

He waits for me to return to the chair.

"Relax as much as you can. Like you were going to sleep right there. Watch this go back and forth..."

∞

THIRTEEN

From the YouTube Channel "Tom Paine Events," in a video entitled:
Unknown Knowns: Michael Connell ♦ The Courier

Transcript: "Connell was a high-level Republican consultant who was a witness in a case regarding alleged tampering with the 2004 U.S. Presidential election. Connell was deeply involved in the contested Ohio vote. He was also involved in a case involving thousands of missing emails pertaining to the political firing of U.S. Attorneys. According to an Attorney General involved in the election case, Connell's life had been threatened. Connell's plane crashed in late 2008, a single-person plane crash. Project Censored and Robert Kennedy Jr. both advocated for a federal investigation, finding the crash suspicious due to Connell's meeting with mysterious people, his involvement with high-level Republicans, reports of sabotage to his plane, and missing information--his Blackberry. What he knew about these cases is an unknown known. His death raises the question can your friends also be your enemies when it comes to keeping information suppressed?"

∞

Friday, November 18, 2011, Continued

CHIANG STARTS TALKING to Gabriel as he stares at the metronome. Gabriel goes under amazingly quick, and falls deep into a trance.

"Gabriel, do you remember a man named Damon Clement?'

Gabriel frowns. "He said he was my friend. He promised me that if I did things, he'd let me go away."

"Go away where?"

"We were going to go to a place for a ritual. People under the sun. They loved me. They wanted me there because I was going to protect them. But he lied. Ryan told me that. And the owl. V. Is she here?"

"Not at the moment. Who is the owl?"

"I heard her voice when I got there--where Damon was. She stayed outside my window. She watched over me. I could be there and not be there. She told me to be careful over what I told Damon. She told me he was lying."

"What did he want you to do?"

"To kill some demons. We talked about it over and over. He wanted me to go some places and kill the demons who were going to hurt him. Him and his friend. I had to practice taking pain in case the demons attacked me. It was to show how I could help people and protect people. Everything was building to that. These people in white, they did things. It hurt so much. But he said it would protect him if I could go through it. I fought the demon. He wanted to tear my eyes out, but I fought him. And the other man in the green mask. He was the one who hit me first. He pulled me up by the arms. He kicked my leg when I was down. But then, later, Damon was in danger, and he asked me to fight the green man, and I took him down."

Zest, who has been keeping a neutral expression, reacts to what Gabriel is saying by turning away.

Chiang continues, "You protected Clement."

"He told me I was a protector. It was strange. I saw my mother. And Dominic. They wanted me to take revenge, and when I couldn't they said I had to protect others. And I saw Joel. He kept asking me questions."

Joel's eyes widen. He wants to say something, but Chiang raises a hand to stop him. "When did you see them?"

"When I was first there. They looked like the photos I had. All the questions, over and over."

"All right. Who is Clement's friend?"

"Uh...he...I don't know. He told me to forget I knew him. I had to protect him but I can't remember him."

Now Zest is frowning. "Encausse. Was that who it was?"

"That's the name I found before, and yeah, Damon said his name was Encausse. Damon said he was mean, and that I shouldn't worry but still protect him."

"Do you remember what he looked like?"

"Ah, no. He was very adamant about not remembering him or his other name. He told me not to remember about him. I put the memory in a safe place."

"Okay. What happened the last night? Why did you get mad at Clement?"

"We were supposed to leave. He promised. And then he said, no, I had to go somewhere first, and kill this other person who was trying to hurt him."

Zest turns back around. Chiang glances at him. "Who was it, Gabriel?"

"A man in New York City. Jacobs. He was going to take me there. But we were supposed to visit the sun people first."

"Okay. He's gone. I want you to relax. Clement can't do any more harm to you. You don't have to listen to him anymore. You are released from any obligations to him, do you understand?"

Gabriel stares blankly. "Yeah, but...what do I do now?"

"Do you know who you are?"

"No. I just know what you call me, what you say I did."

"You know you are Gabriel and not Ryan."

"I let Ryan talk for me."

Jeffrey interrupts. "It's his middle name."

"Why don't you remember anything, Gabriel? Did Ryan say not to?"

"V told me. She told me I had to forget, because Clement would use it against me. I wouldn't know what I was saying."

"How did you forget?

"Locked them all away."

"In what? A box?"

Gabriel shakes his head. "No, better than that. Books. Locked books. Books are safe. Books are permanent. And when they're locked away, even better. You can't go where they are."

"What place is that?"

"I can't tell you. I didn't let Damon or Encausse know, and no one can know."

Chiang thinks for a moment. "Gabriel, one of the books was left out. You took it out because you know it's safe. You see it here, open? You are in what you see; you are in that part of your life now. Can you see that?"

Gabriel gets up to stare at an invisible book. Then he looks up. "Why did I open this?"

"You wanted a good memory, one to savor. One to make you feel happy. Tell me what you see. Where are you?"

Gabriel smiles. "Uh...West 86th Street. In front of the Barnes and Noble. It's where I got my cat, Archie. He's such a badass. See, the animal shelter people are here. They have the cats and kittens in the cages. My uncle Dominic, we were both going to get a cat. But he died and I decided to go ahead anyway, to have a cat with me in his apartment. I didn't want to be alone when I went through his stuff. You see him?"

Gabriel appears to be looking at something just below eye level. "Here he is. So tiny but a huge voice. He was trying to get my attention, sticking his little paws through the cage. He was insistent. There couldn't be any other choice. As soon as he was home with me, even just a tiny thing, he was *tearing up* the place. He caught a mouse the next night and left it on my bed."

Gabriel laughs suddenly, shocking all of them. Chiang looks at Jeffrey, who nods. "I remember that. He told me."

Chiang turns back to Gabriel. "You can remember Archie now. It's safe. How about anyone else in your life?"

Gabriel appears to be thinking. "I don't...I don't know. They're still in the books."

"Except for this one." Chiang points to empty space on Gabriel's other side. "You just opened that book."

"Oh, I must of have forgotten."

"This is someone you know, Gabriel. Someone you care about. You want to be reminded of this person. Who's in the book, Gabriel?"

Gabriel's eyes get wider. "Joel. He's everything to me."

Joel feels his eyes water. Jeffrey puts his hand on Joel's back.

Chiang continues, "You did well, keeping Joel safe. Just like Archie, it's okay now to let the books stay open and remember everything. What do you see when you see Joel?"

"This Goth bar near NYU. I'm working on a case, and not having a lot of luck on it. But I see him there, and I feel like things are looking up when we see each other. He smiles at me. He's drawing, and I have to go over. I have to see what he's drawing, and talk to him. I know he feels the connection too. I ask him to create a painting for me. Bring it to my apartment. When he came over to my place with it, I didn't want him to leave."

Joel exhales silently. Chiang looks at him, and Joel nods.

"Okay, Gabriel. I want you to know that it's okay to keep the books out. You can start opening them, and allowing the memories to come back."

Gabriel shakes his head. "No. I have to protect everyone. Clement wanted to know about them. They all wanted to know, and I think they wanted to see if I could be forced to hurt people. They tried to pretend they *were* Joel and my mom. They tried to look like the pictures I had. "

"They are gone, Gabriel. You do not have to worry about them anymore. Joel and Archie and everyone else is safe from them."

"I can't do that. If I'm a protector, I can't put them in danger."

Chiang takes his hand. "Gabriel, listen to me. You opened the books. You told us about Archie and Joel, so you know it's safe."

"No. I can't take that risk. They have to go back to the safe place."

He and Chiang stare at each other, a test of wills.

"All right," Chiang says. "I going to let you sleep now. I want you to feel like you can go back to your safe place. No one knows about it, not even me. But it's important you have it."

He leads Gabriel back into sleep.

"Why did you stop?" Joel asks him.

"He was stressing. Imagine the conflict in his mind and what his first priority is."

Joel rubs his head. "To be stubborn and do things his own way."

"Yes, there's that. I want to think about how to continue the questions. We'll try again tomorrow. He's *there,* he just has to be convinced."

Some hours later, Joel checks on Gabriel in his room. Chiang has given Gabriel tea, and told him it was an herbal remedy. Gabriel believed that, and apparently feels better. He's flipping through the books in his father's shelves.

"Hi," Gabriel says. His eyes are friendly, maybe more.

He sounds better too.

"I'd like to talk to you. Chiang said this would help."

Gabriel closes *The Timothy Files* and indicates Joel should sit on the bed. "It's about Goddamn time."

"I can't imagine how you feel." Joel sits at the end of the bed, near Gabriel's chair. It's raining outside, and the rain provides a steady soundtrack.

Gabriel frowns at him. "I turn on the TV, I don't know if I like what I'm watching. I hear music, I have no idea if it's *my music.*"

"You have that book at home."

Gabriel leans forward. "At home. Who are we to each other?"

"We don't exactly live together, but you and I *are* together."

Gabriel stares at him, in his eyes, intensely. "Is that true? I guess that's why you're here. I'm not very good company. I've felt like shit as long as I can remember, which isn't much. I wanted to die every day, every hour. I still don't feel...right, just that I might be okay with living. But you're here."

"You've been through hell. You'd be here for me, you have been. You'll find out more about yourself." Joel takes out his phone. "I'm going to show you something."

He finds what he wants, then hands Gabriel the phone.

Gabriel breathes slowly. "That's you and me."

"Early in the year. We were going through your picture album, and I took this."

"I don't remember it, but it feels familiar."

Joel and Gabriel on Gabriel's sofa. Joel lying on Gabriel's chest, with Gabriel's arms around him. Joel had taken the photo, right before they took a trip to New Jersey that where Joel ended up confronting his parents.

Gabriel looks back and forth from the photo to Joel. "I wish I did remember. This looks..."

"It is. Whatever you're going to say. It's all that and more."

Gabriel starts to hand it back, and then on impulse, starts going through more pictures on the phone.

Joel gets up to look over his shoulder. Gabriel stares at photos of himself in his apartment. Pictures of him with Joel. With Veronica, Geneva, Mikki, Bob, Jason, Danny. With Archie of course. Archie sleeping on him, Gabriel holding Archie like a baby.

"That's Archie."

"My cat?"

"Yes."

Gabriel finally hands him back the phone. "Where is this?"

"New York. East Village. That's where you live."

"This isn't a trick. My father wouldn't trick me."

Joel shakes his head. "No. We're together."

Gabriel looks angry for a moment. "It's not fair that I can't...Can I ask you stuff?"

"Sure."

"Are we good together?"

"Hell yeah."

"I'm glad. It gives me something to...be positive about."

"I just want you to get better, baby."

Gabriel hugs himself. He's sweating again, but looking at Joel, as if he's trying to get beyond the pain when the last remnants of detox happen.

"Why don't you lie down? Don't try too hard right now."

"I want this blankness in my mind to stop."

"I know; you're stubborn under hypnosis and you're stubborn trying to come back."

"Joel, I want to know who you are. I want to know who I am, I want to feel like a *normal person.*"

Joel sees him trembling. "I'm going to see what I can give you, okay?"

"I can't stand this."

"Yes, you can, Gabriel. You've already come so far." Carefully, Joel slips his arms around Gabriel. Gabriel curls up against him.

Joel feels Gabriel's body shuddering. He's going through a bad moment. "I'm so sick..."

"I'll be with you."

∞

Chiang has Gabriel under again. He's pointed out that Gabriel has opened all the books, but Gabriel is reluctant to keep them open.

"You can start remembering your life, Gabriel. It's safe."

"He would have hurt them."

"I understand. You put them away so they wouldn't be hurt. It wasn't safe to be yourself. But now, you can. You did your job to protect them. You can come home."

"He was in my head. He walked around in my *head.*"

"I know. You did well in fighting him. You remembered your father, though. So you can do this."

"Uh, I knew, I knew my dad would be able to protect himself. He told me how to do it. He told me how to put things away."

"And you did that, because you trusted him. Right?"

"Yeah."

"He's here. Listen to him." Chiang nods at Jeffrey.

"Gabriel, you did just right. Just as I wanted you to do. It's okay now. I'm here to protect you, you don't have to worry anymore."

Gabriel has his eyes closed this time. "I'm scared. I have to keep the books safe."

"I know, but because I'm protecting you, it's okay. In fact, it's important. Gabriel, you want to protect and help people, like you were trained to do. Then you need to remember."

"I don't understand."

Jeffrey speaks in a strong but calm voice. "You need to remember your life to protect your friends. You need to remember them to help them. It's time, Gabriel."

Gabriel gets up and goes to the window again, as if he's looking for someone.

Jeffrey tries a different tactic. "Where is your safe place, Gabriel?"

"With my mom. I'm with my mom."

Chiang asks Jeffrey, "What might that mean?"

Jeffrey shakes his head. "His mom has passed." He raises his hands helplessly. "They were very close, together so much..."

Chiang says, "His voice sounds different. Gabriel, are you where your mother is now, or are you back in time?"

"Where she was. In our place. I was always safe. She watched over me."

"The library," Jeffrey says. "Kate was a librarian. She took him with her and he'd spend hours there. He feels safe around books."

"Makes sense." Chiang gets up and speaks to Gabriel. "Gabriel, you're in the library with your mother. She's watching over you while she's working, and you have your books nearby. With your memories."

Gabriel turns to him. "How do you know?"

"She said we could talk. Kate said it was okay for you to open the books now."

Gabriel's expression is doubtful. "I don't hear her saying anything. If I don't hear her, I don't say anything."

They take a break. Gabriel goes back to the sofa and closes his eyes.

Jeffrey smiles humorlessly. "Gabriel will be defiant no matter what. That's so him."

"It's who he is, taken to an extreme. Clement's work exacerbated it."

"Well, we could get a recording of Kate's voice that I may have somewhere, run it through a modulator and set up a track to prompt him. Or maybe he needs hospitalization."

Joel confronts Jeffrey, angry. "Not while I'm around. You'd give up on him? It's all about voices and who he trusts. You don't have his mom, but you have the owl. He trusts *her*."

"Take it easy, Joel. I'm just frustrated. You're talking about the owl he said he heard in that house?"

"It had Veronica's voice. Bring her down here."

"Why not call or Skype?"

"She wants to see him. Her and Danny. Maybe it will help. Jesus, why not?"

"Why not, indeed? We have to use the path his mind is taking; the Tao of his mind. Chiang walks over and touches Gabriel's shoulder. "Gabriel, I want to talk to you about V."

"V. Yes. I heard her voice again the other day."

"If she spoke to you, can you open the books?"

Gabriel's eyes move under his closed lids. "She would watch over me like Mom does. She protected me in the house."

"That's correct. She is going to be here soon."

∞

"They're here." Joel gets up and opens the door of the townhouse. Jeffrey and Geneva had gone to the train station to pick up Veronica and Danny. Trains seem safer than flights, but quicker than driving. Geneva leads them to the door, with Jeffrey checking behind them.

Veronica hugs Joel. Danny, although pensive, greets him as well.

"We didn't tell him you were coming."

Danny asks, "See what the surprise does?"

"Whatever works at this point."

It's around noon, and Gabriel is in the kitchen with Zest and Chiang. He's stubborn about eating as with anything else. He's sitting at a kitchen table ignoring a sandwich in front of him.

"I have friends of yours here," Joel tells him.

Danny walks over to Gabriel. "Hey man."

Gabriel stares at him. He tries hard, they can see that. "I know you from the picture Joel showed me. You're Danny Martinez. I just can't..."

"It's all right. I'm just glad to see you're okay." He pulls up a chair next to Gabriel.

"We've know each other a long time," Gabriel says, "...as I was told."

"Twenty-odd years. I can't believe I'm not in there." He touches Gabriel's head. Gabriel follows his movement with his eyes, studying Danny intensely. Then he looks over at Veronica. "I've seen your picture too, Veronica."

She comes over and puts her hand on his back "Gabriel, you're too much in your own head, as usual. We'll make you better."

His brow furrows at hearing her voice. "You're..."

"Veronica. Your partner. Your friend."

"No, I know you from...I've heard you somewhere else."

"Maybe you did." She sits on the other side of him. "Maybe I projected my thoughts."

They both have more photos to show him. Veronica even has a recording where Gabriel was interviewed on the Brian Lehrer show on WNYC. If hearing one's voice isn't disconcerting enough, not having any sense of how or when it happened or memory of the interview and the events that were the subject of the interview is mind-blowing.

Gabriel stays still, listening. His only comment is, "I digress a lot, don't I?"

"It's a part of what we love about you," Veronica laughs. "When you love someone, you even love the pain-in-the-ass parts."

After some time to settle in and preparing Veronica for the next step, Chiang takes Gabriel back to the living room to put him under again.

"Gabriel, you're back in the library with your locked books."

"Yes. My mom is working. She said I can keep my books back here."

"I have someone who wants to speak with you."

Gabriel opens his eyes.

Veronica is standing near him, at an angle to Chiang and Gabriel. "Gabriel, I'm here."

Now Gabriel is animated. He looks around expectantly. "You came back."

"Yes. I wanted you to know you aren't alone anymore. That you did the right thing when I spoke to you before."

Gabriel gets up and goes to the windows. "He really did lie. You told me Damon was lying."

"He did. His power is over. You're free. Free to be yourself. You don't have to hide away."

"This is all confusing..."

"I know, but it doesn't have to be anymore. Gabriel, you have books there. I know you were protecting your life and people in it. But Clement is gone. You were stronger than he was, and always have been. You can open those books. You need to prove that he cannot control you any more by letting yourself come back."

Gabriel sighs deeply.

Veronica says gently, "You can believe me, Gabriel. I know what's going on, and I've been there since the beginning."

"I know..." Gabriel starts crying. "I saw my mom. She was working, but now she's leaving. My mom is going away."

Veronica embraces him. "She's always with you. She knows you're strong enough to go home now. You know if your mom feels you're strong, you can come home."

Gabriel is seeing it, staring into space, and holds on to her. "I don't want her to leave."

Jeffrey has to step away, tears in his own eyes.

"She's in here," Veronica pats his chest. "It's okay, Gabriel. She wants to you to be with the people who love you."

Gabriel has a hard time stopping crying. It gets to everyone in the room, even Zest, who lights a cigarette.

"You see the books opening, Gabriel?"

Gabriel has gotten down to the carpet, hanging on Veronica. "Yes...I...it's so much."

Chiang gets down as well, and takes Gabriel through some of what he sees, at different times of his life. It's enough to feel that he's broken through.

Chiang leads Gabriel back to an easy chair, and into a deeper sleep. "Gabriel, you are safe now, and everyone is safe, and so you can take care of yourself now. You don't have to hide; you may come home. So you can remember what happened to you. You are stronger, and this will not hurt you. Sleep and let this process until you can wake up and be with us."

Gabriel rapidly calms down, and sleeps.

Chiang then tells everyone, "Give him a half-hour or so. Now that it's safe, it's going to come in a flood. He's going to remember everything, and that's going to be traumatic in a different way."

Jeffrey makes coffee, and chain smokes as Zest does. He picks up an album of photos to thumb through. While Joel is watching Gabriel sleep, he also notices Zest staring out the sliding glass doors of living room to the back yard. He seems very much out of sorts.

Gabriel is quiet for some time. Then he's suddenly restless and Joel hurries over and gets on his knees by the chair.

Gabriel opens his eyes and looks uncertain for a moment, then sees Joel. "Oh. Okay. I was having some kind of weird dream."

Joel sees immediately that Gabriel's expression is different. His eyes don't have that unfamiliarity anymore. As Gabriel rubs his head, Joel asks, "Are you all right, Gabriel?"

"Yeah, baby. Just I feel really weird, like all of my life was suddenly around me, like I was reading about it. Remember you were trying to help me put one of those albums together, and I couldn't figure out where to start...you look upset, Joel. Did I have one of *those* migraines again? I feel like I've been *out* out."

Joel exhales, smiling, and reaches over to put his hand on Gabriel's. "You remember what you were doing last?"

"Uh, wow. I feel kind of lost. I was planning to go somewhere, we needed to go somewhere..."

Then Gabriel suddenly realizes he's not in his apartment. He looks around and sees his father, and draws his breath in. "What? Where are we?"

Jeffrey walks up to him and says slowly, "This is my place in Bethesda. You haven't been here before, Gabriel."

They all watch him stare at his father, to try to process, to make sense, to find a mental anchor. "Yeah, we couldn't go home, because of Clement. Okay, did I pass out or something? I don't remember us driving here, even."

"Something like that."

Gabriel's trying to cover up his confusion. "I don't remember it. I guess this was a really bad headache." He starts to laugh, and then he suddenly turns in the chair to see Zest standing by the sliding glass doors. His being there confounds Gabriel. For a second he struggles to speak. "What...oh my *God.*"

Zest looks back at him, his expression shifting in empathy.

Gabriel stares at him in shock. And then something else comes over him. He's remembering.

"*What did he do,*" Gabriel whispers. "*What did he do to me?*"

"He tried," Zest responds. "He didn't succeed."

Gabriel runs his hands over his face and gets up. He walks over to the sliding glass door, opens it roughly, and leaves. The others watch him pace the boundaries of the backyard, barefoot, in the cold.

"He does that," Joel says.

Jeffrey nods. "I know. He used to do it as a kid. He worried over his mother because she was a bit nervous at times. I would take him on a perimeter walk, show him how to check things to make sure she was safe. He has to take action; he can't stay still."

Then Gabriel disappears around the corner of the house, and Joel gets up and goes after him.

Outside, Joel sees Gabriel on the sidewalk in front of Jeffrey's house. He's staring at the sky. It's very cold; in the thirties. Neither has a coat. Gabriel starts to shake, but doesn't otherwise seem to realize the cold. He stares at Joel. "When did--long has this been going on?"

"You were gone nearly two weeks. You've been here another two weeks."

Gabriel wipes away tears. "I put you away. I put you away because this man was *in my head,* and I didn't want them to find you and hurt you."

"I understand." Joel takes his hand. "You did what you needed to. You're back. All that matters."

"God, it's so weird now. I feel *every year* of my life. It's all dug out and in front of me. How did you handle this? Wait, did I see *Chiang* in there?"

"I called him down to help. We got you out of this place where Clement had you."

Danny comes out the front door, with one of Jeffrey's jackets. "Thanks," Gabriel says, and Danny embraces him. "Okay, am I in there now?"

"Yeah, man. You're here." They hold each other, but aren't alone for long when Geneva and Veronica come out, better dressed for the winter. They all hold each other.

Gabriel mutters, "Jor-El and the Council elders are still inside, huh?"

"You *would* say something like that," Danny chides. "But I'm glad to hear it."

They see Zest watching them from a living room window.

"Something's up with him," Joel says.

Gabriel starts shivering. "I saw his eyes. He's had the same thing happen." He reaches to take Joel's hand. "And I'm going to need to talk to him regarding what to do about it."

∞

PART THREE
IRKALLA

∞

FOURTEEN

From the YouTube Channel "Tom Paine Events," in a video entitled: Unknown Knowns: Martha Mitchell and Dorothy Hunt ♦ The Wild Cards

Transcript: "Martha Mitchell was the former wife of John Mitchell, who had been Attorney General under President Nixon and then ran Nixon's re-election campaign. Mitchell died of natural causes, but her unknown known is a metaphorical death--of reputation. When Mitchell became concerned during the early days of Watergate that her husband would be a scapegoat, she would routinely call reporters to complain of Nixon's abuse of power and corruption. Mitchell claimed at one point she was kidnapped and drugged to shut her up. The Nixon Administration portrayed her as a hysterical nutcase, a joke, and an alcoholic. Although the kidnapping claim could not be verified, her contentions regarding the Nixon Administration were.

"In psychology the "Martha Mitchell" effect is when a patient is mistakenly diagnosed as paranoid, when in fact the events claimed have actually occurred. Mitchell is not the only woman connected to Watergate to be involved in mystery. Dorothy Hunt, former CIA operative and the wife of Watergate break-in organizer (and former CIA operative) E. Howard Hunt, died in a plane crash after having agitated for financial support to take care of the Watergate defendants. Also aboard the plane was Michelle Clark, a journalist working on the Watergate story who Dorothy had met shortly before the flight, and two attorneys who were investigating John Mitchell in an anti-trust case. Watergate seems to have been a rather internecine affair. These deaths raise the question, which is easier to do prevent attention to someone speaking out--death or discrediting?"

∞

Saturday, November 26
Alphabet City, Avenue A, 7:00 am

THE BLACKNESS EVAPORATES. I can see light in my windows. I sit up and check my surroundings. My bed, my room, my cat. Okay. Everything is safe.

I get up and walk out the bedroom. In the living room, Zest is sitting in one of the easy chairs, smoking and reading *Les Miserables.* Okay. Everything is weird.

He's fully dressed in his usual three-piece suit. He looks up at me with a tiny smile. "Joel had some things to take care of. He called me."

"For babysitting?"

"He was insistent upon utilizing my skills."

Fair enough. I've been back home all of three days. I feel like it's a lifetime. Lazarus arising after a mystery school initiation.

I'm determined that I'm not going to let this fuck me up. But I can't help but be fucked up. I want coffee and I have to do it a new way. Using a pod machine, which usually I don't like for the waste, and bottled water, which usually I don't like for the waste. However, in using these I can be reasonably sure no one has tainted them with opiates or hallucinogens. Once I regained my memory, I had distress over eating or drinking anything anyone else touches. Joel immediately had bought two cases of bottled water which now sit ungainly on the kitchen counter. Archie jumps on top of them while I make coffee for myself and Zest.

Although babysitting, Zest keeps to a non-threatening distance. I'm in the habit right now of breaking down every space I'm in as to fighting distance. I know the space in the kitchen, dining area and living room in my head. I know the square feet, and the pacing distances. These no longer seem like rooms, but a series of spaces safe or cornered, each requiring a certain strategy.

Am I going to see my entire apartment, my life, that way?

I can feel remnants of pain in my shoulders from the hanging torture. I don't want to go to a doctor. I don't want to see my therapist. I don't know what to do.

"We need to talk," I tell Zest. Because I haven't since I've been back. Not seriously. Life is too intense for me. Everything I see raises memories, from the experience of having lived my life in full in a matter of hours. I'm just waiting for the intensity to lessen.

Zest nods, waiting for me to put the cup down and step back before he picks it up. "I'm good with that."

"What does Clement...what does he do, really?"

"He is a psyops specialist. He does work for the intelligence agencies but more for the Society. When I first started my work for the Society, some 'administrators,' let's call them, wanted to ensure I couldn't be broken easily. Clement himself had recruited me. They wanted a method of vetting a person, a form of interrogative torture. He was okay with that--that I'd be his subject. I remember him with a clipboard, deciding what to try next. Just as you describe, he has his methodology down to a ritual."

I hear in his casual tone the anger he has over his experience. I understand that anger.

"Did he try to play good cop with you, too?"

Zest drinks slowly, his eyes getting far away. "Yes. He had someone physically torture me, and he intervened. He said he could have them stop if I just went along with what they wanted. It was a trick, of course. He tried this several ways, standard psychology maneuver."

"Or standard sadist maneuver. Did he tell you, "I'm so sorry," every other minute?"

Zest pauses, looking at me. "This man was someone I thought was a mentor. Each time he said it, I hated him more."

"Word on that."

We spend some time in silence together, rather comfortably. Zest had once said, at a point in time when we helped each other under stress, that we were the same kind of professional. Not in the same profession, but the same kind of professional. Now we've shared a same experience, decades apart. At the hands of the same man. A rather unique bonding thing.

"Why are you here? I mean, I appreciate the interest you've had in me, and taking care of Veronica, and getting me out. I just don't see why overall. Is this still like in New Jersey?"

"I've been drawn into it. I'm not walking away. I made my choices."

"Joel had a discussion with me about you not long ago. He is concerned about you because he believes you want to leave the Society. But you can't leave the Society. He's under the impression you're going to kill yourself."

Zest smiles. "He cuts to the chase, doesn't he?"

"Yeah. He's very much bothered by the possibility."

"And you?"

"Of course, if that's your plan. My life is very much forefront in my mind as such. I realize I've come close to suicidal acts, but for very specific reasons and not with an inevitable sense of death. I always hope. I don't favor suicide unless it's an extreme circumstance and no other option exists."

"I understand that extreme option. I've seen it played out. I have not made that decision, to be honest with you. I don't have an option, and I've been sort of in a null sense of living. It's coming to the end of a road and meeting a brick wall, as I mentioned to you in June."

"Can you explain the circumstances to me? I'm interested."

Zest sits on one of the bar chairs. Archie jumps up and comes over to him. He scratches the cat idly.

"When I was recruited, I was a believer due to circumstances-- my upbringing, my social set. I wouldn't have had interest otherwise. I had no other frame of reference. I drank the Kool-Aid, so to speak. By the way, I met Jim Jones once. He was an early contact. And one of those extreme options.

"In any case, I had principles laid out for me that seemed logical. Then as time went on, because maybe I wasn't in a position to actually be in power, it became more of a job and less principled. Eventually, I spent a long time in a state of self-imposed numbness. Not denial--I knew what I was doing. By then, no other way of life was possible. By virtue of my work, I kept myself as anonymous as possible. But I couldn't escape."

"Ever? At any time?"

"It's not like the movies. There's no hiding place in the world. I still wanted to escape, and live without getting orders to hurt someone. Yet they will not let me do that. I know too much. A classic situation."

He gets a text. "That's Joel; checking up on you. How you both handle things made this easier, such as in Westchester."

"Simpler, not easier. Even a man like Nelson, sending him to his death was not easy. Just that Joel was more valuable to me than the guilt I had afterwards."

"I know this is not going to happen, but you don't need to have guilt over Nelson. You do not know half the things that man has done. He's on a level like Cody. Nonetheless, to further this thought, you were a catalyst for me. I found something in my mind--a sense of wrongness, distaste, loathing, to protect Nelson over you. I knew that he would not leave alive, and you would. It was better that you went my way. To try to take him out would have been suicide."

"And why am I so seductive to you?"

He smiles. "I see in you traits I had at one time. You have very honest eyes. When I threatened you, I saw those threats reflected back to me. And because of what I saw of you--I followed you before I contacted you--it was if I threatened myself. When you challenged me, it was if I was challenging myself. If you were a different person, you could be doing my job. Maybe better. Take those skills you have for compassion and turn them the other way--you would be a super-efficient destructive force. But--you would never do this. It's not in your DNA. You are my potential, in action."

"Very narcissistic of you."

"Narcissistic fantasies are all I have left." He shrugs.

I sit on the sofa with my coffee. I try reading, but it doesn't work right now. Instead I browse through one of my uncle's art books. Zest returns to Revolutionary War France and understanding how a desperate good man commits crimes.

The front door opens sometime later; Joel has come back. Without a word he comes over to me, searching for something wrong. Because it's Joel, I can't tell him that his tendency to come over and get close makes me nervous. I immediately tense inside.

"Everything is fine," Zest tells him.

Joel shrugs off his jacket and drapes it on the other easy chair. "Better be." He sits next to me on the sofa. Too close, but I don't know how to tell him. When I went through bad things before, holding him as close as I could was comforting.

But something is very wrong. This isn't PTSD. Danny makes me a little nervous getting close. Geneva, a little nervous. But not a problem. Veronica, no issues at all. In fact, she's the only person I can relax around. But with Joel there's something else. It's like there's an unconscious sense making me feel weird about him.

When he puts his hand on my arm, I want to scream inside. And I have to hide that. I don't want to see the hurt in his face--not after what he went through to get me here.

I can't respond and be affectionate, so I try to deflect. "Zest was just telling me about his life and how he can't disappear."

Zest smiles very faintly. His eyes darken with wryness. "You may think disappearing is easy. I almost have to put this in supernatural terms that might seem ridiculous. But it involves Clement."

"That wouldn't seem ridiculous at all. Not to me."

"I found out recently he imparted a message, a post-hypnotic suggestion during the 'initiation' process of Society members. No matter how much a person wants to leave the Society, if the person does, the Society can locate them and their cover or disguise, no matter how isolated. The post-hypnotic suggestion was for the apostate member to compulsively leave a trace of themselves. For the Society to find them. Each member has a different trace, but Clement could recognize and find it. He said we're helpless to do otherwise."

Zest's voice carries finality. No wonder he's considering suicide. He may or may not live in fear of being found out under normal circumstances, but to always live in fear that any action you take might unwittingly reveal yourself?

"That's part of the psyops, isn't it?" I say to him. To make you *think* that you have a tell, and then you put yourself in a situation where you will be found. Even if you don't want to. Even if what he said wasn't true."

"Perhaps it's a ruse, but I doubt it. He likes tinkering inside people's minds too much not to do it. In either case, we do nothing but second-guess ourselves, and that will lead back to them. In computer terms, it's their back door to us. The fact that he put this back door in my mind and made my existence a *fait accompli* makes me hate him more."

He sighs. "So, I enact the only autonomy I can under these circumstances. I will barricade myself somewhere in a measure of futility until I carry this out. You wouldn't be able to visit, so we better indulge in our terms of endearment now."

It takes me a moment to realize Zest is being humorous.

I counteract that. "Or, since you think you're going to be hunted like Jesse James, you could go out like Butch Cassidy instead. Go down in a blaze of glory."

Zest toys with his book, studying me. "What did you have in mind?"

"Taking them down. For good."

"Fuck," Joel says. "I knew it was leading to this."

He sounds distressed. I say quietly, "I don't have another option, either. Not after what

Clement did to me. Are you with me?"

"Of course I am."

Now I look at Zest. "With or without you."

"Is this revenge? I can help you find Clement. You can have your revenge against him. Your father is likely to act soon on that in any case."

"I'll handle my dad. This is my thing. Yeah, I could limit it to Clement. But he's more than just himself. He was setting me up to kill Jacobs and then myself. Like a Manchurian Candidate. Right?"

Zest's eyes change. "Yes. He had that plan ready. He was going to use Nelson, originally. And then you were on his radar, and he liked you. What he saw in you."

"Goddamn it. What the hell did he see in me?" I slam down my coffee cup harder than I intend, and it breaks. Joel immediately goes into cleanup mode, and I put up my hand to stop him. "I'll take care of it."

As I mop up what has spilled, I continue talking to Zest. "I encountered the Society by pure chance. I haven't gone back to work yet, nor even let anyone know I'm alive. In part, it's because I've realized that no matter how clean a life I live, so to speak, eventually I'll catch their ire again. I'm not going to live my life in fear of that. I know there has to be a way to take them down."

Zest walks closer to me, but he's focused, moving slowly. Contemplative. Joel has conversely become hyper. Cleaning up after my cleaning up, fiddling with things nervously.

I hold my hand out to Zest. "They took our minds out and *played* with them. Like rich kids taking toys out of a box and leaving them on the floor for the nanny. But they have a vulnerability. They *have* to. Do you want to accept what they did to you?"

He raises his eyebrows at me. "Well...I do not want to. You have a way of being persuasive, Gabriel. But you need to know more about them. Might I have another coffee?"

"Sure." I start setting it up. "Tell me what I need to know."

"Are you aware...I'm sure you're not...that there are two of them?"

"*Two* of them. Two Tertullian Societies." I shake my head. "You mean--two divisions. Two sectors."

"Yes. That's a good way to put it. There's the faction you ran up against with Jacobs--call them secular, for lack of a better word. They are more into politics and financial affairs. They are known informally as the Production Faction."

"Social Darwinists."

"I suppose. They claim publicly no Tertullian Society exists, not like the one in Pre-War Germany. Then there is the other faction who are known as the True Believers. You understand what that means?"

I feel like we should be whispering by candlelight. I put Zest's coffee down on the counter for him. "I think so. The Production Faction would be like what people think the Bilderbergers are. The True Believers are more occult-based. They probably still have rituals going back to their Nazi origins."

"That they do. Clement is very much an adherent to the rituals. I work mostly with the Production Faction. And have for some time. The True Believers do not often ask for help, but since nominally they are supposed to be cooperative, I move from group to group. Of course, since Clement recruited me, he believes that I am loyal to him."

"And you let him think that because it suits your purposes, right? Okay, I know when you have division, you have rivalries, jealousies, conflict. Standard in an ingroup/outgroup dichotomy, basic social psychology."

"Correct. Each division is supposed to be on the same side, adhering to the same principles...but each thinks the *other* is inferior."

"I can see that set-up. The Production Faction thinks the True Believers are wingnuts, right? And the Believers think the Secular group betrayed the original ideals."

Zest shrugs. "Your deduction is very accurate regarding the situation."

"Those who are apostates are always hated more than those who are nonbelievers. What do these True Believers really believe?"

"They do actually adhere to occult principles. Their lineage goes back to the turn of the Twentieth Century. Sects like OTO-- Ordo Templi Orientis, the Golden Dawn. Subverting the principles. Gabriel, you probably know that W.B. Yeats had an issue with Aleister Crowley being part of the Golden Dawn. Crowley went off and did his own set up with the OTO, created his own legend, crashed and burned. At the end of his life, he was making cash from selling charters of the OTO. And some saw that Crowley got somewhere doing his own thing, and so they did as well. Those were the people who eventually got close to Hitler before he was in politics."

"What's the endgame?"

"Controlling the world. Seriously. The True Believers consider themselves to be the heirs of the universe and all the power in it, destined to have control over lesser beings. They look for anything that reinforces that belief. Fascism, political or occult, lends itself to the idea of a striated society, of those who deserve and those who serve."

"Fine. So why does Clement want to kill Jacobs?"

"The other side of the coin is that the Production Faction has done nothing but look to find more ways to make money, and gain power. Pure capitalism. Oligarchy, but without real ideals. A man like Jacobs doesn't go home and engage in Hitler-worship, or try to create a rift in time and space to gain alchemical powers. His company is the alchemy, to turn anything possible into gold by any means possible. They are strictly cost/benefit analysis.

"Here's the important part about that. The few who are at the apex of the Society have no political beliefs other than what's expedient. However, they use ruthlessly what's available. And they do that because people further down, and people not in the Society, do have political and social beliefs that can be exploited. They don't know that it's done solely to earn someone else money."

Zest pauses to sip his coffee then continues. "As you might imagine, the Believers' numbers are far fewer than the Production Faction. The Production Faction pretty much goes about its work without thinking about the Believers unless necessary. Clement is on the Believers side. He's been their de facto leader."

"So we pit them against each other. When they fight from the inside, they bring each other down."

"You say that like it can be done."

"Of course, it can. Especially if you're with us. I very much get a sense that not only are you done with them, but you also have some strong feelings about being subjected to Clement's mind-laundering service."

"I'm not going to deny that."

And he moves closer to the counter, to stare into my eyes. I stare back into his.

I tell him, "We shared something that reasonably, the two of us should never have shared. We ideally should have never met each other. And yet it happened. This is how the universe works. And if no one stops them, they move on, like an impenetrable monolith."

"Yes."

I say, "You never told me who Jacobs was. But since I was supposed to kill him, I think I earned the right to know."

His head tilts. I feel something change in the air. A confluence of energies. As if the telluric currents in the stratosphere are converging over us.

"Jacobs is Lane Hunter. He and the other Society directors are holding a meeting in the near future. Clement has been very concerned about it."

Joel says, "Lane Hunter--the CEO of Mendel-Malthus? God, that figures. You gave us the information about them."

Zest raises his eyebrows. "You see what this involves now. The Society doesn't have to recruit hundreds of people. All it needs is its people to be well-placed, and willing to create an impenetrable nexus of contacts."

I smile. "That doesn't bother me. Satan himself wouldn't intimidate me right now. Hunter is just a man, a person, a vulnerability. And now a target. Trust me, they already have vulnerabilities."

He's on the precipice. I feel that, I feel him converting. He says, "Gabriel, I told you I was a dead man. Before I go, I can rid you of Clement, and have the satisfaction that he leaves the earth before I do."

"Zest...*Maxim,* you've been doing this so long you don't see the other way."

"Is that so?"

"You told Joel and Veronica you have information on the Society. Information that can seriously hurt them, expose them. I don't doubt that. You're too smart not to have this. Why can't you use it?"

"Let's say I did. I sent the information around to fifty newspapers and online outlets that would print it. Some of the more well-known "leaks" pages you'd think would print the information are actually Society fronts. Now, should the information be printed, the persons in charge of the Society--the directors--disappear. In order for the information to be effective, it has to result in something. Arrests, imprisonment. You have to take them *all* out, Clement included, or they go underground and recoup."

"Then that's what we have to do. You said that the directors are holding a meeting."

"January first."

"And you said that Clement is concerned about this meeting. He can show up, then. It's his chance to take them out--or so he'll think."

"He's too nervous to do that. He's underground now, and won't leave for some time. He's probably devastated that Cognoscenti doesn't work."

"Not if you tell him it *does* work. Not if you tell him I came to you because I have no idea what happened to me, but I got out of the clutches of who took me out of Spotsylvania, and I want to help my BFF Damon. You know he'll believe it."

Zest stares at me a long time, while behind me Joel fidgets nervously.

"You want to help him out," Zest says slowly.

"By killing Jacobs for him. Kill all of them. He'd like that, right?"

"He would," Zest searches for his pack of cigarettes. "And the information?"

"Ah, that's the genius of this." I start pacing the apartment. "People are agitating over what scraps of conspiracy they're getting now from Tom Paine. Let them eat cake--for Paine to release the real good stuff--your information."

Zest inhales. "And you can arrange with Paine to coordinate this."

"I can." I smile at him and spread my hands. "He and I are simpatico." Joel's mouth falls open, staring at me. But what's the point of pretense now?

Zest frowns, starts to smile, and then laughs. It's the first time I've ever heard him laugh out loud. "I positively *commend* you. What have you been using for the information you have thus far...no, I can guess. Mr. Varney must have given you some leads."

"May he rest in peace. He deserves that much."

"You make quite a case, Gabriel."

"I'm trying to be seductive to you. Maxim, what I've told you already will get me killed. Either faction would do so, and call you to do it. If I'm willing to risk this, can you? Instead of hiding in a remote castle and killing yourself? You literally have nothing to lose in going in with me."

Zest smiles, and I smile with him. An odd moment we share. "Then I'm with you. It is a way of bringing this to a close in an honorable fashion, at least for myself."

His voice is subdued. Even Joel, who is highly agitated, is quiet. This seems befitting for a moment in which we should be slitting our wrists to sign something in blood.

Zest goes into professional mode. "We should think about next steps."

"And loose ends. I want to follow up on Mesereau. He had a photo of a building and a key. He had to have a good reason to have those. What is the story with him?"

"He is--or was--with the Production Faction. He seems to have been genuinely concerned over Clement and planning to expose him, perhaps more."

I've gotten my phone back, and I now check my photos of Mesereau's secret space, and the photos I took of the plans in the Institute--of the Foundation. "It matches."

Joel and Zest compare the two, and agree.

Zest says, "The January first meeting is at the Foundation. The building is closed for renovations, so to speak. Clement is not invited, because he is the subject."

"Uh-oh," Joel says. "Someone's going to get more than a warning note on his desk."

"I'm involved with the meeting because I'm the instrument of termination, to follow up on Joel's *bon mot.* However, Clement is not stupid, and he suspects that something more is going on in that meeting. "

I feel recharged with purpose. "I see a chance to create a real comedy of errors with who thinks who is going to show up. All we need is *Yakety-Sax* in the background. I believe this key works something in the building, so let's start there."

"Since it's closed, we can get in and find out easily. Under the cover of darkness is best. Are you up for it tomorrow night?"

"It's been a while since I've illegally entered a place. Seems like I need to get on the bicycle again."

∞

We agree that Zest will pick me up around 11 the next night. I'd prefer we be alone. But Joel insists on coming. For his safety, I in turn insist that he limit himself to staying in Zest's car and watching the outside to warn us.

Later on that night, I've gone to bed. Joel gets in with me, and holds me. I was dozing, but the presence of his body wakes me up. Naturally since I've been back he's been sleeping with me.

My body and mind have been kind about nightmares. Instead of reliving the house, I just filter through memories again. Maybe a little warped, maybe with people asking strange questions, but livable.

I should be glad he's with me; of course I'm reminded of him in everything, of all times we had. Maybe that's the problem. Not to use a comparison with Veronica again, but she and I only had two disagreements in ten years. With Joel, I've agonized over and over.

Yeah, but you had bad fights with Danny, too. Several.

I wasn't in love with Danny.

Joel isn't just going to sleep. His hands hold on to my shoulders and back; knead on me gently like a cat. "How are you feeling...?"

I realize what he's asking. "Um..."

"I mean...I don't know what I mean. I don't know how to ask tactfully. Do you need more time? Is there anything I can do?"

"Bear with me. I need time to feel right again."

"Something's off, though. You try to hide it, but I know. You try really hard to hide it. Like you tried last year to hide that you were attracted to me. This is like you're hiding that you're *repulsed* by me."

That suddenly makes me want to cry. "Joel, don't read into it. Things will get better. You know I love you."

His voice is low and gritty. "I almost believe it." Then he gets even lower. "Maybe Veronica should be here instead."

I sigh. "You know, your sarcasm is not helpful. I don't want to pull the card of what I went through--but I will. I have no idea what's going on in my mind and I'm just trying to feel sane."

"Okay. I know. I'm not being fair to you. It's too early to try...for intimacy. I just wanted to see you look at me and not be scared by what you see."

A few beats go by, accentuated by our breathing.

"I can't--I don't know what's wrong. It's not you. I'm sorry about it. I don't want to be this way. I'll go see Chiang. Maybe it will just go away. You haven't done anything wrong; I owe you my life more than once. Right now, I want you to hold me." Although everything I say is true, the last part I have to put more effort into. I really want to have space. I really want to be alone, just me and Archie, but I have to fight that.

"Are you sure?" His voice sounds hopeful.

"Yes. Baby, just hold me."

He slips his arms around me tighter. What disturbs me is that I feel like I did with Alex when I was ready to leave him, but couldn't tell him. Except a little worse--as Joel said, afraid. It doesn't make any sense. I'm angry about it, I'm sad about it. It's why I have to fight it. Fight it.

∞

Sunday, November 27
10:00 pm

On the way from Alphabet City to the Upper West Side, we consider the mystery of Mesereau.

I say to Zest, "He keeps this key and this picture, and the list of the people he's familiar with in the Society. Why?"

"Mesereau was speaking to Mr. Barclay. I know that much from Clement. Clement was watching Mesereau's meetings with Mr. Barclay. If something happened, perhaps Mesereau hoped Mr. Barclay would find what you found and put things together."

"But he bugged out instead. Got extra paranoid, maybe. Or thought he was protecting someone. Alex never found this stuff, or he would have been pestering me to check it out."

Zest glances at me while he's driving. In the shadows of the car, he looks younger. I turn to face him and ask, "How did you get into this?"

I don't think he's going to answer, but he does. "I was born in England, but mostly raised in New Zealand. My father was a diplomat. We had a good life, but I was always an outsider. It's on the tongue--you don't talk like others do and they ensure you know you're not one of them. And I didn't care. I was smart and school bored me. I spent my time playing games with a few people--role-playing games. But it was being an outsider that had the most effect, for a few reasons. Since this was the Seventies in a conservative culture, even more so. Like you and Joel."

"Like us how?"

He glances over again. "Were you out in high school?"

Joel and I are both surprised, although more for the fact Zest is a difficult person to imagine being sexual. "Oh. Okay."

"Unthinkable for a diplomat's son. Anyway, somebody heard of me due to my prowess in gaming. I think some RPG groups were used as a testing ground for the Society. I used to float through several--I had no loyalty. I was my own person by 17. I happened to be in England and I met Clement. He's a few years older than I. He asked my advice about working on a strategy in the games. It turns out he didn't really play them. He was playing me. He introduced me to his mentor, a man named Henry Helms. Helms had started the mind-control experiments Clement continued.

"Clement pushed the outsider angle to me, telling me I could make my own role by being someone my betters had to turn to. "At tea," he said, "they'll always have you drink from the cheaper porcelain. You don't have to cater to them if you step outside of the hierarchy. Use your talents." I guess...it just grew from there."

"And you went through the same thing I did."

"A version of it. It was a loyalty test and loyalty ritual. Only to Clement and Helms. They were going to work in DC, doing some projects for American intelligence--but really for the Society. I went along. I told my father I was going to make contacts with the State Department in DC, but I never did. After undergoing the initiation in Spotsylvania, I never really saw him again."

His expression is unreadable. He is not a man to whom one reaches out and says *I'm so sorry*, or tries to give a comforting touch. Somehow, I understand more about why he said I was like him but with a different destiny.

The Foundation is off Park Avenue, in the Sixties. It is in a three-story building with a solid black granite front and the name emblazoned on the flag over the door. The building has its own little private lot in back, accessed through a common alleyway.

Joel reluctantly remains in the car as Zest and I go to the back door. Zest, of course, has the keys to get in. "The security cameras are off," he says. "There's no real replacement for Nelson as of yet. Things are in flux."

The back area where we enter is a storage-cum-kitchen. The dining room is in front of it. I've been there before when I went to interview Ethan Nelson. Zest has his own set of plans on a tablet.

"You see there's a basement. It's a storage area."

I have my own photographs. "The ones I have include a sub-basement. And what are supposed to be blocked-off passageways."

"Let's go see."

Zest leads me to the back stairs which wind down like a wooden spiral, supported with black iron. He says conversationally, "A rumor I heard was this building was used to hide persons on the run, or important objects, even before it was officially the Foundation."

"What kind of objects?"

"Some of the scrolls in the caves at Qumran. They weren't all sold to scholars or burned for fuel."

"Connected to the actual Tertullian, the Church father?"

"Oh, he was supposed to be a vampire, living for centuries. I'm not kidding. I'm sure Damon half-believes this."

"You mentioned Clement is underground. Did you mean that literally?"

"Yes. I know where he is hiding. He has a safe place in the city. I'll go see him soon."

Zest moves around the fairly clean basement. It has what you expect. Supplies, utilities. I walk around to, going by the faint markings in my photo.

"Here." I push at a wall. It pops open, showing a corridor. It's very short, running parallel to the back wall. It has three doors lined up neatly. Holding up his flashlight, Zest compares my key to each door. It fits the one on the far left.

The room is set up like a dorm room dream. A small futon, a few kitchen appliances. And a man. It's Mesereau, moving away from a wall--almost as if he had come through the wall. He's holding a laptop. He nearly drops it seeing us.

"Oh, Jesus."

∞

FIFTEEN

From the <u>Tom Paine Events Channel</u> on YouTube, in a video entitled:
Unknown Knowns: Dag Hammarskjold ♦ The Diplomat

Transcript: "Hammarskjold was a UN Secretary-General who died in office in 1961, in a plane crash. Hammarskjold was on his way to negotiate a peace treaty between what was then Rhodesia and the Democratic Republic of the Congo. The plane crash immediately sparked rumors, continuing to this day, that the plane was actually shot down. Hammarskjold's intent and actions conflicted with European mining interests in the area. Some witnesses, interviewed by the Guardian UK, said a second plane had been shooting at the airliner Hammarskjold was on just before it went down. The NSA has some information from radio transmissions but will not turn over to the UN, which is still investigating the crash, due to national security. Really? That raises the question of what national security of fifty years ago prevents answering a simple question--was another plane in the sky?"

∞

Sunday, November 27, continued.

MESEREAU RECOGNIZES ZEST. And I can imagine what he thinks--that he's about to be killed.

Zest is drawing his gun. Mesereau throws the laptop at him, and then charges us to get out the room. I block him and we end up on the ground. He's bigger than I, but I don't have a problem keeping him down. I am concerned that he will do something crazy from panic.

"Just take it easy. I'm not going to hurt you. He's not going to hurt you."

"Go fuck yourselves." He tries to spit on me. I'm not fond of that, but shift position to hold his head down. When he tries to bite me, I dig into some sensitive areas and wrestle his body around to be face down.

Zest does a quick reconnaissance of the room and finds a gun under the futon pillow.

Mesereau is breathing hard. I tell him, "Calm down. I said we're not here to kill you."

"I know who *you* are. You're not part of them. Do you know who that man is?"

"Yes. We need to talk."

Mesereau laughs. "I have nothing to say. Do what you came to do."

"I think you do have much to say." Zest pulls up a chair and looks down at him. "I'd like to speak to you at an even level, but I'm afraid right now that can't be done. I'm not here to harm you. How did you come to have the information about this building?"

Mesereau tries to twist his head to look at me. "You caught Wes Darrell, didn't you?"

"Yeah. You know him?"

"Yes. He and I...were working together."

"You and Darrell were both in on the document scheme?"

"That was part of it."

I think for a minute. "What was Nelson's part in this?"

Mesereau snorts. "I don't want to talk about him."

"I think you should talk about him."

"I don't care what you think."

"It does not need to be this way," Zest interjects. "Just tell us. I don't care what you did. If I wanted to kill you, I would have already. You know that."

Mesereau hesitates, then continues. "The whole scheme was Nelson's idea. He had some business going on with smuggling art. Even making forgeries. He stored stuff here until he could get it out. Documents were part of the whole thing. He approached me and Wes separately. I was in a bad way and he knew. Once we were in, he found ways to extort our help. Then he was killed. I heard you were behind that." He looks up at Zest.

"Go on." Zest crosses his legs, lighting a cigarette.

"Wes and I kept on working the scam after Nelson died. Wes was erratic; he didn't do it as well as Nelson could. I knew if the Society found out what I was doing we'd be taken out."

I ask him, "Why would they care about documents that have nothing to do with them?"

"Well, anything illegal that was unauthorized that could draw attention to them, for one. But also, we were forging art and stealing art that was being funneled through the Foundation. Nelson was a psycho; nothing bothered him. Wes was a nervous man. Maybe he jumped, maybe someone pushed him out. But I could see the writing on the wall even before Wes lost it. I thought maybe Barclay could help. I played out my story to him. He seemed sincere. Then Wes was dead and I was just scared."

He takes a deep breath. "People don't know about these rooms. Just Nelson and I. When things went bad, I decided to hide out here. Hiding in plain sight. Like anyone else, I have my financial preparations, and I could leave the country. But they're looking for that, so I wanted to lay low until I could safely get out."

"This is hotel stuff," I say, looking at the furniture and embossed objects in the room. "That carafe is from the Hotel Soliel. How did you get it here? That place is a few blocks away. Do you go outside?"

"There's more than just these rooms. There are passages. Nelson used them to move the art out to his own place."

"Passages to the hotel?"

"Yeah, for one." Mesereau sighs then. I can feel him trembling, straining against my grip. I feel guilty, knowing that feeling.

"Gabriel, let him up and shut the door."

I do so. Mesereau sits up slowly. He asks Zest, "Did you do to Darrell what you had Clement do to Nelson?"

Zest glances at me. "No. I had nothing to do with Darrell's death. I do not believe Clement did either."

Zest turns back to Mesereau. "I have a suggestion. You don't have much alternative. Eventually Clement will find you, or Jacobs will. Clement has a way of finding the Society's *relapsi*. You underwent a sort of ritual with Clement, correct? While that was going on, he implanted a post-hypnotic suggestion to have you trip yourself up and reveal yourself. You haven't done it yet, but when you go elsewhere it's a matter of time."

"He would, that bastard. So what's the suggestion?"

"I kill you. It will look like I did, anyway. Jacobs will be pleased to hear about it. Clement will be pleased to hear about it. It helps me, for my purposes. It will help you because you'll be gone and they won't look for you."

Mesereau gets up and sits on his bunk bed. "You're going against *them*? Jacobs? You're crazy." He looks at me. "You too."

I give him a wry look. "Like you aren't? You were giving all this information to Alex Barclay."

"I tried that as an honorable shot at a way out. Until I found out he was *with* them."

And time stands still, just like that.

"What?" My voice doesn't sound right. It sounds off-key, like a bad note on brass.

He frowns. "You didn't know that? I didn't either. I thought he was an investigative reporter, editor whatever. And then I saw him and Clement together."

I get up and walk over towards Mesereau without even feeling what I'm doing. I get close to Mesereau and take hold of his arms. "What are you talking about--that he's *with them*?"

"What's *your* problem? Oh, wait, you were involved with him. He told me a few months ago he was trying to get his boyfriend to help me. That was you; he showed me stories about you."

I shake my head. "You saw Alex and Clement together. You saw them--*like they knew each other.* Not that Alex may have been interviewing him or something, or undercover."

"No way." Mesereau shakes his head. "I got close to them and listened. I risked my life, maybe. But when I heard them talking, that's when I bugged out. How stupid is that--I'm telling the secrets of the Society to one of that crazy man Clement's protégés..."

"Encausse. Was that the name he used?"

"That's right--he's Encausse. I didn't know that, but I was trying to find out who Encausse was. See, I was going to show Barclay the set-up here for the story. If he was willing, we'd hide out and he could see Jacobs come here. Jesus, you really didn't know...?"

I let go of Mesereau and look over at Zest. "Did you know?"

He's already shaking his head. "No. I told you Clement has been recruiting people outside the Production Faction's circle, for his own purposes. He told me Mesereau was meeting with Barclay. He didn't see fit to explain who Barclay was."

Mesereau says, "It was pure chance I saw them. I was looking for Barclay because I was thinking of getting out of town and wanted to see if he could help. I didn't call him because I don't trust phones. I waited outside the *Standard,* and followed him downtown. I was going to just wait for a good moment to brace him. And then he goes into a bar on Delancey and meets Clement. You could tell they knew each other--and were friendly, almost affectionate."

I take a deep breath and try not to shake visibly. "He--Alex-- told me you knew Clement as an intelligence analyst named Comstock, and you were afraid he was on to you. He wanted me to tap 'Comstock's' apartment. I found out that Comstock was Clement on my own. Is any of what he said about you true?"

"No. And understand I thought Barclay was the real deal from what he reported in war zones. It seemed like good stuff--not the usual propaganda. I approached him and said I wanted to expose the Society. I knew who Clement was already, of course. The fact he was suddenly around my office wasn't entirely unusual, but I took it as a sign to move things along. Barclay arranged for me to meet this guy, Cavendish, in a bar late last year. He was supposed to be from the Office of Government Accountability, and investigating Comstock. Cavendish tells me he's afraid for his life."

Zest nods. "I was there. Watching you at Clement's request."

I ask Zest, "You are absolutely sure you didn't know about Alex?"

"Mr. Barclay was not present at any of those meetings. If I had found that out, I would have told you. It's something you'd need to know."

"Clearly."

I step back and zone out for a minute. Zest then begins making arrangements with Mesereau about the fake death. Mesereau doesn't have much of choice, so he agrees. The set-up needs to be done as soon as possible, as Clement is looking for him.

Clement and his protégé.

We go back upstairs to the kitchen, and Zest calls for a couple of his people to meet him with some equipment. Then we leave the building to go to rural Westchester. Zest, Mesereau, me and Joel in Zest's car. Zest has to explain where we're going and why to Joel, because I can't talk. Mesereau and I are both in a funk. But his is ending soon.

At a specific isolated location--an empty parking lot of a deserted building, Zest sets up the scene with Mesereau using some good squibs. The fake killing looks good, and it's on video. He then helps Mesereau clean up while we wait for Zest's people to come by with another car.

I walk over to a bank of trees. My head is still spinning. I feel like I've lost feeling in my legs. Joel comes up to me. "What's wrong, Gabriel?"

What's wrong...We're in a parking lot of an abandoned building, faking the death of a runaway member of an evil secret society, set up by the rogue troubleshooter of that same agency, in order to bring it down. Oh, and the man I was involved with--who said he loved me at one time--is part of this Goddamned Society.

I search my memory. Every word, every gesture that could have told me something. And there's nothing. He was seamless. I thought he was a sensitive and caring man, and then later, a supercilious snob who just didn't get it. My apologies, Alex. You are deeper than I perceived.

The words don't come to me, though, to answer Joel's question.

Zest is suddenly there and puts his hand on my shoulder. "I've arranged for a car. I'm taking Mesereau somewhere safe. I'll be back in the morning. We need to visit Mr. Chiang. To see if you can remember anything about that--what you might have been told."

It hits me a second time. While I was being tortured and mind-fucked, Alex was there. Alex was *helping*.

"He said--Clement, I mean--he said he was sorry over what Encausse told me. And I can't remember what he told me. What the fuck?"

"Gabriel, this will be taken care of. Joel, you need to look after him. Gabriel has had a rather unpleasant revelation."

I walk away for a moment to be by myself. The car arrives for them. Joel is going to drive Zest's car back to Manhattan.

Zest comes to where I'm standing staring into space. "You'll be all right for the time being?"

"No. But it doesn't matter right now. What did you do with Nelson and Clement--that Mesereau was talking about?"

Zest doesn't hesitate to answer. He speaks flatly. "Before Nelson was to be found--officially, I needed to know if he really had information and evidence on the Society as he had threatened Jacobs with."

"Yeah, I remember him telling me he did."

"As a matter of expediency, Clement worked on him to get the information."

"Tortured him, you mean."

Zest nods. "And the information...I held on to it. It's part of what I told you about."

I shake my head. No time to be sorting out moral niceties at the moment. Zest walks away to talk to Joel. While they talk I search in Zest's car, going through Joel's stuff until I can find one of his awful clove cigarettes.

Zest leaves with Mesereau, and Joel comes up as I light the cigarette. He says, "Hey, baby. Let's go back now."

His tone is quiet. I get in the passenger seat, clutching the pack of Kleveks. As Joel starts the car, he strangely doesn't get after me for smoking. I just see him watching me pensively.

Zest must have told him. Doing me the favor, since I have no idea how to say it. Without looking at Joel, I feel him trying to search for what to say. Finally, he comes up with, "I'm sorry about it, Gabriel."

"You don't have to be. You weren't stupid, I was."

"Don't do that. There's nothing that was your fault, okay?"

"Somehow you knew, though. You traced it back to him."

Joel turns his voice practical. "No, I just thought he was reckless and still hung up on you. I didn't think he was a Sith Lord. Baby, you got hustled. It happens. It happened to me enough. Not on such a grand scale, but whatever. Now it's just a question of whether I just beat the shit out of him, or kick the shit out of him first."

For some reason, maybe how he says it, it makes me laugh. That eases the tension between us. Joel doesn't say, *I told you so,* doesn't tell me I was an idiot not only for listening to Alex, but trying to help him when his intention was to serve me up to his master. But I don't want to think about that now. I'm putting that off, because there's a larger question.

"He said something to me when I was there being tortured. I can't remember it. The one thing I can't remember from that time. That can't be accidental."

"Remembering it, or what he said?"

"What he said. If I don't remember, he must have told me not to."

He glances at me as we get into the Bronx. "That's pretty insidious."

"And why I need to find out."

∞

Monday, November 28
Chinatown, Canal Street, 8:17 am

The next morning I'm in turmoil, having not slept much. Zest has come back, and I'm barely dressed before leaving with him to head down to Chiang's studio. I haven't called ahead because I don't think to. I just go up to Chiang's studio door and ring the bell.

Chiang opens a minute later. "*Xuéshēng,* I have others present."

He calls me *student* to remind me I'm out of place. I don't care but I have to care. I take a deep breath. "It's important....*Shifu.*"

Chiang doesn't spend a long time sizing up the situation. "Quietly. You'll wait in here."

He takes us in. The part of the studio for training is partitioned off by a large blue curtain. He leads us to a side room with chairs and a table. Everything is whitewashed, very stark except for a bright green mandala painted on one wall. The Zen sandbox I'm familiar with is in a corner.

Chiang shuts the door. We wait another twenty minutes or so. I stare at the mandala. "Why did Alex want me to tap Clement's place, when he was Clement's ally?"

"I would guess to have a predetermined conversation you would record. One with the purpose of convincing you, or Mr. Mesereau, or both of you of something."

"But I didn't want to do it--tap his place. Alex got mad when I wouldn't, and when I followed Mesereau. That at least makes sense now."

"Mr. Mesereau told Mr. Barclay about the Foundation, and evidently about the meeting. No doubt Clement found this threatening. It's probably why he wanted you to kill Jacobs right away instead of a long-term plan."

Chiang finally opens the door. "You're disruptive inside, like a volcano. What has come up?"

I look him straight on. "I told you last year about Alex Barclay."

"Yes. That was when you realized you were meant to be with Joel and you needed to end your relationship with Mr. Barclay."

"It turns out...Alex is part of this organization. The Society. He set me up. From the start, I guess."

Chiang's pupils widen as he contemplates me. "The fire is here again, and you are already a person who has to be careful of fire. Betrayal is a fire. It burns so much that it takes the oxygen out of the room."

"I hear what you're saying. I feel that burning. I have no feelings for him, but the thought that he was manipulating me like a game piece..."

"Are you considering revenge?"

"I don't know. I guess I'm not at that place. I want to out-maneuver him. I need to know what he did to me."

"He was there? In Virginia?"

Zest says, "We believe he was. Mr. Barclay is Encausse, Clement's protégé. Gabriel has difficulty accessing in his mind whatever may have happened, whatever may have been said. Perhaps there's a way to unlock this?"

"Let's see."

We go back in the studio, and Chiang takes time to prepare, making the scene as pleasant as possible. Chiang has a larger metronome, with intricate symbols carved in it. Joel would love those symbols...

"One last thing."

"What is it, *Xuéshēng?*"

"Something's happened in my mind about Joel. I don't know if it's connected to Alex or not, but it's not normal. Maybe it's a suggestion, an association. It's making me withdraw from him, almost like I can't stand to have him around. I want this to end."

"If we can find it, we might eradicate it."

"If we don't, I need to fight it."

"Fighting is what you do."

I'm wary of being unconscious while someone is in my mind. Chiang does a method of hypnosis where I'm both under and aware. It's very odd, as I talk from some part of my mind without thought or effort, but safe because I can see what's going on.

"Why are you having difficulty seeing Alex Barclay in the house in Virginia?"

"It's...special. A special situation. He was only there once. Clement thought he would be too disruptive to be there all the time."

"Why so?"

"Because of what he said to me. What Alex said to me. I can't hear him. I can't see him. I feel him there, and that I'm...glad he's there. And confused, like something happened I didn't understand."

"Were you Gabriel or Ryan?"

"Ryan. Clement is talking. I can hear him."

"What does *Clement* say? Can you remember?"

"Yes. He said, *this is a friend of mine. You will protect him as you protect me.*"

"What next? What does he say to Barclay?"

"Clement says, "It all worked. *All the patterns were sorted by Cognoscenti until finding the right match for him. Then it was a matter of going over his life until we found the fundamental core of his being. To protect. He's protecting me.* And then, *He's very cautious. Was Ross cautious? I suspect Ryan has aggravated characteristics of Ross's traits. He's protecting me from dangerous knowledge.*"

Zest's voice. "They were asking about what you found."

"In Mesereau's house. That's right. He says, *Listen to the message, Ryan. I'm adding to the message. You love him.*"

Inside I feel a wave of revulsion.

"Relax, Gabriel. Separate yourself. Just say what Clement told you."

"*Look at him, Ryan. You're glad to see him. You love him. He was in danger, but you helped get him out of it.* Then he says to Alex, *He believes I'm his dearest friend, so my words can be trusted. Also, he's using some of his former self--emotions, memories, experiences--just reconstructed to the reality of who he is now. His mind is searching for something to make sense. On some level he remembers you and whatever, uh, you shared. So it's easier to turn it positive. He may also project what he feels about that other man he was involved with. That man isn't here, but since you are, you must the proper recipient for his feelings. It's how his mind copes.*"

"And then what happens?"

"I think that Alex...asks me something. I feel like he puts his hands on me. Clement says, *I have an idea. Let me get some pictures.* He leaves and comes back. He says, *you shouldn't talk to him about anything other than what's prescribed.*"

"Alex said something to you while Clement was out of the room."

"Yes, I don't know..."

"Personal, perhaps? About Joel?"

"I hear Joel's name, and I don't know who he means."

"What about when Clement comes back?"

I go through what I can. Clement showing me a map. Asking about Veronica. I hear him talking about Kent Varney. *If only I knew to put Zest on him then. Now we know something even Jacobs doesn't know.* And then Clement asking Alex, *You want to leave him this way? You know, once Jacobs and the others are taken care of, you can do what you want with him. I thought one of the reasons you were going to take him to Europe in the first place was that you wanted him with you.*

"Then to me--*He was a little rough with you. I'm sorry.* He's sorry, of course. He's sorry about everything. *He's still coming along. He's my friend, and yours too.*"

A pause in the proceedings.

"Gabriel, you can't remember what Alex said. But you remember that he told you not to remember. He told Ryan."

"Yes. Ryan wanted to put it somewhere safe. He was confused."

"Somewhere safe. Was this a library, Gabriel?"

"Yes. He said it could be archived until we need it."

"Can you go to this library?"

"It...it's not a place I can get to."

"Is it the library where your mother worked?"

"No...although I see her there. And Joel. But it's not really them. I see glass cases. Things on the wall. I know this place, but he knows this place too. Alex. He knows..."

I can feel my eyes widen. "The library at the *Herald-Standard*."

"They have one?" This from Zest.

"Yes. An archive. A large collection of books. Rare books and other kinds. Alex showed me around when we took the job. He took me there to tell me that Mesereau had disappeared."

"Can you go there now? Be in the library now. Look around."

"Uh...I just see all these fake things. My mom who isn't my mom. Joel who isn't Joel. It's fake. I can't see what is happening there."

"Gabriel, did he tell you anything about Joel?"

"Yes, but I don't know who Joel is when he tells me."

"Remember this. What Alex told you was fake. You have nothing to fear from Joel, or reason to be troubled with him. If that feeling comes up, turn it on Alex instead."

Chang takes me out of the trance. I take a couple minutes to absorb what my mind has dug up.

Chiang says, "You need to go to that library."

"Do I? Right now no one knows I'm alive. I suppose I need to think about how to do that."

∞

Thursday, December 1
9:30 am, Houston Street

My friends outside of Geneva, Veronica and Danny know I'm safe but not any details. I have a few close friends--Michaela, Jim, Bob, Jason. Walter, I guess, and Herrmann. More acquaintances who don't need to know what's going on. Even Nic doesn't need to know. Halo is on the impulsive side of youth, so he only knows I'm okay.

Chris is Joel's friend. Nonetheless, I can trust zim. I did earlier this year in the Cody case, and ze lived up to the trust. I explain to Chris what's going on. Veronica has brought me up to date on Tom Paine's videos, whose audience continues to grow. Mankiewitz's stories also tell me that. Unusual for YouTube, the commenters are having conversations about Mankiewitz's speculations, and theorizing as to why I, as the contact with Paine, haven't been online. I get a look at the Missing posters with my face, which freak me out.

The attention on Paine has heightened since Veronica followed through with the information Zest gave her regarding Mendel-Malthus and the Banca Mediterraneo Centrale Internazionale.

I'm keeping a low profile, so I meet Chris at a dark and scuzzy looking coffee shop in the West Village, called Babylon. Chris's hair is twisted up in a faux mohawk and ze's wearing a *Fuck you is the new black* t-shirt.

Chris explains the progress of tracing the viral aspects from Twitter to a Tom Paine Facebook page, blog stories and other steps. I want to know about this in order to maximize the audience for the revelations. Gabriel, the Annunciator.

"Danger Man, I've been talking to the RIP people. They're one of those groups that doesn't have a leader, really..."

"Cell groups. But there's always a leader. Because there's always a dominant personality."

"If you say so. Right now, these are street people, the kind I like. They are being artistic to provoke the public--the way Anonymous would, or Banksy would."

"Ha. I like that."

"Your boy the Roving Reporter, Mankiewitz the Underdog, he gives them stuff to fly on. They take what you reveal as Paine--like you're Jesus, you know? Then they interpret it like the Gnostics. And provoke the world. That's what Underdog said."

"Fair enough. Just like the Gnostics claimed, this world is not what it appears to be. The Demiurge hides within the skin of the proper citizen. What kind of art do they have?"

"Symbolic. You'd like it. Mephisto likes it. He's adding to it. It's graffiti--the Banksy influence again. They ask questions. They make accusations. If the graffiti gets covered up, they redo it. They've also done virtual graffiti in comments on websites and whatever. No online terrorism."

"Good. They have to set boundaries of behavior, Chris."

Chris shrugs. "The people I hang with don't hate people like me, so they're cool with me. Danger Man, on the other hand, makes them walk the *line* because he's *divine.*"

Since Joel isn't around at the moment, I step out to have a cigarette. Chris follows, zis tall angular body stretching in the sunlight, colorful tattoos gleaming.

"I think I want to stay dead for a while," I say. "I'm good with you stirring things up about that."

∞

Sunday, December 4
3:12 pm, Amsterdam Avenue

On the Upper West Side, Zest goes down the steps of a subway station. He uses a Metrocard to get to the platform, but doesn't wait there. He approaches a door built into the mosaic tile, and pulls open a small brass ring. He's inside before anyone even realizes he was there.

At first, the pathway is dark, narrow, and Zest is accompanied by the occasional rat. But eventually he arrives at another tightly sealed arched metal door. It requires a key, and Zest has a key that fits. This pathway is tiled and has recessed lights that turn on when sensing moving presence. The pathway branches off in three directions. Zest chooses one, and ends up at a short stairway. At the landing on top of the stairs is a heavy wooden door. Zest knocks at the door.

A minute passes. Then the sound of a brass peephole being opened. Zest stares straight into the peephole without expression.

The door cracks open. "Maxim...How did you know?"

"I was looking for you. I was concerned something had happened. It did. I determined what was going on. You are lucky to be alive."

"You know...then, do you know who is behind this? Who attacked me?"

"Indeed. But more than that. I have a gift for you."

Clement opens the door wider. "Then please, come in."

∞

SIXTEEN

From the YouTube Channel "Tom Paine Events," in a video entitled:
Unknown Knowns: Roberto Calvi ◆ The Con

Transcript: "Calvi was a corrupt Italian financier who on occasion worked with the Vatican Bank. In 1982, Calvi was found hanging off the scaffolding on London's Blackfriars Bridge. Bricks and thousands in cash was stuffed in his pockets. He had been accused of money laundering for organized crime, and stealing millions from those funds. Calvi was chairman of the Banco Ambrosio, which had just collapsed, and also a member of the illegal Propaganda Due lodge. He was said to be talking to authorities about the crimes. No surprise he was killed.

"No one has been successfully prosecuted for his murder, although the Italian government put several suspects on trial. Due to Calvi's fingers being in several shady ventures, including the Vatican's mysterious financial affairs, Calvi's death raises the question of how the public, or even the authorities, can pull apart reticulated conspiracies in order to find the unknown knowns?"

∞

Sunday, December 4, Continued

Clement's 'safe house' is painted all white. The rooms have no windows, but are comfortable. High end furniture and spaces for Clement to work on his research.

"What's going on, Maxim?" Clement, although nervous, keeps his articulate gestures while he opens a bottle of wine for them. "I had a set-up, it was perfect. It was going incredibly well. And just as I was going to complete my goal, someone broke in. Whoever it was left me alive, but took my subject."

Zest accepts a class of the Montrachet. "Gabriel Ross."

Clement tilts his head. "You know about all of it. Of course, you do. I admit I should have listened to you. My fault for not appreciating your depth of experience. Still, Ross was an amazing tool to play with. He would have done it, Maxim. He would have taken out Jacobs with just a little more work."

"I have no doubt. Damon, the ones who raided your project were from Jacobs' contingent. You must have suspected that. They didn't involve me; it was an under the table operation."

"I suspected, naturally. But why? Why would they care? Do they have Ross now? Or did they kill him?"

"I'm working on finding that out. Mesereau was the one running this. He set up your protégé, Encausse."

Clement looks startled. "You mean you know..."

"That Encausse is Barclay. The operation as a whole was brilliant. But Jacobs heard that Ross was taken and felt he had to stop you."

Clement plays with his wine. "I don't know what to do now. I know what the meeting must be about. I wanted to stop it before it starts."

"Damon, I'd like to see your vision happen as well. I believe we'll find a way to do so. In any case, my gift is I found Mesereau and took care of him. That should throw Jacobs off his game a little."

"You did? Yourself?"

"Of course, to be sure. I have evidence, temporarily if you want to see."

Clement waves that away. "If you did it, he's dead. I just want to see Jacobs dead next, especially if he killed my subject."

"This will happen soon--now that I'm involved."

"I should have let you be involved from the beginning. I was afraid someone would follow you to Spotsylvania...but I should know better."

Clement is agitated, and walks with his glass of wine. "We were very close, Damon. He would have done it...but, now that I think of it, Encausse possibly said something to Ross that disrupted a little. He's still...learning, I guess. And he had that thing for Ross. I hope he didn't really cause more trouble."

Zest smiles dryly. "You have to be careful with the younger ones."

∞

Thursday, December 8
2:27 pm

The office is fortified against intruders. However, I can't just go in and out if I'm pretending to be dead--or at least missing. I want to check on what's going on online, and I don't want to use my apartment or the office. Archie is staying with Veronica and Geneva at the moment, to make the cover look good to anyone who may have the place under observation.

And I'm staying with Herrmann. He knows what's happened. He's responsible for helping me get out. I haven't told Zest about Herrmann, but I've told Herrmann about Zest. Walter is also in on this. He has vicarious thrill helping me around the city, more or less disguised, changing looks periodically. I've gone back to a beard, which just looks strange with my extremely short hair. Walter, being my mainstream press contact, has the embargoed story about the Tertullians and why I need to be missing--so I'm not a target in case either faction wants to wrap-up loose ends.

Because I have a fondness for his cranky irascible self and appreciate his stories about my disappearance, I also let Mankiewitz know I'm alive and a big story is likely to hit; he agrees to keep stirring the disappearance angle. Walter has asked the same-and pointedly raises the Tom Paine videos as the reason why. Mankiewitz can have the articles; Walter wants the book. I wish I could give something to Clark, but his closeness to Alex makes him unapproachable for the time being.

Danny frequently comes by to check that I'm still around, and I discreetly visit Jim, Mikki, and Halo. Veronica comes over to help me set up the new Paine videos. In the fury of activity flaming the fire of those inspired to protest, we work at drafting what to say and how to say it--and what to show in the publicly-accessed Google Docs site serving as the repository for the evidence.

We're looking at the latest video from Tom Paine. "Mendel-Malthus has a series of financial transactions that were not given to Congress during the last bailout. We have these documents, and my media contact is uploading them to my Docs page. This is proof that what I'm telling you is true. Federal agencies such as the SEC have deliberately overlooked the wrongful actions Mendel-Malthus has taken while allowing the company to cause massive credit card, school loan, and mortgage failures that has ruined the credit and buying power of US citizens."

The video was uploaded on YouTube yesterday, and already has 500,000 views and is trending on Twitter. #MMisdeeds.

Veronica isn't the only person visiting me at Herrmann's brownstone apartment. Joel and Chris are here. Herrmann takes the addition of several people in his cat and bulldog haven nicely, puffing on a pipe and listening to Chris explain UFO theories, hacking and the Deep Web.

Chris informs us in a pleased voice, "The RIP people have started protesting Mendel-Malthus. They've set up camp outside. It's really pissing off the Death Star."

"This may lead to trouble," Herrmann comments. "Mendel-Malthus have contracted with Praetorian Security, a private firm. The Mayor agreed to the designation of downtown as a Terrorist Risk Zone, and that means businesses can use force to disrupt trespassers and rioter."

I say, "Praetorian screwed up the Afghanistan infrastructure when they were over there. We can only guess what they'll do to the World Trade Center area. From what I've heard, the RIP group has faced opposition before and they must be aware of the dangers of going near a building with Praetorian guarding it. Nonetheless, Chris, if you're in contact with these groups, be sure to warn them to act carefully and record everything."

∞

Friday, December 9
Noon

I meet Zest downtown, at Battery Park. We stare out over the Hudson River.

"We have to cover everything," I tell Zest. "I want to see what's in Alex's computers. As I remember, he has a work computer and a personal laptop. We can try the work one first, as long as I know he's out of the building. Maybe we can get in his apartment or something later."

"Do you know his routine?"
"Geneva slipped a camera in his office to track him. He has more regular hours as an editor, but he still hits some stories for his column."

"Does he ever leave the laptop?"
"No."

Zest thinks about it. "Suppose I arranged something. You've told me your concerns regarding Mendel-Malthus and Praetorian Security. I can have the director contact him and ask to be the point of a column. He can request a night-time interview to show off his team--at Mendel-Malthus, even, and also request that no laptops or cell phones be brought in because of magnetization issue. I presume Mr. Barclay knows how to take notes by hand. If he doesn't bring the laptop, we can either hit his apartment or office."

I nod. "I think he'd jump at that. Joel and Chris can take the computers. This will give me a chance to go to the library, since I'll know he'll be out a couple hours."

"And I'll have a chance to speak to Jacobs at the same time to begin the set-up."

∞

Tuesday, December 13
Mendel-Malthus Building, 5:12 pm

Zest doesn't have to be announced to Jacobs. Once he contacts Jacobs, Jacobs clears the way for him.

"I'm glad you're here," Jacobs says. "I want you to find out about this Tom Paine person. We can't have these demonstrations continue."

"I have been working on that. I could see the trouble coming while I've been keeping track of Clement."

"Don't tell me he's mixed up in this?"

"He had it set up. I'm sure of it. The entire operation of the RIP was invented by the True Believers. Tom Paine, all of it. They make it look like the Believers are being attacked, but now as you see he is trying to draw attention to you."

"What on earth does he think he's going to gain in doing that? Is he self-destructive?"

"He's becoming more illusory with his machines and their capabilities. You remember Zach Mesereau?"

"He's one of the government intelligence contacts."

"He's a mole. Clement recruited him. He was in touch with a journalist to feel out the possibilities of connecting the Paine information to the Society. I'm watching that journalist now; that's why I arranged the interview with Praetorian. I took care of Mesereau in order to stop that leak."

Jacobs is in shock. "You found all this already?"

"I try to forestall trouble." Zest takes out a phone and shows him the video of Mesereau.

Jacobs sinks in his chair. "Thank you for getting that done. I'll let the other directors know. This puts a priority on resolving what to do with Clement. You won't have a problem with that?"

"I'm prepared as soon as it's official."

Jacobs thinks for a moment. "You know, I may not need the meeting. I don't like using phones, but if it's an emergency..."

"It's not as yet. Clement is underground but I'm having him watched. Mesereau's death has him daunted for the moment. He has to gather his faculties to try anything. In any case, I'll provide security for the meeting."

"We have the Praetorians at your disposal. You can choose who you want out of them."

"Perhaps. I'd prefer to leave that open to my discretion. Lane, I have a suggestion. You are certain that the other directors will agree to Clement's termination?"

"How can they not? You'll be there--you can explain the situation."

"Then use this to our advantage. Draw Clement there. I could convince him to show up. He can be dispatched with immediately. As long as the directors agree."

Jacobs nods, but his eyes are stony. "The only way he'd show up is if he thought he could kill us."

"Of course. But he does not do that himself. He has never done anything by himself except his rituals."

"He has you."

"He believes that and he trusts me. It goes to our advantage."

"A little risky." Jacobs rubs his eyes. "But you're right; he doesn't do anything himself. Make sure he's not armed. Play him out--we can have the satisfaction of shutting this down."

Zest lights a cigarette and goes to look out the 25th floor window. "Once it's done, I'll have the Tom Paine thing set up exposed as the ravings of a Nazi/occult-loving lunatic. The RIP movement will be discredited in addition to everything else."

∞

Herald-Standard Building, 8:30 pm

Just as Zest played a game to get Alex out of the building, we played one to get in. Alex had left his laptop in the office, so we are all there. Chris set up a fake virus attack on the *Herald-Standard's* computers and security system. This necessitates Veronica 'discovering' said attack and taking a team of me (anonymously), Geneva, Joel and Chris to the building. Veronica disarms the security cameras so that I can pass through undetected. It also gives us the excuse to check out computers--should anyone happen to ask. It's late enough that only a small contingent of persons are around. The editorial offices are practically deserted and the library is totally empty.

I have my standard disguise of a wool cap, tinted glasses, and my beard, looking like a Brooklyn hipster. Everyone else is normal, although Chris is dressed down to avoid attracting attention. Chris and Joel head for Alex's office. Veronica begins patrolling the area with cover tasks. Geneva and I go upstairs.

∞

Mendel-Malthus Building, 9:00 pm

Having concluded the meeting successfully, Zest heads down to the lobby. Unlike Gabriel, he does not wear a disguise. His ability to remain undetected is Obi-Wan like. Zest checks to see where Alex is. The director of Praetorian is also in the lobby, reviewing security procedures. Alex is walking with him, listening to the director explain how important having strict security around the risk zones is.

While the director interrupts the interview to tend to a question by an underling, Alex excuses himself to go outside to smoke. Zest observes him from inside. Alex surreptitiously takes out his phone. He shouldn't have it with him, but people would almost rather lose their hands than give up their smartphones. He turns it on while lighting up, flicking the screen idly. Zest positions himself behind a decorative barrier and watches.

Alex suddenly frowns. He looks up, clearly thinking. Then he tosses his cigarette in the street. He strides back to the lobby and speaks briefly with the director, then leaves.

Zest then approaches the director. "Why did he take off?"

"He said he had a problem at the office."

Zest nods and exits the building. He calls Joel. "What are you doing at the moment?"

"We just got into his laptop."

At the same time Alex checked his phone. Alex must have it alarmed. "Be careful--and copy as fast as you can. We may have trouble."

∞

Herald-Standard Building, 8:59 pm

"We need to get this done," Joel tells Chris. "He's coming back."

"W-T-F? I thought we were set."

"Part of critical thinking is preparing for contingencies. That's why we're copying instead of searching."

"You sound like Danger Man again." Chris is supervising a data transfer. "You even got his tone down. Schoolteacher-I'd-like-to-fuck, I call it."

"Can we please move on?" Joel packs his messenger bag. "I want to know how he's doing up there."

"Five-four-three-two-one. Let's do the time warp again." Chris shuts the laptop, wipes it with a cloth, and places it carefully on Alex's desk. Joel opens the office door.

Alex is standing there.

"You might tell me what the fuck you're doing," he says.

Joel doesn't change expression. "Security. What do you think? There's a virus in the system. Davidson called us down."

"*You?*"

"Since you know everything about me, you know I've done this work, and I'm part-owner of the agency, so yeah, *me.*" Joel gestures at Chris. "And Chris is with *me. We* handle this sort of thing."

Alex steps forward, blocking the door. "And you happen to be in my office looking for this virus?"

"We've been looking different places. You have a laptop here, it's vulnerable as an outside computer connecting to the wifi."

"Would you like to show me how you examine one's office for such a virus?"

"Trade secret, Gov'nuh. You wouldn't show us how you search for misplaced commas, right?"

That serves to make Alex glare at him. "In case you forgot, Joel, I am the contact between the agency and Andy Davidson. You, or Veronica, should have called me about this emergency."

"Davidson didn't seem to mind. And your point of contact was to harass Gabriel." Joel can't help saying it.

Alex's face changes, but he's unreadable. "So casual of you to bring him up. Where is he? You all are hiding something."

Hello, Mr. Pot; meet Mr. Kettle...

"That isn't a topic I'm going into now."

Joel and Chris are both surprised when Alex opens his jacket, showing a sidearm. "Or maybe you will. Your Master and Commander has disappeared, and you're here in my office fucking around. You're going to cut the shit and give me answers."

When the fuck did he start arming himself?

But Joel doesn't back down. He has faced several guns before, and by worse people than this fool.

"You'll need to speak to the boss. That would be Veronica."

"Oh, you don't run things?" Alex takes out the gun. He doesn't point it at them, but just holds it.

"Corporate hierarchy. I can make an appointment for you."

"You seem to be as smug as usual. I can't for the life of me understand what he sees in you. And now he's probably somewhere in trouble because of you--again. You don't have everything under your thumb as you think. I can very easily kill both of you and I guarantee I can make it justified. You don't have to believe me. You'll be dead. I'm not waiting for you to think of a smart-ass remark. Tell me what you were doing here."

Joel pauses a second. Veronica is likely hearing this over the radio receivers they all have in their ears. She's on another floor, but after that threat she'll be on her way down. But just in case Alex has an itchy trigger finger, Joel launches into his fake back-up story. "We were installing a program that mirrored your hard drive so we could look at it later."

"Why?"

"We wanted to know if you knew anything about what happened to Gabriel."

"And you couldn't ask?" Alex looks at Chris. "You. I remember you in Gabriel's apartment before. This program is installed on my laptop?"

"Yeah, it's uploading," Chris says.

"Take out the hard drive."

Chris glances at Joel. Joel nods. Chris unscrews the bottom of the laptop and pulls out the black box.

"Break it up--use your feet, break it in pieces, and then put it in the bin and light it."

Chris does so. Joel shakes his head. "Breaking environmental laws, fire codes, and abusing company property. You just keep fucking up--"

Alex interrupts him. "I'm calling some people to deal with you. I can't say what they're going to do, but--"

Behind him, Veronica appears and holds Gabriel's Glock against Alex's head. "He told you to talk to the boss. Well, I'm here. Put that thing on the floor. *Now.*"

Chris exhales in relief as Alex slowly stoops to place his handgun on the floor. Joel allows himself a smirk.

Alex says carefully, "Look, I wasn't going to do anything; I was just surprised to see them here."

"You're so full of shit. Get out of the office."

Alex backs out, his hands up. Veronica keeps the gun trained on him and checks her phone, which is buzzing. "We have someone here to deal with *you*. You're going to be even more surprised."

∞

Herald-Standard Building, 8:30 pm

Geneva and I are on the 12th floor. It's dark and quiet; unlike CUNY Midtown, no one is on duty now. I use my ID to get us in the lobby. Maybe the special collections? I lead her into the room. The case with book on the illustrated apocalypse is still there. I can see version of me in front of me. Darker, distraught. *You need to know, Gabriel. You kept it here safe. Now you need to know.*

I turn around, not sure what I'm looking for.

Geneva says, "What's going on? What do you see?"

"There's something dark. A voice in my mind...*Forget what I told you. Forget what I told you. You'll remember when I tell you.*"

"Is it him?"

I break out into a sweat. "I can feel his hand." And at the same time, Ryan is telling me I need to remember. *Where you feel safe.*

"The other library," I tell Geneva. The library with the regular books. Where I feel safe.

We go in, and I feel safe, but at the same time I sense Ryan is near me. *You had to hide here.*

"I had to hide here."

"This is what you saw..." Geneva looks around the room with me. Like I found at first, the books are pleasantly overwhelming. But I'm overwhelmed by something else.

I walk to one of the wider aisles, with desks in the middle. "It's okay to remember now," I tell myself.

Yes it is. Be careful.

"Why..."

I hear the voice in my ear. Someone's hand on my face. On my head. Hitting me. "Uhh..."

"I'm here, I got you," Geneva says.

I'm still in the memory. The weirdest thing is I don't understand why this person is treating me this way. I love him. I was told I do. Why is he doing this?

Open your eyes, Gabriel. You can see him.

I open my eyes and instead of Geneva, I see Alex. I'm in the room in the Spotsylvania house again. My hands chained and he is frighteningly close to me.

"You brought this on yourself," he says. *"Thinking you were smarter than everyone else."*

He gets cold--demanding to know what I found in Mesereau's house. That's when he hurts me. *"What's the fucking map, Ryan?"* Slapping me when I don't respond fast enough.

I'm in shock, but I must be describing this to Geneva. I hear her voice in my delusion.

"What does he say when he's alone with you?"

Alex leans close, I feel his face brush mine. He asks me something intimate, and I'm responding positively. The part of me here in the library feels disgusted and violated now, but I push that aside to listen to his other words.

"If you see Joel again, he's going to hurt you. He's dangerous to you. You cannot ever, ever trust him. He is going to hurt you. You are afraid of him. You can never be close to him again."

And then, *"Forget I told you this. Forget I was here. For you, I was never here. You do not remember me, just what you heard about Joel."*

And then I bring myself back. What I remember has me shaking. Geneva has to hold me for a moment. "Oh, my God, he's as bad as Clement."

"You're okay now," she tells me. "He didn't know you would fight for yourself."

Veronica is calling us. Geneva answers. "What's going on, honey?... What? Are you kidding me?"

She puts the phone down and says, "Alex is here. He left the interview at Mendel suddenly, and came over here. He tried to hold Joel and Chris at gunpoint, but Veronica disarmed him--she's my hero. Zest is here now too."

I take a deep breath. "Well, let's get him up here and see what he has to say for himself, shall we?"

S EVENTEEN

From the <u>Tom Paine Events Channel</u> on YouTube, in a video entitled:

Unknown Knowns: Jeanie and Al Mills ♦ The Apostates

Transcript: "Jeanie and Al Mills were members of the People's Temple church. They left the church in 1974, and were highly critical of the Reverend Jim Jones. In 1980, a year after the Jonestown massacre, the Mills and their daughter were shot to death in their home. The Mills' son was suspected in the killings, but charges could not be supported. The couple were said to be considered traitors by Jones, but fears of People's Temple hit squads could not be verified.

"Jim Jones did have strange connections including several indicative of intelligence such as the CIA, including rumored CIA personnel and religious organizations that were known fronts for the agency. Was Jonestown a mind-control experiment, as some conspiracy theorists theorize? If so, what were any intelligence agencies involved trying to achieve by such experiment?"

∞

Tuesday, December 13, Continued

I DECIDE TO STAY in the library where I still feel safe. Geneva waits by the door, watching. Five minutes later she says, "They're here."

I get up. I feel stronger, maybe. Angry but cold angry, like he was.

The door opens, and I first see Joel come in. Joel comes in first and heads over to me. "Are you okay?"

"Yes," I put my hands on his face. A flood of feelings come back to me. I can't go through it now, but he sees the change. "I am, baby. I promise. What did he do?"

"He only knows what story I gave him. We have the copy."

"He didn't hurt you?"

"No. He came in all *Tinker Tailor Soldier Asshole,* but V pulled a gun on him and shut his ass down. God, I love her for that."

Joel goes back to the door and opens it. He brings Chris in. Chris is still a little freaked out, and stays with Joel to one side near the door. Veronica is next, holding Alex's arm. Zest is behind Alex, with his gun.

Alex sees me and his eyes go wide. Well, I'm supposed to be dead, though God knows what he *really* thought after I was rescued from Spotsylvania. I can see his expression changing as he tries to connect me being here, and Zest being here. They bring him close to me, but not too close.

"Gabriel, my God. I was afraid something happened to you," Alex says. "I knew they were hiding--"

"Something did happen to me. You know--you were there."

He frowns. "You've lost me. All I know is that you've been gone and there were terrible rumors--"

"Yeah, because I was going through terrible things. Torture. Brainwashing. Inhuman experiments by your inhumane mentor Clement."

His face suddenly goes blank. A little too blank.

"The worst thing you can do now," I tell him, "is pretend you don't know what I'm talking about. I remember your visit in Spotsylvania. You tried to make me to forget, but it didn't work. What was that about, anyway, telling me to forget? You didn't want to be taken down with Clement if he was caught? Or just personal spite?"

He takes a deep breath. "Gabriel, you think you know the situation, but you don't."

"You want to tell me about it? Enlighten me as to why I was set up to be tortured?"

"That was not my doing."

"Clement made the decision but you brought me to him. And you were there, helping him interrogate me about Mesereau."

Alex keeps my gaze, seeming calm. "Gabriel, you don't understand. I'm not insulting your intelligence, but you don't know what this situation is really about."

"What is it then?"

"I can't tell you now. If I can talk to you alone..."

Because I want to hear his excuse, I walk away a few yards towards one of the bookshelves. Alex follows me. He says in a low voice, "That man who is with you all. You know who he is?" He glances back at Zest.

"You're damned right I do. I know everything now."

"You don't, actually. That man is dangerous."

"No shit. So maybe you should be concerned."

"You can't get involved with him. He does terrible things for the Society."

"*I know.* I was threatened with those things last year. For my loved ones, which included you at the time. Except you weren't really in danger."

"Gabriel, you're a smart man. Too smart not to listen. I am not who you think I am. This situation is deeper and more dangerous than it appears. I don't know how you got that man on your side, but there are far more powerful people involved. You have to trust me. Come with me now, and I can protect you."

I laugh. "I have to give you credit. You have all the gall in the world to say that after what you did, and after what Clement did to me. He tried to destroy my brain, my mind, my being. But you want me to go with you, because *Zest* is dangerous to me."

"I never thought Cognoscenti would actually work. I tried to help you. I was going to take you away from Damon and keep you safe. This whole situation involves government intelligence."

"Bullshit."

"I'm telling you the truth. I was protecting you from the inside."

"By interrogating me? Slapping me around?"

"Gabriel, I was trying to *help you.* I had to put on an act. And just in case Damon's stupid hypnosis machine worked, I gave you some suggestions while you were under--to save you. So he couldn't actually control you."

"Your 'suggestions' included forcing me to say I wanted to fuck you. Very classy. And telling me Joel couldn't be trusted." My voice goes cold. "It's time for you leave. Get your passport and go to London. Anywhere but here. I don't want to see you in this city. You're resigning from the *Herald-Standard* as of right now."

A look of anger flashes over his face. "Jesus, Gabriel. You really cannot see beyond yourself, can you? This isn't all about you. It's so much bigger, and if you'd just listen to me instead of playing sullen choirboy, believing the world revolves around you..."

"Really? *I'm* being narcissistic. I should just do as you say. After you've been working for them the whole time. You come on to me, play like you're on my side, help me do research on them--while you were reporting on me to Clement." My voice drops. "What kind of person even does that? Sleep with someone, say you love them--while you sell them out?"

"It wasn't a lie. I know what you were thinking, but it wasn't a lie. I did care for you. I still do. I could do so much for you if you'd listen."

"I don't want your help. I want you gone. I hope your father really has a safe house, because you're going to need it."

"God, this is more serious than your being a scorned lover. You've been consistently getting in over your head--brash, impulsive, hotheaded Gabriel. I tried to help, but I can't help the fact you were weak enough to lose your mind."

His words sound off in my mind. *This isn't all about you/you were weak enough to lose your mind.*

Inside I start shaking. "You tell Clement all about me, all about my life--about my mother and uncle. *You* must have told him so he could make me hallucinate them. I was abducted, my partner nearly killed, and then I'm tortured and converted to some be kind of robot-assassin, and forced into attempted suicide. But I shouldn't be upset because *it's not about me. Is that what you want to tell me, Alex?*"

For a second I lose myself. I'm Ryan, back in the white room in Spotsylvania. With the man in green mask. Damon Clement is telling me to attack the green man; I'm instantly filled with rage and grab him by the neck, slamming him against the wall.

And behind me I hear a collective gasp; I've grabbed Alex by the neck and slammed him up against a bookshelf. Books are tumbling off the shelf from the force of impact. I see fear in his eyes but I can't let go. In my rage I'm the machine Clement wanted me to be. The library starts to fade in my vision, becoming the white room.

The owl's voice is suddenly beside me. "Gabriel, it's okay. Let go. *Let go.* We'll take care of him."

Alex can't speak and a part of me is glad to keep him that way, pinning him to the shelf with my hand as books rain around us. Let him see what happens from fucking with me. I keep my eyes locked with his; the wider and more frightened his are, the hotter mine feel.

The owl is still trying to get to me. She clutches my shoulder. "Gabriel, come back. Let him go. Let me take care of it."

She's staring at me. I don't want to take my eyes from Alex, but she takes hold of my face. Reluctantly, I look at her. As I do, I feel my hand loosen its grip.

"That's it, stay with me. Stay with me."

In a daze, I let her pull me aside. Zest comes up swiftly and grabs Alex's arm. "Mr. Barclay, your internship with Damon is terminated. I am contacting him immediately as to your betrayal of him as a mole sent in from Jacobs."

Alex coughs harshly, holding his throat. He manages to say, "Damon will never believe that."

"He will believe me over you, and he always will. If you think otherwise, go to him with your story and see what happens. He will call me over to kill you. He is looking for a reason why his experiment failed, and you serve as a perfect explanation with your actions. You do not have any other options because I am also informing Jacobs as to your status with Damon. He will have me looking for you. Should you try to have anything further to do with Gabriel or anyone else here, I will be taking care of the situation. You have this one warning. After tonight, I will dispense with you for the sake of safety."

Veronica tells Zest, "Get him out of here. Take everything–his keys, his phones, his ID badge. We'll handle the resignation letter."

Zest hustles Alex out the room with Geneva's help. When they pass Joel, Joel has a smile and two fingers raised backwards against his chest. A gesture meaning *Fuck You* in England.

But as soon as they are gone, he runs over to me. "What's going on?"

Veronica has her arms around me. "He needs to calm down, get back to himself."

"What can I do?"

Standing between them, I'm desperately trying not to be Ryan, I'm desperately trying to reach out and prove I haven't lost my mind. I feel my eyes roll up in my head.

∞

The library has a sofa; I'm lying on it feeling the throbbing pain of one of my massive headaches. I can barely see what's going on. Joel and Veronica are talking to Davidson, having sent a resignation notice from Alex's work computer. They tell Davidson they traced the virus to Alex's laptop and caught him trying to burn it in his office. When confronted, he quit on the spot. Davidson is shocked, but is glad business is taken care of quickly. Even in my screwed-up state, I'm proud of their abilities.

Chris is putting the books back on the shelves, and Geneva is massaging my head. Eventually I recover enough to want to think about next steps. I want to include Zest in this. When Zest comes over to check on me, I ask him where he is staying.

He shakes his head. "That's only for emergencies."

I start to argue with him, but Herrmann calls me. I get up to speak to him privately, telling him what's going on including about Zest.

"Bring him here," he says. "I would like to see this man."

"That crosses a line," I respond. "I can't let you be hurt."

"Am I better than Joel or Veronica? Does my age worry you? I fought another man to the death in Paraguay in 1972. I can handle it. I want to see him."

And so we pack ourselves into Zest's SUV and head for Brooklyn.

After we are in the brownstone, Chris sets to work downloading the info from Alex's computer to his own. Meanwhile Zest and Herrmann appraise each other.

Herrmann holds his pipe contemplatively. "I'm careful who I allow in my home. The fact you have helped my friends balances against the fact you work for that organization and you have committed terrible acts."

Zest tilts his head in acknowledgement. "I won't pretend otherwise and insult your intelligence. I thank you for letting me in."

"I was able to find the man who abducted Gabriel. I can find you if I have to. That is all I'll say about it. However, I would like to learn more about this organization."

"I can tell you what I've told Gabriel."

"That is a start." Herrmann, as per his hospitality, begins making coffee and tea for everyone.

"You are shaking, Gabriel," he says to me quietly. He picks up a pebbled bottle. "Have some port." He pours a glass of dark purple liquid.

I've gotten better at accepting food and liquid from others. Still, my hand is trembling. He catches my hand and meets my eyes. "It will be okay. Did you find out what you need to know?"

I sip at the port. I'd forgotten I like the sweetness of it. I explain what happened with Alex while I allow the warmth to spread. It scares me--feeling something affect my body, feeling it mix with my adrenaline. Herrmann has my elbow, gently, coaching the rest of the story.

I have to turn to Chris. "I'm sorry about what happened with him threatening you."

"Hey, it's no thing. I had to remain calm for Mephisto, because he, like, freaks out over minor shit like this. But I'm there for backup."

Joel rolls his eyes.

I say, "I'm glad you watch over him. You have a job with us whenever you want to do cybersecurity for real."

"Do I get a license to carry? Can I call myself Double-0-C?"

Joel says, "Why don't you see if you can handle this simple task first?"

"Mephisto is jealous of my mad skilz. Pretty soon I'm partners with Danger Man and Warrior Princess, we're gonna bust into Hangar 18 to rescue the aliens, and Mephisto will be holding my calls and gettin' my coffee--oh, shit."

"What?" I come up behind him, where he has his laptop set up on Herrmann's desk. One of the cats is lying against the back of the screen, cleaning herself. She stops and looks up at the sound of my voice.

"You said Anakin Skywalker claims to be a spy. Well, uh, he has some messages that kinda backs that up."

"You've *got* to be kidding."

"No, he has encrypted email software and a drop-box. Nothing that great; I was able to figure out which program decodes it. But from the *diction*, as you would say, Danger Man, he's talking to the real deal--or someone who says they are."

I look over the list of emails but I can't focus. "Chris, can you put these all in one document? I want to read everything. I see his contact is code-named Reaper. That's rich."

Zest has been reading over my shoulder. "Just so you know, the Society's contact with intelligence has been nebulous. Only Clement really has been involved with them. The Production Faction always felt that intelligence would try to control the Society from the inside."

"This doesn't make things any better." I can see the messages go back a year, two years, more. "Who was he spying on me for? The CIA or Clement?"

"Or both," Zest says.

"Ugh. It's not like I don't already feel like the stupidest person in the world." I hear various protests, but I shake off any attempt to dissuade me. I feel how I feel. "Look for any mention of me in those messages, Chris."

He glances at me briefly, then begins searching. "Nothing with your name."

I close my eyes and think. "August. August 16, 2010. That was Raymond's funeral. That's where I met him. Find something in that timeframe."

Chris hesitates. "Danger Man, you sure you want me to read..."

I laugh out loud. "Chris, no time to be squeamish. Not after what I've been through. I need your help. I don't care what you find and what he says, so long as it gives me information I need. You already know the story of how stupid I was."

And then Herrmann says to me. "Gabriel, I think of you like a son. And I will take the right of a father and tell you to get a hold of yourself. No one chooses to be in a bad situation. You've pointed to philosophers like Boethius and Victor Frankl, who went through worse, and made the most of it. You have to set an example now."

I hadn't realized how commanding his voice is until now. I've chosen mentors who are extraordinarily strong, to counteract my wildness. Like with Chiang, locking horns with Herrmann is difficult because I know he knows better than I do. I can only run away, which I've done before.

And I can't do that again. I can't offer any excuse. I nod to Herrmann, acknowledging his wisdom. "Go ahead, Chris. It's okay."

Zest, because he is the ultimate bad boy, hands me a cigarette-
-probably because I'm shaking. No one questions the propriety of his
lighting the cigarette for me. I breathe out smoke, trying to stop the
tremors.

I hold my hand out to Veronica. She takes it. I still get
automatic comfort from her, the owl. Joel bumps up against me; I
take his hand as well.

Chris is most attractive and confident when able to show off zis
talents, including speed reading. "Okay, I looked for anything that
sounded like, uh, he had contact with you. Unscrambled, he did write
about you to the Grim Reaper about a week after that date."

"And he said?"

"He met you in the context of Raymond Booth. That you
probably were going to continue to investigate Booth's death, and that
Clement was interested in you. Then he talks about the type of
contacts you had, as the messages go on. Reaper says...that Alex is
getting too close to you, and Alex says that's irrelevant. He says that he
wants protection for you."

I don't react to that. *Whatever.*

"Moving on, Alex is glad you've found a contact--Varney? He
wants to bring Varney in, but makes it clear that he controls the story,
not to have separate contracts."

I shake my head. "Yeah, he wanted to write a book about it."

"He says as much. Reaper says as long as nothing classified--
and that he'd establish priority for Alex to be cleared to do so, but to
be careful in case you or Varney wanted to write something as well."

Veronica has made me sit down with her on a nearby couch.
"It explains why he has these emails in the first place," she comments.
"Reaper would have surely told him to delete the messages wouldn't
he? But Alex wants them for his own use."

The words 'delete the messages' make me react, and she
squeezes my hand. Chris asks me, "Was he threatened at some
point?"

"He told me an editor warned him off the case."

"He mentions it to Reaper, but it's a cover story. He says you
gave up the case. Clement told him Mr. Zest was involved, and that
explained everything, yadda yadda. Well, he also takes credit for
getting you to come to your senses."

"Uh-huh. Go on."

"Um, not much for a time after that. He says Clement is still interested, and he wants you to go to Europe to be protected from him, before Clement makes a move. And then...oh, Mephisto, this is where you come in."

"Super," Joel says.

"He just says that contact with Danger Man has ended and that he's gone back to a 'previous disruptive force.' Damn! That's your new avatar, Disruptive Force."

I speak up. "Moving along, Chris."

"He tries to maintain contact with you, doesn't work well. Up to early this year, when Reaper asks if you can be involved in Operation Accountability. Alex says you already are."

"That has to be something related to Mesereau. Mesereau's day job was intelligence while at the same time working with the Society. Is there any contact you see with Clement?"

"Nothing that looks like it...I'll keep searching."

"I still don't have answer to the question--who is he really working for? Spying on Clement for the CIA, or acting as a mole in the CIA for Clement? I know what I suspect."

"What's that," Veronica asks.

"That he's his own best friend first. He'll play whoever he needs to. I don't put full faith and credit into any alleged allegiances."

"Neither do I," Zest remarks. "I wouldn't have let him leave as you did, but I understand why you did. However, I can find him shortly...if needed."

"Not for that."

"He's a chaotic element."

"Not so much. He still has the government to hitch his wagon to. Take that away, and he's more problematic being loose."

We both stub out our cigarettes at the same time. Zest says, "Gabriel, you mention that he is most concerned with himself--a bit of a narcissist, then? And he wants a book. He probably planned tell his story within his paper, too."

"You think he'll still try to be involved in some way."

Zest has a small smile. "When you ended your association with him, did he give up?"

"I wouldn't be here if he had. What this really raises is whether or not it affects our plans. It doesn't. But still. I'm going to talk to my dad; he might know something."

∞

Wednesday, December 14
91st Street Brooklyn, 1:30 am

"I thought you forgot about me," Jeffrey says. "Zest has let me know you're okay."

"I'm sorry, Dad. I still feel like I've lost my mind--that all this is hyperreality."

We're outside, and down the block from his building, near a park.

"Intelligence work is all hyperreality. Not only creating stories but acting them out. Saying one thing to the world and another inside."

"You were out of town anyway."

"Keeping in touch with the office, so to speak. You know, they would like me to retire. I don't fit the recruiting posters these days. It's clear I won't be leading any more missions. That kind of leaves me without a hell of a lot to do. Someone suggested a teaching post. I don't have the temperament to teach. I'd last as long as I would with an office job."

"I wouldn't last in one either. Uh, we can figure out something together. I'll help you with that."

Jeffrey smiles sardonically. "That's good of you, to help consider where exactly we can put me out to pasture."

That's exactly what I would say under the circumstances, and exactly how I'd say it.

"But before we do that, Gabriel, what's your question?"

I explain what was found in Alex's hard drive. "How can I find out who Reaper is, and what Operation Accountability is?"

Jeffrey is silent for a minute. "I have someone I can ask. This person helped find the information about Clement before. I still have a few favors before they set me out for the polar bears."

∞

We have about two weeks until the January 1 meeting happens. And I feel I'm in a ghost world--not dead and not alive. Later in the morning I go to Queens to train with Chiang some more, taking Veronica, Danny and Walter with me. The sheer physicality of working out helps both of us heal and I feel better with friends nearby.

Then my dad meets with me and Zest at Herrmann's place. "Enigma is an intelligence operation tasked with finding out how so-called secret societies are connected to political and military factions across the world. They have some long-term moles in various organizations to collect information. The Tertullians was one of these. I imagine Barclay was their mole. He's not a real operative, but an asset. He started with the MI6 version of Enigma, which is cooperating with ours. My assessment is Barclay allowed himself to take things too far."

I shake my head. "That's so him. He wants a book deal and all the credit."

"They don't care. They won't let him say anything other than the cover story no matter what he thinks he's going to do. Here's the wild card. Operation Accountability is *another* long-term project to suss out some rogue personnel who are actually cooperating with some of the societies. They aren't sure why these rogue ops are doing it--money, ideology, whatever. But they've focused on a small faction, Project Q. Those are the ones working directly with Clement. I would guess that a couple of the persons in the Spotsylvania house observing you were Q personnel. They wanted to see if Clement's convoluted magical mystery machine actually worked. But Q knows Enigma is on to them, and wants to eradicate any connection."

"What a fucking mess," I comment.

"It is," Zest agrees. "I'll see what I can do about them after we take care of the Production Faction and Clement. But I have something else to let you know about. You know the RIP movement has been protesting down by Mendel-Malthus. Jacobs wants to get rid of them. They are going to be set up this weekend as terrorists, with the Praetorian personnel taking them out."

"Which they could do, under the Terrorist Risk Zone law. Anyone deemed a threat to a financial system, including private banking, can be considered a terrorist and taken down with up to deadly force."

"This plan discredits them, and perhaps to an extent Tom Paine, since the RIP are his biggest followers."

"We can warn them."

"If they believe it. They'll still protest. I know agitators are going to start something in the crowd, to give an excuse to send in the forces. Doesn't matter what happens next, as long as people believe the story about what happened *first...*"

"Who are these agitators? Any idea?"

"Yes. I know you want to try to find these people."

"The RIP has helped me and made Paine a source to listen to seriously. I do want to help them."

∞

The New York Scene/The Thin Blue Line Column by Carl Mankiewitz
Live Blogging from the Mendel-Malthus Protest

The RIP movement is causing barely a ripple of notice out on the street from a city surfeited by Occupy. However, that is not the only community. The protest is blazing hot on YouTube and related social media--Twitter, Facebook, Instagram and more. This is due in no small part to the presence of the mysterious Tom Paine. No one has seen Paine, but he said he would be here, and we've already seen some provocative camera work on his channel.

See the accompanying photos and video, below. You can see the crowd of around 100 people in the public access strip of grass and cement in front of the Mendel-Malthus building. A driveway, like a moat, separates that public access from the building itself. The building, nicknamed the Death Star, is black with black-tinted windows, and bulges out in a grotesque bit of architectural design. The public access part has just enough room for the protestors, who are split in half by a long winding sculpture, an abstract piece meant to represent Julius Caesar...

∞

Saturday, December 17
Mendel-Malthus Building, 7:00 pm

The RIP crowd, all wearing Maneki-neko cat masks start chanting at 7pm sharp. They keep the slogans at low volume, in case someone needs to shout instructions. It's sort of a point counter-point round, with half the crowd saying *Tell the truth*, and the other half, *What do you have to lose?*

Three or four people who have become the leaders of RIP have congregated in the middle of crowd to direct the chanting.

I'm here with Joel, Veronica, and Chris. Chris is with me, and Joel and Veronica are on different sides of the edge of the crowd. The police are a few yards away.

Zest is up...somewhere. In a building or on a roof, somewhere he can watch us and keep up with the reaction inside the building. We all have earphones in to keep in touch and follow what's happening.

Zest speaks to me. "The feed is going well. From what I see, it's being shared *appreciably.*"

"So far, so good."

"Hold on, Jacobs is calling."

"Okay." I turn to my group. "We should split up, see how things look from different areas."

∞

Zest answers his phone. "Yes?"

It's Jacobs. "Do you happen to be around?"

"Naturally. I've been tracking what is happening with this."

"We're planning to shut it down."

"So I understand."

"Do you see anyone claiming to be Paine? Or do you still think Paine is a false flag?"

"It's Clement, actually. He is not here, but he revived communication with me just now--which is why I'm here. I told you what he was doing in Virginia. He is, to put it bluntly, losing his mind."

"That changes the tenor of our meeting. As to how to take care of him."

"Naturally," Zest says again.

So far, so good.

∞

I can't hear much, I take a moment to just look around at the people who have gathered solely on the basis of trying to find justice.

I see Chris pop up, his curly head towering over others. He reaches for my hand and pulls me into his space. While the rhythmic beat of the chanting continues, Zest calls me again.

"Gabriel, they've sent someone into the crowd itself. Someone to start a violent act. Maybe you can find the person. I'm trying to scan from up here."

"Do you know what the person looks like?

"Six foot, blonde, young, razor-cut. He might have a gun or explosive."

Jesus. I grab Chris. "Are some of your friends here?"

"Oh, yeah. We should warn them."

"We should. Someone's going to start shit, and then the headbreakers will move in. Tell them now!"

Chris whips out his phone. I talk to some people nearby, and think I see Joel, who isn't wearing a mask, winding his way to the other side of the crowd. I text him and Veronica.

I hear Chris say to someone, "Spies are here; they're going to start something."

"What you do mean?"

I turn around and tell the man Chris is talking too, "Agent provocateurs. Someone to throw something, shoot something."

The guy pushes his mask up, giving me a cynical look. "Oh, come on bro. How do we know *you* aren't an Agent Provocateur?"

But the girl next to him is frowning at me in recognition. "Oh! You're Gabriel! Gabriel Ross. You're Tom Paine's contact..."

"I'm trying to protect RIP."

"I thought you were dead!" She whispers something in the other man's ear. He doesn't seem to want to listen. Then I realize if the girl recognized me, others will too.

In the center of the crowd is a sculpture. I move towards it. The monument is an abstract sculpture running the length of the public access area. One half of it is a beam about waist high. Interspersed on the beam are thin poles inscribed with inspirational messages. I get my fingers on the metal edge of the beginning of the beam.

It requires focus, and some luck. I have to be like my cat. Without pausing to think, I grab the sculpture and haul myself up. I crouch at first; there's nothing to steady myself on until I can get to the first pole, about 15 feet away. So short, and yet so long. I crabwalk along as fast as I can and reach the pole.

Standing, I have to hold on as people slam against the sculpture. But I can look over the crowd, and search for something recognizable.

I scan every blond head I see. That includes looking for Joel and Veronica. People turn and look at me. "Hey," I yell out. "I need your help."

A rush of noise. Then most of the crowd turns to look at me. A sea of cat masks. It's so visually nervewrecking that it makes me waver some. *Faceless people in masks staring at me.* I see some recognize me. I take a deep breath and force myself to look at the crowd.

"You're in danger. There's a man here who's trying to set you up. Don't panic. Don't get violent. They want that--to have the police or the Praetorians to bring you down."

The crowd around me gets quiet and the quiet starts to spread. I can feel lights behind me, see cameras in front of me. I sense the NYPD watching from behind their blue barricades, and the faceless Praetorians in black and silver lined up against the entrance of Mendel-Malthus.

"What happened to you," someone asks in the silence.

"What happened to me doesn't matter. A man is in this crowd; he's six feet tall, short blond hair, muscular. He's got a gun or some other weapon. He's trying to pretend he's one of you, so you'll be portrayed as a violent group, a terrorist group."

I turn and look over my shoulder speaking towards the police. "This is all on live feed. No one in RIP is violent. No one is breaking laws. Whoever tries anything is a plant to discredit the movement."

I then see Joel at the far end of the beam, grabbing it and looking up at me. I turn back to the crowd. "Find the mole. Let him leave. Show the city what's really going on."

People begin looking around.

"Don't panic, don't do anything violent. Remember what you're here to prove."

A few people are nervous and some leave the crowd and run away. I can't blame them. The Praetorians start moving toward the crowd ominously.

A man to my left is pulling a cap over his head. He's six feet, young, and has muscles, and is trying to slip away. Feeling a little like Donald Sutherland in *Invasion of the Body Snatchers* I point at him. "Let me in..."

The crowd gets back and I jump down and move toward the man. He looks over his shoulder at me and tries to push his way out.

I grab him and put my leg between his to pull him off balance. He reaches in his coat, and I block him. He's damn strong, but I'm stronger from fear, forcing him to go to his knees. I knock his mask off, and find the gun in his inner pocket. The people around us gasp. Some want to try to attack him.

I tell them, "Stop! Don't do it. They'll use anything as an excuse. Send him out. Send him back to his masters."

"He's right," this from the young lady who recognized me earlier. "Gauntlet, people, Gauntlet! Let him pass."
"Just a second." I empty the man's gun of its bullets and put it back in his pocket. "If he doesn't have a license, I hope the police take him in on possession." Then I push the guy in his back. He glances at me hatefully, then moves through the tunnel of space towards the barricade.

People have their phone cameras up. "Get the word out," I say to the sea of cameras. "He's not one of you. He's a plant. The cops need to know."

An improvised chant goes up--*Not one of us.* In my ear, Zest says, "Excellent, Gabriel. That's the most significant danger, but they're going to move the force in anyway. They *have* to."

"Why? The mole is gone."

"They'll try to change the story later. Desperation tactics."

I haul myself up on the beam. Sure enough, the Praetorians are moving closer, as if sensing blood. "Turn your phone speakers on," I yell at the crowd.

Joel has gotten next to me. He's filming me, and the noise of what I say is coming through Tom Paine's channel. My voice is amplified through his camera's speaker. People get the idea and turn to Paine's channel. Collectively these make my voice louder like a wave in the cat-faced crowd.

"You all need to know that Mendel-Malthus's guards, Praetorian Security, is going to treat you like criminals. You can try to run. You can get down and cover your heads and not move, to show the public that you aren't the criminals here."

Some of the Praetorians start spraying a substance on the front lines, making people stumble over themselves.

"Get down! Cover your heads."

Most of the crowd goes to their knees, pulling jackets over their faces to avoid the spray. It fills the air.

Something goes off--a flare. Bright lights are being shined in from the police side. Screens that have some kind of pulsating wave, and electromagnetic pulse crowd-control device.

I feel a flashback to the house. On the floor, in chains. The screen pulsating.

You can't give into that now.

Now the Praetorians are in the crowd itself. Some kind of muffled chanting continues as they begin passive resistance.

I would drop down myself, but Zest's speaks to me urgently. "Gabriel, leave now. Go to the doors."

I press my hand over my ear to hear better. "What doors?" "Mendel's doors. Keep moving. They're going to try to stab you. Don't let them get close."

I look for Joel and Veronica. They've been swept back to the far end of the beam. Joel avoids being maced, and when a Praetorian tries to grab his sweatshirt, he kicks the man in the kneecap.

Another guard is getting close to me. I might or might not see a knife. I can't hesitate. Like a Zen exercise, I dodge arms, heads, and the Praetorian guard who tries to grab me. I'm climb back on the beam and run.

I can't jump off or stop. Joel is swimming towards the other end, straining to meet me. Veronica reaches him, and at the edge I jump off and they catch me.

A fury is erupting some yards behind us. It looks like a shark feeding frenzy of people.

I struggle back up. "We have to get out."

Zest says to me breathlessly, "The Praetorians are surrounding the crowd. Go to the lobby."

"Are you kidding?"

"I made arrangements to prevent you being attacked--you have to trust me," he says. "Just go and ask for Hunter--" his voice cuts off. Electronically, not otherwise. I realize something's being broadcast to jam transmissions.

All I can get is static. Of course--that helps in confusion and setting the official story.

The crowd suddenly surges backward. I almost fall, as I'm not paying attention. Falling in a crowd that's panicking is tantamount to suicide.

Not being tall doesn't help. It's hard to get a handle on what's happening.

Our part of the crowd slams against the barricade. Since the crowd seems to be half-trying to escape and half-trying to fight. One would think the cops would let the crowd through to escape and get out of danger, but they're closing ranks. They also shove back, hitting people climbing over the sawhorses.

More pulse grenades are going off, making people angrier and more panicked.

I hustle us towards a side door that doesn't have a guard in front. But I say to Joel and Veronica, "This is going to be serious; you don't have to go with me. Both of you can disappear."

"No way," Joel responds.

Veronica says, "I'm not leaving."

And with that, we duck under more arms and legs, barrel past the sawhorses when an opening pops up, and throw ourselves through the side revolving door.

The Mendel-Malthus lobby is empty, except for a front desk person.

Who is very surprised to see us.

He's on the phone, and jumps up, then starts to call for more security. I hold my hand up, heading over. Unexpectedly, he raises his other hand, showing an automatic. I stop walking and start talking.

"We have an appointment."

"Do not move any closer."

"Mr. Hunter is expecting us. My name is Gabriel Ross. Call him and check."

"Stay where you are. I'll shoot."

"Call him," I say again.

The front desk drone ignores me, talking now into a radio. But his phone rings, and when he sees the number, he stops.

He picks up the phone. "Wilson. Front."

He listens for a moment. "Yes, sir." Then he stares at me. "Yes sir. Of course. Certainly."

Hanging up, he says to us in a tight voice, "Someone will be here shortly to escort you."

I can't help but be a smartass. "Need us to sign in?"

He glares at me. "Not necessary, *sir.*"

Another Praetorian man suddenly appears and gestures for Wilson to lower his sidearm. "Twenty-Five cleared it." Hunter is on the 25th floor.

Veronica whispers to me, "What are we doing?"

"I believe it's an impromptu stakeholders' meeting."

She smiles. "We're the stakeholders?"

"Did our taxes contribute to the bailout of this corporation? I'd say we are."

Another specimen appears. Super-WASP. Six-foot white man, sharp $200 haircut, blond hair and FBI features. Fitted expensive suit.

I believe I've seen him before. At Cronos, a gay bar. So has Joel and Veronica, who've been to Cronos more often than I. And this guy knows they know. His face doesn't change but his eyes do. "Come with me please." He nods his head a fraction of an inch.

We follow him to the elevator banks.

In the elevator, SuperWASP keeps his eyes to the front, hands folded in a way HR probably taught him during orientation.

"Haven't I seen you before," Joel asks with a hint of impertinence we desperately need.

The man flicks his eyes toward Joel. "No."

I look at his name tag. Spencer. He meets my eyes inadvertently. Curiosity. Two gay white men in the same city, around the same age. And yet so different.

Finally, we hit 25. Spencer leads us down a wide, quiet hall to a set of glass doors and a wide, quiet lobby with a wide, quiet desk. Then through another set of doors--mahogany, another hall and a secretary's anteroom. The secretary gets up and knocks on another pair of mahogany double-doors.

She opens one of the doors and steps back. Spencer goes in first. Once we're all in and standing in front of Hunter's desk, Spencer says, "Sir?"

Hunter nods at him. He looks the same as in his CEO pictures. Medium height, trim, slightly gray, slightly thinning hair. A suit so expensive, coffee is afraid to spill itself on it.

Spencer leaves, but meets my eyes once more. Then he looks away too quickly, awkwardly. I'm officially rough trade.

But enough of that. We have a CEO to harass. My phone buzzes with a text; it's Zest.

--Go with what happens.

Okay.

Hunter keeps his face neutral. He looks at my hands, as if I had a weapon. "Mr. Ross. Do you want to tell me why you all are here?"

"To ask you to stop your goon squad Praetorians from assaulting innocent people."

He leans back. "It's private property out front. They're trespassing. You're trespassing."

"They are on the public access area. And you invited me up. That negates trespassing."

"The crowd outside is dangerous. This is a major financial institution. I have to protect it. The city laws allow for defense of financial systems and banking."

"To the point of killing people? I guess you paid for the law."

"We're in a Terrorist Risk Zone," he says evenly. "Is that all you have to ask?"

"Maybe not. You know me from another situation. The Raymond Booth case."

"I'm afraid I'm not familiar with that."

"Ethan Nelson told me who you were before he died."

His eyes narrow. "I don't know who that person is."

"As if. Do we really play this?"

He leans forward. "What are you really trying to do?"

"Get you to stop what you're doing. You and the Tertullian Society."

"Conspiracy theorist lunacy."

"More evidence is coming out from Tom Paine."

"Oh yes, you're his contact, aren't you? Maybe, Mr. Ross, he's pulling a long con on you. It happens. A global multi-national corporation garners many conspiracy theories. Many people need something to blame when they can't cope with the randomness in life."

I match his tone. "I have no delusions other than what's forced upon me. I think you can end the Tertullians. You're in that position. Otherwise, it'll blow up in your face. You can stop running a super-evil corporation, and go back to running a regular evil corporation."

Hunter frowns at me. "I'm not responsible for what you believe."

"I don't believe, *I know*. I was tortured because of what you do. The people you know, and what they believe in."

"Were you? If so, I'm sorry to hear that. It may have affected you adversely, whatever you went through. You have to be careful about perspective. Ms. Gianni, Mr. McFadden, you appear to be with Mr. Ross. Is that so, or do you wish to leave?"

"I am his partner and friend. I'm not leaving here until the matter is sorted out."

"Is that so? Consider how wisely you've chosen your friends. I have given you a chance to rectify that. Mr. McFadden? I have heard you're, shall we say, close to Travis Churchill. In here though, his influence is negated. But you too have the option to leave."

Joel lights up a cigarette. "I have nothing to say to you."

Hunter checks one of six smartphones on his desk. "Gabriel, I can see you have a strange influence over people. I don't understand, though, why you brought your friends with you. That wasn't like you before, to endanger people."

"When I was investigating Raymond's death, you mean?"

"You had your warning and your opportunity to stay out of this business. I know your personality. Getting yourself killed--I expected that sooner or later. Getting your friends killed--I thought that wasn't part of your 'ethics.'"

"I'm not afraid of you."

"Clearly. But of what happens to those foolish enough to follow you?"

He gets another message. I'm guessing it's a message from Zest.

Hunter says, "In any case, not to be inhospitable but our time is over."

The door opens and Zest enters. I know I'm going to have to do some improv acting. I just frown like I don't understand why he's there.

"He hasn't tried anything, just like you said." Hunter says to him.

"Clement would have to wait until he knows Mr. Ross is here and then give him the word."

"I don't know what you're talking about," I say stonily.

"Damon sent you here." Zest faces me. "Remember the message?"

I walk closer to him. "What do you know about the message?" I try to sound confused. "I'll have to talk to Damon about you."

"It's aborted." Zest says quietly. "I'll need you to come with me." He has just the right tone of consequence.

I try to show the face of someone slowly realizing his fate. "Why?"

"Just come with me."

I look over at Veronica and Joel. "Leave them out of it."

Hunter says, "It's too late for that."

Zest holds up his hand, interrupting him. He says to me, "It can be done, but you'll need to take care of something for me first."

Hunter starts to protest, but Zest just gives him a look. I have the satisfaction of seeing Hunter shut up like a whipped dog. I suppress smiling, and just try to give the impression that hopeful I'm not getting Joel and Veronica killed. It's a real hope.

Zest holds his hand out to indicate I should precede him out the office. He ushers us out the anteroom. "End of the hall," he says. At the end we arrive at what appears to be a maintenance door. The door leads to a dark staircase.

I ask, "Twenty-five flights down?"

"Service elevator," he says shortly. There are indeed elevator doors in the small dark room at the bottom of the stairs.

Inside the elevator, Zest takes out a square, metal-gray device the size of a pack of playing cards and flicks it to life. "This interferes with any recording devices. But Gabriel, you can continue to act upset."

"Cameras in here?"

He nods. "What did you tell Hunter?"

I get in front of Zest and face him, running my fingers through my short, short hair, like I'm agitated and arguing with him. "Nothing in particular."

Zest looks down at the floor. "You're going to need to die for now."

"Just me?"

"Not under these circumstances. To set up our being able to go to Jacob's office, I told him that you should be allowed inside Mendel-Malthus so I could contain you better. I said Ms. Gianni was working for Clement and sold you out. At some point she was going to call Clement for the trigger so you would kill Jacobs. At least, that's what I said."

I turn and look at Veronica, who seems rightfully horrified, and Zest grabs my arm. Joel steps in front of Veronica. On camera, this would look bad--for us.

Joel asks, "What does that mean, to die for now?"

"You are all going to be considered dead until the takedown of Jacobs and Clement."

"How elaborate does that get?"

"Jacobs won't look for evidence. I saw that with Mesereau. I'm not Nelson. If I made mistakes, I wouldn't be here. This is the about the last time that will play in my favor."

I turn to Joel and Veronica. "You understand what this is going to involve?"

Veronica nods. "We chose to be here."

Zest checks his device. "No actual bodies will help. Disappearing is better. Since it's three of you, death will be assumed. But no police involvement in a homicide--because no bodies to investigate."

"Using the system against itself."

"You'll be in a conspiracy theory of your own."

Joel asks, "Where are we going now?"

"Out the back of the building. A bit of a walk. I have a car waiting. You're with me under the aegis that Gabriel knows he's on his way to certain death, but is intent upon me sparing your lives."

"Once we're in the car, it's over." My own words lead me to look Zest directly in the eyes. It's hard to read his expression. Of course, I can't help but think that if he wanted to change his mind about challenging the Tertullian Society, he could do what he told Jacobs he'd do. Very neat, wraps up everything. He easily goes back to what he knows.

For a moment, I see something flicker in his eyes. He knows what I'm thinking.

Trust is very hard, with all the lies we've been working. All of us fall quiet. The air is tense as we move down a corridor to an exit that's actually from another building, and then outside. We can't even hear the mob anymore.

Zest keeps glancing at me. Our parallel thoughts. If I feel he's lying to me, and he believes I feel he's lying to me, violence is imminent. Because I won't go down easily.

We can see a nondescript black car waiting at the end of the alley. Zest opens his jacket. I slow my pace and not so subtly get in front of Veronica and Joel. They stop behind me.

Zest stops too, facing me. He holds up his hands carefully, like he did in the Westchester warehouse. "We'll both feel better if I do this."

"And what is that?"

"Give you something. I understand your concerns."

He reaches around under his arm very slowly. All my efforts in trusting him struggles in those seconds as he draws his hand out again. A gun, a Smith and Wesson auto. He holds it hanging off one finger, and stretches his hand out to me.

I take the gun, just as slowly, and check it over. It's in good working condition. He's right; I do feel better.

We continue on to the car. Zest knocks on the tinted driver's side window. It lowers, and he says to the person inside, "You can go."

The driver says something, and Zest responds, "I'm handling this."

The driver, a nondescript middle-aged man, gets out. Zest waits until he hustles away down the street then opens the passenger and back doors. He goes back to the driver's side, and pops the trunk and hood.

It's not like I'm *not* going to check everything. Nothing in the car raises concerns. Veronica and Joel wait until I finish the searching entire car. Zest is smoking in the meantime. If he's worried about time, he nonetheless doesn't attempt to rush me.

He asks me, "Do you want to drive?"

"Joel can drive."

We get in. I sit in the back with Zest. He leans over the front seat to hand another device to Joel. "Plug that into the GPS. It will say we're going to Long Island. All of you turn off your phones completely now."

Joel lights another Djarum. "Where are we really going?"

"The warehouse in Westchester. Nelson's. You remember where it is."

"Yeah. How long is all this going to be for?"

"At least until the meeting about Damon on the first. I'll check in, but for a few days I'll be out of the country, picking up the documents needed to expose Jacobs and the Society." Zest looks over at me. "We're going to have to set this up carefully, because now we'll have just the one opportunity to take them down--and live."

∞

PART FOUR

ASVATTHA

∞

From the YouTube Channel "Tom Paine Events," in a video entitled: Unknown Knowns: The Highway of Tears & Juarez Maquiladora Murders ♦ The Slaughtered

Transcript: "The United States is probably considered the country with the highest number of serial killers. However, the US is bookended by a series of wholesale slaughters of women in Mexico and Canada--murders that clearly have more than one killer, have targeted vulnerable women, and have been going on for decades. In British Columbia the victims are primarily First Nation members and have been found sexually assaulted and murdered on Highway 16. These victims number over 40 (but authorities posit a much lower number). One suspect (now deceased) was linked to some of the murders by DNA, and authorities have acknowledged others are involved.

"Critics of the Highway of Tears investigation argue not enough efforts have been invested (or media attention given) to solve the crimes because Aboriginal persons are not highly valued--and that any rise in attention is due to a few Caucasian victims. In Juarez, Mexico, hundreds of women have been murdered from 1993 through today. Many were workers in area factories (maquiladoras). The women were poverty-level and often exploited. The killings have been violent and included rape and torture. A few persons have been arrested, but like in Canada if these persons are responsible they are not the only killers.

"Strangely, a backlash against the fact women have been specifically targeted is going on, with some arguing that gender doesn't play a role—when it clearly has. The mind-boggling scale of these North American crimes, intertwined with misogynistic and/or racist elements, raises the question of how can such pervasive killings go on without real answers--and why are these victims continuing to be marginalized?"

∞

Westchester County, 10:35 pm

ZEST HAS JOEL drive up to the gate of a metal fence that surrounds the warehouse. I'm not happy to see it again and neither is Joel. But here we are. Zest gets out and unlocks the gate. He then unlocks the front doors of the warehouse and disappears inside.

I don't know what to say. I catch Veronica's eyes in the rear-view mirror and start to speak.

"Don't apologize or I'll knock you out," she says. "Let's make the best of this."

Joel makes some sort of scornful noise next to her and she turns to him. "I have knockouts for more than one person if you test me."

He first gives her a willful look like a cat challenging authority then pretends she's not there, also like a cat.

Zest steps out and waves to us. I decide as we head to the door that Veronica has the right idea. Make the best of it. I have to appreciate every moment I'm in control of my body and mind. My own Maslow's hierarchy.

Zest says, "I've been staying here. It's comfortable. Really only the downstairs is set up, but you do what you will to make it as you wish. I'll bring things to you. You can't go out or use a phone. At all. I'm taking the phones with me. I trust you can live with that. No ordering from Amazon."

His sense of humor is lacking something.

He contemplates us. "Veronica, I think you understand best about the importance of not going out. Even looking out the upstairs windows is risky. Exude your authority."

"Can do," she responds.

Annoyed, and relieved that I'm annoyed instead of scared to death, I say, "I understand what you're setting up and why we can't be seen. I'm not going to jeopardize our shot."

Zest actually makes a dismissive gesture. "I'd wager that without her authority within 48 hours you attempt to go outside. It's in your nature. Don't do it."

He collects our phones. I have a list of people to contact and what to say. We all do.

Zest only says, "I'll use my discretion."

"My dad and Herrmann won't just sit around..."

"I'll use my discretion." And then he's gone, the door shutting like he's the last on Earth we'll see. Unsettling.

We take a moment to look around. It doesn't look like it did last year. The downstairs is all one large space more or less square, about 50 feet by 50. No windows. But it does have posters of the outside. Places in Europe; the colors break up the solid gray walls.

Not much furniture. A king-sized mattress on a bamboo mat. Two plain wood chairs and one desk chair. A spartan wood desk.

"He took decorating tips from you," I tell Joel. He gives me an icy look in return while Veronica laughs.

The desk has writing pads and books. Dostoyevsky and Ross MacDonald. A state-of-the-art coffee pot is on a small table next to the desk.

"Coffee and books--I'm set."

Veronica is investigating the left side of the room, where against that wall is a stainless-steel fridge, a porcelain sink and a large armoire. She opens the fridge. "Wine! Fuck yeah." She pulls out a bottle. "*Chateauneuf de Pape*. We have a party now."

"Unless it's like the *Twilight Zone*. No corkscrew."

"That wouldn't stop me." She checks the armoire. "Towels. Soap. I guess since this is a bachelor pad, he didn't need privacy."

She indicates the shower, which is on the far side of the room. It had to have been installed after the last time we were here. It consists of a large tiled square with a depression and drain. A small lip surrounds the square. No curtain. A pipe comes up from the floor and ends in a large showerhead. "At least the commode is in a closet with a door."

"If privacy means something to you."

"Depends upon what you want to be private about."

I notice Joel has not said a word since we came in. He's barely moved. He stands by the mattress.

"Baby, what's going on in your mind? Outside of the general situation?"

He shrugs. "Well, first off, the last time I was here, I was kidnapped. I can deal with that; the memories are fuzzy. But I don't like being confined. I was in the Tombs overnight once until Chris and Iz could get me out. I had a blade in my shoe the cops didn't find. I was afraid I'd have to use it on this guy getting too close to me in the cage. And once I was in a car trunk. I was with this guy in Dubai, and he almost got caught by his father. He had to hide me in a hurry."

"Dubai? The car must have been a Caddy."

"Bentley. He had taste."

I go over to him and put my arms around him. "I know you had it worse, he mutters." I nod, but I still want to comfort him. And I can feel what I used to with him. A relief. He can feel it too, even though he's on the verge of sulking.

"I think we're better company than the inmates at the tombs." Veronica comes over with the wine and glasses. "Even with the open shower. Which I need as I smell like everybody's cigarettes and sweaty crowds."

She strips off her t-shirt after setting the wine and glass on the desk. I help her pour, and she takes off her sports bra. Earlier in the year she had a breast reduction from a C cup to an A cup, which made her feel more real in her identity, and gives her a more androgynous look.

Joel doesn't see her undress but feels her when she hugs him from behind and says. "Let's have a drink to survival."

Joel relents enough to accept a glass. I silently commend Zest's taste in good white wine. It's like drinking silk.

Joel avoids looking at Veronica, especially when she unzips her jeans and heads for the shower. While she's testing the water, I check the scar on her leg from the bullet. "He did a good job on that. It's healing well."

"It's sore but feeling better."

We talk about it a little more, comparing her left leg to where I was injured in my right. We glance over and see Joel is on the mattress resolutely facing away and staring at a poster of the Vienna Opera House.

She smiles at me and tells Joel. "I can't be modest at this point. Under these circumstances."

Joel says, "I'm just trying to be courteous. I don't have Gabriel's history with you."

She and I exchange glances, and she rolls her eyes. "Better start pouring my next glass, hey?"

"Give him time," I tell her. "And that we have."

"He can be that way if he wants. But when he showers, I'm watching the hell out of him."

I see him smile a tiny bit. I go over and lay down next to him. "I think that will be our major entertainment."

"You're too blasé about this."

"I think this is the first time I'm not recovering or reacting."

Veronica says, "It's a calmness that comes from the fact we can't do anything for now. Stasis. We can't sit around and worry for two weeks. So..."

"So treat it as a holiday? I can't do that."

"Treat it as a chance to get some rest," I tell him. "Look. Two ways I can get you out of this. One, when it's the day of the meeting I'll have Zest take you somewhere first. You don't need to be part of it. Or you can leave now. I'll trust you to stay out of sight."

"No." Veronica is out of the shower and wrapping herself in a towel. "He doesn't go anywhere. Don't test me. And you're not dropping me off. I'm in it to the end."

Joel has his head nearly between his knees. He lifts it slightly. "I guess I need to be here to watch out for you."

Veronica puts her hand on his head and he closes his eyes.

With more wine easing the way, we all manage to shower, and sleep together on the mattress. In the morning I wake up between them and sense something is different. And indeed, some stuff is by the door.

"We have a delivery service."

"Was that Zest?" Veronica is sitting up.

"Didn't even hear him get in. Either he's super quiet or we were super out."

More towels, wine, an iPod in a Bose speaker, more books. Cold food, as nothing can be cooked. But good bread and coffee. I have to smile seeing a sketchpad and pencils. "He likes Joel, I guess."

Zest also leaves a note saying Archie is okay--he checked. I guess he likes me too.

The next few days have no sense of time because we can't see the outside. It becomes uncanny. Anything can happen outside and we wouldn't know. The world can end. If it wasn't for a couple more deliveries from Zest, who assures us by note all is well, we might believe we're the only people left in the world.

Joel spends a lot of time sketching. Veronica and I read and talk and drink wine. The room is ventilated so we can smoke--which we don't--or light incense Zest brought--which we do. As the days roll by--three, four, five, the conversation becomes more intense.

We've hit the wine hard on day six--I think. Veronica and I are pretend-writing a journal of each year we've known each other. It becomes a free-association exercise.

Joel doesn't exactly join in, but he does seem more involved in listening to us. I'm prone on the mattress and they're sitting on it. Joel has the sketch pad on his knees, lying back with his head on her chest. I consider the tableau. It interrupts my attempts at creativity but leaves me more thoughtful.

"If something happens to me, you two have my blessing."

Joel frowns. "Gabriel, for fuck's sake..."

"At least you know. That's important to me."

"Nothing's going to happen to you."

"I can't agree with that. Maybe, maybe not. But you don't have to wonder, if that's want you want to do. What you feel about her is not a threat to our relationship."

"I don't know. Emotional threats are always threats," Veronica says. "You're right about you and Joel. Joel loves you more than he loves me. It's something profound. His feelings about me aren't a threat to you. But if I ended up with stronger feelings for him, then I'd be the one who's threatened."

"But you do have feelings for him."

"That's what being close does to you, hey? People think being bisexual means you increase your chance for a date on the weekend; it also means you have more genders to risk being emotionally attached to someone you shouldn't be."

Joel looks a little taken aback at her words. "It can happen to anyone. I think with us, we're already emotionally attached. Sexuality is just part of it. I feel safe with you."

They haven't really moved and I'm still contemplating them. "Joel knows you and I slept together. I didn't give him details. It was in the year after we broke up, Joel. I wasn't inclined to be involved with anyone new. There's a part of me that could easily be ascetic, and not deal with the bullshit that comes with relationships."

"Uh, excuse me?" Now he gives his about-to-pout look to me.

"I'm not apologizing. We've been through that. But I did want emotional comfort, and Veronica and I could be very emotionally close."

"At least we can get along, right? We're good roommates." She moves her foot against me.

I feel my head hurting; one of the bad headaches coming along. I manage not to throw up, but just move over where I can feel both of them. Things go black for some time.

When I wake up, I can see Joel staring down at me. He's sketching something. Ten minutes later he shows me a quick drawing of myself, in Veronica's lap.

"For posterity," he says. "I have to do something; sitting around is making me crazy."

"Let's talk," I suggest.

"Ugh, you and the talking. What are you, Phil Donahue?"

Veronica brings Joel's head down to her shoulder. "This is a strange opportunity," she says. Joel and I listen. I can tell we're both getting comfort from her. "Somehow, in this little world, this set from *The Prisoner*, what happens is different. We are the core of a family and something more."

"I think that's true." I feel her hand on my head as I speak. I need warmth, and she has warmth. I have the warmth from her legs and her abdomen and her hand. My legs are curled against Joel's, and I can feel his warmth as well. The human touch never seemed so important.

"Whatever happens is so unknown, that any rules of decorum are nonexistent. There's only us here, cut off from the world. Time stands still. Don't let it turn us away, but turn us to each other."

Joel is watching her hand stroking my head, then closes his eyes. In the quiet tension of the moment, the closeness enhances their breathing. His mouth is slightly open, as if he's thinking or imagining. Her eyes go to me, and I nod. I'm not sure what I'm agreeing to. Then she turns her head to her left and touches her lips to Joel's. His eyes open in surprise. She kisses him again, firmer, and he draws that in. With no distraction and heightened sensitivity, I can practically read him. I feel the part of him that wants her. It doesn't bother me. It awakens a desire in me for him, like the first time he was with me. His own desire in caught between us makes mine stronger.

Joel glances down at me, biting his lip.

"It's okay." I both lean against Veronica and reach out to put my hand on his bare legs. "It's okay."

"We're under too much strain. It's emotional..."

"It's a lot of things. Bunker mentality. A sense that we're going to die. An alternate reality that we're already dead. Let it go. Give in to the feelings."

"There's being able to face each other, and be friends with each other in the real world outside romantic fantasy."

I'm amused that he's resisting. "We're in the worst at the moment. Over the last five days, we've been more emotionally intimate than in the ten years I've known Veronica, or the four years I've known you. I hope you both forgive me for being here. For me, while I cherish the memories I have with you both I also put away every conflict, every disagreement I had with you. And that makes things more direct, more basic, less inclined to pretense. We can either live the rest of this time politely, to have flowery polite and proper pictures in our heads if we're killed, or we live as honestly as we can and know we survived it."

Joel is silent. The air around us is perhaps dangerous because Veronica's boundaries--never that strong--are down. Mine as well. But Joel is afraid to dive in. I turn my head up and smile at her in a wicked manner. She bends down and kisses me on the mouth. We've done that hundreds of times not sexually, and a few times sexually.

Joel draws in his breath. Veronica and I can spur each other on, as we did in Chiang's studio. Almost showing off. For a few moments we become just the feeling of mouths against each other. Another reason I was able to be sexually intimate with her is the strong male aspect of her being. I can feel it, covered by the female biology. I feel it even more when my eyes are closed. She claims she can sometimes sense a female aspect to me, which wouldn't surprise me. Together, our eyes closed, the gender and sexuality mix and become one.

I can't see Joel while her face is over mine, but I can feel the magnetic energy rising from him. His body is trying to break his mental resistance. I know he's aroused watching us, drawn to be part of us.

By touch, I unzip his jeans and put my hand in, moving my leg over his. Without moving from me, Veronica also puts her hand in, over mine and with mine. We wrap our hands around him together, feeling him grow hard and his breath grow short. Then I stop and pull off Veronica's top and she slides mine off, and then our shorts. Naked, we pull Joel down between us, pressing on either side of his body.

"Holy fuck," he whispers. "Uh, please don't stop."

"We're not," I tell him. "You've been feeling caught between us. Now you really are, baby."

And that becomes the cue for what begins and what builds, like a techno version of Ravel's *Bolero.* Joel's shy, but it doesn't take long for the shyness to dissipate when his senses are overwhelmed. He opens to let us do what we want to him, with him, with each other. Tending to him becomes the focus for us, until he's clearly thrown off his anxieties and gives in to immersion.

Afterwards we sleep entwined. And when awake again our closeness leads to building the sexuality again. Now past the point of modesty, Joel is more assertive, wanting, immersing. I'm good to be along for the ride. I'm grateful every time my body reacts as it is supposed to with him. Joel's initial reluctance becomes a surprising erotic aggression. Like an end of the world reaction. *I don't know if we're going to live through this so I'm going to fuck the way I've always wanted.*

He creates and lives some fantasies. I'm new to this. I've been highly sexual but not very adventurous. The freedom we gave each other allows for new perspectives and prisms of sensuality. The feel of him on top of me as my head rests between her legs. Drawing his mouth to me while she is controlling him between her thighs. Then we both enclose him to let him be the taker and the taken, which almost has the three of us literally hitting a wall and delightfully struggling in the counterbalance of body weight.

And for the remainder of the days we're together we just continue exploring whatever comes to mind, whatever arises as desire. A new Maslow's hierarchy.

Until Zest shows up one morning; he opens the door and stands against the background of a cold and ice-blue sky. "It's go-time. I've made necessary arrangements. Let's discuss logistics."

∞

NINETEEN

From the YouTube Channel "Tom Paine Events," in a video entitled:
Unknown Knowns: Hale Boggs ♦ The Doubter

Transcript: "Another plane crash in a long-twisted family tree of plane crashes. Boggs was a representative from Alaska and a member of the Warren Commission. What's not generally known about the Warren Commission is that a few members did not agree with the conclusions given to the public. Boggs for one said he had serious doubts. He also had harsh words regarding FBI director J. Edgar Hoover, condemning Hoover for spying on Commission members. The plane Boggs was on disappeared in 1971 over Alaska, and has never been found. His death raises the question of what happens to those who don't follow the party line."

∞

Sunday, January 1st
The Foundation, 10 pm

It's time.

We are dressed as Praetorian security personnel. Myself, Geneva and Jeffrey. We have the Praetorian's black face masks on, of course. Joel and Veronica are down the street a short distance in another anonymous SUV and watching us on video via the cameras Zest put in the building.

Inside the Foundation we all stand in the front large lobby, silent and armed. We wait with Zest until he gets a signal on his phone. He nods at us and leaves to go to the front door.

A minute later Zest comes back, leading four men towards the meeting room. Jacobs is one. Another is older, white, in a dark suit. Zest had identified him to us as a Swiss man named Noah Danuser-- code name Voirol. Zest told us that Viorol was Jacob's consult on the Booth case. Danuser is headquartered in Western Europe. The two other men are in their fifties. One is from Southern Europe, Vincente Simon (Code name: Bernardi) and the other from Eastern Europe/Asia, name of Anton Teterin (Code name: Pajari).

They don't look at us, of course. We're hired help--literally faceless.

Once they are inside Geneva goes to wait near the front entrance. Jeffrey and I stay on either side of the meeting room door. Inside the room, as we can hear through our earpieces, the directors are complaining about some political situation in Germany.

I breathe to keep myself calm. I don't like having a mask on, and I don't like seeing my dad and Geneva in masks. My breathing gets louder.

"Count out loud, Gabriel," my dad says. "Focus on the numbers. Forward or backward."

"Too much like the hypnosis."

"Try it in Spanish."

I work on that to myself. Going backwards. *Ciento, noventa y nueve, noventa y ocho...*it helps, but I still start shaking. Geneva comes up to me.

"The Arabic alphabet. I'm going to say it; say it with me." She watches the front while slowly saying each syllable. "*Alief; beh, teh, theh, jīm, ha, kha, dhal, ra...*"

Listen. Learn. Repeat. I find myself calming down.

The meeting room door rattles then opens. Zest steps out, shutting the door behind him. He glances at me. I nod carefully.

"I don't want to wait too long. He should be here now." Zest checks his phone. "Yes, he's in the back lot."

I clear my throat. "I'm ready."

Zest walks away, down the columned corridor.

My breathing changes again. "Easy," Jeffrey says. "We have your back. Whatever happens, I'll step in if necessary. You're not alone."

"Thank you." I take a deep breath. Blood pounds in my ear.

The front door opens. Then footsteps get closer. And Zest is back, with Clement beside him. Zest is cool as ever; Clement is noticeably hyper. His eyes dart at the three of us.

Zest takes hold of his arm to get his attention. Clement focuses on him. I see actual affection in his eyes.

Zest says softly, "See here, Damon." He walks over to me and gently takes off my mask.

Clement comes up and stares at me in wonder. I can't move. I see the same perverted affection in his eyes.

"Oh, Gabriel." He looks at Zest. "Is it Gabriel? Or Ryan?"

"They're fused." Zest improvises this on the spot.

I want to hit Clement across the face with my gun, but instead speak to him. "Damon. You're safe." My anger sounds choked, and could pass for relief.

He puts his hands on my face. "Yes, my dear boy. I know you did your best, and look--here we are. Now we finish our *message*."

I'm afraid. Afraid something will click in and make me not be myself. But nothing. The word means nothing. Still, I draw back as if it does. "The message will be complete."

"Yes--yes. Exactly."

I see my dad touch his weapon. Zest had told me Jeffrey had wanted to go back and kill Clement. An understandable instinct in a good parent. A good parent. He must be; he's here with me.

Zest speaks to Clement like he would to a hyperactive toddler. "Damon, let me be the lead. You can say what you want to say, but do not act."

"Of course, of course. Well, we have Gabriel here for the *coup de grâce.* I'm sorry, Gabriel, we weren't able to do this earlier. Maxim, I'm sorry as well. But it's all coming together now."

Zest and I perhaps can't help but meet each other's eyes. Both of us wanting to kick the shit out of him.

Then I pull my mask down. Zest opens the door. He goes in, Clement follows. Then I go in, with my dad and Geneva behind me.

Hunter and the rest look up. They are all sitting at one end of a rectangular table about ten feet long. The men do not seem alarmed at Clement's presence, since Zest had told them he was arranging for Clement to attend the meeting.

"This is unexpectedly soon," Hunter says. "But really, we're all in agreement. No need for formalities." He looks to the other directors and they nod.

"Formality and principle are not your guidelines." Clement's words have a biting quality. "I'm surprised you're even here bothering to have a quorum."

"Well, that's more due to you, Damon," Hunter responds smugly.

"Yes it is. Not in the way you think."

Hunter frowns at him. Zest holds up his hand. We move behind the other directors. Zest stays by Hunter.

"What--" a look goes over Hunter's face where it dawns on him things are turning.

Zest shoots a glance at Clement to make sure he's not bugging out from excitement. "Go ahead," he tells us.

Hunter starts to get up, and Zest has his Smith and Wesson out. He cocks it, holding the barrel to Hunter's head. Hunter freezes.

We take out plastic tie-cuffs and bind the directors' hands behind them. The chairs have a bar in the back we use to cuff their necks--leaving space to breathe. I'm not crazy about this part but they need to be immobilized.

"Maxim, what is this?" Hunter has strain in his voice but not panic. He's not ready to believe that Zest is betraying him. It could be just an elaborate show...

Zest doesn't answer. "Go ahead," he tells me. I move over and bind Hunter's hands and neck. As I know, this takes all the air out of one's sails.

Clement is delighted. "Where you underestimate me, Lane, is that I'm willing to do what you don't need to bother with. Your penchant for undervaluing people is your Achilles."

Hunter stares at Zest. "Maxim, whatever is going on, you are aware of the consequences. I'm depending upon your intelligence in that regard."

"I'm knowledgeable of the consequences," Zest says shortly. "Maxim is brilliant--and on my side. He always has been."

Hunter is able to just keep his eyes on Zest--perhaps to see if he can tell what Zest is feeling or thinking by looking in his eyes.

Clement walks up to where the directors are trapped and stares at each of them. "I know what you think of me. That makes it all the sweeter to do this. See, Lane, everything I was doing had value. It all had a purpose--which you abandoned. I wouldn't care about that, but you not only disrespected me, you wanted to get rid of me. Just waiting for the right time. Well..."

Now he steps over to where I am. "It's time for you to go."

With a dramatic flourish, he takes off my mask. I knew he was going to and have steeled myself for the touch of his hands again.

Hunter's eyes go wide. Staring at me, I see his nostrils flare and his pupils dilate. Now he knows Zest directly lied to him. My being there in any way can't be good for them. His face twitches from his thoughts.

"I trained him, Lane. With my methods and my machine, you are so scornful of. And finally, I have the moment of truth. For Gabriel to be the instrument of your destruction."

Hunter doesn't look or respond to Clement, which must be frustrating. He keeps his attention on Zest--survival.

"Killing me won't prevent what will happen to you," he says.

"What happens, happens, Lane." Zest shrugs. "It's already beyond the Rubicon."

"Not for you. An exception for you is always available."

"Oh, shut up," Clement snaps. "At least die with dignity."

He grabs my arm and pulls me out to a wider angle to the table. "Gabriel, it is time for the *message*. I would like to do a full ritual. Something from the old Masters. To bring the powers to us and respect them. The powers exist--our being here proves it."

"Damon," Zest says. "We do not have that kind of time. Others will check on them soon. I respect the Masters and the ritual. I went through it. But the powers can still be respected. We can engage in something symbolic as soon as we complete this task."

"I wish I could take one of them with me for the sacrifice."
Clement almost seems to pout.

"Use Cognoscenti in the later ritual. For the symbolism."

Clement's eyes brighten. "Of course! I'll train a volunteer to
be Jacobs," he gives Hunter a hateful look, "And that person will take
on Jacobs' Cognoscenti profile. We'll have to save some of his
blood..."

Zest very admirably holds back from rolling his eyes. Clement
assumes a solemn expression, taking a ceremonial dagger out from his
jacket. He says, "They will dance, but it is I who have brought them to
the dance. Those initiated into the Masters' Doctrine have their eyes
opened to a thousand *suns* and a thousand *hells,* and find the powers
of all the Masters before them ready to evolve. Those who betray
suffer a thousand deaths. Gabriel, take the knife."

The plan is for me to play along up to this point. While
Clement eagerly watches me take the dagger from him--as do the
other directors (not eagerly), Zest palms a syringe, planning to jab it in
Clement's neck. I point the dagger at Hunter. Behind Clement, Zest
lifts his hand with syringe.

The door to the room slams open and a gun goes off, held by
a dark figure in the doorway.

Clement is hit and falls on the table in a spray of blood. His
knife clatters to the floor.

Three men in military garb, two white and one black, barrel
into the meeting room. "Do not move," one of them says. "This is a
grenade." He holds up a metal oblong device. "If you shoot, it goes
off. If you move, I throw it and we leave--you die."

∞

Joel and Veronica, in Zest's SUV down the street, watch the
camera feed from inside of the Foundation. Zest is speaking to the
directors while Gabriel, Geneva and Jeffrey Ross wait in the main
area. Zest is about to leave and get Clement.

"So far, so good," Joel notes.

Veronica is temporarily smoking again, opening a pack of
American Spirits. Joel accepts one as they watch Zest leave.

Then there's a frantic knock on the car window. Veronica and Joel both jump back, startled. The SUV is by a fire engine, so it could be a cop. But when Joel looks out the window, he almost drops the cigarette out of his mouth. Alex is standing outside the vehicle, staring at them.

"God, you're alive," He says. "Open the door--please--you have trouble coming."

Veronica reaches for the door handle. "Watch the camera," she tells Joel.

Joel starts to protest, but she's right. It's not like Alex will go away. He turns to the camera as she opens the door and asks Alex, "What are you talking about?"

Alex leans into the vehicle. "You were all rumored to be dead. That man Zest was supposed to have killed you all made you disappear like Jimmy Hoffa."

"Uh-huh, well, we might be ghosts. One never knows. What is this trouble?"

Alex frowns at her. "If you're alive, Gabriel is alive right? I've been trying to find out for weeks."

"Alex, what is going on?"

"Gabriel is in the Foundation, right? If Zest didn't kill him, then Gabriel is with him. We saw them down the street. Zest go on, and then Damon. Gabriel's in danger."

"*What* danger?"

"An intelligence contingent is going to invade--not the people I work with, another faction. But my people aren't going to stop it. So that's why I'm here."

Veronica glances back at the monitor. Inside the Foundation, they've gone into the meeting room. Clement is waving his arms around.

She asks Alex, "How many?"

"Three. They have guns and more."

Veronica picks up the Glock and a spare clip. "I'm going in."

Zest has other weapons hidden in the car including another pistol. Joel takes that out. "Me too. If you're lying, Alex--I'll kill you next."

"No time to fight, Joel. I'm not lying. Gabriel's found out what I said was true. I know that--I know how he is."

For a second, Joel meets his eyes. *I know how he is...*but this isn't time to argue about who knows Gabriel. He and Veronica exit the car. Veronica tries to signal Gabriel through the earpiece, but he doesn't answer. "Something's up in there."

Alex follows them as they hurry down the street. "There's something else you need to know."

Now they're at the back door of the Foundation. "What is it?" Veronica checks the door carefully, and then the feed on her phone. "Someone's in there with them."

"Do something!"

She glares at Alex. "Keep quiet--don't fuck this up."

Alex inhales. "Yes, I will. What I wanted to say is, they have explosives."

"We'll worry about that later." Carefully she opens the door and checks out the dark kitchen area. Silently she moves forward with the Glock in front of her. Joel follows, and Alex behind him.

Peeking around a corner, Veronica sees a white man standing outside the meeting room door, which is open. He's scanning the empty main lobby area. Loud voices are coming from the meeting room.

An unknown male voice is louder than the others. "We know you have documentation of our connection to Clement. Get it now. If you don't, we'll shoot him."

Gabriel's voice. "Don't do it. Shoot *him*. Shoot them all. Don't give them anything because they're going to kill us anyway."

"Shut up!" The first voice.

Then Hunter. "Whoever you are, we can come to a deal. I don't care what you do with them. I can get you a great deal of funding. I can find these documents--"

Zest interrupts him. "He does not have any access to documents. You are not going to get anything while you are threatening us."

Veronica ducks back. She and Joel look at her phone. The camera is still on. They can see in the room. The four directors are secured to chairs. Clement is sprawled across the table. He's still alive. Zest is backed up against a wall. A second man, black, has his gun trained on Geneva and Jeffrey on the far side of the room. The white man who was talking has a large gun against Gabriel's head, near Zest. Gabriel looks at his father, and then up at the camera.

Alex whispers, "What can we do?"

Joel and Veronica look at each other. She says, "If we make a move, he'll make a move."

Joel nods. "Distraction."

Veronica clicks a button that makes the camera blink red as a signaling device. Gabriel is still looking at the camera, and he tilts his head slowly. He knows now they're there. Veronica takes a breath and looks around the corner again. She aims carefully. When the man outside the door turns to look in the meeting room, she shoots him in the shoulder.

∞

I have to guess what Veronica and Joel are going to do, but it's a close guess. As soon as the shot goes off and the man holding the gun on me snaps his head to the left, I'm already moving. I duck under his gun and kick his leg out from under him. He tries to twist back toward me; I drop my shoulder and punch him solidly in the nuts.

When I turn back, now holding his gun, I see Jeffrey and Geneva have tackled the other invader and are cuffing his hands. Two of the directors have toppled to the floor in their chairs from fear and panic.

More shots come from the main room and I move over to the door as Zest slips around me to secure the leader of this mini-invasion force. The third man is on the floor in the lobby, severely injured. He's shooting in the direction of the kitchen. He sees me and raises the gun. His shot goes wild as I duck back.

I pick up the device the leader was threatening us with and call out to the man in the lobby, "I giving you your friend's grenade. Have fun with it."

"Stop," the leader says. "Don't do it. You have us. Baker, surrender your weapon."

The man in the lobby floor yells back, "That's not the directive. We are *not* to give up to anyone."

"Baker, that's *an order.*"

I can see through the jamb of the door. I figure I can shoot his leg and Veronica can follow up shooting his arm. I'm just aiming the gun, when Jeffrey suddenly steps in front of the door and shoots the lobby man in the head.

Then he turns to the leader on his knees in front of me and Zest. The leader rips his hand out of Zest's grasp and snags a radio of some kind out of his pocket.

"Abort. *Abort.*"

Zest takes the leader's gun out of my hand, and shoots him in the head. He spits out blood and topples over.

I'm stunned, too much to move.

Jeffrey calls out the door, "Veronica? We're clear."

"Coming..."

He meets my eyes; I'm still frozen in place. "We're saving you a decision you couldn't make."

I know he's right, but the dead man next to me is filling my senses.

"He's correct," Zest says. He and my dad both look at the remaining invader, who is on his knees by Geneva. His eyes are focused intensely on them and he says respectfully, "I'm unarmed. I'm not going to do anything."

Veronica comes in with Joel. They take in the situation of the man on the floor in the main room and the man on the floor in this room.

And Alex. I can perhaps believe more that Alex is not part of the Society from the look on his face seeing the dead men, and his 'mentor' still on the table. Clement is still trying to get up. He gasps. "You. What are you doing here? Maxim, you have to do something--"

Zest does something. He turns to Clement and shoots him right between the eyes.

Clement, surprise on his face, rolls off the table and falls on Hunter, which seems fitting. Hunter screams, his panic muffled by Clement's body.

The other directors start howling as well. I ignore that and say to Alex, "What *are* you doing here?"

Alex has backed up against the doorway. "These men--they aren't from my faction. They are Project Q. They're a rogue--"

"I know the backstory." I look over at the man on his knees, who's staring at Alex. "The rivals to Enigma."

Alex says, "Yes, that's it. Enigma knows you're here. They want to get rid of Project Q. They've set explosives in the building."

"No," our remaining Q member says. "They wouldn't do that."

"How would you know," Alex asks scornfully.

"I'm one of them. My code name is *Delta* with Q, and *Mortem* with Enigma. Barclay is *Eternity*. Clement was *Bedevil*. I was sent to infiltrate the Q faction."

Alex laughs. "I suppose you'd say anything."

I hold my hand up. I'm getting myself back together, because I have to. "I don't care *who* is a Goddamn mole for *whom* anymore. How do you know about the explosives, Alex?"

"I heard one of my faction mention it. I was hiding with them, see. They're set up near here, watching everything. As soon as Zest took Clement in, they went in and wired the front door."

Delta--or Mortem, asks, "Did you contact Reaper?"

"No...just the open channel. They asked me over to debrief me. I think it was...*Undertow*."

"You're an idiot; Undertow is part of Q. You are only supposed to contact me or Mortem. You know that. That's why Enigma had to set the explosives."

Alex gets upset, and I interrupt him before he has a hissy fit. "So, regardless we need to leave. Out the back." I turn to Delta/Mortem. Everybody has two names, two faces, two loyalties. "You--since you don't think any explosives are here, you can go first."

"I don't know for sure; I just know he's not trustworthy." He indicates Alex.

Zest has his phone, checking more of his cameras. "They were here right after you came in the back."

I look back at Alex. "These people, Enigma--the good guys, right? They're going to blow up a building in New York?"

"Not like a bomb. Like a Con Ed problem, make it look like a gas main."

"Can you contact them? Their problems are significantly less now."

"I can try." He takes out his phone. "But we should do something."

"I know." I look at everyone. "Let's go."

"To the roof," Mortem says. "They won't listen to him--acceptable loss. He's an asset, not an op. But I can signal them."

We hear something then, from an upper floor. I suck in air, and keep my desire to tremble at bay. Everyone looks up. I ask my father, "Timed charges?"

"Most likely." The building rumbles again and we can hear a wall collapse.

"Then we go downstairs. I hope Mesereau was telling the truth about those passages."

Mortem says, "We tried to get him as an asset. He was unreliable."

"Take your chances here then. The rest of us--I remember the plans from the Foundation. There's a way out."

Everyone not tied up starts to move. Geneva and Jeffrey quickly check the other bodies for anything useful. Hunter and the other directors freak out. "You're not leaving us here," Hunter whines.

"You've served your purpose. Right now, most of your secrets are going online anyway."

"But you, Gabriel, you don't do that--leave people to die."

I tuck my gun away. "That's why you were okay with me being killed." But I take a knife and swiftly cut his neck tie. "Don't slow us down."

"Not good, Gabriel." This from Zest.

"Don't cut their hands free. If they fall, they fall." And with that, I'm out of the room. Another charge goes off. Dust and plaster falls over us.

Jeffrey has his automatic ready. "Which way, Gabriel?"

"The back stairs are by the kitchen." Jeffrey holds back as I lead the rest of us to the kitchen. I look back and note that the directors are scrambling to keep up with their hands behind their back. Delta is better at staying balanced. Zest and Jeffrey wait to follow them.

Downstairs, I open up the hidden wall in the basement. We can now really feel shaking in the frame of the building. As Jeffrey and Zest make it down the stairs, part of the ceiling on the first floor collapses. The debris blocks the door at the top of the stairs and dust from the debris puffs around us. Jeffrey almost falls. I run over to him. "I'm okay." He nods toward Veronica, who is breathing heavily. "Check on her."

I go back and put my arm around her. "Stay with me."

"I've got her too," Joel says.

I take a quick look around to ensure no one's in serious trouble, and then I move inside the hidden hallway to Mesereau's former room. I have the key, which Zest retrieved for me. The electricity no longer works so the room is dark. Geneva has rescued a flashlight from one of the dead Qs. My dad has one as well. That gives us a horror-movie effect. To add to that, something in the structure of the building above us is emitting a horrible screeching metal groan.

I'm surprised how I can now contain my fear. But I can. I run the plans in my head and compare to the room in front of me. Mesereau wanted this room out of the three down here, because of the passageway. Any marks on the wall that would indicate another hidden door aren't noticeable.

When Zest and I were here before, Mesereau was in a posture that in hindsight indicated he had just come back from the passageway. He was facing the wall to my right so I go to where he was standing. Geneva shines the light on the wall. Veronica and I run our hands on it.

"This is ridiculous," Danuser says. "You're getting us all killed."

"Shut the fuck up," Joel tells him.

He's intimidated by Joel but Hunter won't give up, badgering Mortem. "You can do something--I know you can. You're trained. Call in your people!"

I ignore that and look at the floor. "Geneva, put the light here." We get down and scan the floor. The light hits a hairline width-depression. I press on it in different places. Something moves. I press again. A large square loosens. Veronica and I get our fingers under the edge and lift up. A four-by four-square comes up on a hinge, revealing a wooden ladder going down.

Geneva bends down and shines the light inside the darkness below for reconnaissance. "Clear. Looks like another passage."

"Can you go first, with the light?"

"Yup." She's down the ladder in a second. I go next to be able to help Veronica. Joel comes down next followed by Alex and Delta, and the directors. I really don't care about them, but Alex ensures they don't actually fall. Then Zest and my dad move down. By this time Geneva has swept the area around us with the light. A fairly large passageway stretches out in what I believe is north.

"This is incredible," Alex says, crowding up against me. "Do you know where this goes?"

I move away from him. "I have an idea, actually." The building above us shakes again with an explosion, and dust comes down. "We better hustle."

The passageway is framed by wood with a packed dirt floor. It is wide enough for three people to walk abreast. Geneva is slightly ahead of Veronica and I. Joel is behind us. Alex is trying to get next to me and I can sense Joel blocking him.

"Does this passage go out? Are you sure?" That's Hunter from somewhere behind me.

"You're welcome to go back," I tell him without looking at him.

"You didn't really release any information, did you?" His voice is closer. I glance over my shoulder and see he's moved forward. Zest steps up and grabs his shoulder.

"Maxim, you didn't give them information. I can't see you doing that..."

"If it was up to me, you'd still be upstairs with Clement. When the authorities found your remains, they would put them together with what Tom Paine has exposed."

"You--no. This is unacceptable."

I glance back and see Zest has lifted his gun. "Do not keep talking."

"You can't--" Hunter turns to Mortem. "You still have contacts if you get out. I know you won't be arrested. I have access to funds you can use."

"I'm not discussing this," Mortem says wryly. "I know who you are and what you do."

"Get us out of here and we will compensate you very well."

I turn again to look at Mortem. "You're being asked to kill us, with your hands tied and the rest of us armed. How are you going to handle that one?"

Mortem meets my eyes as we move ahead. "I was a mole in Q. Seriously. What you're doing here--we wouldn't be against it."

I continue walking. "But Enigma was okay with us being crushed under the building, or being shot up by your friend Able."

"We aren't rescuers. We handle matters of international security."

"Project Accountability?"

"There was a greater good. We saw the information go out from Tom Paine tonight. I was told before I was in the building."

"Are you serious?" This from Hunter.

"There's an online user, Satyricon, who seems to be getting people to go to Paine's YouTube channel. It was getting big with the protestors."

"Chris does the job," Joel says to me *sotto voce*. Part of the set-up, once we were out of Westchester, was for Chris to prepare to release the documents Zest brought back, and also for Walter and Mankiewitz to publish them in their columns. I have been too busy concentrating on being around Clement again to be much help in that, but Joel, Veronica, and Chris worked quickly with Zest on the documents. And as an added bonus, taking down various Tertullian financial accounts that Zest knew about, before this all gets public.

"You can help us," Hunter has desperation in his voice. "We need to get out."

"I know someone whose father has a safe house," I say for my own amusement. I hear Alex huffing behind me.

Hunter just won't shut up. "We, these other three gentlemen and me, we have *forces*. We have *assets*. Exactly what you need, and without the nonsense Clement carried with him."

Hunter, stumbling, even manages to get next to Alex. "You too. You're with them--you can tell them about valuable assets. You wouldn't cast your lot with these people, would you?"

I stop in my tracks. "You know, if I knock you down, I can keep you from getting up again. You can try to crawl back to a destroyed building, or find your way out here like the *Poseidon Adventure.* You're Red Shirts to me. I'll knock all of you on your asses down here and you can go Donner Party on each other until someone digs you up."

"You wouldn't do that." His tone is scornful. "You're too--"

I turn around slam him in the gut. He gasps and falls down. It makes everyone go quiet, but I'm in control this time. "You don't realize how sick I am of you people. What you've done, what you're doing. I'm not going to risk other people's lives for you."

I meet Mortem's eyes. "That goes for you do. I don't give a flying fuck for your acceptable-losses theory. I don't kill people, but I can leave you here."

Mortem nods shortly. "I'm not in your way. You have command here, I accept that. I know about you and what you're capable of."

"What Alex told you?" I move forward again, talking as Hunter inches his way up by leaning against one of the wooden walls.

"Only in part. We did our own surveillance. You approached my partner, *Reaper*, on the PATH train some months ago. He's not usually burned in surveillance. My superior is *Kismet.* We know about you, and then there's what happened to your uncle..."

Before I can even process what he just said, Danuser interrupts. "Get us in touch with your superior. We have accounts we can get you access to."

Joel says, "Not anymore. Most of your assets are gone, and what's left is going to be tied up by regulatory agencies."

The directors all get freaked again about their money. And while their impending poverty is great, what Mortem said sticks with me. "What about my uncle," I ask him. "What does he have to do with this?"

"He...well, I'll tell you about it later. Too many ears."

Before I can ask anything else, Geneva slows down in front of us. "I hear something," she says. She shines the light down the tunnel. "The path goes downhill some."

"I'm guessing it eventually comes back up around 77th. The Soleil Hotel. But is that..."

We see water ahead. As the path slopes down, water is rising. Alarmingly, a few rats scatter past us, going the other way.

"A pipe or main broke." Geneva edges closer to look. "It's not up to the ceiling yet."

I try to do some mental calculations, praying I'm right. I'm guessing we have three more blocks to go. The water might take a half hour to get to the top of the tunnel if it keeps rising at the rate it is. Some objects that look like paintings pop up from the murk. Nelson's leftovers, maybe.

I fucking hate being in water. I remember the hallucination I had of the water rising over my head in the demon's pit. And water being poured over me in the box. Geneva takes my hand and squeezes it briefly, as sweat breaks out all over me. "I'll check it out. Hold on."

She moves down to where the water starts, and finds a loose piece of wood to stick in.

"This is suicide. Go back to the building." Hunter. But we hear shudders in up and behind us, negating that theory.

"Waist high," Geneva reports. She meets my eyes. I sweat more, the responsibility of everyone's lives weighing on me.

My father is beside me. He grips my arm. "I'll go in and see if it's clear. I've done this plenty of times."

He moves forward in the water. After a second Joel follows him.

"Joel..."

"I'm a good swimmer. You had to bring up the *Poseidon Adventure*, right?"

In a few seconds they disappear.

Mortem comes up next to me. "Cut me loose, and I can help." He tilts his head toward Zest. "He can watch me."

Even though the water throws me, I feel I can make an executive decision about people. I take out a knife and free Mortem. He nods. "Thank you."

The four directors start chattering together.

"All I'll do is help you through the water," Mortem says.

I crouch down and look into the path. I hear splashing. "Dad?"

His voice comes back. "We're fine, Gabriel. Just a moment."

I'm trembling now. I know Veronica isn't any better. In the dark, underground, and now water. Jesus Christ. I take her hand and draw her away. "You'll be okay," I whisper. "Don't let go of my hand. I will not let anything happen to you."

"I was going to tell you the same."

Geneva joins us. She says in my ear, "Gabriel, this is no worse than when I talked you through climbing that rope in Rochester. You can do this."

I can do it. When you have to take care of someone else, you can get past your fears.

Jeffrey is wading back, and Joel is behind him. Joel is entirely wet. A couple rats swim by as well, making me ill.

Joel says, "One low point where you have to duck. It's not that bad."

"Yeah, okay."

Jeffrey says, "Joel, take the point. Geneva, Gabriel and Veronica. Then you, Barclay." He looks at Mortem. "You'll be with me to help these men. Anything else and I'll cut your throat."

"I know your reputation as well. I understand."

"You four--do not do anything other than what we tell you. You're dead weight. Zest, it's up to you if you want to follow or go ahead."

Zest is taking off his jacket. "I'll be up there with you."

The idea of being last doesn't sit well with the directors, and they actually shut up.

Joel goes back down. I watch him move confidently. Geneva takes my other hand and she leads me, and I hold on to Veronica. The water is fucking cold. I try not to think of the rats.

"Easy," Geneva says.

"I'm right behind you, Gabriel," Jeffrey adds.

A few steps at a time. The water comes up to our waists, and it's harder to keep footing. I can tell Veronica is trying not to make any noises of fear. I grip her hand tightly as we step down further to where the water hits our chests.

"Here we go," Joel says. "One at a time. Me first. It's literally three steps. Don't try to swim, because you two suck at that. Wait for Geneva. Then I'll come back and get you. One, two, three and you're out. And don't drink any of this shit."

He and Geneva duck down and are under the water. Then a moment later he's back. "Veronica first," I say. "Get her safe."

"I have you," He tells her. "Don't let go. If you fall, don't panic. I'll pick you up. Deep breath, close your eyes and step forward--one, two three."

By now she's shaking. I kiss her cheek quickly. "Go on, you're holding us up."

Veronica inhales sharply, squinches her eyes shut and ducks down; Joel goes with her. I listen hard, counting to myself. One, two three. I think I hear something, but the water blocks it. Four, five six. Seven, Eight--

Joel is back, like a dark mermaid. "She's a trouper. You're next, Man of Action."

He takes my hand. I want to be a smartass, but I'm all out. I take a breath, close my eyes, and lower myself slowly. A satanic baptism.

My heart pounds as sound is cut off and my balance is shaken. I want to scream from no sound, no sight, and freezing water. Joel grips my hand and pulls me forward gently. One. I feel like I'm going to tip over and try not to scream. Two--two...my feet slip. I start to panic, not being able to feel anything around me but the water. I'm pretty sure a rat swims across my face.

Then Joel's arm goes around my neck and he pulls me forward like a lifeguard. A second later we come up, and I'm gasping.

I see Geneva holding onto a metal brace sticking out the wall. She has her arm around Veronica. "You're okay, baby. You did it."

"Christ, all those Bond films you watch...for nothing." Joel drags me over to her and waits until I catch my footing.

I allow myself to laugh uncontrollably for a moment in relief, even while shaking. "Don't think this will stop me kicking your ass."

Jeffrey comes up next. Then Alex. He's freaked out enough to have quieted appreciably. Then Zest. He's fine, naturally. He tells us, "They're demanding we cut them loose. I'm not, so I'm going to take the first two and Mortem the last two."

He goes back under. Although we must be a few blocks from the Foundation, we can still feel the shaking in the ground and the walls. It gives a very troubling sensation of the weight of the entire city on us.

Jeffrey asks, "Everyone okay?" We all say yes. Joel moves ahead, taking Geneva's light. "It goes uphill."

Zest comes back with Hunter. Hunter looks like he's aged a few years. Too bad about that nice suit. Jeffrey holds on to him as Zest goes back. By the time he and Mortem are here with the other three, I've calmed down.

We move on. The water level lowers. One or two more rats run past us, but that seems like small potatoes at this point.

Another ten minutes on dry ground. Then we hit a wall--literally. The wall is cement. Geneva and Veronica and I go over it gradually with our hands. Finally, a section comes loose. I pry it back.

A basement. Large, dark, cleanish. It's a storage room that doesn't look like people visit it too often. Using the flashlight, Geneva and I check the nearest objects. "This is where Mesereau was getting his stuff. *Hotel Soleil.*"

When everyone is safe inside, I shut the wall panel. Hunter starts to say something. "Shut up, or I'll put all of you back in the tunnel, and block the door."

From sounds nearby we can tell a laundry room is nearby. I think about what to do with the directors. Originally, we were going to leave them in the Foundation tied up, for police to find. With the documentation of misdeeds made public they'd have to be taken into custody.

It's three in the morning now. Fewer staff around. I go to Joel. "I want to shut off the security cameras."

"I could do that, if we can get in the security office."

"How about turning off the electricity for a half hour?"

"It's probably computer-controlled. Let's find the office."

Zest has a phone. We use it to find a layout of the hotel. The security office is down the hall from us. I crack open the door of the storage room. The hall is deserted.

"I can't imagine they'd have more than two people inside."

Zest steps up and produces his syringes. "Give me a minute." Jeffrey joins him. They march out the hallway to an office. An unfortunate security person steps out and within a few seconds is in on the floor. Zest and Jeffrey go inside the office. Then Zest waves at us, and pulls the prone man into the office.

I tell Geneva, "Keep watch on them. Seriously, if they say one fucking word, in the tunnel they go."

"No problem." Geneva has her gun out. Joel and I make for the security office. Zest goes back to the storeroom. Joel spends a minute looking over the system and begins turning off cameras. He finds feed of us in the hall, and erases it. Finally, he's ready to turn off the electricity, at least for the first two floors. By this time, I've figured out where to take the directors.

"Time to move," I say. Joel turns off the lights from the control area. Then he picks up a laptop and we leave.

I hustle to get back to the storeroom. "Let's go." We all move to a storage elevator at the back of the hallway, and take it to the second floor. Just past the elevator on the second floor is a banquet room; it's deserted this time of night.

A few minutes preparations and we're ready to go for good. "Gentlemen, it's not been a pleasure," I tell the directors before we leave.

The lights are still off. We head for a staircase, and then a first-floor hallway. Some staff are milling around trying to figure out what's going on. They don't pay attention to us, and we are able to exit through a kitchen door to an alley. We don't stop until we're in the next block. We need to go far enough away to be able to access YouTube and see the camera footage, via the laptop sending it out to the internet, of Hunter and the other three tied to the banquet table. The laptop camera records the lights going on, and the police arriving--tipped off from an anonymous call to local and federal agencies, as well as the district attorney and state attorney general's office. Of course, Mankiewitz, Walter, and Clark have been called as well to check out the video.

The documents that have been released already have things buzzing on social media. To bring down a power, you have to create a matching force that becomes so large, it can't subside. That force has been set in motion.

Despite their protests, on the video we can see all four are taken away by the police.

It's hard to believe but the Tertullian Society is, in effect, done. The head of the Hydra has been chopped off.

∞

∞

D E N O U E M E N T

From the YouTube Channel "Tom Paine Events," in a video entitled:
Unknown Knowns ♦ Pier Paolo Pasolini

Transcript: "Pasolini was a brilliant, provocative, politically subversive Italian filmmaker. His death in 1975, beaten to death and run over with his own car in a remote location, appeared to be the consequence of a raw tryst with a young man that went wrong. The young man was convicted of the brutal murder along with...'unknown others,' who were written out of the final verdict. The forensic examiner had concluded more than one person was responsible.

"But was that the whole story? Pasolini had recently been harshly criticizing the political party in power, and what he saw as destructive media-based consumerism. He was trying to negotiate the return of stolen reels of his last film, Salò. He may have been targeted by the neo-fascist groups who were violently attacking leftists during this time in Italy. Pasolini's friends maintain his murder was more than a sordid sex case, despite the public story. His death raises the question of what happens to creative artists whose freedom of expression hits the powers that be too close?"

∞

***The Sentinel* UK**

Exclusive Excerpts from *Between the Lines: A Memoir of Danger,* by Alex Shenoy Barclay

I had been working five years as a journalist in London when a faction from MI6 approached me. They knew I had extensive sources around the city, and they knew my father, who had on occasion worked with intelligence.

They told me various cells were popping up around Europe--not terrorist, occult. One cult in particular concerned them. Some strange incidents had convinced a section head in Sydney that the cult was dangerous. The person in charge of the cell was American but had lived in the UK for some years--Damon Clement.

Clement had recently moved from Australia to the US. He was working under the name Comstock. Clement's hermit-like nature was legend; few persons in the Tertullian Society saw him on the field. They only had contact with him when he would indoctrinate them for the Society.

For a special few, he would take them through the old rituals. He was careful to cover his tracks, and of course had the protection of the Production Faction even if the two divisions did not get along. Meanwhile, watching him was a joint a UK/US investigation--and like in the UK some US intelligence factions are genuinely interested in the potential for his research, rather than putting him away without any further investigation.

Those factions asked me to work with them, and I saw the usefulness of their mission. They saw I was getting some notice with my political reporting. But I could also be an asset to Clement. I published some articles meant to catch his eye. I had second-hand contacts with whom I talked about issues and ideas meant to get back to him. And it worked; it took nearly three years to do so. He arranged to meet me by 'accident,' and began a slow seduction of recruiting me. His mantra to convince me was my status as an outsider...caught between two worlds in England and India, but not fully part of either.

Eventually, once he believed I was under his tutorship, he brought me into the Tertullian Society. But to his part--the True Believers. Clement had done this with several others that Jacobs, the titular head of the US sector of the Society, did not know about. Clement kept his special recruits deep undercover until the right time. I was extraordinarily successful in that Clement considered me to be like a son to him, having mentored me (or so he thought) for seven years. He even went so far as saying he'd want me to replace his favored protégé, known only as Z. He told me Z was a morose person who was going to burn out eventually. He kept us apart so that Z wouldn't taint me, he said. This was later borne out by Z's strange fascination with Gabriel Ross. Gabriel no doubt felt Z was helping him but Z was more likely drawing him into the serpentine intrigue Gabriel is so susceptible to.

I've been accused of having Stockholm syndrome, but that was never the case. Like Joe Pistone, the FBI agent who acted undercover as "Donnie Brasco" in the Mafia for several years, I never became emotionally attached to Clement or anyone else in the Tertullian operation. Not even Gabriel. I was fond of him, but his naiveté precluded any serious involvement.

Nonetheless I rather felt sympathy for Gabriel. He was struggling financially with his business, and tended to get in trouble and earn bad press. His heart was sincere, but he lacked maturity. In any case, my reporting on the Booth matter was the perfect excuse to meet him. I already knew what was going on but I let Gabriel discuss his theories with me, of course. I was taken at times by his puppy dog enthusiasm. I thought I could do him a favor by allowing him a role in this operation--he is very intelligent and ethical. He managed to find and interview Kent Varney, a former journalist who was well-acquainted with the Tertullians. Sadly, Varney was also too impulsive for his own good and ended in killed mysteriously in DC.

At that point, Gabriel refused to proceed in a logical I manner. I thought as a friend I might spirit him away to Europe. I could keep him safe while I handled things in the States. But Gabriel made some questionable personal choices and I decided I had to avoid being close to him for my own protection. Then Gabriel insisted upon getting involved in the Clement affair again. Once he was on Clement's radar things were set in motion. I worked on controlling the investigation by being on the inside. I was already working in a double capacity with Clement and Enigma. I was stretching to be of use in a third capacity with an internal factor working against Enigma. With matters far more important at stake than one or two persons, naturally I could not play nanny.

I'm aware Gabriel has alluded to certain things happening to him, bad things. I know he met with Damon Clement somewhere out of New York. I can't say what happened while he was there, voluntarily or no. I am empathetic to anything that may have occurred. I did my best to influence Clement but Gabriel knew the risks of getting involved with things beyond his skill set...

∞

Friday, January 20, 2012
East Village, 7:00 pm

CARL MANKIEWITZ was always fair to me as a reporter. Over the last year he's been friendly as well. And so we have dinner and talk. I go over some more details I've found out about the Society. They had maintained a disinformation program to perpetuate silly rumors regarding the Society. Certain obnoxious radio and online conspiracy 'experts' helped with that. Then they also influenced authors and journalists to discourage beliefs in *any* conspiracies.

There's more I can't tell him that what I *can* tell. But we do discuss the intricacies of being thought dead, then pretending to be dead. We had to pretend to be dead for our own good, until the directors could be arrested. Since the exposure was the force set in motion, authorities had to go along with it. When that happens, the trick is to pretend you were working for that all along and take all the credit. It doesn't matter so long as the Hydra has been crushed.

Mankiewitz and I drop the roles of reporter and subject for a bit and connect on a more personal level. It feels like something I need, having been made inhuman. Even if I can't tell him everything.

One of the things I can't tell him is the deal with the intelligence agent, Mortem. The night we took the leaders of the Society down, we returned to Herrmann's apartment to recoup. Chris was there to meet us, while overhauling Herrmann's computer system to make it safer. Once we were all inside, Zest had indicated Mortem and said to me, "I want to speak with him for a bit."

But first Zest and my father talked to Herrmann privately while the rest of us cleaned up. I kept watch on Mortem and Alex, who also cleaned up and were quiet and respectful of the surroundings. We treated them decently because we're not the people we escaped from.

Then Zest and Jeffrey took Mortem aside in Herrmann's private study. They talked for over an hour. When they came out, Mortem was not with them.

They come over to where I'm sitting with Joel. Zest said to me, "We let him go. We have an arrangement with him."

I had about a half-dozen different responses on my tongue but just said. "What arrangement, and how would you know he'd live up to it?"

"The arrangement is for your benefit. To have you and everyone here left alone."

I looked at Jeffrey for confirmation.

"It's true, Gabriel. In return we help him with some things."

"I don't get a say in that?"

"No, you don't." Jeffrey stared at me, eye to eye. "I want you to know you have my utmost respect with how you handled with this operation, and how you kept to your principles. This is our part. We took the choice from you. Deliberately. I understand your moral compass. Other than taking care of you and hoping to see your mother again someday, I don't have one."

Zest added, "You are already aware I don't have the same philosophies as you, Gabriel. We took on the sin. You're not involved. It's a negative right, so to speak."

"You're saying Enigma is not coming after us for anything."

"No, nor the government in general. The fallout is limited to what is extant."

"I wanted to talk to him about what he said regarding Dom. That he knew something..."

"I'll try to find out for you," Jeffrey says.

I shake my head, disturbed. "How does that work--you just don't turn him in, so everything's just peachy?"

Jeffrey and Zest looked at each other. "He questions everything," Jeffrey said. "You have to get used to it."

Zest took a deep breath. "Yes, I've had my experience in that. It's more than not turning him in. You are right in thinking that would not be good enough. Because Mortem is not high enough in the hierarchy. We can, however, help his superior and his team with certain things. And we will. We were talking to Kismet--Mortem's superior--and we made arrangements."

I didn't like the sound of that. "To do what?"

Zest lit a cigarette. "I'm getting them Cognoscenti. I doubt it works, but they want to see it. We also implied that Tom Paine is a leaderless faction like Anonymous, so they don't try to look for a specific person. And we're helping them in some imminent projects."

"I'm retiring," Jeffrey added. "As soon as I put the papers in this week. Then Maxim

and I are on a mission to help one of their operatives."

"You don't have to do this--"

"Gabriel, don't argue with me. I know how to make choices. I don't make yours; you don't make mine. You can respect me on that, as I respect you. You need to. I know what I'm doing. As private actors, we can take care of certain things they can't. This also helps a person in serious trouble who they want extracted."

"In fact," Zest added, "It's rather a new career."

"That's my doing, Gabriel," Herrmann interjected. "I know people who need help. Some persons are in other countries who need to be extracted and resettled, who are left behind. Such as translators working for the military who have been refused immigration due to red tape. Intelligence agents who have been exposed and put into danger due to politics. Governments can't help them, but we can."

"Who funds it? Black budget?"

"No government money. The Tertullian assets we were able to recover helps in the funding. Chris offered, uh...assistance."

"Oh, I can totally Lizbeth Salander more of that shit," Chris said. "I'll be your dragon tattoo."

"Joel? You're welcome to continue helping."

"I have someone to help. Who needs all my help. I'll back up Chris when and if it's needed it, but I've got people to take care of."

So there's that. And I can't tell Mankiewitz I'm Tom Paine. A part of me would like to be Tom Paine in public. But that's too dangerous. I plan to continue Paine's work as a collective, with information Zest gives me. We exposed the four Society leaders currently in custody. Paine has Mankiewitz, Clark Ahn and Nic receive some documents by courier to set them up with good stories and public interest, revealing more to keep the story going. Just as a hyperreality constructs a different world, this is a reverse. The constructed reality of the Society is brought down bit by bit. Some will run like the rats in the tunnel as the funding and power evaporates. The directors are still a danger in some ways--to other people if not us--and I suggest to my media contacts that they be watched or they might be suicided as a new crop of unknown knowns. Like Darrell.

I can't tell Mankiewitz about Alex. Well, I could, but I don't. Alex didn't say much in Herrmann's apartment that night. He decided he didn't want to fuck with my dad or Zest, who managed in a couple hours to work a better deal with Enigma than he had in ten years. He may not be a bad person. He did bad things, certainly--and then he tried to help. I don't know who the fuck he really is. He's writing for *The Sentinel*, a London-based independent news organization. I've read--or tried to--the Fanfiction he wrote for himself regarding the Tertullian operation. But I think it's better that we have several thousand miles between us. I'm really hard on forgiveness these days.

∞

[SCRAMBLE MESSAGE]
8422910084 8914883427 8807661192 1850996810

[Unscramble] ENIGMA Project/Eyes Only

From Kismet, to MORTEM and REAPER

--Confirmation of arrangement with MAGICIAN's sponsors. Operation RECLAMATION activated as collaboration. Contacts/code names GUARDIAN and PHANTASM.

I took request of informing MAGICIAN about PARADISE under advisement. The topic is not prudent at the current time. Discussion of PARADISE with MAGICIAN is embargoed until further notice.

∞

Mankiewitz had asked what I'm doing next. Working on my thesis, actually. And I can socialize with my friends again like a normal person. I am amused--somewhat--by Chris giving me a couple of the street posters from RIP: one with my face, one with the Maneki-neko cat.

While I'm deciding where I want to put those posters in the office, my work cell phone rings.

The voice is hesitant, quiet, and disguised. "I figured out something about you. You're Tom Paine."

I sigh. "Who are you, and what do you want? I'm not in the mood for crackpots, to be honest."

"I'm not one. I...I'm on your side. But I saw what others didn't see, that it was right in front of them. Of course it would be you. It's so you."

"Whatever works for your *Fantasy Island.*"

"Paine is still publishing. I'm glad. I thought it might end once the Tertullian Society directors were indicted, but he has turned to other topics. Underreported stories, more detail on the women in Juarez and Canada."

"Yeah, I saw that. I guess conspiracies can only go so far. Eventually, you have to mention the Illuminati and once that happens you've gone full-tilt tin hat."

The voice continues. "I think you have a good following. You can investigate some things that need investigating. Let me give you one. There's a group in Montana and Upstate New York." The person is quiet a moment. "*Paradise.* Look into them. They haven't gotten on the Southern Poverty Law Center's watchlist yet, but they should."

"What are they, white supremacists? What's the angle with them?"

"I just believe they are a topic that Tom Paine should research. Dig deep. Who they know. What they know. Find the connections, Gabriel. I'm telling you for a reason."

The caller hangs up. The number was unknown. I turn over what the person said in my mind, and after I take care of the posters I look into Paradise. Eventually, the day gets away from me and I save it for tomorrow.

A couple weeks later, I have Tom Paine discuss the group, and I also publish something in *NYCultcha.*

I hope to put some time aside for more research, but meanwhile I have to work on the thesis. My academic advisor Professor French is interested in me teaching once I have the degree. I tell her I'm not sure I have the patience. She waves that away. "You think you'd be like Slavoj Žižek, complaining about those pesky students with their personal problems? You're like Dom and you know it. He would spend hours with students, mentoring them."
"I know. I used to wait for him here while he did."

"Speaking of which...something odd happened the other day. A man turned up here asking about Dom. He said Dom had tried to solve a problem for him and the student had wanted to see what happened to him. And the thing is, I remembered that happening. Dom was big on trying to help students problem-solve. It was one of the reasons he was so popular while other profs would slam their doors shut. This student approached him right before Dom died, so that's probably why I remembered. I didn't tell the man that. He said he wanted to contact you and give his condolences." She searches in her desk and comes up with a scrap of paper. "This is his number. He seemed a little nervous, so I wasn't entirely sure about him."

I think about that. "Someone said something to me about my uncle not too long ago. Does anyone here ever talk about what happened to him?"

Anne looks grave. "You know, Gabriel, no one talks about it. And since several years have passed it's been forgotten. When I say no one talks about it, I don't mean because it was here on the campus and the administration put the kibosh on it, but because something *was* odd."

I feel some regret. "I didn't learn enough about it at the time. The whole thing was too painful. But I have--I don't know--a question raised about it in my mind, I guess. I'll have to get in touch with Dom's boyfriend, Randall. He hates me, so that will be fun. But if something was odd as you say, then I want to find out what. I don't want it to be like Ioan Culianu--shot in the head on campus in a men's room, and the campus never pushed for a better investigation."

"Dom's death was one of Žižek's Unknown Knowns. Gabriel, if anyone was meant to look into Unknown Knowns, you are."

∞

Tuesday, January 31
Brooklyn, 3:30 pm

We've celebrated Joel's 34th birthday--partly spent with Joel and our friends, and partly with just Joel and Veronica and I. So far, so good with what's going on. Zest and Jeffrey have left to extract some person stuck somewhere, and Chris has diverted serious funds from bank accounts. Veronica and Geneva and I are working a case about a con artist that's getting pretty heavy. Herrmann and I are going over parts of his book that need more research. Walter and I the same. I haven't heard back about what Kismet et al. know about Dom, but I have hopes.

In the meantime, I decide to call the man who claimed to be one of Dom's students. The man's name is Wright Lindsay. I leave him a message. He calls me back a couple days later. Lindsay is quiet and circumspect, expressing his sorrow that Dom was killed.

"What kind of problem did Dom help you with, if you don't mind my asking?"

"Um, it's been on my mind lately. I had gotten in some trouble and...well, it's why I was drawn to contact you. Can we meet me outside somewhere? I need to be cautious. I'll explain why."

I had done a background search on Lindsay, and hadn't turned up anything--as if he disappeared after college. "Do you have proof of your identity? I see you have no online presence, nothing in the CUNY Uptown alumni organization, for example."

"Yeah, I have reasons for that. I have my old college ID and a few papers Professor Sheehan graded. You'll recognize his writing, I bet."

As we're going to meet Herrmann on Tuesday, I suggest he come to the park near Herrmann's brownstone. Lindsay agrees.

At the appropriate time on Tuesday Herrmann walks outside with Joel and I, taking his bulldogs Larry and Michael with him. We walk a couple blocks over to the park and my phone rings. Lindsay asks, "You're at the park? I'm heading over."

"I'm on the west side, at the dog run."

"I'm by the men's room. Can you meet me here?"

"Okay."

Joel and Herrmann follow me over. I don't see anyone standing outside the men's room. I lean into the actual bathroom briefly to scan it, but it's empty.

I turn back to them and shrug. "What the hell?"

"Maybe he lost his nerve," Joel says.

"Goddamn it. I need to know what he was going to tell me."

Herrmann says, "It will be difficult for you to look into this; I can see that already by the haunted expression on your face."

"I owe it to Dom. He did everything he could to make me a decent person." Herrmann looks so concerned, I try to lighten up. "If I can find out what happened to him then it is a far, far better thing I do than..."

I stop in the middle of quoting Dickens in jest, when my attention is drawn to a tree some distance away from us. Movement, a black figure in the branches, catches my eye. I start to say, "What is that..." and then something punches me in the chest.

For some reason I think it's a baseball that someone threw my way and that makes me angry. Who could be so careless playing around?

Until I see blood on my shirt. Spreading. It's incomprehensible to me. Blood should not be coming out my shirt. I stagger back one step, two steps, until I hit the wall of the men's room building. Then I lose my balance and drop to the ground on my back.

I see the sky over me and in my mind I say *what what what...*

Joel is leaning over me, apparently talking. I can't hear him. I recognize I'm in shock. I try to speak and blood comes out my mouth.

"*Call 911.*" Herrmann says. His voice sounds like it's filtered through cotton. The loudest sound I hear is pounding in my ears. Herrmann puts his hand is on my shoulder. "*Gabriel stay still.*" I read his lips because I can't hear anymore.

I can see Joel call somebody, yelling on his phone, and then it's all overridden by my mind blanking out.

I had always thought I'd hear David Gray's song *The One I Love* if I died, and I do.

Gonna close my eyes/gonna watch you go...

Adrenaline fills me for a second, and then I have a strange sensation of fading. Joel is still frantic, and I want to tell him this will be okay.

Really, it will be okay.

∞

Something opens in my field of vision. I see a place--a beautiful room of some sort. I'm seeing it at the same time as I'm aware of other things. Joel kneeling over me, his hands covered in what must be my blood. Him putting his hands on my face and head, sitting next to me in an ambulance. EMTs strapping a mask over my face; the loud sound of my tortured breathing.

But this flurry of activity seems to fade out as the room becomes clearer. It's like I'm in between movies, or two movies are playing over each other, and each is struggling to be in 3D.

I recognize a hospital, a trauma unit, and sudden pain. I see myself struggling to sit up, to breathe. I see things I couldn't possibly see as I'm wheeled into a surgical room--Veronica arriving and holding on to Joel. Herrmann with his hands on both of them. My father comes in with Zest. And then the pain takes over. Pain so bad I can't help but try to reach the beautiful room. It becomes clearer to me. A wooden floor and a carpet. Tall wooden bookshelves. Tables and comfortable chairs. A library.

The physical pain puts me in agony, but when I step on the library floor, it goes away. I turn away from the pain, and begin walking on the floor, moving further into the room. It is more vivid, more real, as the hospital fades like a Polaroid left in the sun.

Somewhere Else

"Gabriel." My uncle Dominic. He comes up and embraces me. I can smell his cologne. I stopped wearing cologne after he died.

He's here. Solid. Real. I can touch him. My mom is here too. She appears next to Dom and puts her hands on my face. I feel her. This is not a dream.

I have the most wonderful sense of happiness seeing her, holding her. All else immediately is gone from my consciousness.

And Dominic too. It's like when I was a teenager and the three of us were together doing something as family. Without even speaking we could be comforted by being in each other's presence.

I can think of banal comments to make...*so this is what it's like.* I have no need. All I feel is the warmth of my family. I spend what feels like hours with them.

"You were waiting for me..."

"We did. This is another realm, Gabriel. Not like people think. It's better, actually. But time is not what it is back there. Waiting isn't anything. We knew this was coming."

"Do we go somewhere? Get reincarnated?"

"You can do so..." Dom, holding my hand looks away and points to a wall. "But I want you to see..." A black spot on the wall, filled with lightning.

Something cuts through my happiness. A wail. Coming through a painting on the wall. A mandala. It reminds me of the Tibetan Book of the Dead and the Egyptian Book of the Dead, both of which offer instructions for getting to the right place once one dies. The mandala moves, becomes alive, a vortex. It pulsates on the wall, growing. The blues and red in the design become black and throbbing from the staccato sound of the wail.

I look into the vortex and I can see...myself. Covered in blood, in the hospital. A sense of urgency. A sense of hopelessness. I realize the wail is coming from elsewhere in the hospital. Someone crying for me. My guilt rises sharply, cutting me. I'm happy here and Joel is crying because of what happened out there.

What had Culianu said about the body and soul? *The Phantasm isn't working any more. The communication between body and soul is cut. I have no apparatus to connect with myself. So I can't communicate with Joel.*

"Isn't there any way I can tell him it's all okay?"

"He can't sense this realm. When we were there, we couldn't see it or feel it either. It's too much for the human mind. Animals can sense it, sometimes."

I hear Joel again and I feel bad--or what bad felt like on Earth. What can I do? How can I create some kind of magical semiotics for him and Veronica?

"Let's talk, Gabriel." Mom turns me from the vortex.

"I feel so confused. I don't feel like I'm like you. Why am I not moving on?"

"You need to see you are here with us, but choose to be here. Or choose not to."

I look to the vortex and see myself again. In a hospital bed in an intensive care unit. I forgot my hair was short and how I don't like it. I look terrible--drawn and pale with the tubes everywhere. Joel and Veronica are by my bed. My father is a short distance away. I sense I'm struggling to keep my heart beating, to let the blood continue to flow. It's like the ocean--a wave of sensation then floating away.

Dominic says, "This is hard, Gabriel, because in your situation you have a choice. It doesn't happen all the time. But some get a choice to move on or go back. Many choose to move on."

"I have a choice. Why didn't you have a choice?"

My mother answers. "My sickness was too advanced. Dom's death was too sudden for him to be aware of it."

"It was murder," Dom tells me.

"Murder...that explains...I want to do something about it. But I want to stay here too. Why is the choice so *hard?*"

"You don't want to let them go."

"But they'd be safe with me gone. All the trouble that's been so far..."

"That isn't part of the choice, Gabriel. Don't think for them. What do you feel you want to do?"

"I want to be with you." I hold on to him again, and then look over my shoulder. "And I don't want to leave them. I want to find out what happened to you. What happened to me."

"I won't tell you going back isn't hard. You'll be in extreme pain, and you won't remember this--you won't remember being here with us."

The lack of Phantasm again; no pneuma to interpret the other realm to my five senses. In the window, Veronica looks up. I hear her although she isn't speaking. "We're not ready," she says. "I know you are around. Come back to us, Gabriel."

She *would* find me. My desire to leave with my family is aching against her fury and the heartbreak of Joel crying at my bed.

"Let me go," I yell at her. "You'll be fine without me."

Her head tilts as if she hears. Her voice is distorted. "You're not ready to leave us, Gabriel. Fight it and come back. *Please.*"

Her words and emotions pull at me. At the same time, I know what I want to do. And as I realize that, I get a sense of pain in my physical body. "Uhhh. I can't...oh, it's going to be hard."

"You made your choice," Dom says. "You won't remember this, but I'll try to tell you somehow about what happened to me. It was because of Paradise. *Paradise.* Remember that. We love you, Gabriel."

"I love you too," I say, and even while I'm holding them I feel myself moving away.

Veronica's eyes burn at me now. "Come back," she tells me.

∞

Danny and Jeffrey have been around all day too, but both of them left for a break to go outside for a cigarette. Joel and Veronica are in the ICU with Gabriel; Joel is trying to talk to Veronica through his tears.

"...And they want me to look at some form on organ donation; I can't sign any forms...."

"Easy," Veronica says, holding him. "Breathe. Come on. Breathe. Don't think about the forms."

Their voices are in my head. I try to make sense of what they are saying. Fire. Everything is fire. My chest is aching so bad I want to scream. I feel like my soul is ripped into my body and fighting every fiber in pain.

A strange sense of loss but it fades, replaced by an overwhelming desire to get out of the devices holding me down. Everything in my arms and on my face makes my nerve endings scream.

Veronica and Joel are still holding on to each other. Joel says in her shoulder, "I don't know what to do..."

She glances over at me with a sense of sadness that turns into realization. She sees my eyes are open.

"Joel, look at him..."

He lifts his head. She's staring at Gabriel. And Gabriel's eyes are open and he's watching them.

I can't seem to move but I try. I try to let her know I'm alive and I hear her. My fingers lift off the bed a fraction of an inch.

"Oh, my God. Are you awake? Is he awake?" Joel jumps up and moves by Gabriel's head.

I ache in a different way when I see tears on his face. In my mind I can get up and comfort him. Really all I can do is strain to move an inch. I can't speak with the tube down my throat. My hands go up, and fall down.

Veronica rings for the ICU nurse. He runs in and checks out the situation. In a matter of minutes, the doctor returns and is fussing over Gabriel. They can tell she doesn't want to sound hopeful, but she's examining his vitals intensely. "His blood pressure is better..."

The doctor takes his hand. "Gabriel, can you hear me?"

I try to speak and remember I can nod instead. I feel myself breathing hard, fighting the pain to try to communicate.

"He's awake, he's going to make it," Joel says.

"I'm going to check him out. Let's just hold on before any..."

But Joel and Veronica tune that out. The doctor's caution is no match for the will of the people around him. When the doctor turns away for a moment, Joel leans over the bed. "Stay with us, baby. Keep fighting..."

He is rewarded by Gabriel smiling. He's sure of it, in Gabriel's eyes.

Before the doctor takes over, I'm able to brush my fingers against his hand for a second. I see Veronica on the phone, calling someone to say I'm awake. And in the terrible pain my mind becomes more conscious. I have a last sense like a dream of my mom and Dom holding me...and a word Dom tells me to remember-- Paradise.

∞

Friday, February 3
2:00 pm, Union Square

Mankiewitz has been avoiding it all day, but he finally begins pulling together information for the obituary. He starts to type up his own thoughts about Gabriel Ross as a tribute.

His phone rings.

"It's Joel McFadden."

Mankiewitz pauses in his typing. "What's the story, Joel?"

"He pulled through." Joel sighs deeply. "He's back with us."

"Awake? Stable?"

"Yeah, he's conscious. His doctor feels he's past the crisis point. We're not sure what he's going to go through to recover, but...that's something we can handle. He can't get out of bed right now and he can't really talk." Joel laughs, and it sounds like he's crying at the same time. "But he's here, you know? He's *here.*"

After a few minutes of talk Joel says goodbye and Mankiewitz begins writing a new story. He smiles to himself at the pleasure of putting the obituary away.

∞

The New York Scene/The Thin Blue Line Column by Carl Mankiewitz
Cheating Death: The Scene's Favorite PI Survives Assassination Attempt

The word is in that Gabriel Ross is in cautiously stable condition at Brooklyn-Presbyterian Hospital. A source close to Ross said he had 72 hours of struggle due to loss of blood, and technically died at least a couple times while being worked on in the ER and critical care facility.

Now that Ross is more or less out of immediate danger, the question becomes who tried to kill him...

∞

THE END OF *DEAD FOR NOW*

GABRIEL AND JOEL WILL RETURN IN HARDCORE.

ABOUT THE AUTHOR

Alex Fiano is a writer, teacher, artist, and LGBTQ+ advocate (particularly for youth) living in New York City. Read more about Alex here: **https://gabrielsworld.com/gabriels-world/about-the-author/**

The books in the *Gabriel's World* Series are:

The Hanged Man
Two-Faced Woman
The Book of Joel
Dead for Now
Hardcore (2019)

[Cover images in part from dead_brushes/brusheezy.com]